THE

CABINETS

OF

BARNABY

MAYNE

ALSO BY ELSA HART

City of Ink

The White Mirror

Jade Dragon Mountain

The

CABINETS

of

BARNABY
MAYNE

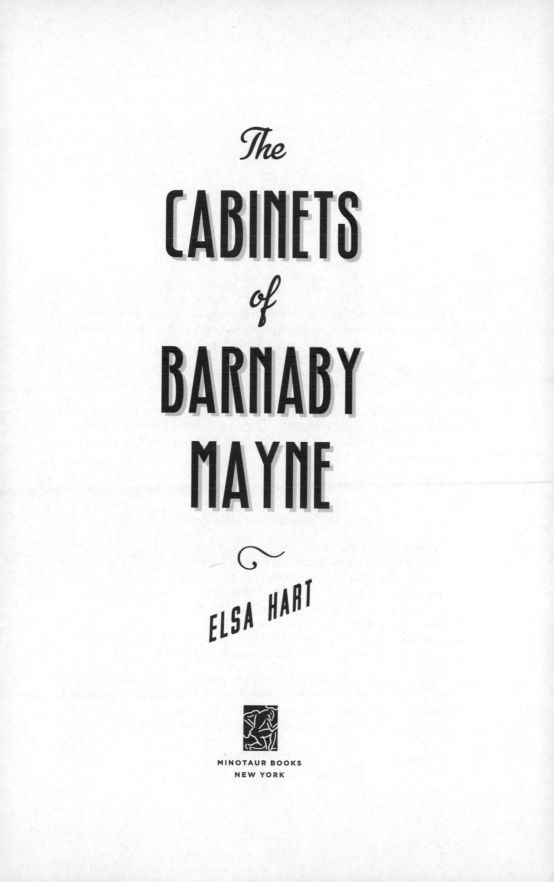

ELSA HART

MINOTAUR BOOKS
NEW YORK

First published in the United States by Minotaur Books, an imprint of St. Martin's Publishing Group

THE CABINETS OF BARNABY MAYNE. Copyright © 2020 by Elsa Hart. All rights reserved. Printed in the United States of America. For information, address St. Martin's Publishing Group, 120 Broadway, New York, NY 10271.

www.minotaurbooks.com

Designed by Jonathan Bennett

Library of Congress Cataloging-in-Publication Data

Names: Hart, Elsa, author.
Title: The cabinets of Barnaby Mayne / Elsa Hart.
Description: First edition. | New York : Minotaur Books, 2020.
Identifiers: LCCN 2019059161 | ISBN 9781250142818
   (hardcover) | ISBN 9781250142825 (ebook)
Subjects: GSAFD: Mystery fiction.
Classification: LCC PS3608.A78455 C33 2020 | DDC 813/.6—dc23
LC record available at https://lccn.loc.gov/2019059161

Our books may be purchased in bulk for promotional, educational, or business use. Please contact your local bookseller or the Macmillan Corporate and Premium Sales Department at 1-800-221-7945, extension 5442, or by email at MacmillanSpecialMarkets@macmillan.com.

First Edition: 2020

10 9 8 7 6 5 4 3 2 1

To Elizabeth Blackwell and her *Curious Herbal*

THE
CABINETS
OF
BARNABY
MAYNE

CHAPTER 1

It has been suggested that the surface of the earth was once smooth, and that beneath it was an abyss filled with water. After many years, the crust of the earth became dry and brittle. At a command from God it cracked, and the waters that had been trapped within surged and roiled through the broken land. Thus the Flood was not a deluge from above that covered the mountains, but a welling from below that created them. The world inherited by man was but the jagged ruin left by that great devastation.

This was just one theory that was being debated in Signore Covo's coffeehouse one drizzly spring morning. The year was 1703. Queen Anne occupied the throne, and for the citizens of London, there were enough new laws, new wars, and new books to sustain any argument. But Covo's was popular because it inspired a more fanciful variety of conversation. Its walls and ceilings, encrusted with objects intended to provoke wonder and speculation, made serious gentlemen feel comfortable entertaining thoughts of subterranean giants, unknown civilizations, and even, with the appropriate tone of deprecation, magic.

Upstairs, Signore Covo reclined in a chair before the hearth, legs outstretched, affecting the casual elegance his

English companion would expect from a secretive Italian noble. Wearing a bemused half smile, he watched Mr. Simon Babington, silver-buttoned and bewigged, pace across the floor.

"I am not an ignorant man, Covo. I know that through a glass lens, a man may observe living creatures in a drop of water. Fiery *Noctiluca* holds no mystery for me. And as for corpuscular philosophy—"

"Not even Newton himself could confound you," said Covo.

"And he has tried," said Babington. "He has tried. So you see there is much about the world that I understand. But for all my knowledge, I cannot fathom how a man as aloof, as conceited, as *uncooperative* as Sir Barnaby Mayne has attained such clout in our community."

Covo rotated his hands so that his steepled fingertips pointed to an ornate clock standing in the corner. "Time," he said. "It has a deleterious effect on youth, but there are advantages to its passage. Mayne has spent forty years funding travelers and having their briny crates delivered to him from as near as France and as far as China. He knows which letters to write, which parties to attend, which societies to join, and which monographs to debate. He has played the game, Babington, and he has played it for a long time. I cannot help but admire the old obsessive."

"Admire him?" Babington exclaimed, with an indignant quiver of his cheeks. "He knows I've been pursuing an edition of Palissy's *Fontaines* for more than a year, but instead of alerting me to the rumor that one had surfaced in Lovell's Bookshop, he sniffed it out and bought it for himself. It is against all etiquette. He isn't even interested in hydrology! He only wanted it because he knew I did. Prior to this, if I had come across a *Picatrix* or a *Liber-Razielis* I'd have told him at once. But no longer. No longer."

"You might ask to borrow the book from him," said Covo, pleasantly.

"And take my place among the toadying supplicants begging for access to his cabinets? It would please him too much. No, Covo. What I want is revenge."

"What exactly are you asking me to do?" Signore Covo's eyes slid to a pair of rusty swords displayed above the mantelpiece.

Following the look, Babington blanched. "Of course I don't mean—What sort of man do you think I am?"

"What sort of man do you think *I* am?" asked Covo curiously.

The question prompted an uncertain laugh from Babington. "I really cannot say."

"Tell me, then," said Covo, "what manner of revenge you intend."

Babington cleared his throat. "I want to take something that Sir Barnaby wants."

"You have a particular item in mind?"

"Not just one item." Babington lowered himself to the chair opposite Covo. "Is the name Follywolle familiar to you?"

"Naturally. He was one of you." By *one of you*, Covo meant the set of gentlemen who considered themselves collectors. They were known for dedicating their disposable income, and in some cases their indisposable income, to the acquisition and display of rarities of art and nature.

"Then you know Follywolle is dead," said Babington.

Covo nodded. "Several months ago, at his wife's family estate in Sweden, where he had lived these past ten years."

"He kept his whole collection there," said Babington. "And now that he has gone to await the Resurrection, his widow intends to auction it." He shuddered. "The man is to be pitied. His life's work. Evicted from its shelves, predated upon, torn to pieces."

"A tragic fate," said Covo.

Babington, not noticing the mocking smile that curved Covo's lips, carried on. "Of course Sir Barnaby has a contact already in Sweden."

"Whom he has asked to pick the carcass, if you will," murmured Covo.

Babington frowned disapprovingly. "Some respect, Covo, really."

"My apologies," said Covo. "I was charmed by your metaphor and could not resist the opportunity to extend it."

"My point," said Babington, "is that Sir Barnaby's contact in Sweden is to send him a catalogue of all the items to be sold at the Follywolle auction. What I want is to ensure that Sir Barnaby is prevented from acquiring a single object he desires."

Covo repressed a sigh. What children these collectors were. "Mayne is a savvy competitor," he said aloud. "He is hardly likely to discuss the items upon which he intends to bid."

"Which is why I have come to you," said Babington. "Is this not precisely the kind of service you offer?"

"Allow me to clarify," said Covo. "You wish me to discover what Sir Barnaby Mayne intends to purchase from the Follywolle auction without alerting Mayne to the fact that his privacy has been compromised?"

Babington's gaze grew distant as he fixed it on a desirable future. "Yes," he murmured. "Yes, that is what I want.

I want Sir Barnaby to choose from among the books, birds, bones, shells, and statues those he believes will most complement his cabinets. I want him to clear spaces on his shelves for his new acquisitions while he waits in eager anticipation for their arrival. I want him to instruct that poor curator of his to prepare lines in the registers. And after the crates are delivered to *my* door instead of to his, I intend to publish a monograph on whatever object he craved most."

Covo drew in his long legs, planted his hands on the arms of his chair, and rose to his considerable height. "I believe I understand what is required of me. I presume you are similarly cognizant of what I require of you?"

Babington's rapturous expression soured as he removed a heavy purse from his pocket and counted out coins. "The rest when I have what I want," he said. Covo accepted the coins with a short nod.

As Babington moved to the door, his gaze wandered over the walls and ceilings of the chamber. "Your décor grows more dense every time I visit. What is this?" He pointed to an arrow that dangled from the ceiling, tied with a length of golden thread.

Covo's expression grew more serious than it had yet been in the course of their conversation. "That is the arrow of an elf queen. They say that when allowed to swing freely, at midnight on the full moon its point will lead its owner to treasure." Covo paused delicately. "A prize for any collector."

"Come now, Covo. Do you take me for a credulous man? I will not condone you making a mockery of a serious pursuit." Babington's tone was chiding, but his gaze lingered on the arrow. Covo smiled inwardly. When Babington had gone, Covo stood for a long moment in thoughtful stillness, watching the arrow swing.

CHAPTER 2

The London residence of Sir Barnaby Mayne comprised two adjacent houses near the center of a stately terrace in the fashionable neighborhood of Bloomsbury Square. Cecily Kay, obeying the instructions Sir Barnaby had given in his letter, knocked on the door of number seven. She was surprised when the first sound to reach her from within was of shattering glass.

Several moments passed before the door was opened by a maid whose dark eyes, soft features, and undefined chin called to mind the countenance of a young squirrel. She appeared anxious. Cecily's keen nose detected a sharp odor wafting over the stoop, and an explanation suggested itself. She looked at the maid sympathetically. "A broken specimen jar?" she asked.

The maid's face registered bewilderment. "Yes, my lady. How did you know?"

Cecily, who was almost a head taller than the other woman, nodded over her at the interior of the house. "*Spiritu vini*," she said. "I must assume that in the home of one of the most esteemed collectors in England, the smell of strong alcohol at midday may be attributed not to afternoon carousing, but to the project of preservation. That, in com-

bination with the sound of breaking glass— I hope no one
has been injured?"

"A *mop*, Thomasin!" The words arrived disembodied on
the doorstep as if the house itself had spoken them. The
maid gave a nervous start and glanced over her shoulder.

Of the qualities of life on land Cecily had missed during
the two months she had spent at sea, hillsides textured by
leaves and dotted with flowers ranked high while extended,
formal welcomes ranked low. She was more than happy
to release the maid from her duties at the front door. "Go
ahead," she said quickly. "I can manage."

"*Thomasin!*" the hoarse, impatient voice called again.
The maid spun around, hurried to the far side of the room,
and disappeared through an interior door. Cecily turned to
her possessions, which the coachman had stacked beside
her on the stoop before driving away. They included a battered, salt-stained trunk and three neat bundles of pressed
plants. Cecily moved the bundles inside first, then dragged
the trunk over the threshold. She closed the door, patted the
grit from her hands, and surveyed the room.

It was a large square chamber lit by two windows facing
the street. The door through which the maid had gone was
directly opposite the front entrance. There was another door
to Cecily's right. With the exception of the space taken up
by doors and windows, the walls were lined from floor to
ceiling with cabinets, the top halves of which were fitted
with open shelves, the bottom with wide, shallow drawers.
Display tables filled the center of the room in such a dense
arrangement that the spaces between them were only wide
enough to permit the passage of a single person. Every
surface—every inch of oaken shelf and every tabletop from
corner to corner—was covered in stones. It was as if the

very foundation of the earth had been disassembled and set out again in neat rows of boulders, rocks, and pebbles, each tagged with a red paper label.

Cecily had seen collections before, but never one vast enough to require that an entire room be devoted to the matter and substance of mountains, caves, deserts, and coastlines. The thought of all that awaited her in the rooms beyond filled her with anticipation. She bent eagerly over the table closest to her and examined the label attached to a nondescript green stone. *A kind of Smaragdus,* she read, *which, being heated red hot, shines in the dark for a considerable time, about one-sixteenth of an hour.* Its neighbor was a spherical gray rock identified as the *Eagle Stone, named for the common opinion that the eagle carries it to her nest—*

"Who is that in the Stone Room?" The same voice that had summoned the maid cut off Cecily's perusal. She crossed the chamber as quickly as she could, holding her skirts tight to keep them from catching on a corner as she squeezed between the display tables. When she opened the inner door, she found herself facing a spacious landing punctured to her left by a dim stairwell. On the other side of the landing from where she stood, a long, dark hallway extended toward the back of the house.

"Sir Barnaby Mayne?" she inquired of the gloom. As her eyes adjusted, she discerned two figures at the far end of the hall. One appeared to tower, stork-like, above the other.

The reply was impatient. "Yes? Yes, who is it?"

"Cecily Kay."

"You have arrived too early, Lady Kay. Have a care where you step. My curator has broken a jar."

Cecily advanced cautiously. Spheres of candlelight clung to the walls, caressing the corners of paintings. As she entered the hallway and drew nearer to the figures, she realized that the one who had appeared so tall was in fact perched on a step stool in front of a shelf crowded with jars. At the base of the stool, glass shards gleamed wickedly from a spreading pool of liquid. The alcohol fumes stung her eyes. With no rug to soak it up, the puddle was expanding, sending out sluggish arms toward the buckled shoes of Sir Barnaby Mayne.

Cecily would have known him to be the master of the house at once, even if she had not recognized him from the portraits on the frontispieces of his published books. Though age had made him frail, thinning his cheeks to translucence and carving furrows around his eyes, the authority he projected over the space around him was unambiguous. His shoulders, encased in black velvet, appeared broader than they were, as if they were appropriating breadth and volume from the darkness surrounding them. He wore a gray wig that rose high above his brow and fell in luxurious curls down his chest, framing the pristine lace that cascaded from his collar.

He spared her only a glance before returning his attention to a glistening gray lump near the center of the puddle. "As you see, Lady Kay, you have arrived not only early, but at an inopportune moment. My curator has selected the hour before the tour begins as an ideal time to demonstrate his capacity for clumsiness, a defect I make every effort to identify *before* I offer employment. I will not tolerate it, Dinley."

The man standing on the stool stepped down gingerly into the puddle. Cecily judged him to be in his early twenties. Gaunt cheeks and angular features were gentled by a pair of large, dark eyes. Cecily was not certain whether to attribute the tears that glazed them to the fumes or to his employer's reprimands. "I—I will obtain a new jar," he managed.

"Action at long last." Sir Barnaby put a hand to his heart in mock surprise. "I thought him afflicted by paralysis. *Well?* Why do you linger? Every moment the specimen is exposed to the air hastens its decay. *Go.*"

The curator scurried away. Cecily, heedless of the puddle dampening the hems of her skirt and petticoat, crouched to examine the gray lump on the floor. It was an aquatic creature, long-since deceased, with a body resembling that of an eel. Its open jaws, which increased the size of an already disproportionately large head, bristled with needle-like teeth as long as her little finger. "I've seen a fish like this before," she said. "Is it the vipermouth?"

"Mine is the only specimen in England," said Sir Barnaby. If her astuteness had impressed him, he gave no indication of it. "Do not linger so close," he added coldly. "I will not see it damaged further."

Cecily stood and surveyed the shelves above the step stool. By the light of the nearest candle on the wall she could see the fins, scales, and sinuous coils of fish and snakes suspended inside the glass jars. A door beside her creaked hesitantly open, spilling light from an adjacent room into the hallway. She stepped out of the way.

"Something was broken?" The question, delivered in a heavy accent, came from a man with an appearance of general dishevelment. His clothes, though fine, sagged at the knees and elbows. The skin around his eyes was swollen with fatigue, and the unkempt mass of curls on his head looked less like a wig than like a gray cat posing as a wig to escape pursuing hounds. As he spoke, he extended a foot forward.

"Stop!" Sir Barnaby's explosive exclamation came too

late. The newcomer's heel met the toothy head of the fish with a wet squelch. He hopped backward in dismay. "Ah, Sir Barnaby, I did not see." Still balancing on one foot, he picked up a sodden cloth from the floor and scraped it over the bottom of his boot. A fragment of the ruined creature dropped from the sole of the shoe. "I am most sincerely sorry," he said, sounding mortified.

"You have destroyed it." Sir Barnaby uttered the words in a voice like a pestle grinding against an empty mortar.

The man quailed and closed his eyes tightly for a moment as if he thought he could escape by taking cover behind his eyelids. When he opened them he noticed Cecily and seized the opportunity to address someone other than his enraged host. He executed a tremulous bow. "My gentle lady," he said. "I am Helm. Mr. Otto Helm. A visitor to your England from my country of Sweden."

Cecily, perceiving Sir Barnaby to be too much in the grip of anger to facilitate the introduction, introduced herself.

"Kay," murmured Helm. "Kay. Kay." He rubbed his forehead. "Ah, yes. Kay. Of course. I am knowing the name of your husband. He is in the office of consul, yes? In Constantinople?"

Cecily recognized in Helm the fatigue of a traveler worn out by the sustained effort of existing in unfamiliar spaces. "You are nearly correct," she said kindly. "He is in Smyrna."

"Smyrna, of course," said Helm. Interest lit his weary features. "If you yourself have traveled in the Levant, perhaps you would speak to me of the wonders you saw there. Did you happen upon any serpents? I have a particular interest in serpents."

"I did," said Cecily. She was gratified by the question. This was exactly the sort of discourse she had hoped awaited her in the Mayne house. But before she could continue, Sir Barnaby interrupted.

"I would have thought," he said acidly to Helm, "that my books and specimens would be sufficient to occupy you." He turned to Cecily. "Mr. Helm is here today to make a study of the serpents in my collection. I make every effort to accommodate the requests of scholars, but I have just been reminded of why I do not like to crowd the house."

Helm was looking up at the jars on the shelf. "Ah," he said mournfully. "I see you keep serpents here, too. I hope I have not most unfortunately trod upon one of them."

"It was not a serpent," growled Sir Barnaby. "It was a very rare fish. I suggest you return to the desk provided for your use. If you require assistance locating a specimen, Dinley will help you after he has finished here."

As if he saw in the words of his displeased host a chance to make amends, Helm answered with as much animation as his uncertain English allowed. "Ah, indeed I am in no need of aid. How could I be? Your system of arrangement is the most orderly and comprehensible of any I have seen in my travels. It is a great pleasure to me to conduct my study in the house of Mayne. Also as I have much enjoyed the company of yourself, and of Mr. Dinley, and of your lady illustrator, who expressed to me such sincere interest in the coloration of scales—"

"If you desire further speech with Mrs. Barlow, by all means seek her out," said Sir Barnaby, putting an impatient end to Helm's praise. "I have no time to converse with you now."

"Yes, yes, of course," said Helm meekly. "I will go to my work. I am most sorry for the loss of the fish." He bowed again to Cecily before backing slowly into the other room and closing the door. The silvery chime of a standing clock proclaimed the hour of one. Thomasin arrived, mop and bucket in hand, accompanied by a man of middle age whose forearms were flecked with flour and who exuded a fragrance of herbs.

Sir Barnaby addressed Cecily. "John will take you to your room and assist you with your belongings. The tour will convene in the Stone Room at half past two. The clocks in the house keep accurate time, and I insist on punctuality."

Dinley returned carrying a jar, which Sir Barnaby informed him coldly would no longer be necessary. "You will have to make a note to acquire a new specimen," he said. "Which of my correspondents will be making the journey through Gibraltar this year? Livesy? Scarcliff? Watson?"

"W-Watson, I believe," murmured Dinley.

As Cecily followed John up the stairs, she listened to Sir Barnaby fling demands at his hapless curator.

"Have you replaced the wire in the jaw of the hartebeest?"

"N-not yet."

"And the butterfly boxes? Are they dusted?"

"No. I intended to—"

"Your incompetence requires no explanation. I will be in my study. If the house is not ready when my guests arrive, you will answer for it."

A memory returned to Cecily, of a sailor stooped over a gleaming fish lying still on the wooden planks of the harbor at Gibraltar. Cecily had asked him why it was called the vipermouth. *Because,* he had responded, *like the viper, it swallows its prey whole.*

CHAPTER 3

The guest bedroom that was to be Cecily's home for a week appeared to prioritize the comfort of the collection over that of a person. The laden shelves that lined its walls were free of dust and soot, while the blue velvet curtains around the bed were faded and moth-eaten. Whorled shells and the spiny husks of sea urchins covered not only the desk by the window, but also the seat of the chair drawn up to it. The wall above the dresser, instead of being fitted with a mirror, was hung with a vast tessellation of mounted fish jaws.

Cecily, unperturbed by the arrangement, regarded with pride the three rectangular bundles she had arranged neatly on the floor. The leather belts that bound them were stained and rough, but remained tight. The edges, formed by hundreds of sheets of stacked brown paper, were still crisp. She knelt beside one of the bundles, loosened the belt, and carefully lifted the board and top sheet away to examine the plant resting flat beneath.

She smiled. It was dry. The leaves were intact. The translucent petals of its three flowers retained their pink color. She reflected with pleasure that after a journey of two months through storms on land and sea, the plants appeared less waterlogged and wind-chapped than she did. A brief in-

14

spection satisfied her that the rest of the specimens were, for the most part, in equally good condition. She reassembled the stack and pulled the belt tight again.

When she had exchanged her boots for clean slippers, she went out onto the landing that separated her room from the one opposite. The space, though windowless, was expansive enough to be considered a chamber in its own right. It was dedicated to a display of corals, which filled the shelves in tiny kingdoms of pink and white. According to a longcase clock with a loud tick, the time was half past one. There was still an hour before the tour was to begin. Cecily eyed the closed door of the other room. Sir Barnaby had not forbidden her from exploring.

It should have occurred to her to knock, but the quiet upper stories of the house seemed so devoted to the collection that she did not expect to encounter another living being. She opened the door, stepped inside, and halted abruptly as the woman seated at a desk in the gray light of a window turned to see who had come in. Cecily apologized, but even as she offered the polite excuses appropriate in the event of intruding upon a stranger, she began to feel that the woman was not a stranger at all.

The woman seemed to be having a similar reaction to the sight of Cecily. She leaned forward in her chair and fixed Cecily with an intent stare. Slowly, she lowered the paintbrush she was holding. Its bristles left a bright smudge of blue on the paper resting on the desk. All at once the woman leapt to her feet. A cloud of pencil shavings scattered from the folds of her skirt to the floor as she crossed the room. "Cecily!" she cried.

The face of a girl appeared in Cecily's mind. She heard as if from a great distance a child's voice calling, and saw the open door of a cottage framed in tangled vines. Memory supplied her with a name. "Meacan?"

Before she could take a step back, Cecily found her arms held in a warm half embrace. "It *is* you," said Meacan. "After a hundred years! *Cecily Goodrick*."

The sound of her maiden name heightened Cecily's sense of disorientation. "It's Cecily Kay now," she managed.

"Barlow," announced Meacan. "I'm Meacan Barlow."

The two women regarded each other. It had not in fact been a hundred years since they had last done so, but twenty-five. Cecily had been the shorter of the two when they were girls of nine and ten, and was now the taller. Her dark hair was laced with silver and her eyes were a forthright blue. She had the lean, sturdy posture and wind-grooved skin of hard travel, and had not been back in England long enough for the sun to retreat from her burnished cheeks or for her chapped lips to heal. Meacan, in contrast, had rounded and softened with the accumulation of years, and the lines of her face were more suggestive of laughter and tears than of nature's gusts. Her hair, which had been a haze of yellow when she was a girl, had darkened to sparrow brown, and was mostly but not entirely confined by its pins.

Cecily and Meacan had met during the reign of the Merry Monarch, in the year 1678. Opinions popular at that time included the belief that all Catholics were conspiring against the king, the acknowledgment that allowing women to play the roles of women onstage might be of some benefit to theater, and the feeling that marriage was best avoided by gentlemen gardeners, as it interfered with their work. Meacan's father, one of the most respected gardeners in England, did not conform to this expectation. He not only had a wife and children, but did not like to be parted from them.

When Cecily's father hired him to spend a year beautifying the grounds of the estate, the gardener brought his family with him.

Had James Goodrick not been a lover of books who studied even the least tolerated philosophies of his time with interest, his daughter might never have become acquainted with the daughter of the visiting gardener. As it was, he had recently been inspired by the principles of the persecuted Quakers to give Cecily a broad education. When he learned that there was to be another girl of about Cecily's age on the estate, he extended the services of Cecily's tutors to her. So it was that while their fathers sketched parterres and debated the placement of trees, Cecily and Meacan became first classmates, then friends.

Meacan shook her head in wonder and released Cecily's arms. "You don't look as if you've come from Durham," she said. Her attention shifted from Cecily's face to her dress. She scrutinized the muted purple fabric. "And I haven't seen silk of this color in any of the London shops. Where have you been?"

"In Smyrna," Cecily answered. "My husband was appointed consul there seven years ago."

Cecily read the curiosity in Meacan's eyes and hesitated. She thought of the confidences they had shared while navigating the gnarled lower branches of chestnut trees and wading through wilderness ponds as tadpoles tickled their feet. That had been a long time ago. The familiarity between them had faded like an old tapestry exposed to years of blanching sunlight. And Cecily was unused to discussing matters of the heart.

Her marriage, though better than many, was not a convivial one. She wished that as a young woman of nineteen she had been more discerning, but Andrew's apparent desire to learn more of the world had charmed her. Andrew, in turn, had been delighted by his bride's eager questions when he believed the source of her enthusiasm to be her fascination with *him*. By the time Cecily realized that Andrew's chief interest was in wealth, advancement, and other women, and Andrew realized that his wife had an embarrassing habit of demonstrating knowledge superior to his, it was too late. Their disappointment in each other had simmered until, two months earlier, it had boiled over into outright hostility.

She saw that Meacan was waiting for her to continue and cleared her throat. "I wished to make a visit home, but as the Company's present negotiations with the Ottomans require my husband's full attention, he has not accompanied me." She forced a smile. "But tell me about yourself."

To her relief, Meacan appeared eager to expound upon the past two decades of her life. She had been married and widowed twice. Her first husband had been an actor, her second a printer. From her first marriage she had a son, now sixteen and apprenticed to a clockmaker. Though, she added good-humoredly, he had inherited from his father a mind both quick and quickly distracted, and she would not be surprised if this time next month he'd turned his attention to a new profession. She asked after Cecily's family. Cecily explained that her parents had both departed the world peacefully, and that as their only child, she had inherited her father's estate upon his passing.

"And the gardens?" asked Meacan, after offering her condolences.

"The steward informs me they are well tended and more beautiful every year," said Cecily. "It has been a long time since I saw them myself. When we are in England, we make our home at my husband's estate in Lincolnshire."

Her words recalled them to their present circumstances. Meacan fluttered a hand to indicate the house enclosing them. "Why have you come here?"

"I wrote to Sir Barnaby," said Cecily. "To ask if I might consult his cabinets. While I was in Smyrna, I made a small collection of plants, many of which I cannot identify with any certainty. I understand his repository of dried specimens and botanical books to be among the most comprehensive and well ordered in the country."

"Ah." Meacan's eyes, a changeable green, twinkled with cheerful mockery. "So you are one of *them*."

"Them?"

Meacan tucked her chin, narrowed her eyes, and pressed her lips together in a caricature of Sir Barnaby. "The collectors," she intoned. "The noble scholars. Finding God's Truth in the veins of leaves and scales of lizards and colors of shells. Arranging them all into little piles. Giving them names no one can remember." She relaxed her expression, returned to the desk, and tapped a finger on a half-finished sketch. "Not that I resent it. You enthusiasts keep the poor artists employed."

Cecily connected Meacan's words to the pencil shavings and the paintbrush. "You're an illustrator?"

"A *sought-after* illustrator," said Meacan, with pride. "Currently in Sir Barnaby's employ. He intends to publish another catalogue of his most wondrous wonders."

Cecily glanced around her at the room. Like hers, it was fitted with display cases, but the atmosphere here was softened by evidence of human habitation. A froth of petticoats covered a chair. A cloak and a gown hung from the corners of a cabinet, partly obscuring its contents. The items arranged on the dresser had been swept to one side to make room for combs and ribbons. "You're staying in the house?" she asked.

Meacan nodded. "For the better part of a week already, and I'm hoping to keep the room for the season."

"But where do you usually live?"

"I keep an apartment in Ludgate Hill," said Meacan. "Only at present I find myself not *quite* solvent enough to pay the rent, so I've let it for the season."

Cecily had moved to the desk and was examining Meacan's half-finished drawing. A unicorn shell filled the page, its ghostly twirls sketched with delicate assurance. The shell itself rested beside the paper, its red label affixed to it with string. Cecily was impressed by the likeness, and said so.

Meacan assumed an affronted air. "I don't know why you sound surprised. I told you I was sought-after."

"The last time I saw you," said Cecily, arching a dark eyebrow, "you were persuading me to fill our tutor's boots with berries."

Meacan laughed. "I have since acquired the patience and decorum of an old oak."

Cecily was about to reply when her attention shifted to a large book lying open on the desk to a page dense with colorful illustrations. The subjects—common butterflies and beetles—were familiar to Cecily, with one exception. She bent to look at the outlier more closely. It appeared to be an insect of some kind. Each segment of its body was decorated with a different pattern in a wild variety of hues. Its multitudinous legs alternated in color, and it had three separate sets of wings. On its forehead, between two bulging and expressive eyes, was a bright blue horn, the paint of which was still wet. Not far from it, the brush Meacan had discarded rested in a blotch of blue.

"I've never seen a creature like this," said Cecily, fascinated. "What is it called?"

Meacan's expression was serious. "This," she said, "is the *alphonius barnobios bittelbug.*"

"The what?"

"Ah," said Meacan. "Perhaps you know it by its other name. The *belonmia speciama mercantilia sepherens.*"

Cecily, beginning to be skeptical, shook her head.

"And I thought you such an authority on Latin names," said Meacan loftily. "The common name, then. This bug is known as the *Illustrator's Revenge.*"

"Revenge?"

"Mmm."

Cecily looked at the page again. She had assumed it to be part of a sketchbook. Now she saw that the text was printed. She flipped to the frontispiece and read the title, which proclaimed the book to be a "new and compleat" treatise on the insects of Wales. She looked at Meacan, aghast. "Are you—painting in a published book?"

"I am," said Meacan.

"But this book is a resource for scholars."

"It is, yes," Meacan agreed. "And its author should have paid me for my work." She pointed to the printed illustrations. "These are all mine. A month of labor. And not a *farthing* of what I was promised. They're all the same, you know, *the collectors.* Fists as tight as buds in winter." Her eyes dropped proudly to the glistening chimera. "Whenever I come across a copy of the volume, I make a small addition."

"Why?"

Meacan raised her brows as if the answer was obvious. "In the hope that it will bring ridicule to the author, of course. They so dislike being ridiculed. *Reputation*, you know."

The spell of camaraderie that had been cast by the chance reunion wavered. Cecily felt a rush of irritation. She had come, after a journey of two months, to what she had anticipated would be a sanctum of scholarly order, only to be greeted by a smashed fish, a curmudgeonly host, and an old friend turned defacer of books.

Meacan crossed her arms over her chest. "You aren't going to betray me, are you? You look as annoyed as you did when I rearranged your father's library."

"Rearranged it? You pulled all the books from the shelves, made a small fortress of them, declared yourself a queen, and invited the hounds inside to be your courtiers."

"As I recall," said Meacan with a sigh, "they rose against their monarch and toppled the kingdom."

Cecily nodded. "I am still finding paw prints on the pages."

Meacan let out a peal of laughter. "Are you really?"

Cecily pointed to the painted bug. "Does the world not contain enough to bewilder the mind without your introducing deliberate confusion to earnest endeavors?"

"Bah." Meacan made a dismissive gesture. "You think too highly of collectors."

"Why should I not think highly of them?"

"Because," said Meacan, slipping her brush behind her ear, "they are, most of them, men. *Wealthy* men. With obsessions. And Sir Barnaby is among the worst of them. You *are* to join the tour today, I assume?"

"I am."

"Then take my advice. Keep your elbows close to your

sides, and if you pick something up, be sure to return it to its exact place. Guests are not exempt from his temper. And don't cross Martha, either."

"Martha?"

"The housekeeper," said Meacan. "Martha is married to John, who mostly does the cooking and gardening. She's been employed by Sir Barnaby since the day the carpenters came to put in the cabinets, and is as devoted to it all as he is."

"And the maid, Thomasin?" asked Cecily. "Is she related to them?"

Meacan shook her head. "Thomasin hasn't been here long, and won't stay long, if you ask me. She doesn't like dusting skeletons. And that's the whole household. Oh, and Walter Dinley, of course. Stay close to him on the tour. He's clever, but he's as gentle as a doe. Sir Barnaby doesn't deserve him."

"Then you won't be joining the group?" asked Cecily.

"Sir Barnaby doesn't like to crowd the rooms," said Meacan. "He's asked me to make a drawing of the sweetbay in the garden while it's in bloom. I intend to occupy myself with that pleasant task, and then return here until we're called to supper. But Cecily?"

"Yes?"

Meacan drummed her fingers on the desk. She started to speak, stopped, drew in a breath, held it, and exhaled slowly. Finally she lifted her eyes to meet Cecily's. "It's good to see you again."

As Cecily made her way out of the room and down the stairs, she wondered what it was that Meacan had meant to say, and what had kept her silent.

CHAPTER 4

When Cecily reentered the Stone Room, she found Sir Barnaby and Walter Dinley standing with their backs to her, each positioned before a window. In the light, without the shadows of the house to prop him up, Sir Barnaby appeared smaller and more frail than he had earlier. Dinley's worn brown jacket was flecked with the dusty detritus of innumerable drawers and cabinets. Over their shoulders, the carriages and passersby looked blurred and unstable through the thick glass.

A rattle and jingle of reins, followed by a knock, announced the arrival of another guest. A man in the early years of middle age, he was dressed expensively. His well-tailored waistcoat was subtly embroidered with silver flowers. The cravat meticulously wrapped and twisted around his neck was trimmed in lace. Its ends were tucked fashionably through a buttonhole of his jacket. He wore a voluminous wig that overwhelmed his features and exuded a halo of jasmine-scented powder. He addressed himself at once to Sir Barnaby.

"Wondrous," he said, lifting his hands high in a gesture of all-encompassing praise for the shelves around him: "At last, the day has come." He dropped his hands, divested

himself of his hat and sword, and searched for a surface designated to receive them. Finding none, he propped the sword
by the door and set the hat on top of a knobby stalactite, all
the while maintaining a steady patter. "As I remarked only
yesterday to Norbury, who did me the great honor of inviting me to supper—a great honor, though nothing of course
compared to that of the present moment—as I remarked,
after he guided me through a room in which he has installed
a veritable *congregation* of mummies, not only of cats and
crocodiles but, I am very nearly convinced, of a true *dragon*,
but before we examined his diverse sepulchral lamps of the
ancients, unless I am mistaken and it was at *Wyville's* house
that I saw the sepulchral lamps—" The man paused, adrift
in his own speech, and cast about for the idea that had initiated it.

Sir Barnaby prompted him impatiently. "As you remarked
to Norbury—"

The man's expression cleared. "Yes, yes, as I remarked to
Norbury, I have anticipated this day with such fervor that
I have been able to think of nothing else all week. At last I
am to see, in full and in daylight, the mightiest collection
in London. For not only is yours the most *vast*, the most
comprehensive, the most *colossal*, but surely it is also the key
by which man shall unlock the hidden secrets of the earth.
Eh, Sir Barnaby? *Non vi* . . ." He faltered as Sir Barnaby,
apparently no longer listening, returned his attention to the
window.

Recovering quickly from the slight, the man renewed
his smile and greeted Dinley with casual familiarity before
addressing Cecily. "Humphrey Warbulton," he announced
with a bow.

Cecily introduced herself.

"A moment," said Warbulton. "I make an effort to acquaint myself with all the names in our little community of collectors and travelers. Your husband—is he a fellow of the Philosophical Society? No? The Society for the Study of Quadrupeds? The Shipwreck Speculators? The Butterfly Enthusiasts? Ah, but of course. *Kay*, consul at Smyrna." Warbulton's expression turned hopeful. "I would be most grateful for an introduction."

Cecily started to reply, but stopped when she saw that Warbulton's attention had been suddenly captured by one of the display tables, from which he plucked a thin, conical stone. "Sir Barnaby," he said eagerly, holding it aloft. "Sir Barnaby, do you remember last month's meeting? The Fossil Society? Mr. Gare's presentation?"

"Gare's a fool," grunted Sir Barnaby.

The reply seemed to delight Warbulton, who turned to Cecily, proffering the stone. "Mr. Gare," he explained, "attempted to convince us that this should properly be called a *tonguestone,* as it is in fact the tongue of a serpent *turned* to stone by Saint Paul the Apostle after he was shipwrecked on the isle of Malta. Sir Barnaby not only offered *unassailable* evidence to the contrary, but set Mr. Gare down *so roundly* that—and I have not yet communicated this amusing addendum to you, Sir Barnaby—that Mr. Denby whispered to me that if Gare's face was any indication, the man's head was hot enough to—to *cook* every louse in his wig." Warbulton let out a hoot of self-conscious laughter.

Cecily, exhausted by Warbulton but curious about the stone, took it and turned it over in her hands. Its surface was smooth and gray, and it was about the length of her little finger. She squinted at the label. "Petrified remains of an antediluvian squid," she read.

Sir Barnaby swiveled his head without turning fully around. He was scowling. "I must insist the objects not be removed from their places," he said. "And do not clatter so recklessly through the shelves." The second comment was directed at Warbulton, whose cuffs of fine lawn were alighting like birds on one rock after another.

As Cecily returned the stone to its place, another carriage drew to a halt outside. It seemed to her that both Sir Barnaby and Dinley tensed in anticipation as they waited for its occupant to come into view, and relaxed when they saw who it was. Cecily judged the new arrival to be about fifty. Dressed in a suit of very pale gray wool, he carried himself with the easy assurance of a gentleman wealthy enough to replace his wigs when they itched and his shoes when they pinched. His healthy complexion and trim figure suggested that he had the means to eat and drink what he wanted, and the discipline not to indulge in an excess of either. In one hand he held a bulky doctor's case, in the other a book bound in red vellum.

"As promised," he announced, handing the book to Sir Barnaby, "I convey to you from the darkness of time the *Liber Iuratus Honorii*, complete and in fine condition."

Cecily saw for the first time Sir Barnaby's eyes light with excitement. He took the book and began an inspection of it. "Yes," he murmured, turning its pages. "Yes, this does appear to be complete."

The newcomer smiled indulgently. "As I mentioned yesterday, I thought of you the moment I saw it for sale. It is a rare delight to give you a book you do not already possess." He turned. "How are you, Dinley? You are pale."

Dinley attempted a smile. "Only—only a little tired."

The man looked concerned. "You must improve the

quality of your rest. I suggest an infusion of Saint John's wort, to be drunk an hour before bed. Many of my patients have found it exceedingly effective."

Dinley thanked the man, who then turned to greet Warbulton and Cecily. "I'm Giles Inwood," he said. "You must be here for today's tour."

Warbulton crossed the room, his coat catching on the corners of tables and flashing its lining of orange silk. "But we've met before, Mr. Inwood. You must remember. The demonstration of the diving bell?"

Inwood's forehead creased into lines of polite effort. "I'm afraid I—" His expression cleared. "Ah, yes. Were you not the gentleman who volunteered to enter the bell and be submerged?"

Warbulton nodded so forcefully that his wig shifted forward. "I was, yes. And now that we are friends I will tell you that the experience was *most* unpleasant. A terrible pressure in the head and deprivation of the lungs."

In the desultory conversation that followed, Cecily and Inwood were introduced. She learned that he was, in addition to a collector, a physician and close friend of Sir Barnaby's. He had not come to participate in the tour, having seen his friend's collection on numerous occasions, but declared that he would make himself comfortable in the house until the time he was expected to call on a nearby patient.

It was nearing half past two when a new voice spoke, not from the front door, but from the inner door that opened into the dark hallway. "Is this where I'm to be?"

The attention of every person in the room fixed instantly on a woman in whose face youth and beauty met in undeniable accord. Her skin was like translucent stone, delicately tinted by the pink and blue life that flowed through the veins beneath it. Her guileless eyes, bright as forget-me-nots, regarded them all with nervous excitement. "I've—I've come for the tour."

Sir Barnaby frowned. "*Whence* did you come?"

The young woman's brow crinkled in a moment of confusion, then smoothed. "Oh, my apologies," she said quickly. "I've come from the garden. I—I misdirected the carriage, and was left in the alley behind the house instead of being brought to the front. I thought I would be obliged to walk the length of the terrace to enter, but when I knocked on the door in the wall, I was admitted by the kind woman making a sketch of the sweetbay tree. She told me I had come to the correct house."

Meacan, thought Cecily, glad that someone had been there to assist the girl, who did not look as if she was accustomed to taking carriages through the city alone.

Dinley looked, if possible, more pale than he had before. "The—the *alley*?"

"Whatever fool of a carriage driver left you there should be hauled to the constable," said Inwood. "That alley isn't safe for an armed man, let alone an innocent girl."

"You must be Miss Alice Fordyce," said Sir Barnaby. "You are younger than your letter led me to believe you would be. Have you no escort?"

Again, she was apologetic. "I was to come with my aunt, whom I am visiting. This morning she was not feeling well, and I—I persuaded her to let me come alone, for I am only in London for a short time, and have such a wish to see your cabinets. I have been told they contain all the wonders of the world."

The words, delivered with such sweetness that even Sir Barnaby could not scowl at them, were still hovering in the room as the clock on the mantelpiece chimed two thirty. There was another knock on the door. Sir Barnaby started to attention and opened it himself.

"You look disappointed," said the man who stood on the threshold. His features, clothes, and bearing were so conventional as to make him, in Cecily's eyes, difficult to distinguish from any number of landed gentlemen occupying the middle rungs of financial complacency. As he stepped inside, he fixed appreciative eyes on Alice Fordyce. "Allow me to correct myself," he said. "Not disappointed, but distracted. And how could you not be? You did not tell me you had acquired a living goddess of beauty for your cabinets. Martin Carlyle, miss."

The girl looked down and murmured her name. Reluctantly, Mr. Carlyle shifted his gaze to take in the rest of the company. "Ah, Inwood," he said. "Is there word on the wreck of the *Nuestra Señora*?"

Inwood gave him a cheerful smile. "Well met, Carlyle. I didn't know you were an investor."

"I?" Carlyle chuckled. "Certainly not. I can afford to appear in society *with* gamblers. I cannot afford to be one of them."

Cecily was not surprised to hear Warbulton's voice chime in. "I don't believe I've seen you at any of the lectures, Mr. Carlyle. Are you a collector?"

"Merely an appreciative visitor," said Carlyle.

"You must visit my collection, then," said Inwood. "I'm to lead a tour Monday a week from today."

Carlyle inclined his head. "I'm obliged to you. Certainly, I will attend."

Inwood addressed the group. "You are all most welcome. I have a number of antiquities in which I take some small pride, though I will warn you, my cabinets are not nearly so full of marvels as the ones you will see today."

Warbulton, who seemed incapable of repressing speech for more than a few moments at a time, spoke again. "I have a collection," he said. "It is, I admit, in its infancy, but what better example could I choose to follow than that set by Sir Barnaby, who has assembled here this veritable paradise on earth, this replica of Eden, this world of wonders—"

Sir Barnaby broke in. "It is past time. Dinley?"

Dinley took a circuitous path between the tables, squeezing awkwardly past the other guests, and bolted the front door. Sir Barnaby cast a final, irritated glance out the window. "Our company is not complete, but if our purpose is to visit each room before supper, we can delay no longer."

The visitors assembled as best they could. Sir Barnaby's eyes moved over the room, looking not at the faces of his guests, but at the shelves he had so meticulously assembled over the course of his long life. "The project of a true collector is a noble one. And yet there are those who denigrate our efforts. Who would call our houses *knicknackatories*, our labors frivolous, our devotions impious. But time will make fools of our detractors, for the shelves you will see today contain no less than the future course of all knowledge toward the secrets God left for man to discover. Let us begin."

CHAPTER 5

From the Stone Room, the group followed the same path Cecily had taken that morning down the candlelit hall to the shelves of specimen jars. The enclosed space still smelled faintly of alcohol. They paused while Sir Barnaby drew their attention to a number of rare snakes and fish, among them the small but reputedly mighty *shiphalter*, named for tales told of its power to change the course of ships by attaching itself to their hulls.

Three doors led out of the hall. The first, which Sir Barnaby indicated but did not open, was the entrance to his private study. The second, set in the rear wall of the house, led to the garden. The third, through which the tour continued, connected the house they were in to the house adjoining it. Sir Barnaby explained as he ushered them into the next room that he had been obliged to purchase the second property to accommodate his expanding collection. Because the two buildings shared a wall, adding new doors had proved a practical means of facilitating movement between them.

Recognizing the place where Otto Helm had taken his unfortunate step onto the vipermouth, Cecily was not surprised to see the Swede hunched over a desk in a corner of the room, his nose almost touching the side of a specimen jar.

The heavy, unmoving coils of a snake were visible through the breath-clouded glass. Helm had a notebook open before him and was whispering under his breath as his pencil rushed across the page. Absorbed in his work, he made no effort to introduce himself to the group. His whispered count of scales and the scratch of his pencil continued as Sir Barnaby pointed out notable specimens among the skeletal serpents winding up walls and watching from jars.

The tour left the Serpent Room and continued up a dim stairwell. Over the next hour and a quarter, they shuffled through the Artifact Room, the Bird Room, and the Beast Room. Even Cecily, who prided herself on her ability to maintain her bearings, became disoriented amid vast displays of vases, boxes, swords, coins, feathers, eggs, nests, insects, bones, pelts, horns, and claws. It was nearing five o'clock when they reached the library. At the center of the room, an enormous skull was displayed on a solid, low table.

"Is it a giant?" Alice Fordyce peered into a cavernous socket large enough to encompass her golden head. The skull was almost as tall as she was. Its brow was a smooth plane of yellowed bone, its massive jaw curved like an arm bent to cradle an infant.

"Many scholars have believed so," said Sir Barnaby. "There was a Jesuit who claimed he had identified several of these skulls by name—Goliath, Asterion, Orestes, even Polyphemus himself."

"A *cyclops*," breathed Alice.

Sir Barnaby's tone was dismissive. "That is all simply Catholic credulity. I have made a careful study of the bones. It is my opinion—and I am supported in this by the fellows of the Royal Society—that though the noble brow and jaw do resemble those of a man, the skull belongs to—"

"An elephant!" The word burst from Humphrey Warbulton, who had already removed three books from a shelf, fanned their pages, and set them on a table. "It is an elephant, isn't it?"

Sir Barnaby motioned for Dinley to replace the books. "How reassuring," he said, "to know that Mr. Warbulton can guide you all through my collection, should I fail."

Warbulton, seemingly oblivious to the acid in Sir Barnaby's voice, approached the skull. He wedged himself between Cecily and Alice, knocking Alice off-balance as he placed a hand on the elephant's jaw. Alice reached for a table to stop her fall. One of the elephant's teeth clattered to the ground.

"Take care!" cried Dinley.

Warbulton picked up the tooth and attempted to reinsert it into its place. He fumbled, and another tooth fell to the floor. "It doesn't *look* fragile," he said, with an apologetic wince.

"Miss—Miss Fordyce," said Dinley. "Your hand."

Alice had righted herself and was looking at her palm. Blood was welling in little beads along a thin wound. She glanced around her in apparent surprise. "I don't know what happened."

It was Carlyle who picked up a pale pink shell from the table on which she had caught herself. The edge of the shell glistened red. Alice stared at it, then at her palm. "It's only a scratch," she said. "There is no need to be concerned."

"On the contrary." Dinley's voice was unexpectedly firm. "It must be bandaged at once."

"Oh, but that isn't necessary," said Alice. "I have a handkerchief in my pocket that will suffice."

Dinley was adamant. "I will escort you to the kitchen,

Miss Fordyce. John has a good store of salves. We cannot risk infection."

A crease appeared between Alice's brows. "I assure you, Mr. Dinley, there is no need."

Carlyle chimed in. "Do not deprive us of our fair companion, Dinley, I beg you."

Sir Barnaby concluded the matter. "In this instance, Mr. Dinley is correct. Miss Fordyce, there are objects in my collection more dangerous than they appear. A dead creature may retain its venom, after all, and even I cannot say for certain which ancient weapons may have been dipped in poison to heighten their efficacy."

Alice, her expression now touched with fear, followed Dinley out of the room. Sir Barnaby spoke after them. "If Inwood is still here, you might consult him."

When the two had gone, Sir Barnaby lectured the group briefly on the system he employed to maintain his registers, a set of forty volumes bound in matching blue vellum. The depleted tour then proceeded up the staircase to a spacious landing. Like the one outside Cecily's room, it was furnished with cabinets. The theme of the display was not immediately obvious. In addition to vases, books, corals, and statuettes, the shelves contained bones, stacked and rolled papers and textiles, and several large wooden crates. An odor of salt and moldy straw permeated the space, reminding Cecily of the creaking compartments of a ship at sea.

"It became clear to me," Sir Barnaby began, "that there is among my guests a fascination with those travelers who have attained a certain degree of notoriety. As I count many such adventurers among my correspondents, I have dedicated this small chamber to their current endeavors." Sir Barnaby gestured to a section of a shelf. "Here you will find items sent to me by the pirate Samuel Goring." He gestured to another section. "And here are butterflies and illustrations contributed by that unusual female lepidopterist whose exploits have garnered such attention."

Cecily's attention was drawn to an open crate resting on a table. Its battered sides were covered in circular patterns of dried mildew. Bits of bright silk, glazed porcelain, and filigreed metal peeped out from protective wrappings.

"If you are careful, you may handle the items," said Sir Barnaby.

Carlyle reached over Cecily's shoulder and pulled a porcelain bowl from the crate. He examined it appreciatively. "This is a color I haven't seen. It glitters as if there is gold suspended in the glaze."

Sir Barnaby nodded. "You will also find in that box, among other wonders, a scarlet butterfly very well preserved, and a cow bezoar as large as a hen's egg. But you have not brought your sketchbook today, Mr. Carlyle."

Carlyle replaced the bowl. "I've lost interest in the activity," he said with a shrug. "I envy you, Sir Barnaby. The endurance of your passion. Do you never tire of making labels and keeping registers?"

Sir Barnaby frowned. "I consider the maintenance of my shelves a duty to God and to science, not a trifling passion."

Warbulton joined Carlyle and Cecily at the crate. "Who sent it?" he asked.

"Anthony Holt," said Sir Barnaby.

"*Holt*?" Warbulton nodded eagerly. "Oh, I know all about him, of course. Impossible to be one of *us* and know nothing of Anthony Holt. I've attended all the readings of his letters at the Society. Do you have news of his latest exploits? Some tidbit, perhaps, that I might share at the coffeehouses? To what distant shore does he now sail?"

"To those beyond the reckoning of our maps," said Sir Barnaby. "Anthony Holt is dead."

"Dead?" Warbulton's eyes widened.

"Lost at sea," said Sir Barnaby. "The letter arrived yesterday. It is most unfortunate, as he had promised his next box would contain several items of particular interest to me."

Cecily looked at her host in surprise. There was no trace of grief in his tone, and she saw none in his expression. A step on the stair announced the return of Walter Dinley. He was alone. Miss Fordyce, he explained, had been more shaken by the incident than she had initially believed herself to be. He had summoned a carriage to return her to her aunt. "And," he added, proffering a thick folded paper to Sir Barnaby with an unsteady hand, "a courier just came with a message for you."

Sir Barnaby snatched the letter from Dinley. He tore it open and read silently. When he finished, he folded it, his face intent. "A reply is required," he announced. Offering no further explanation, he started down the stairs.

"But the tour—" said Dinley.

Sir Barnaby spoke without turning. "Continue it."

When he had gone, the abandoned guests turned to their new leader, who looked if possible more pale and anxious than he had yet that day. Dinley began a halting and inarticulate itemization of the room, starting with a *capricorn beetle* sent to Sir Barnaby by a correspondent in Norway. He continued for a few minutes before he stuttered to a halt in the middle of telling them about a barnacle sent from the Isle of Ascension. "I—I should go to the kitchen," he said.

"To check on preparations for supper. Perhaps it would be best if—that is, I am sure Sir Barnaby would not mind if you continued on your own. Or if you wish to return to an item of interest, you could do so. And reconvene when—when Sir Barnaby has finished."

Cecily, unenthusiastic about the prospect of being left alone with the loquacious Warbulton and the uninspiring Carlyle, inquired where she would find Sir Barnaby's collection of dried plants.

"The Plant Room," said Dinley. "It's—it's next to my room. Upstairs and through the connecting door."

Cecily thanked him, and departed. She emerged from the dark stairwell into a furnished garret. The single long room extended the entire length of the house. Gabled windows set into the sloping ceilings offered a view of the street from one end, and a view of the garden from the other. More than half of the space was dedicated to antiquities, the shelves populated by warriors, nymphs, and gods chiseled in marble, cast in bronze, or fired onto the rounded sides of ancient urns.

The remainder of the room offered insight into the labor required to maintain the collection. Rows of empty specimen jars gleamed like bubbles on the floor. On a low table, an assortment of tiny birds waited to be mounted on wooden stands. A half-complete skeleton sat next to a pile of bones. Cecily surveyed the clutter of labels, pencils, quills, papers, and pots of paste and paint. In a corner, tucked beneath the roof and surrounded by crates and towers of books, was a bed. Beside it was a chair with a coat draped over it and a pair of worn boots beneath it.

"So this is how the curator is accommodated," said Carlyle, who had come up the stairs behind her. "I would hardly call it a room."

Cecily did not answer. She had located the connecting door to the other house. She glanced at Carlyle and was relieved to see that the antiquities appeared to have captured his attention. The old floorboards creaked loudly under her feet as she entered the Plant Room and closed the door behind her. To the unknowing observer, it would have appeared to be a second library. Certainly it *was* a library, of a sort. Cecily knew that within the bindings that lined its walls was a vast, dried garden. Here, impossibly, spring flowers bloomed beside autumn ones, and the approach of winter carried no promise of change.

She went first to the volumes set out on the long table at the center of the room. With gentle confidence, she slid her hands between the pages, assessing the fragility of each plant before she turned to the next. Their names were written on each sheet in unwieldy blocks of Latin and English and languages she did not know.

Cecily's parents had each contributed to her enduring fascination with plants. Her father's obsession had been with the trees and hedges and flowers that gave shape and permanence to his land. Her mother's had been with the careful maintenance of an herb garden outside the kitchen. Both had pored over books and catalogues of the newest and rarest plants growing in nurseries and apothecary gardens. But neither they nor Cecily had ever seen a collection to rival Sir Barnaby's.

Her absorption was so complete that when the clocks in the house below announced in a scattered chorus that it was six o'clock, she could hardly believe that a whole hour had passed. She looked regretfully down at the thick whorled flowers of a *Phlomis* collected in Spain. She would happily have forgone supper and conversation for another hour of

acquainting herself with the room, but she had to acknowledge that she was hungry and tired.

She wondered why no one had come in search of her.
She had been aware of movement through the house, of
the creaking of floors and rumbling of stairs, but no one
had passed through the Plant Room. As she descended, she
expected to come across one of the other guests. Her sensitive nose picked out pipe smoke, wig powder, and traces
of malodorous city mud scraped onto stairs by booted feet.

But she saw no one until she entered the dining room
on the ground floor, where she found Inwood and Carlyle
deep in conversation. The table that filled the center of the
chamber was already laden with dishes. Steam rose from
meat pies and fresh baked bread. Boiled eggs bobbed and
gleamed in a pool of dark broth. Green salads festooned
with fruit and sprinkled with flower petals brought spring
color to the darkly savory spread.

The two men were discussing the ongoing war between
Sweden and Russia. ". . . Tsar's forces have captured the
fortress at Nyen," Carlyle was saying. "I heard he's going to
make it his new capital, which suggests he is confident the
victory will endure."

Inwood answered amiably. "I would not underestimate
the Swedes. Their young king continues to show his mettle
not only in war, but in government. I've heard nothing but
praise for his legal reforms." He noticed Cecily and smiled.
"Lady Kay. Have you seen Sir Barnaby?"

"Not since he excused himself from our company," she
replied. "Did the tour never reconvene?"

Carlyle bent to sniff a dish of thick puce-colored soup.
He grimaced. "Smells of rotting seaweed. If he insists on
impressing us with foreign fare, why not a cask of rare

madeira?" He straightened. "In answer to your question, we were all quite abandoned, left to wander alone through Sir Barnaby's fair Eden."

"I've never known him to neglect a tour," said Inwood.

"Then let us fetch our erstwhile host," said Carlyle, his eye on the meat pies. "He cannot intend for us to have a cold supper. His purpose was to answer a letter, was it not? Perhaps he fell asleep in his study."

The three of them went together to the closed door in the hall opposite the specimen jars. Inwood's knock was met with silence. "Sir Barnaby," he said, and knocked again. "Sir Barnaby, are you there?"

"You'll have to knock louder than that to wake a sleeping man of his age," said Carlyle. He took a turn to rap on the door. Cecily thought she heard the shuffle of feet inside the room. Inwood turned the brass handle. The door was unlocked and swung open easily. Inwood stepped inside and stopped. Cecily heard his intake of breath, sharp and shocked.

The face of Walter Dinley confronted them, his eyes dark pools of panic in his white face. He stood in the center of the room, a knife gripped in one shaking hand. His knuckles were streaked with rivulets of red. In front of him on the floor, lying on his side so that all they could see was an expanse of black velvet and a tumble of gray curls, was the still form of Sir Barnaby Mayne.

Dinley spoke first. His voice was trembling and unnatural. "I—I killed him! I will no longer—no longer be so—so disrespected. We argued and I killed him! I killed him!"

"Dinley," said Inwood, his voice hoarse. "Get away."

Dinley didn't move. "I killed him," he said. "I killed him."

Inwood lunged. Dinley stumbled backward. It seemed

to Cecily he would be trapped in the corner of the room, unable to escape unless he could force his way past them into the hall. She didn't see the other door until he had hurled himself upon it. In an instant he had thrown it open. Clammy air rushed into the room. He fled. The knife fell from his hand, chiming as it hit the stone veranda. It was Carlyle who shoved Cecily aside and went in pursuit, pausing to sweep up the fallen blade. Both men tore across the garden, gravel clattering behind them. Dinley reached the far wall first and disappeared through a door into the alley beyond.

Cecily turned back to the room. Inwood had dropped to his knees beside Sir Barnaby. She watched his fingers move with practiced assurance from the fallen man's wrist to his lips. The physician's shoulders slumped. She knew before he spoke that Sir Barnaby Mayne was dead.

CHAPTER 6

From their perches on oaken shelves, stuffed birds stared down at the body of their former owner. Sir Barnaby's eyes were open, but the ferocious blue fire that had animated them was gone. His wig was askew, exposing a mottled scalp. Bright ruby stains dappled his snowy white scarf. Beneath him was a rug decorated with geometric spirals and jagged diamonds in shades of burgundy and brown that made it look as if it were patterned in channels of blood.

It was Thomasin who summoned the other occupants of the house. The maid appeared at the open door to the hall, looked inquiringly into the room, and began to scream. Her cries drew John and his wife up from the kitchen. The two stayed only long enough for Inwood to tell them what had happened before they left to cry murder from the front steps. Bells began to ring through the parish and shouts to fill its streets.

Meacan, apparently alerted to danger by the tenor of the cries, entered the room clutching a stone axe in one hand and a battered Viking shield in the other. Both objects bore bright red labels. She paused in the doorway to take in the scene, and only lowered the weapon when she saw Cecily. Warbulton arrived last. Unlike Meacan, he seemed not to have perceived any threat within the commotion, but called cheerfully from the stairs to ask whether supper was ready. When he reached the study, he backed into the corner farthest from the body and, upon being told what had occurred, began a steady murmur of incoherent lamentation.

Inwood completed his cursory examination. He gently drew the edges of Sir Barnaby's shirt closed. "It was the wound to the heart that killed him," he said. When he looked up, Cecily thought he seemed older, as if he had come near enough to death for it to claim a little of him, too.

"This cannot be," said Warbulton. "It is impossible. It is too atrocious, too terrible."

"*Dinley?*" The single word was uttered in an incredulous tone by Meacan, who had taken up a position by the door, still holding the axe in a loose grip at her side. Her expression was wary, her attention alternating between the room and the dim hallway. "You are certain," she went on, "that it was *Walter Dinley*? The same man who apologizes to furniture when he bumps into it? Who can piece together broken seashells for hours without once losing patience? I've never even heard him raise his voice, let alone— You say he *confessed?*"

"His words were unambiguous," said Inwood. He stood and went to the open door to the garden. He remained there, his back to the room, looking out at the plant beds and paths. Cecily stepped away in deference to his emotion. She was familiar with seeking comfort in the quiet abundance of living leaves and flowers.

Her retreat brought her to the desk positioned against the wall between the two windows. She looked down at the dark wood. It was bare except for a neat pile of papers at one corner, a folded length of black velvet at another, and a sticky gleam of blood stamped in a telltale shape at its center. It was only part of a handprint, but the thumb, two fingers, and cleanly halved palm were unmistakable.

A glance at the body confirmed that Sir Barnaby's hands were bloodied. In her mind she saw the dying man, still standing, press them to the fatal wound on his chest as if to imprison his escaping life. She saw him stumble and fling out an arm in search of support, his body desperate to deny the inevitability of his fall. She saw the hand come down hard on the smooth wood. A moment of hope, perhaps, as he touched that familiar surface. And then—Cecily tensed her shoulders to repress the shudder that moved up her spine.

The room smelled of old books, tallow, and accumulated smoke. As her shock lessened and she became more aware of her surroundings, Cecily's keen nose also detected a faint odor of camphor and roses. It was a cramped space, constricted by the wall that divided it from the hallway and by the cabinets that encroached upon its center. Most of these were fitted with doors of solid wood that concealed their contents, but the shelves that were visible contained a vast assortment of objects. Conch shells gaped like open mouths. Furred hides overlapped scaled ones. Turtles and crabs and other small armored creatures alternated with snuffboxes and statuettes. On the mantelpiece, an undulating backbone led Cecily's gaze along its knobbly path to a row of milky crystal orbs set in ornate stands and a ticking clock encased in ebony.

One corner of the room was occupied by a wooden wheel taller than Cecily by a head. Narrow ledges were spaced evenly around its circumference, each supporting a book held open by a strap. A sturdy cane stool was positioned so that by turning the wheel, a reader sitting on the stool could consult multiple books with ease. A worn Turkey-work chair was positioned near the unlit hearth with a low, cluttered table beside it.

The chatter outside grew louder, heralding Carlyle's return through the front entrance. Sweat stood in beads on his brow and mud spattered his stockings. The knife was still in his hand. He set it down on a shelf near Warbulton, who drew away, pointing a shaking finger at the bloody blade. "Is that—is that what—"

"I thought I might have need of a weapon if I apprehended him," said Carlyle, raising an eyebrow at Warbulton's evident terror. "I wish I could tell you the blood came from the villain."

Inwood turned from the garden door. "Dinley remains at liberty?"

"For the moment," said Carlyle as he straightened his wig. "If he'd stayed in the alleys I might have overtaken him, but he found his way to the street." Carlyle gestured toward the front of the house. "He threw himself into a crowd gathered around some mountebank selling cure-alls. By the time I'd pushed my way through, he'd vanished."

Inwood started toward the hall. "We'll have to summon the parish constable—"

Carlyle stopped him. "It is already done. The man is also the local butcher, but he appears to take his office seriously. He declared to me that as far as he understands the law, an employee who kills his master is as bad as a traitor to the Crown. By the time I left him he'd roused ten men to the hunt. Come sunset, Dinley won't be able to ask a rat in an alley for help without being handed over. I wouldn't be surprised if the morning finds him already drawn and—"

"Enough," said Inwood. "There are women present."

"Speak freely, gentlemen," declared Meacan. "No need to be delicate when we're all in the same room with the same sight before us."

Her words made Cecily notice for the first time that they were not, in fact, all in the room. She wondered why Otto Helm had not appeared, but before she could ask, Thomasin tearfully announced the arrival of the undertaker. It was clear as soon as the man entered, assistants in tow, that the space could not accommodate them all. Warbulton, gray-faced, muttered the word *brandy* like an incantation and slipped out. Carlyle followed.

A dark wave of exhaustion swept over Cecily. Hunger, hard travel, and the day's events were taking their toll. Her knees trembled as she left the study. She went to the dining room only long enough to procure bread and a bowl of vegetable stew. No one challenged her when she departed with the dishes. She had to think hard to remember where her bedroom was. The crowded cabinets, connecting doors, and dark stairwells confused her. She was only certain she had found it when she recognized the familiar outlines of her own weathered trunk and bundles of plants.

Her windows looked down to the street. Through the thick, uneven glass she watched the other guests go. Carlyle climbed into the first coach that was summoned. Warbulton stumbled out after him to wait for the next. An enormous feather protruded from the brim of his hat, twitching aimlessly behind him. When a coach stopped for him, his attempts to climb into it were hindered by his dress sword, which swung on its sash and barred the door until he managed to dislodge it. The last to leave the house was Inwood, who accompanied the undertaker and the body. Curious neighbors collected around them and formed a kind of procession down the street, their hats and cloaked shoulders darkening as mist turned to soaking rain.

Cecily had just set the empty bowl aside when she heard a soft thud at the base of her door. She opened it to find Meacan, a cup in each hand, one foot raised to tap again with her toe. "Brandy," Meacan announced, lowering her foot. "I'm certain you need it as much as I do. My heart feels touched by frost and all the skeletons in the house seem to be turning their skulls to look at me."

She thrust one of the cups at Cecily, entered the room, and settled herself on the window seat. Her skirts bunched around her in ridges and valleys of stiff linen, turning the pattern of straight stripes on the fabric to one of crooked paths. "Sit," she said, motioning for Cecily to take the chair by the desk. "Drink your brandy, and tell me what happened."

"But you already know." Cecily set the cup she had been handed down amid the sea urchins on the desk and took a seat. "We found Walter Dinley standing over Sir Barnaby, the knife still—"

Meacan interrupted. "Still in his hand, yes. *That* picture has been sketched for me already. But how did any of it come to pass? What was Sir Barnaby doing in his study? Where were you and the others? I have not been able to wrest a clear account from anyone." Meacan lifted her free hand and counted on her fingers. "Martha could tell me nothing. Nor could John or Thomasin. They were in the kitchen all afternoon. I tried to question the man who assumed authority—the doctor with the sort of eyes that suggest you are friends even before you have been introduced—but he was busy making arrangements with the undertaker. As for the other two, the first was concerned only with effecting his own departure, and the second, the gilded one, was shaking like a mouse in the shadow of a cat. He didn't speak a word."

It was not difficult for Cecily to match Meacan's descriptions to their subjects. "The one who took so much responsibility upon himself is Giles Inwood," she explained. "I believe he and Sir Barnaby have been acquainted for many years. The others are Martin Carlyle and Humphrey Warbulton."

Meacan propped an elbow on a knee and leaned her head on her hand. Her fingers disappeared into her hair. "So that was Warbulton?"

"You know the name?"

"They've been talking about him."

"They?"

"The collectors." Meacan took a drink. She settled her shoulders against the wall of the alcove, secure in her command of the subject. "For men who consider themselves so learned, they are remarkably oblivious to the possibility that a woman who is drawing may be listening at the same time. Humphrey Warbulton is a textile merchant with a vast fortune who is determined to secure a place among the gentry. He had taken it into his mind to earn their respect by establishing himself as a collector, as several have done before him. Of course, to be a collector one needs connections, and the circle does not open to just anyone. His fate is under discussion."

Meacan's expression turned speculative. "Inwood's name is familiar. Carlyle's I have not heard before." She gestured Cecily forward with her cup. "Now I implore you. Do not leave me in ignorance any longer. Tell me how the master of the house met his doom."

Cecily welcomed Meacan's request, and not just because she wanted to oblige her old friend. She was eager to impose order on her own thoughts for the first time since feelings of shock and distress had scattered them. But to her surprise and chagrin, she found as she attempted to relate the events of the afternoon that her memories of the day were not easily assembled. The harder she tried to put them in their correct places, the more they slid away like drops of water on a swaying lotus leaf.

It was the tour of the collection, she decided, that had compromised her control over her own perception. She had passed through so many realms of nature and artifice in the space of a few hours that she could not hold the whole path in her mind. Had the clocks been chiming three or four when Sir Barnaby had shown them a vial of golden sand from the Tagus River? Had it yet struck five when they stopped beneath the outstretched wings of the albatross? She did her best to give a clear account, beginning with the accident in the library that led to Alice Fordyce's injury and early departure, and ending with Dinley's return bearing the letter that had been delivered by courier.

"And that was the last time I saw Sir Barnaby alive," she concluded.

While Cecily was speaking, Meacan had emptied her cup, discarded it, and plucked an urchin from the desk. "And Dinley?"

Cecily explained how Dinley had attempted to continue the tour only to abandon it minutes later, and how she in turn had extricated herself from the company of Warbulton and Carlyle in order to seek out the Plant Room.

"So the three of you each went your separate ways," said Meacan slowly. "And you saw and heard nothing more until you, Inwood, and Carlyle found Sir Barnaby."

"Nothing pertaining to his murder," said Cecily. "Did you?"

"Not a raised voice or a rushed step."

There was a short silence as both women retreated into their own thoughts. Meacan's brow was furrowed, her gaze on the spiky urchin she was rotating between her nimble fingers. Cecily's eyes fell on the three bundles on the floor. Her mind moved from the plants within them, patiently awaiting names, to the wealth of information waiting upstairs. "I wonder," she mused aloud, "whether I will be permitted to stay."

Meacan pinned her with an astonished gaze. "Why would you want to?"

Cecily indicated the bundles. "I collected more than a hundred plants, and I came here expressly to identify them. Without names, they can be of little use to scholars and apothecaries, and would better have been left to grow without interruption."

"Well, it isn't up to me," said Meacan. "But I would not choose to sit alone in that dry garret garden studying dead leaves and squinting over Latin in a house where there has been a murder. It will give you bad dreams."

"What you refer to as a *dry garret garden*," said Cecily with asperity, "is the result of years of dedicated effort. I can think of few better ways to honor Sir Barnaby's memory, and to ease the passage of his soul, than to put his shelves to the use for which he intended them."

Meacan lifted her shoulders in an irreverent shrug. "I suppose it will give you an advantage over the others. You'll be here first, before the frenzy begins."

"The frenzy?" It was Cecily's turn to be taken aback.

"The scavengers coming to pick the bones," said Meacan.

"I refer, of course, to the bones of the collection. They'll be visiting in droves, dressed in mourning, each claiming to have been one of Sir Barnaby's closest friends. And all the while they'll be scrutinizing the cabinets for what they hope to acquire, should it come up for sale. And if it *is* sold, there will be a tremendous squabbling over toads in jars and headless statues and trays of butterflies."

"Do you dislike them all so much?"

"Dislike them?" Meacan leaned forward and set the urchin back on the desk. As she shifted, the stripes on her dress changed course. She sat back and they altered once more. "On the contrary. As I told you before, I rely on them for sustenance. I am like one of the tiny, glimmering fish that swim close to whales and share their food while keeping a wary distance from their thrashing tails."

Cecily considered what Meacan had said about the collection. She looked around the room. The objects displayed on the shelves were slowly disappearing, as if night was creeping into the house from inside the cabinets rather than from the windows. "Do you think the collection will be sold?"

"We will find out soon enough," said Meacan. Following the direction of Cecily's look, she frowned at the walls. "I thought this house had an evil feel to it the moment I stepped inside. I should have guessed Death was nearby, sharpening his scythe. There were omens, you know."

Cecily raised a brow to show her skepticism. "Accuse me of credulity if you like," said Meacan. "But you can't tell me not to believe a portent after it's been proved true. On the day I accepted Sir Barnaby's offer of employment, he received me in the dining room. When I entered, I thought at first that a meal was set out before him. Then I realized the table was covered in insects. As if that was not unsettling enough, the specimen he held in his hand was none other than the deathwatch beetle." Meacan gave an eloquent shudder. "That night I dreamt of mermaids. *Turn away from a venture*. That's what it means to dream of mermaids, isn't it?"

"More so for sailors than for illustrators, I think," said Cecily. And because she considered clear thinking and honest observation to be antidotes to fear, she continued. "As for the deathwatch beetle, which is a *Scarabaeus* much like any other, it has been heard and seen by many who have survived long after the encounter."

"And yet Sir Barnaby lies dead," said Meacan.

Cecily sighed. "And would lie dead still, had he handled a hundred beetles or none." As she spoke, her thoughts returned to the study. She saw Sir Barnaby's open eyes and the ruby-speckled scarf around his neck like the red and white feathers of a bird. The vision changed and she saw Walter Dinley's face. There had been no anger in it, only devastation. She could not imagine what had moved such a seemingly gentle person to such sudden violence. "If only Mr. Helm had still been studying his snakes," she said, half to herself. "He might have heard the altercation and alerted the house before it was too late. Do you know what took him away?"

"How could I? I never spoke to the man."

Cecily cocked her head. Helm hadn't mentioned Meacan by name, but what other lady illustrator could he have meant? "He told me you expressed interest in his work," she said.

There was a pause before Meacan answered. "Oh yes," she said. "The Swede studying snakes. I'd forgotten."

Her voice held a false note. Each woman heard it, and each was aware that the other heard it, as well. A sudden constraint settled over them. It was as if an intruder had entered the room and reminded them with a wicked grin that they were strangers. The trust that had come from remembered childhood friendship retreated like a light that disappears around a bend in a tunnel, leaving only an uncertain glow for them to follow. Meacan didn't volunteer anything further about Helm, and Cecily didn't ask.

"You must be too tired to make sense of another thought," said Meacan lightly. She uncurled herself from the window seat and stood. Her eyes were expressionless smudges of shadow in the gathering darkness. "Rest will do us both good." She went to the door and left without another word, leaving Cecily looking after her, wondering why, mere hours after the murder of their host, this woman she was no longer sure she knew had lied.

CHAPTER 7

At nine years old, Cecily was a quiet, serious girl whose favorite place was the schoolroom filled with books, maps, and burnished instruments that promised conversance with the stars. When her father told her that she was to share her sanctum with a stranger, she awaited the arrival of the gardener's family and her new classmate with trepidation.

She never forgot her first sight of Meacan. The girl who descended from a cart laden with potted plants looked like the proud attendant to a fairy queen. Leafy garlands obscured the sturdy wool of her dress. Her hair, as fine and fair as mist around her freckled face, was festooned with blue and purple blossoms. She seemed fully aware of the effect of her appearance, and directed a smile of courtly majesty at the cottage that was to be her family's home for the year. The spell was broken by a cry of exasperation from the gardener, who had been unaware that his daughter had spent the afternoon turning the plants he had carefully selected on behalf of his new employer into frills and furbelows.

Despite their differences, friendship came as naturally as sunrise to the girls. In the schoolroom, Meacan accepted Cecily's authority, if not that of their tutors, and followed her enthusiastically down paths of ink and vellum to ancient citadels, lost libraries, and utopian islands. Meacan, in turn, showed Cecily that curiosity need not be confined to the house. Gardens could be explored, skirts knotted up for ease of movement, and disciplinarians eluded with a combination of advance planning and bravado. As hedges, lawns, and parterres took shape around the Goodrick home, Cecily and Meacan ventured ever farther beyond its bounds.

One chill October day ten months into their acquaintance, Meacan appeared before Cecily quivering with excitement. A film of spiderwebs clung to her shoulders. She had been investigating an attic room, she said, and had found tucked within an old and brittle book of hours a message written in a cipher she could not interpret. Cecily took the proffered book and opened it. The blue and gold initials were as bright as if the scribe who illuminated them had dipped his brush into the sunlight pooled on his desk and mixed it with the paint. The paper Meacan had found folded inside was mottled with age, its contents written in scarlet ink.

It had been a month of sorrow. The Goodrick family had welcomed a son, only to see him depart the world less than two hours after he entered it. It was not the first time death had visited the house on that terrible errand, and the grief that hung about the rooms was tinged with bitterness. Cecily could make little of the fragments of discussion she overheard concerning heirs and inheritance, but she was sensitive to the despair that had begun to etch itself onto her parents' faces.

Meacan's discovery shook Cecily from her stupor of gloom. As the gusts of an approaching storm began to rattle the windows, she examined the odd message with eager interest, wondering what stranger or ancestor might have created it. Had she been a few years older, she might have questioned why a document of seeming antiquity was written not in runes or minuscules, but in modern cursive. Her doubts might have deepened several hours later when, its ciphers broken and its riddles solved, the revealed text directed its reader to a ruined castle less than an hour's walk from the estate, where the worthy adventurer would find the lost sword of King Arthur, the blade Excalibur itself.

But her child's mind, alight with the thrill of revelation, did not admit doubts. Instead, she permitted the message and its mysterious author free rein over her imagination. She did not even notice that Meacan had remained uncharacteristically quiet, allowing Cecily to puzzle through the acrostics and allusions on her own.

It was easy for the two girls to slip unnoticed out the kitchen door, through the fragrant herb garden, and around the back of a hedge maze into the woodlands. The household was preoccupied, not only with mourning, but with the task of hosting an eminent nobleman on his way to Scotland. Meacan in particular had studied the man with fascination. The curls of his black wig fell almost to his waist, and he wore the voluminous petticoat breeches popular at court that year. By the next, the fashion would be spoken of with wincing embarrassment by most who had adopted it.

The air outside was heavy as if, like the grieving house, it contained more than it could hold. The storm that had been coming closer all day was almost overhead. They should have turned around when the birds stopped singing, but neither of the girls was paying attention. By the time they began to climb the hill to the castle, black clouds had consumed the sky and they could hear thunder. The wind grew stronger. Cecily's skirts pulled urgently at her legs, as if the fabric itself was trying to tug her back to the house and to safety. She heard a crack and turned to see the limb of an old oak crash down across the path behind them.

The battlements of the abandoned keep grinned like jagged teeth. Nothing was left of the ruin but stone, stubborn against the ravages of time that had rotted the pennants on the walls and the people who had hung them there. To reach its single remaining hearth, they had to ascend an exposed, uneven set of stairs. When they reached the top, it was Cecily who knelt and crawled into the cold fireplace as the first drops of rain fell.

Enclosed in stone, she reached as high as she could and ran her hands over ledges and crevices, not minding the tickle of spiders against her skin. Each rumble of thunder was louder than the one before. Meacan urged her to hurry. Just as she was beginning to feel foolish, Cecily's fingertips touched metal. Awkwardly, because the sword was heavy and difficult to manipulate in the confined space, she freed it and brought it out to where Meacan waited. They had only moments to marvel at the jeweled hilt and the blade etched with vines and flowers before a sudden clap of thunder startled Cecily so much that she dropped the sword with a clatter to the ground.

Dark patches spread across the floor around them as the rain became a downpour and soaked the stone. Cecily retrieved the sword. She could barely see Meacan in front of her as they fled down the stairs. A false step sent Cecily tumbling. As she struck the ground a white flash of agony filled her vision. Meacan was beside her in an instant, helping her up. But as soon as Cecily put weight on her right ankle, she crumpled.

They tried again. Meacan supported Cecily on her right side, and they used the sword as a cane for her left. It was no use. Progress was impossible. They hobbled back the short distance they had gone and found a place for Cecily to huddle under a stone doorframe. Meacan pressed a kiss to her cheek and disappeared, the rain closing around her running form like a curtain. Cecily was left alone. Each flash of lightning turned the walls around her white, and she felt she was trapped in a ghostly realm. She drew her knees to her chest and waited in miserable anticipation for the next onslaught. The sky presented all the visages of death that her frightened child's mind could conjure.

It was like this that her father, Meacan's father, and two of the servants found her. She was taken up into adult arms and carried back to the house. By the time they arrived, she was reduced to mortified weeping. Her last memory of the day was of the visiting nobleman demanding to know how his best dress sword, which he'd last seen when he had wrapped it in velvet in his own home and tucked it into his trunk, had come to be covered in mud and in the possession of two undisciplined girls.

Lying in the guest bedroom of the Mayne house twenty-five years later, Cecily recalled the aftermath of the event. To everyone's relief, her injury had been minor. The terror of the day had long since faded, and on another night, Cecily might have smiled at the thought of how Meacan had hoped to cheer her grieving friend by arranging an adventure for her. How she must have labored over the project, crafting her riddles, counterfeiting signs of age upon the sheet of paper, liberating the oblivious nobleman of his sword, and making the journey to the castle alone at dawn to conceal the prize. It had emerged during Meacan's pale-faced confession that the plan had come to her when she discovered the sword during a covert exploration of the nobleman's room. She had meant to reveal the truth to Cecily as soon as their quest was complete, and return it to its place before anyone knew it was missing.

Cecily knew why the memory had returned tonight as she drifted in and out of sleep, and why it made her uneasy. However good Meacan's intentions had been, on that day she had demonstrated a reckless disregard not only for rules, but for reality, that had brought them both perilously close to real harm. Today, real harm had been done. Cecily wanted to believe that Meacan was still the same well-meaning girl she had known, but she could not dismiss the possibility that while Meacan's waywardness had remained with her through adulthood, her goodness had not.

And yet what possible connection could Meacan have to the evil that had been done in the house? Whatever Meacan was hiding was surely her own business, and nothing to do with the murder. The circumstances of Sir Barnaby's death seemed clear enough. Strange, yes, that the quiet curator who had demonstrated no inclination toward violence should kill his employer. Strange that Sir Barnaby had abandoned his guests so suddenly. Strange that Otto Helm had disappeared.

Sleep eluded Cecily and she rose. She was relieved that she had thought to set her own tinderbox on the dresser by the bed. Even with fatigued fingers she had no difficulty lighting a candle. The flame drew breath. The light through the jaw of a shark on the wall cast a yawning, distended ring of shadow teeth on the ceiling that moved as if she was seeing it through water.

Cecily's awareness of the shadow drew her gaze to the spiderlike shape cast by her own fingers on the wooden surface of the dresser. The image of the bloody handprint on

Sir Barnaby's desk intruded on her thoughts. She realized that something about that print had bothered her, and it had not only been the image it conjured of a dying man. It was something else. Something about its shape. She spread her own hand flat. The question that had been flickering in the back of her mind flared brighter.

The answer to the question was in Sir Barnaby's study. She knew she should wait until morning. But the long hours of night stretched in front of her, and before she could stop herself she was retrieving her wrap from where she had draped it over a chair. Its frayed edge caught on the edge of a sea urchin. She freed it. The wool had a familiar, comforting fragrance of the dried lavender she kept in her trunk. She covered her candle with a lantern and stepped out of the room.

The pale face of the clock on the landing told her the time was quarter to three. There was no light under Meacan's door, and no sound from within. Cecily started down the staircase, her toe searching carefully for each step before she lowered herself onto it. Every creak seemed loud to her ears, and she had to remind herself that she was not doing anything wrong.

She reached the landing of the ground floor and entered the Serpent Room. The desk at which Otto Helm had been working was still surrounded by the snakes that had not been put away. She could just see their looped and coiled forms in the light of her lantern. Serpentine spines wound like curving ladders up the wall. Her apprehension mounted as she passed through the connecting door into the other house.

The study door was open. The last time she had seen the room, Sir Barnaby's body had been in it, and though it was no longer there, she skirted the place where it had lain. Her light did not reach the corners of the room. A vision rose unbidden before her of Sir Barnaby standing just out of sight, watching her from within the darkness, hidden among his possessions. She steadied herself and held the lantern before her as if it could ward away waiting ghosts.

The handprint was no longer wet and glistening, but it was still visible on the desk. The line that cut down the center of the palm was as crisp and clearly defined as it had been in her memory. She brought her own hand down to hover over the print. A rush of gratification swept through her. She had been right. For the shape to have been halved so cleanly, a surface other than the desk must have received its other half. There had been a sheet of paper there when the bloodied hand had struck.

Where, then, was the bloodstained page? Cecily was certain it had not been on the desk earlier that day. She riffled through the papers piled at the corner, then got to her hands and knees and examined the floor. Slowly, she sat back on her heels. The house was silent. The light of her lantern was reflected in the mirrors, crystals, and glass-eyed birds arranged around her in the dark. It was a long moment before she acknowledged the truth of what she had come to the room to confirm. In the final moments of Sir Barnaby's life, there had been a document on the desk. That document had disappeared.

CHAPTER 8

Dawn entered Sir Barnaby Mayne's house slowly, gray and tattered from its journey through the nets of cloud and smoke that covered London. Dingy light crept over scuffed floors and climbed the faces of cabinets. From the recesses of shelves, red labels began to emerge like bright rose petals scattered over yellowed bones, bronze statuettes, and the pearlescent interiors of shells.

Cecily was accustomed to dressing alone, though she had employed maids at various times during her travels. She wore stays that laced in the front, and could manipulate with ease the pins and ties that were required to hold even the simplest dresses in place. In Smyrna, her appearance-conscious husband had dictated much of her wardrobe. A close adherent of fashion, he had presented her with ostentatious petticoats, hairpieces that increased her height by a foot, and gowns of patterned silk with long trains. Cecily was not puritanical, but she was practical. She liked dresses in which it was possible to ascend a roadside berm in search of a glimpsed tree or stoop on a path to harvest an unfamiliar herb. She had brought back to England only the clothes she had selected herself, which, while elegant, were comfortable, durable, and easy to clean. That morning, she put on the same purple-gray linen gown she had worn the day before, and went downstairs.

She was craving fresh air. Though she knew she would not find it outside on a misty, soot-dense London morning, she nevertheless left the house through a door in the Serpent Room and entered the garden, an enclosed rectangle that extended from the rear of the residence.

It was clear that Sir Barnaby had not been among the collectors who treated their gardens as extensions of their collections, filling them with rarities and challenging skilled gardeners like Meacan's father to keep them alive in London soil. Preferring to devote his attention to his shelves, he had settled for a courtyard that was merely fashionable. Neat boxwoods separated graveled paths from flower beds filled with silvery germander, marigolds, pinks, and lilies. A soot-stained statue of Athena posed dutifully on a central pedestal. There was a humble greenhouse, a modest assortment of potted kitchen herbs, and a carriage house set into the far wall. The whole space seemed to be looking up at the residence with faint resentment, as a child might look at a sibling it knows is preferred.

The exception to this otherwise unremarkable display was the tree in the far left corner. Its dark green leaves had a waxy sheen, and heavy white flowers rested like birds at the ends of its slender branches. Cecily knew it was the sweetbay because Sir Barnaby, proud of the specimen that was one of only four growing in London, had published several essays about it in the *Transactions*, all of which she had read with interest. She followed the gravel paths until she was enveloped by the tree's spiced lemon sweetness.

A stone bench dusted with pencil shavings testified to Meacan's presence there on the previous day. Cecily's attention moved from the bench to the back wall, where she saw a door half hidden by a curtain of privet. This, she surmised, must be the door through which Alice Fordyce had arrived, and through which Dinley had made his escape. She went to it, stopping on the way to glance inside the carriage house. It came as no surprise that Sir Barnaby had not used the space to keep a carriage, but to store exceptionally large and unwieldy collection items. Bronze and marble sculptures stared out from the cobwebbed gloom, in company with colossal bones. A golden face and bands of hieroglyphs gleamed from a painted coffin.

The wall of the garden was high and crowned with shards of glass to deter thieves. Cecily unbolted the door and looked out. To her left and right, a narrow road pitted with puddles extended along the garden walls of the adjacent properties. Across the road, a dreary field stretched away from her. The mist that blanketed it was fetid and stagnant, as if it had been there a long time. Within it loomed the gnarled and twisted shapes of trees. She heard the faint buzz of flies.

"Lady Kay!" The cry came from behind her. John was gesturing from the now-open door of Sir Barnaby's study. "Come back to the house!" he called. "It isn't safe out on the road!"

Once he was assured that she was coming back, John disappeared back into the study. Cecily reached it in time to see him finish rolling up the burgundy rug. Grunting with the effort, he dragged it into the corner behind the book wheel. Thomasin stood ready with a mop, which she submerged into a sloshing bucket as soon as the rug was out of the way. Martha was observing the other two in a posture of command.

The housekeeper was a woman of about fifty who appeared to possess the same physical strength as her husband compacted into a much smaller form. Her slender bones were armored by sinew visible in taut cords at her neck and forearms. In one hand she held the knife that had killed Sir Barnaby, in the other a damp cloth discolored by rusty stains. "You had best not step inside, Lady Kay," she said. "The floor isn't clean yet."

Cecily remained obediently on the veranda. John skirted the spreading arc of Thomasin's mop to join her. "I hope you'll forgive my calling to you so roughly," he said, nodding over Cecily's shoulder toward the back of the garden. "They call that place the dueler's field. Stay more than a few days in this house and you'll surely hear a pistol shot from it or the strike of steel at dawn. But there's more bad business there than just dueling, especially when the mist sits heavy on it."

"I am grateful to you for the warning," Cecily reassured him. "It did seem a forbidding place. Have you seen Mrs. Barlow?"

"She has gone out," said John. "We hear the two of you are old acquaintances."

Cecily nodded. "We haven't seen each other in many years. Has she—" Cecily considered her words. "Has she got on well here?"

"Oh yes," said John. "Mrs. Barlow has been very good company. Until yesterday, this house was as happy as I've ever seen it."

"Mrs. Barlow isn't careful enough with the objects," muttered Martha. "Smudging them with fingerprints, leaving them out after she's finished making her drawings, putting them back too near the edges of shelves. Someone employed here should know better." Martha, still holding the knife, was now alternating her attention between it and the shelves. There was a hint of uncertainty in her look.

"Did it come from the collection?" asked Cecily, indicating the weapon.

Martha frowned. "I dust the room every two weeks and I've never seen it before," she said. "And it doesn't have a label. The master was very diligent about labels."

Cecily's eyes dropped to the blade. "May I see it?"

After a moment's hesitation, Martha handed the weapon to her. To Cecily's eye, its appearance would have been malevolent even if it wasn't associated with murder. Its hilt was a branch of white wood that had been polished, but left in its natural, twisting shape. It was capped by a silver pommel set with three glittering black gemstones. The iron blade was etched with markings almost too faint to see. If they came from a language, it was not one Cecily recognized.

"*Thomasin!*" The cry came from Martha. Thomasin had inadvertently knocked a bird from a shelf behind her with the handle of her mop. It had toppled to the floor, where water was quickly soaking its tufted blue feathers. Martha snatched up the bird and cradled it, daubing at the moisture with a corner of her apron. Then she delicately separated the feathers and blew on them. She returned the bird to its place. "This is why he never let the new maids do the dusting," she said.

Thomasin slapped her mop loudly over the floor. "And what do you think will matter most to Lady Mayne? Having the room clean of her husband's blood or keeping some old birds dry?"

"This has nothing to do with Lady Mayne," said Martha. "And you'll be out of the house if I hear such insolence from you again."

"You aren't the mistress here," Thomasin shot back. "And make no doubt of it, I'll be gone from this place the moment I find a position that suits me."

Martha's look could have frozen a pond on a summer's day. "You will treat the collection as if the master himself were in the room. Do you understand?"

"If you have no more need of me here, Martha," said John, cautiously interrupting. "I'll just fix Lady Kay something to eat and start preparing a noon meal."

Martha gave them both a nod of dismissal. She held out her hand for the knife. Cecily gave it to her. After a moment's deliberation, Martha returned it to the shelf where Carlyle had set it. Rather than cross the wet floor, John led Cecily along the veranda and down into the kitchen from the outside. "Martha didn't intend any rudeness to you, Lady Kay," he said as he stoked the fire. "I hope you don't see it that way. She's been employed by Sir Barnaby longer than any of us, since before she and I were married. He trained her to care for the collection more than he ever taught her to serve ladies such as yourself. Now, do you take breakfast? Cup of ale? Toast and butter? I've some anchovies and cheese if you like. It will be goose pie and salad at midday."

Cecily accepted the ale and toast, which were soon set before her. While she ate, John worked with gusto, cleaning and chopping vegetables and herbs spread in fragrant bunches across the sturdy central table. "Is Lady Mayne expected soon?" she asked.

He nodded as he used a cloth to absorb moisture from a bowl of lettuce. "This afternoon, assuming she's in a fit state for the journey, poor woman. The estate's a mere two hours away."

"Does she come to London often?"

"Oh no," John replied. "Not above three or four times in the past fifteen years that I recall. But many of the fruits and vegetables for Sir Barnaby's table are delivered from the estate, and I will say she keeps a fine garden. Just this month we've had alexanders for pottage, elderflower, parsnips, lettuce and rocket, celery, shallots, onions also, and artichokes. Do you care for artichokes?"

"I enjoyed them in Venice," Cecily replied.

John looked interested. "Yes? And how were they served there?"

Cecily considered for a moment. "I believe they were broiled."

"That's common," said John. "I myself am of the opinion that they should be served raw. A good oil over them, not too strong. Vinegar, salt, and pepper. Though it's hard to say that's better than an artichoke fried in butter with parsley. You can preserve them, too, dried or pickled, though if dried you must keep the leaves from touching."

Cecily's thoughts remained on the Mayne estate. "And is it a large family?" she asked.

John examined a leaf and cast it aside. "Artichokes? Oh, I don't know about the families and names in Latin you scholars use."

Cecily corrected him gently. "I was referring to the Mayne family."

"Oh, yes." John looked slightly embarrassed. "The Mayne family, of course. I can tell you Sir Barnaby had no children. Martha says the estate is to be divided between the widow and a distant cousin."

"And what will happen to the collection?"

John heaved a sigh. "That I don't know, but it will be a shame indeed if it's not looked after when he spent so many years laboring over it." He paused and looked at Cecily from under wiry gray brows. It was an assessing look. "Try a radish," he said, and handed a single translucent sliver across the table to her.

She took a bite, enjoyed the crisp texture and heat of it, and thanked him. "I am reminded that Dioscorides and Pliny both celebrated the radish above all roots," she said. "And that a radish cast in solid gold was one of the decorations in the Delphic Temple."

John looked pleased. "Don't know much about the ancients myself, but the first time I ate a radish raw, like this, so thin you can see through it, was a revelation to me, Lady Kay, a revelation. I'd never thought to do anything but boil and fry and bake a vegetable. But now I say eat them raw whenever it's the season for it. Sir Barnaby took some persuading on the idea, but Mr. Dinley was a great help to me in that."

Cecily saw his expression fall as he spoke the curator's name. "You and he were friends?" she asked.

John hesitated, then appeared to conclude that a person willing to sit in a kitchen and speak of radishes could be trusted. "I'd have said we were. He always came to tell me what he read about new vegetables coming to our English gardens. On several occasions he persuaded the master to put a little money toward the greenhouse so that I could attempt my own experiments with new seeds." John fell silent.

Curiosity nudged Cecily forward. "Did he and Sir Barnaby often quarrel?"

"Quarrel?" John reached for a bowl of tansies and began to clean them. "No, Dinley wasn't the sort to quarrel. Sir Barnaby shouted at *him* often enough, to be sure, but Dinley never seemed to take offense. He seemed—" John searched for words. "He seemed a *contented* fellow, Lady Kay. Quiet, diligent, happy to be part of the master's work. No matter how hard I think on it, I cannot understand what could have made him do such a terrible thing."

Martha's voice reached them from the kitchen door. "We all believed we knew Mr. Dinley's temperament." Cecily turned and saw the housekeeper enter, Thomasin behind her carrying the bucket. The water inside it was darker than it had been, and the rags bunched in the maid's hand were tinged a sickening pink.

"But we were wrong," Martha continued. "And no pleasant memories of Mr. Dinley reading letters to us from distant shores can survive what he did. They're dead along with the master. Walter Dinley is a murderer and a thief, and if there is justice in the world he'll be punished for it."

Cecily's thoughts went instantly to the missing sheet of paper. "A thief?"

Martha nodded. "He stole the jeweled pistol from the Artifact Room, and that's only what's obviously missing. It was in a glass case at the center of the mantelpiece."

"He didn't have a pistol when I saw him," said Cecily.

"Then he had it hidden in his jacket," said Martha. "Or left a sack of stolen objects in the alley before he committed the foul deed."

The explanation did not make sense to Cecily. She recalled Dinley's words. *We argued and I killed him.* Everything about the scene suggested that Dinley had killed Sir Barnaby while in the grip of a sudden, violent rage, not in the commission of a premeditated theft. If Dinley had wanted to steal from the collection, surely he had subtler means available to him. And if he had taken the gun for its death-dealing power, why hadn't he used it? "We were all surprised when Sir Barnaby left the tour so hastily," she said. "Did you see him when he came downstairs?"

"See him?" Martha's eyes narrowed. "None of us saw anything. We were all here in the kitchen."

"What of the message that drew him down?" asked Cecily. "I understand it was delivered by a courier."

Martha nodded. "I saw the man approach." She gestured to the narrow strip of glass that gave the occupants of the basement kitchen a view of the feet, hooves, and wheels passing on the street outside. "I heard him knock, and I would have sent Thomasin up to admit him had not Dinley arrived at the door first."

"But didn't the courier wait for an answer?"

"If he did, he stayed outside the house," said Martha. "We never spoke to him."

Cecily could see the expressions of the three servants becoming withdrawn. Her questions were making them nervous. She tried to make her voice sound merely sympathetic. "To think," she said. "Mr. Dinley was in the kitchen with Miss Fordyce only a little while before it happened."

The three of them looked at her blankly. "Miss Fordyce," said Thomasin slowly. "Was she the pretty one in the beige gown?"

Cecily looked at them in surprise. "Yes. He brought her here, didn't he? To clean and bandage the cut on her hand?"

"Miss Fordyce never came into the kitchen," said John.

"But Mr. Dinley was adamant," said Cecily. "He said you kept salves."

"I do," said John. He gestured to a shelf lined with neatly sealed bottles of various size. "But I'm telling you the truth when I say no one asked for them yesterday."

"What became of the young lady?" asked Thomasin.

Cecily stared. "She left. Dinley put her in a carriage. Didn't you see it through the window?"

"No carriages came to the house after the guests arrived," said Martha.

"Then Mr. Helm did not depart in a carriage?"

Thomasin answered. "The foreigner? No, I saw him go on foot." Martha and John nodded affirmation of her words.

"Do you know where he went?"

"No," said Martha. "And it surprised us to see him go. He was supposed to stay to supper. Sir Barnaby was clear on that."

"At what time did he leave?"

John spoke thoughtfully. "The eggs had come to a boil, and I thought to myself the timing would be just right to serve them at six. It must have been something like a quarter to the hour."

"So close to when it happened?" asked Cecily. At a quarter to six, the fatal argument might already have begun.

"It *was* a quarter to six," said Martha slowly. "It was the last time I noticed the clock, thinking all was as it should be. The front door closing when he left was the last sound I heard from upstairs before the screaming."

CHAPTER 9

ady Mayne's arrival later that afternoon necessitated a hasty emptying of the carriage house to make room for her coach. From the window of the Plant Room, Cecily watched John wrestle an assortment of enormous bones into a corner of the garden, then drag the painted coffin through the gravel to the house. It was not until Lady Mayne had interviewed the servants and installed herself in a chamber adjacent to the master bedroom that she sent her maid, a severe young woman named Susanna, to bring Cecily to her.

Cecily had spent the afternoon in pursuit of plant names. With her own specimens stacked beside her, she searched the Mayne collection for matching ones. She pulled bound catalogues and journals and indices from shelves. She read letters and traced her index finger over faded maps, following the routes of other travelers. With great care, she slid specimen sheets out from dense piles. She squinted to count dried petals and sepals and to decipher descriptions made imprecise by the cold, illness, fatigue, or haste of the collectors who had scrawled them.

The work cleared her mind and renewed her energy. By the time Lady Mayne summoned her, she had not only confirmed that the sweet-smelling plant with pale pink flowers she had collected and pressed two years ago had been given the name "*Salvia orientalis Absinthium redolens*" by an earlier collector, but had also arranged her puzzlement over Barnaby Mayne's death into a list of questions. She would not assign two plants the same name if there were discrepancies between them. It only followed that she would not accept what appeared to have happened as truth until she could make sense of it.

First, there was the matter of the missing gun. She had gone to the Artifact Room and located the empty glass box in the center of the mantelpiece. A label attached to it described a snaphance pistol of Spanish make etched in scrolls and florals and set with semiprecious stones. She did not believe Dinley had taken it, and she wanted to know who had. She also wanted to know why Dinley had lied about putting Alice Fordyce in a carriage, where Otto Helm had gone, what message had been delivered by the courier, and why a document had been removed from the desk. Finally, she wanted to know what Meacan, who to her knowledge had not yet returned, was up to.

With these questions turning over in her thoughts, she followed Susanna to Lady Mayne's door. The room they entered was dim, the windows already draped in the black silk of mourning. If the chamber had ever been intended for use by the lady of the house, it had forgotten itself long ago. The collection had filled it, as it had filled the other bedrooms, like sediment ushered up a beach by a rising tide. Where the walls were not lined with cabinets, they were studded with turtle shells, antlers, and dried crustaceans.

Lady Mayne sat in a chair by an unlit fire, a candle on the table beside her. Her skin was as densely lined as the surface of an icy pond cracked by a fallen stone. The hair visible beneath her widow's hat was gray. She sat very still at the center of the chair as if she was afraid it would tip over if she moved. Behind her on the bed, a white cat slept.

Cecily's condolences were accepted with a tremulous nod. Lady Mayne started to speak, but her lips trembled and she pressed them together. Cecily offered to return at a later hour, but the widow shook her head and gestured for Cecily to approach. At last the quivering lips relaxed. Lady Mayne settled more deeply into her chair. "It—it is the *odor*," she said in a tight voice. "It has been years since I endured a journey into the city." She indicated the chair opposite her. "Sit, please, Lady Kay."

A glance at the chair made Cecily pause. Resting on the red woven seat was an open box subdivided into sections, each of which contained a brittle husk of a beetle. Lady Mayne noticed her guest's hesitation and craned her neck forward to look. She sucked in her breath. "Susanna," she snapped. "How am I to receive callers when even the chairs in my own bedchamber are being used as pedestals for—for *insects*?"

The maid hurried over from the edge of the room, where she had been draping black cloth over shelves. She seized the box, set it on the floor, and slid it roughly under the chair with her toe.

"I apologize," said Lady Mayne stiffly as Cecily took a seat. "My husband had no consideration for the comfort of his guests. I am mortified."

"No apology is necessary," said Cecily, somewhat taken aback. "To assemble and maintain a collection as remarkable as this must have required your husband's complete dedication, a quality for which I have nothing but admiration."

"Is that so?" Lady Mayne's lips curved in a small, bitter

smile. Her eyes, pale as raindrops on glass, focused on a distant point in her memory. "When we were married, my husband had his butterflies and his books, as so many educated gentlemen do. I imagined—you know how we women spin fantasies of times to come—I imagined that if God should grant us long lives, my husband would lean on a silver-topped cane as he pottered through our house showing guests his little collections. I would indulge his habit of buying books. A few antiquities, perhaps." Lady Mayne's gaze returned to the present. "Instead—" She stopped and indicated the walls around her with a listless hand.

"The Mayne collection became one of the most consulted in England," said Cecily.

"Consulted?" Lady Mayne cocked her head as if she did not understand the word.

"By scholars," said Cecily. "I know at least ten books of reference, essential books, that could not have been written without the aid of Sir Barnaby's cabinets."

"He used to tell me these displays would lead men to truths of *great significance*," said Lady Mayne. Her voice was soft and cold as falling snow. "But that is not what I see. When I look at these walls, I see paths leading into realms of idleness and madness. And have I not been proven correct? Was not my husband's murderer mad? Might it not have been these very shelves that made him so?"

Cecily had no intention of challenging a grieving woman's views on the pursuit of knowledge, but Lady Mayne appeared to be waiting for her to speak. "Did you know Mr. Dinley?" she asked.

"I did not need to know him," said Lady Mayne. "I met enough of them in the past. The collectors and their curators, the travelers and their patrons. Oh, they each had their particular obsessions, but it was what they had in common that made me retreat to my room and utter my prayers. It was the way their eyes burned like coals. They frightened me. Sometimes, even *my husband*—" Lady Mayne stopped herself, but the words she had been about to utter hovered between them. *My husband frightened me.*

After a short silence, Lady Mayne sighed. "Mad or not, it makes no difference now. And if the villain escapes the hands of the law, he will not escape God's justice."

Cecily hesitated. She had heard the finality in Lady Mayne's tone. The widow accepted the explanation she had been given. Perhaps it would be wrong to introduce uncertainty to the mind of a woman seeking calm in the wake of bereavement. But wouldn't it be worse to allow a lie to be perpetuated if there was a way to correct it? "Lady Mayne," she said, deciding on honesty. "I am troubled by the circumstances of your husband's death."

Lady Mayne looked surprised. "Troubled, Lady Kay? In what way are you troubled?"

With the clarity and concision that was natural to her, Cecily explained. She told Lady Mayne about the courier, the print on the desk, the unexplained departure of Alice Fordyce, and the missing pistol. She spoke of Dinley's temperament, and the surprise expressed by those who knew him that he was capable of such violence. The only item on her list of which she made no mention was the possibility of Meacan's involvement. "I do not wish to cause you further distress," she concluded. "But it seems to me very possible that Mr. Dinley either had a more complicated motive for the murder of your husband than he led us to believe, or that he did not commit the crime at all."

Lady Mayne had listened politely, but without any evidence

of strong emotion. "Did Walter Dinley say that he killed my husband?" she asked when Cecily had finished.

"He did, but—"

Lady Mayne interrupted. "I have known women of your disposition," she said, not unkindly. "I believe you mean well. But Lady Kay, not only have I never met the man who killed my husband, but I have seen little of my husband since the day we wed. I did not know him. I did not follow his affairs. As to the exact circumstances of his death, I have no desire to learn more of them. I intend to remain in this house long enough to fulfill those obligations required of me by law and custom. When I have done so, I will return to a life that I do not expect to change significantly from what it was. If you will be so kind as to spare me, I do not wish to speak of this again."

A rustling and crunching broke the silence. Cecily located the source of the sound near the hem of her skirts. The white cat had dragged the box of beetles out from under the chair. They were scattered, red and turquoise and black, over the carpet. It was using its claws and teeth to tear one to pieces. Susanna shooed the cat away and began gingerly to drop the beetles back into the box.

Lady Mayne turned her attention back to Cecily. When she spoke, it was as if their previous exchange had never occurred. "I understand that your husband's estate is in Lincolnshire, and that he is serving as consul in Smyrna?"

"That is so," said Cecily.

"The coffee comes from that part of the world, doesn't it?" Lady Mayne waved a weary hand. "I believe the coffee is much to blame for these obsessions that overcome gentlemen of intelligence. The drink exerts its will not only over the mind, but over the passage of time. They go into those coffeehouses together and become so lost in idle speculation that they forget their families, their devotions, and their duties. Your husband did not return to England with you?"

"His work at the consular office required him to stay."

"But you must be eager to return to Lincolnshire. What prompted you to break your journey in such an unusual way?"

As Cecily explained that she wished to identify the plants she had collected over the course of her travels, Lady Mayne's expression became coldly critical. "We must take care, Lady Kay," she said. "Curiosity was Eve's weakness." She lifted a hand and fluttered it at Susanna. "Can you cover that shelf, also? Yes, yes, if the cloth will reach."

She turned back to Cecily. "You must allow me to assist you as best I can in finding accommodation elsewhere. Doubtless you will wish to depart before evening?"

Cecily drew in a breath. "I had hoped, Lady Mayne, if it would not be an excessive burden, that I might stay a few days more. To complete my work."

Lady Mayne's brows lifted in surprise. "Surely that is not what you wish, Lady Kay. The bedrooms here offer no comfort, and the servants are so woefully trained that I am ashamed to call myself their mistress. This will be a place of mourning. You cannot really want to stay here?"

"It is a visit I have long anticipated, Lady Mayne. I can assure you my presence will not be an intrusive one."

A thought occurred to the widow and her eyes narrowed. "You do not intend, I hope, to make further inquiries into my husband's death? To do so would not only be against my express wishes, but would violate the sanctity of a house in mourning."

"My only intention is to complete the work I came to do," said Cecily.

After a moment of silent consideration, Lady Mayne nodded. "Then you may stay," she said. "I am, for the present, mistress of this house, and I would not turn away a guest to whom my husband promised accommodation. But I will advise you to complete your work with all possible efficiency. The collection is not to remain here long."

Cecily maintained an expression of polite interest. "Oh? What do you intend for it?"

Lady Mayne's lips compressed. "Your question would suggest that I have some power in the matter. I assure you, I do not. My husband made arrangements for it all long ago, arrangements of a legally binding nature. The collection is to go to another collector, a man in whom my husband placed absolute trust. The only function of the widow in these circumstances is to facilitate the transfer."

"I see," said Cecily. "And is this friend to take possession soon?"

"As soon as it can be effected. I have already sent for him. Indeed I suspect the footsteps now ascending the stair are his."

They were. The door of the room opened, allowing in a little more light, and Cecily was confronted with the affable features, now lined with concern and sympathy, of Giles Inwood.

CHAPTER 10

Gentlemen visitors to the office of the consul in Smyrna often expressed delight when they discovered that the consul's wife collected plants. How charming, how *unconventional* a pursuit for a woman, they would exclaim. Lady Kay must allow them to assist with any identifications that were puzzling her. Almost invariably, they made this offer in the expectation that they would glance at what Cecily had found, make a pronouncement, and enjoy the affirmation of an attractive female as the Aegean air, perfumed by cinnamon and cloves arriving in Persian caravans, blew gently through the windows. Instead, these interactions usually ended with the gentleman making an abrupt excuse and leaving, either out of boredom, or out of frustration with the stubborn woman who treated every tiny discrepancy as if it meant the difference between bittersweet and deadly nightshade.

Cecily *was* stubborn. And she was too committed to her questions for Lady Mayne's injunction to deter her from pursuing their answers. She did understand that she would have to proceed discreetly. When she reentered Sir Barnaby's study after leaving the widow's chamber, she was prepared to explain to anyone who challenged her that she was perusing the bookshelves for herbals and floras.

It was the first time she had been in the room alone and in daylight. Except for the rug rolled into the corner and the knife resting conspicuously on the shelf, it looked as it must have when its owner was alive. The book spines pressed together on the shelves formed an uneven surface, a testament to the frequency and excitement with which they had been consulted. The cane seat of the stool in front of the book wheel was indented, the volumes on the wheel open to the last pages Sir Barnaby had read.

She went first to the desk, and examined one by one the papers piled at one corner. There were seven distinct documents. The first three were invitations to lectures at the Royal Society pertaining, respectively, to microscopic observations of rainwater, unusual circular arches seen in the air by Edmund Halley, and various species of insects found in the bark of decaying elms and ashes. The next two were requests to visit the collection. There was nothing remarkable about either. The sixth exerted a stronger claim to her attention. It was a letter written by the captain of the ship called the *Salamander* reporting the death of the traveler Anthony Holt. Cecily had to hold the paper close to her eyes to decipher the water-blurred text. *To Sir Barnaby Mayne,* she read.

> *It is my understanding that you are the benefactor whose generous patronage has these past eight months placed Anthony Holt under my care. It is with deepest regret that I write to inform you that Mr. Holt was taken from this world on the eleventh of January this year. Three brave sailors were lost with him in the storm that struck our vessel not long after we departed Chusan.*

That any survived must be counted a miracle. The waves rose
so high that it seemed to me the very mountains of the earth
could not have withstood their might.

Mr. Holt held you ever in great esteem. I believe you occupied
in his affections the place of a father, his own having disowned
and renounced all connection to him some years ago. It is for
this reason that I direct my letter to you. May it bring you com-
fort to know that Mr. Holt conducted himself with intelligence,
wit, and admirable valor. His loss will be keenly felt by all who
had the honor of his acquaintance.

Cecily set the letter down and picked up the final document. It was a printed booklet identified by its title page as a catalogue of items to be sold by the widow of the late Mr. Follywolle at an auction to take place in Stockholm the following month. Cecily paged through the hundreds of listed books and objects, a handful of which had been circled and annotated with bidding instructions. Among the circled items were books on diverse subjects, a skeleton of an armadillo, a snuffbox made of jasper, a Roman urn, and a preserved chameleon.

She put the papers back as she had found them and turned her attention to the open shelves. Of the miscellaneous objects Sir Barnaby had elected to keep in his private study, a considerable number appeared to be artifacts of alchemy and magic. She caught her own reflection in a mirror of black obsidian that, according to its label, had belonged to the sorcerer John Dee. A closer examination of the crystal orbs on the mantelpiece revealed that there were sigils and pentacles engraved on them. Sir Barnaby's interest in occult studies was also evident on the bookshelves, which

contained no botanical volumes, but did contain an assortment of grimoires and books of spells.

As Cecily returned a well-thumbed edition of *The Discov-
erie of Witchcraft* to its place, she wondered what it was that
Sir Barnaby had found so compelling about the subject.
Though she disagreed with Puritanical condemnation of
the study of magic, it had simply never ranked high on the
list of subjects that attracted her attention. She considered it
somewhat old-fashioned, its proponents vulnerable to char-
latanism.

She moved to the book wheel, where the theme was the
same. The open volume positioned in front of the stool contained instructions for the design and production of magic
rings. As she turned the wheel, pages printed with pentacles,
incantations, and lists of spirit names creaked past. She had
just turned past a book open to a hand-sketched illustration of a parrot skull haloed in cryptic symbols when her
thoughts were interrupted by the sound of footsteps in the
hall.

Giles Inwood entered the room. His eyes were shadowed,
his cheeks deflated. He looked startled to see her.

"Mr. Inwood," said Cecily. "I apologize. Perhaps I am not
permitted to—"

He made a small gesture, brushing away her apology. "You
may go where you wish, Lady Kay. I understand you are to
remain a guest in this house. Allow me to tell you how much
I admire your dedication to your work. Sir Barnaby would
have—" Inwood cleared his throat and looked around the
room. "Forgive me," he said softly. "It is difficult to be in
this place again. I find myself filled with the hope that he will
return at any moment."

Cecily nodded her understanding. Inwood collected himself and gave her a look of professional assessment. "You appear tired, Lady Kay. You cannot have slept peacefully. May I suggest an infusion of Saint John's wort—" He stopped again as a spasm of emotion crossed his face.

"Mr. Inwood?"

Inwood drew in a long, steadying breath before he answered. "I was recalling that I spoke those same words yesterday to that—that *villain* Dinley. Saint John's wort to soothe the nerves, I told him. What a fool I was. I should have observed the signs of mania."

"You could not have predicted what would happen," said Cecily.

"You are kind, Lady Kay, but I was well acquainted with Dinley. I could see that he was not himself. The man I knew was not nervous by nature. As a physician I am compelled to wonder whether he might have been bitten by a mad dog or ingested some pernicious herb. Hemlock root has been known to cause madness. I had a case last month of a woman consuming hemlock that had been mixed in with parsnips."

Cecily thought it unlikely, having encountered John's passion for roots and vegetables, that the cook would ever make such an error. "Did you inquire in the kitchen?"

Inwood nodded and winced slightly. "I did. The reply I received was, shall we say, *adamant.*"

Cecily smiled. She wanted to speak frankly to Inwood. He seemed a calm, intelligent man genuinely grieved by the death of his friend. But there was a good chance that if she told him what she had told Lady Mayne, he would report their conversation to the widow. And that wasn't all. If Cecily *was* correct, if there was more to Sir Barnaby's death than it appeared, she could not trust him.

"I must thank you," she said after a moment. "For allowing me to stay and make use of the Plant Room."

Inwood's eyebrows lifted. "You owe me no thanks. I had no part in the decision."

"Lady Mayne is mistress of the house, of course," said Cecily. "But I understand Sir Barnaby left the collection to you."

To her surprise, Cecily thought she saw grim amusement move over Inwood's face like wind through the leaves of a tree. An instant later, his expression settled back into one of grief. "Yes," he said quietly. "My friend has done me the honor of entrusting me with his legacy."

He picked up an opalescent shell from the shelf nearest to him and sighed as he touched a finger gently to its red label. "As for your gratitude, Lady Kay, you must direct it at Sir Barnaby alone. It will be my pleasure to host you at my own estate once the collection is housed there, but it will always be the Mayne collection. It didn't only *belong* to him, you see. His very self is bound up in it. Sir Barnaby is here, now, still alive within these cabinets. Every object, every choice of where to place it, every label written—he is here. I feel as if I could speak to him, and he would answer."

The words, though spoken with almost reverent affection, chilled Cecily. She felt ever more strongly as if they were in the presence of a ghost. "You and Sir Barnaby must have known each other for many years," she said.

Inwood set the shell down and returned his attention to her. "I was still a student when he became a kind of mentor to me. Our interests diverged as we grew older, but it is my opinion that this very divergence helped us remain friends."

"How so?"

"Collectors," said Inwood with a rueful smile, "can have

trouble staying on good terms when they are seeking to acquire the same objects."

"I see," said Cecily. "Then I take it you did not share Sir
Barnaby's interest in the occult."

Inwood showed no sign of surprise or discomfiture. His
eyes flitted to the crystals on the mantelpiece with the same
detached skepticism Cecily herself felt toward them. "I did
not," he said lightly. "But it had fascinated him for some time."

"Was he—" Cecily hesitated.

"Practicing?" finished Inwood. "I cannot say for certain. He knew the subject was not fashionable, and did not
speak of it often. When he did, he claimed that his interest
was merely theoretical. He offered the usual justifications.
To make a record of vulgar belief, and to strip the objects
of their mystery. But I knew him well—I believe he cared
rather more than he admitted."

"And Dinley? Did he also study it?"

Inwood frowned at the mention of Dinley's name. "I do
not believe so."

"Has there been any progress in the search for him?"

Inwood's frown deepened. "None, but the constable and
his men have not relaxed their efforts. He will be found."

"You mentioned," said Cecily, "that Mr. Dinley was not
usually a nervous man. He appeared to me a very gentle
person. Had Sir Barnaby expressed concerns about him to
you? Or reported any previous altercations?"

"Not to my knowledge," said Inwood. "Sir Barnaby and I
dined together only the day before yesterday. Dinley's name
never entered the conversation."

"Only the day before yesterday? Then you and Sir Barnaby must have discussed the upcoming tour."

Inwood nodded. "We did, yes. He was particularly eager for the guests to see the Holt box. He had just found out about the poor fellow. But he spoke mostly of an auction catalogue he was looking forward to receiving. He was hoping to acquire several books and specimens he felt the collection was missing." The faint smile returned to Inwood's face. "He was an elderly man, Lady Kay, but he had no intention of dying."

"He had just showed us the Holt box when he left us," said Cecily. "I have wondered what it can have been that drew him away. Did you happen to see him when he came downstairs?"

"I did not. I didn't even know the tour had ended until Carlyle told me."

"Then you didn't see Mr. Dinley come down either?"

"I did see Dinley, but that was earlier. I was in the hall when he came down with that lovely young woman—I recommended bistort to slow the bleeding."

"But you didn't go down to the kitchen with them?"

"No, and I don't believe they were going downstairs. I think they were going out to the garden."

A knock on the front door of the house prevented Cecily from asking another question. They listened in silence. The stairs creaked as one of the servants ascended from the kitchen. A moment later, a shriek rent the air. Cecily, who was closer to the door, rushed into the hall just ahead of Inwood.

Thomasin was standing at the entrance, one hand covering her mouth. On the threshold stood the swaying form of a man. One side of his face was a mask of dried and fresh blood. He wore no coat. His shirt was ripped and filthy. His wig was a ghastly ruin of matted tangles. As Cecily reached him, he staggered and fell forward into her arms. It took all her strength to control him as they sank together to the floor. She looked down at the battered features and recognized them. It was Otto Helm.

CHAPTER 11

As is often the case for those who exert themselves beyond their capacities in order to survive, Helm's condition deteriorated rapidly once he understood that he was safe. He remained on the floor, propped up in Cecily's arms, and seemed only vaguely cognizant of where he was. Cecily heard running footsteps in the house behind her, but Helm's weight prevented her from turning.

"What happened?" The voice was Meacan's. She entered Cecily's vision a moment later, followed by Lady Mayne's maid, Susanna, who stood aghast at the scene before her. Meacan appeared to have spent the day outside. The hems of her skirts and petticoats were dirty, and her dress was flecked with the unavoidable muck flung up by churning carriage wheels. When she saw Helm, her eyes widened, then flickered for an instant to meet Cecily's before she returned her attention to him.

Helm, who had thus far produced only a string of words in Swedish separated by whimpers of pain, made a halting attempt at English. "Thieves," he said hoarsely. "In the alley." His eyes filled with panicked tears. "My bag," he managed. "My notebooks."

Inwood's voice was at once consoling and authoritative.

"That is not important now, Mr. Helm. We must see to your injuries."

Helm struggled to speak. "I wish not to be . . . trouble," he said in a barely audible voice. "Help me . . . return . . . my inn."

"Out of the question," said Inwood, as he and Cecily eased Helm into a seated position with his back against a craggy boulder tagged with a red label. "From what I can see, it was by luck alone you made it this far."

Lady Mayne did not come downstairs, but upon being apprised of the situation expressed shock and concern. She agreed at once that accommodation should be given to the wounded man. As there were no unoccupied guest rooms in the house, she ordered that Helm be made as comfortable as possible in the bed that had been Walter Dinley's. She instructed the servants to take their commands from Inwood and to keep her informed of the condition of her unexpected guest.

Before they addressed the problem of conveying Helm to the uppermost level of the house, Inwood asked John for a list of salves, ointments, and medicines available in the kitchen. He nodded approvingly when John confirmed that he always kept aloe to hand. "And hyssop?" he asked the cook.

John's face fell. "I did have some, but it occurred to me to test the bitterness of it in balance with sweet figs and I'm afraid I used it all. The apothecary isn't far, though. Just beyond the end of the terrace." John started to gesture east, then dropped his arm with an expression of dismay. "But it will be closed. This is the time Ashton and his wife were to join a party of herbalists on a journey to Kent."

Meacan interjected. "Their son is minding the shop." The

group, with the exception of Helm, turned inquiring eyes to her. "I am acquainted with the family," she explained.

"Then I will require hyssop," said Inwood. "Also water germander and valerian. And if this younger Ashton knows his trade well, anything else he recommends for cuts and bruises."

"I'll go," declared John. "Won't take above a quarter of an hour."

Inwood stopped him. "I will need your help to carry the patient upstairs."

It was decided that Thomasin would go to the apothecary. Cecily watched her set out with a basket over her arm. The lines of tension that ran across the maid's forehead and from her nose to the outer corners of her mouth had deepened over the last two days. Once outside, she looked back at the house with obvious loathing.

While John and Inwood struggled up the stairs with Helm between them, Meacan and Cecily waited at the base of the stairwell, ready to follow once the others had made sufficient progress, or assist if called. Meacan stood with her head tilted back, staring up into the gloom. From above, they could hear John and Inwood's grunts of effort interspersed with the thump of Helm's boots against the stairs and his yelps of pain. Meacan's arms were crossed tight across her waist. There was a small indentation on her right cheek.

"You used to bite your cheek like that when you were angry," Cecily remarked.

Meacan did not unclench her jaw. "I *am* angry. If they wanted his bag, they could have given him a push and snatched it. They didn't need to beat the poor man."

Cecily wasn't entirely sure what to make of Meacan's comment, which sounded sincere, but struck her as odd given the well-known dangers of London's streets. Cecily doubted even the most naïve resident could traverse them without seeing a flash of an imagined knife. And Meacan was not naïve. "He is fortunate he found his way to safety," she said. "And that Inwood is here to minister to his injuries without delay." She paused. "When he is recovered, perhaps we will be able to resolve the question of why he left the house so suddenly."

Meacan's gaze remained on the stairwell, her expression unchanged. She spoke casually. "It has been suggested to me since I returned from my errands that you've asked more than a few questions already today."

"When did you return?" asked Cecily.

Meacan's cheek relaxed and a corner of her mouth quirked into a smile. "And from what errands, you will ask next? For all your admirable qualities, my dear old friend, I cannot compliment your subtlety. I returned an hour ago. My errands are my own affair, but to satisfy your curiosity, I will tell you that I was visiting my tenant and making inquiries into future employment."

Cecily didn't know whether to be irritated at the hint of mockery in Meacan's tone or relieved by the warmth in it. "From whom did you hear that I've been asking questions?"

Meacan lifted a hand in a vague gesture that could have referred to all the occupants in the house, or to the house itself. "I also heard that Lady Mayne gave you permission to stay," she said. "I myself have yet to meet her. I was on my way to do so when I heard the commotion and came down to find you holding poor Mr. Helm. You'll have to change your dress."

Cecily looked down at herself and noticed for the first

time the dark smears of blood on her bodice, skirt, and
sleeves. "Easily done," she said, but the thought of the injuries required to leave such stains sent a shiver up her spine.
There was no longer any sound or vibration upon the stairs,
only distant voices from the top of the house. They started
up together. The candlelight on the walls threw gleaming
phantoms across the oil paintings. Mounted corals reached
out like crooked fingers grasping for their hair.

Meacan exhaled with a shudder as if she was cold. "The
collection is changing," she announced ominously. "Everything looks sharper and more poisonous than it did before."

"I expect it is only our perception of it that is altered,"
said Cecily reasonably. "We cannot dismiss from our minds
what we have seen these past two days."

"No." Meacan let the word drop decisively. "No, it is the
collection. It's as if it knows its master is no longer here and
is preparing to defend itself."

"That is fantasy," said Cecily firmly.

They had reached the first landing. Meacan nodded toward the open door of the Beast Room. The skeleton of a
hartebeest stood at its center, its black horns twisting up
to points from its white skull. It was watched by the stern
head of a lioness mounted to the wall behind it. The claws
and scaled belly of a crocodile strung from the ceiling were
visible through the top of the doorway. "I thought I saw that
crocodile move this morning," said Meacan. "And I'd swear
I heard a snake hiss at me from inside its jar."

Cecily recalled the distorted shadow of the shark's jaw on
her ceiling. "I am sure you did not," she said. "And even if
we were to entertain this delusion, I would point out that
the collection does not need to defend itself. There is not

going to be an auction, or, as you put it, a *frenzy*. The entire Mayne collection is to be transferred in its entirety to the care of Giles Inwood."

"Is it?" Meacan dropped her dire, prophetic tone. "That is very interesting."

Cecily drew in a breath. "Meacan," she said with quiet gravity. "Do you know something about the death of Barnaby Mayne?"

They had started up the next flight of stairs. Meacan stopped and put a hand on Cecily's arm to halt her. "I know exactly what everyone else knows," she said in a hushed voice. "Why would you ask such a question?"

"Because last night you didn't want to tell me you had spoken to Helm, and because there are inconsistencies in the way the murder appeared to take place."

"What inconsistencies?"

"Confide in me, and I will tell you."

"I have nothing to confide." Meacan glanced up and down the stairwell. Its center, outlined by the angled spiral of the bannister, presented a hollow plunge to the depths of the house. There was no sound of a step or a breath to be heard except for their own. She looked at Cecily. "And as for your inconsistencies, of course there were secrets in the house that day. This is one of the oldest collections in London. If that silent lioness on the wall could speak, she could share enough secrets to addle even the most orderly mind."

"Then you think—"

"I think it is unwise to follow a path leading from a murder into the realm of the collectors. It is a shadowy place full of illusions. And it isn't safe."

A door creaked open above them. Susanna's clipped voice

called down. "Is that Mrs. Barlow on the stairs? Lady Mayne is waiting for you."

Meacan gave Cecily a final, inscrutable look. "Trust your old friend. Limit your questions to the names of plants," she whispered. "If you don't, I fear you will find yourself in trouble." And with that she was gone, leaving Cecily uncertain whether she had just received a warning or a threat.

Cecily continued up alone to the garret. John and Inwood had navigated the piles of crates and books on the floor and deposited Helm on Dinley's bed. Helm had fallen unconscious, and for the second time in two days, Cecily watched Giles Inwood perform a perfunctory examination of a still and bloodied body. "The skull is intact," he said. "I am confident of it. But the arm is broken and a rib is cracked. Whether the ankle is sprained or fractured I cannot yet tell."

John left to boil water and prepare salves in the kitchen. When he returned some minutes later, Thomasin was with him. The maid's affect had changed. There was color in her cheeks and a sparkle of energy in her eyes. Cecily didn't know whether to attribute it to the fortifying fragrance of the basketful of medicinal herbs she carried, or merely to the brief reprieve she had enjoyed from the house.

Inwood examined the contents of the basket with satisfaction and sent John and Thomasin back down with instructions for their preparation. "You may leave me to my patient, Lady Kay," he said. "Do not be overly concerned. His wounds are not as grave as they might have been. It is fear and exhaustion that has overcome him."

Cecily, accepting the dismissal, turned to go, then paused. "I should ask," she said, "how you think it best to inform him of what has occurred."

Inwood looked confused. "Inform him—"

Cecily looked at the unconscious man. "About Sir Barnaby," she whispered. "I do not think he knows."

Inwood's expression cleared. "Of course. You are right. He should be spared undue shock or distress." He lapsed into thoughtful silence. "He will wake, unfortunately, while I set the bone, but after that he will sleep. It will be best to wait until tomorrow, when he is rested, to tell him. Perhaps you would be so kind as to do it?"

"Of course."

"Good. I would stay myself, but I have—" Inwood hesitated. "I have several urgent matters of business to which I must attend. I will examine him again when I return in two days. Summon the apothecary if his condition worsens."

"Two days?"

"Has Lady Mayne not told you? Sir Barnaby is to be brought back to the house so that those who mourn him might pay their respects. You may expect to see every member of the collecting community here."

"I see," said Cecily slowly. "I presume then that Mr. Warbulton and Mr. Carlyle will be among them? Even perhaps Miss Fordyce?"

"Almost certainly," Inwood replied. "It will be a mournful reunion of our small company."

CHAPTER 12

The sun, burning out at last at the end of a long spring day, flared its final rays through the smoky sky and into the window of the Mayne herbarium. Books and pressed plants radiated outward from where Cecily sat at the long rectangular table in the center of the room, her head bowed low over a plant resting on a sheet of brown paper. Its thin branches formed paths across the page, each one leading to a translucent purple flower.

She glanced up. Through the connecting door to the other house she could just see Helm. Since Inwood's departure four hours earlier, she had kept watch over him. John and Martha had made frequent visits, John to adjust and replace poultices, Martha to tidy and rearrange the space around the patient. Cecily had not spoken to Helm other than to reassure him, on the several occasions when he woke in fretful confusion, that he was safe. At present he was sleeping soundly, his breathing quiet and even.

Satisfied that Helm's condition had not worsened, Cecily returned her attention to the plant. She set her pencil to the corner of the page and completed the last identification the day's fading light would permit. *Origanum* of Sipylus.

After she had finished writing and set the pencil down she remained as she was, staring down at the specimen.

She had a clear memory of the day she had collected it. The weather had been hot, the sun reflected white off marble ruins. Andrew had been hosting a gathering of merchants and ambassadors from Constantinople. Ever willing to indulge what he termed Cecily's *botanical habit* when it removed her from situations in which the presence of his inquisitive wife was, in his view, an embarrassment at best and a liability at worst, he had arranged for Cecily to visit the nearby Mount Sipylus.

Cecily recalled how the light had played like scattered diamonds over the little streams that cooled the air and carved their shapes into the earth. The guide had led the party to a cave nestled on the mountain's shoulder. It was said to be the tomb of Tantalus, that son of Zeus sentenced to stand for all eternity by a pond from which he could never drink, beneath a tree the fruit of which he could never eat. Cecily's attention had been drawn at once to the cascade of purple petals and soft green leaves around the entrance. She had taken a single plant and pressed it that evening, alone by candlelight.

A creak of the floor brought her mind back to the Mayne house and announced the return of John, who urged her to go downstairs and take her supper. Lady Mayne had eaten already. After thanking him, Cecily took her time to make sure the herbarium was tidy, the books and specimens returned to their proper places. She looked once more at Helm. Cleaned and salved and bandaged, he looked much less ghastly than he had. Luck had indeed been with him.

Her path to the kitchen took her past the door to the library. From within, she heard the sound of heavy pages being turned.

Curious, she entered the room and found Meacan sitting on the floor in front of a partially denuded bookcase, her skirts pinned down by books scattered like lily pads around her. The sunset light through the window had turned the gilding on their covers to fiery veins. A porcelain cup half full of coffee was perched on an open volume. The cup, not quite heavy enough to weigh down the page, had slid to the inside margins, and was tilted at a precarious angle. A crumpet glistening with butter rested on the burgundy cover of the book beside it. Cecily, perceiving the grease already seeping into the dark leather, rushed forward, picked up the crumpet, and returned it to the empty plate nearby.

Meacan looked up from the book resting open in her lap. She was not wearing a cap, and her face was surrounded by bramble-like curls. "How is Mr. Helm?"

Cecily lifted the cold coffee cup from the center of the book and set it on the nearest table. "Still asleep," she answered. "But why have you pulled all these books from their places? Have you anyone's permission to do it?"

"I have more than permission," said Meacan. "I am fulfilling the terms of my employment."

"Your employment? Who has employed you?"

Meacan turned a page. "Lady Mayne. She wants the collection to be inventoried before it passes to Inwood, and she has hired me to do it."

"*You* are going to inventory the Mayne collection?"

Meacan raised her head, an eyebrow quirked in challenge. "Do you think I am unqualified? I have existed within the cluttered shelves of the collectors for years. The good librarian and I have that in common."

Cecily was confused. "The good librarian?"

Meacan nodded at the elephant skull. Looking at it,

Cecily had to acknowledge that the gently curving jaw and sad wisdom of the brow suggested the careworn visage of a guardian. She turned back to Meacan. "You spoke so disparagingly of the house and the collection. I thought you wanted to leave."

Meacan shrugged. "Employment is employment." She lifted the book she was holding and turned it around so that Cecily could see its pages. "And I never said there was nothing of interest in this house. Here, for example, is fairy ink." She tilted the book so that it caught the light and Cecily perceived that certain words sparkled and glittered an iridescent silver gray. She lowered herself to the floor and touched one of the letters lightly. It was rough against her fingertip.

"A bit of paste and crushed Muscovy glass," said Meacan. "You can be certain I'll be making use of this technique from now on. I'm only sorry that I wasn't the one to think of it."

Cecily tried to clear her thoughts. "An inventory of the entire collection is a momentous undertaking. Weeks of work at a minimum. Months, to do it thoroughly." She paused. "Lady Mayne told me she intended to have the collection out of the house as quickly as possible."

Meacan closed the book of glittering pages and set it aside with a look of unconcern. "Evidently she changed her mind. But how difficult an endeavor can it be? Sir Barnaby kept his registers as diligently as a clock keeps time."

"I don't doubt it," said Cecily. "But how do you mean to match each entry in the register to an item in the collection?"

Like a ship's captain debating which island to sail toward, Meacan looked out over the books stacked around her. "I am in the midst of devising a method."

"I see," said Cecily doubtfully. "What books are these?"

"A few are registers," said Meacan, gesturing vaguely. "And the others are the ones that seemed of interest to me when I looked at them."

In matters of organization and method, Cecily knew her value. She decided in that moment that, while the truth of Sir Barnaby's death could forever elude her, she had before her now an opportunity to assist in the preservation of his collection. A part of her wondered whether Sir Barnaby himself might appreciate the latter assistance more than the former. "Perhaps I can help you devise an approach," she said.

Meacan looked pleased. "Would you?"

"I will have to familiarize myself with the system before we begin," said Cecily. "Where is the first register?"

A short search led to the oldest of the blue-bound volumes in which Sir Barnaby had recorded his acquisitions. Cecily opened it to the first page. Thin penciled lines divided it into five columns. They contained, respectively, the name or description of each object, the acquisition number assigned to it, the date it was acquired, the price paid, and the location of the object within the house.

The first entry was dated the first of September, 1659. Sir Barnaby must have been in his twenties then. The handwriting was youthful and confident. Cecily exhaled in admiration. Even when the number of items in his cabinets could be counted on one hand and arranged on one table, he had known that his collection would require a system by which to order it. Forty years had yellowed the paper, but the entries on it retained the energy and enthusiasm with which they had been written.

She turned the pages and picked up subsequent volumes, rustling through the years. New hands showed the coming and going of various secretaries, but Sir Barnaby's own writing maintained its dominion over the expanses of paper. Interests swelled like waves, only to recede and be replaced, among them quadrupeds, medicines, antiquities, fossils, amulets, costumes, vases, birds, insects, shells, shoes, eggs, and boxes. As the collection had grown, so, too, had the difficulty of organizing and maintaining it. Cecily could almost feel the heat of mental exertion as the pages became more and more crowded with symbols and revisions and annotations.

Sir Barnaby had recorded the value of objects only when he had paid for them, which in many cases he hadn't. It was clear that as his collection and reputation grew, the number of fellow enthusiasts eager for their specimens to be included in it had increased. *Twenty-three butterflies encased in glass sent by Lord Edgeware. Six birds from Father Kamel in China. A horn of the fish that is called unicorn.* Cecily was so absorbed that she hardly noticed Meacan lighting candles, and was startled by Meacan's voice. "Are you looking for something in particular?"

"I was admiring Sir Barnaby's ability to maintain such orderly registers."

"I see," said Meacan. "I suppose, coming from you, that does sound like an honest answer."

"Why wouldn't it be?"

Candlelight and shadow moved across Meacan's features, making her expression unreadable. "I thought you might still be trying to reconcile those little inconsistencies you mentioned earlier. You can trust *me*, you know, if you wish to discuss them."

Cecily dropped her eyes to the open register. "I decided to take your advice," she said, the dishonesty tasting strange in her mouth. "I was meddling without good cause into matters beyond my understanding. What happened in the study is as clear now as it will ever be."

When there was no reply, Cecily glanced up and caught Meacan giving her a hard look. After a moment, Meacan sat down again and set a candle on the low table beside the coffee cup. "In that case, tell me how to accomplish this inventory you predict will be so difficult."

Cecily took a sip of the coffee and grimaced at the cold bitterness of the brew. "The location column indicates the room in which each object is housed," she said. "F&S for Fish and Snakes, Q for Quadruped, A for Artifact, and so on. Some columns include more specific locations. EW must be East Wall. S3 is Shelf Three. D6 is Drawer 6."

"Yes yes yes," said Meacan, yawning. "Details to address in the morning."

Cecily gave her old friend a stern look. "You must not approach this endeavor frivolously, Meacan. It is one thing to exact petty revenge by conjuring nonexistent bugs. It would be quite another to corrupt the order of the Mayne collection. Do you not understand that these specimens are to be resources for scholars and philosophers?"

"If you're here simply to lecture me . . ." Meacan muttered.

Cecily sighed. "I suggest you approach the endeavor one room at a time. The registers are in chronological order. You will exhaust and confuse yourself if you proceed by searching for a single fossil in the Stone Room followed by a single egg in the Bird Room followed by a volume in the library and so on."

"My path would resemble that of an excited housefly," Meacan agreed. "But how is it to be avoided?"

Cecily frowned, enjoying herself. "You should begin by choosing a room."

"The Aviary," said Meacan.

"You mean the Bird Room."

"Mm."

Cecily ran a finger down the open page of the register and stopped at the entry for the *Toucan*. "You'll have to go through all the registers in order and make a list of every object he put in the bird room."

"Easy enough."

"It will take time. Once you have that list, you'll take it to the Bird Room and begin your work there, say at the top left corner of the easternmost wall, one object at a time. Find the object on your list and make a mark beside it."

"As I said," said Meacan. "Easy enough."

"It won't be at all," Cecily corrected her. "Sir Barnaby may have done everything in his power to avoid inconsistencies and mistakes, but in forty years he cannot have avoided them entirely. You will find objects in the rooms that are not in the registers, and objects in the registers that are not in the rooms. You will have to make separate lists of each. And of course there will be missing labels and incorrect labels and illegible labels."

Meacan slumped down against the wall. "Why," she said, "did he have to acquire *so much*?"

"Because," said Cecily, "if his goal was to keep a record of the whole world and its history, where was he to stop?"

CHAPTER 13

By the following morning, Helm was awake and capable of clear speech. Though the bruises on his face were livid and his ankle was so swollen that he could not rise from the bed without assistance, Cecily was relieved to see that his eyes were alert, attentive, and unblurred by fever. The destroyed wig had been removed, and a soft velvet nightcap had been found to cover his head. She related the events of the previous evening as sensitively as she could, watching for signs of distress in the wounded man. He did give voice to a shocked cry when he learned that the person he thought to be his host was dead, but after that he listened with calm attention to the rest of her account.

"I have no doubt of your truth," he said when she was finished. "But the circumstances are for me difficult to believe. I thought the nature of Mr. Dinley to be most—" He searched for a word. "Most *docile*." He paused and added more quietly, "And yet it is true a man who is not violent may suddenly become so."

"You are not alone in your amazement," said Cecily. "According to those well acquainted with Mr. Dinley, he never gave any indication of a temper. We did wonder whether you heard any part of their argument before your own departure."

"I?" Helm's blue eyes held Cecily's. "No. Why would I be hearing something of it?"

"Because you were in the room closest to the study, and because your path out of the house must have taken you past its door at around the time the argument between them began. You did leave at a quarter to six?"

"Yes, if you say, but I did not remark the time."

"The servants were surprised to see you go. They thought you were to stay to supper."

Helm's gaze shifted to his feet. "A small mistake. I had another supper engagement I remembered most suddenly." A spasm of pain crossed his face.

"Can I be of assistance?" asked Cecily quickly, silently chastising herself for bullying the injured man.

Helm's face relaxed. "I thank you. I am recovered." With his good arm, he raised to his lips the cup Cecily had brought from the kitchen and closed his eyes in appreciation of the fragrant infusion. "We were speaking, I think, of Mr. Dinley," he said. "Who, to me, was most affable and patient."

"I did not realize you had any opportunity to converse with him at length," said Cecily.

Helm started to nod, then winced at the movement. "In the morning when I arrived," he said. "I was obliged to offer my apologies to my host. I wished most fervently to be among the group to tour the house, but alas, I had not the leisure. It was required of me to devote the day's hours to the serpents my master in Sweden wished me to study."

"Then you are employed by another scholar," said Cecily.

"I am in the position of assistant in his research," said Helm. "It is his present work to compile the serpents of the world into a book by which they may be placed correctly in their proper classes and orders. For that purpose, I am sent to visit collections in England and in France so that I may observe for him the serpents he has not in his possession. It is a most laborious effort, for he wishes such exacting measures as a count of scales on the bellies of every creature, a count, you understand, it is most difficult to make through the glass of the specimen jar. But do not think I complain. Serpents have, for me, a fascination." He paused. "Forgive me. I have lost the direction of our conversation."

"You were speaking of your arrival at the house."

"Ah yes. I was most distressed that I could not avail myself of the tour. I requested if I might see briefly the rooms before I began my work. As Sir Barnaby could not himself guide me, Mr. Dinley offered most kindly to do so. I felt toward the man a great sympathy."

Cecily hesitated. She was conscious of Helm's pain and the drowsiness that would soon descend upon him thanks to the potion of valerian and hops, but for the moment he appeared comfortable and glad of the company. "Did Mr. Dinley appear troubled to you?" she asked.

"It was the contrary," answered Helm at once. "He seemed to me—how do you say it? He seemed at the height of spirits."

The answer gave Cecily pause. This was not the Dinley she had encountered, who in the aftermath of the viper-mouth incident had appeared so shaken. "On what subjects did you converse?"

"On many diverse subjects," said Helm. "I had questions in the rooms, which he answered with much patience."

"I believe you also spoke at some length with Mrs. Barlow." Cecily watched his face carefully, though she had little insight into the expression hidden within the swelling bruises.

"I was most enjoying of her company," said Helm at once, his eyes kindling with warmth. "A kind, attentive, and beautiful lady. She was most interested in my work."

"Then—she really did simply ask you about your work? You have no other connection to her?"

"To Mrs. Barlow? But of course not."

Helm appeared so in earnest that Cecily could not think of a way to probe him further on the matter. She returned to the subject of Walter Dinley. "When Mr. Dinley took you through the rooms, did he speak of the upcoming tour?"

This time Helm hesitated before he answered. "Only that he—he was in happy anticipation of it. He told me so when he was assisting me in locating the serpents I required. He was most helpful to my work." Helm stopped. His eyes filled suddenly with misery as his gaze dropped to the bed linens rumpled around him. "When I woke in that dark alley," he said after a moment, "I told myself I was the most unfortunate man in London. My arm that was broken. My return home that would be surely delayed. My—" His voice caught. "My notebooks, my work, my observations all lost." He heaved a shuddering sigh. "What ingratitude, when I possess still my life."

Helm's distress at the loss of his notebooks struck a chord of sympathy in Cecily's chest. An idea occurred to her. "Where were you attacked?" she asked. "Perhaps someone could be sent to search for your books there. I am sure the thieves had no interest in drawings of snakes and counts of scales. If we are lucky, they were discarded and might yet be found."

"It is not possible," whispered Helm.

"We can at least try."

"No." The word burst from Helm with surprising force.

"No," he repeated more calmly. "You see, I do not know where it happened. I made the decision, a foolish notion, to return by foot to my inn when my supper was concluded. I lost my way, and cannot tell you where I was when I was set upon. They left me in a stupor. When I arrived again at my senses, it was night and I was without money. My requests for help were to no good. As was said by Mr. Inwood, it was by luck only that in my wandering I came alive to this place. My notebooks, I must accept, are lost to me."

"And yet you are here in the house with the serpents again," said Cecily encouragingly. "And at least some of what is gone may be recovered. I find often that when I am forced to repeat work I have done already, I do a better job of it."

Her words appeared to cheer Helm slightly. "That is so," he murmured. "And I *am* here." He looked across the garret at the shelves filled with antiquities. "Because of most terrible circumstances, I may after all peruse the Mayne collection."

"When Inwood says your ankle can bear weight," said Cecily. His words had recalled to her something else he had said. "You mentioned Sir Barnaby could not guide you himself in your abbreviated tour that morning," she said. "Was he otherwise occupied?"

"Oh yes," said Helm. "He was making his wishes for the catalogue."

Helm had a good command of English, but in this instance Cecily thought he must have misspoken. "His wishes for the catalogue?"

"Ah," said Helm. "It is an explanation of some length. Perhaps you are not to be interested?"

"On the contrary, I am most intrigued."

"Ah, yes," said Helm. "Like me, you are of a curious mind. I will explain it to you. You are aware, perhaps, that Sir Barnaby had many—what is the word? Many correspondents, many agents in distant places dedicated to that which was of interest to him?"

Cecily nodded her understanding. Helm continued. "He has one such agent in Stockholm, in Sweden, my home. A Mr. Shaw. It is a small city, my lady. Many acquaintances are mutual. Mr. Shaw learned that I was to make a journey soon to London, and that I intended to visit the collections here. He asked if I would make to Sir Barnaby a delivery of a catalogue—a list of such books and objects as were to be sold at auction in Stockholm. It is always more reliable, when it is possible, to convey messages in such a friendly way."

"I see," said Cecily, remembering the catalogue on Sir Barnaby's desk. "Was the collection by chance that of a Mr. Follywolle?"

Helm's eyes brightened. "Yes, yes, exactly so, my lady. Mr. Follywolle, I should say the late Mr. Follywolle, who lived many years in Stockholm and made a collection of great popularity there. Many serpents. His poor widow, in circumstances sadly reduced, is to make an auction of it."

"And you delivered a copy of the auction catalogue to Sir Barnaby."

"Just as you say. When I arrived in the morning yesterday I gave to him the catalogue at once, and explained to him that if he wished to make upon it some markings for the information of his agent—what was of interest to him, what prices he would pay—I could convey it back again to Sweden. It is comprehensible to you? My accent is not so strong?"

Cecily assured him she understood perfectly. He went on. "Sir Barnaby took the catalogue to his study to make the marks upon it before his guests arrived and required his attendance. He told me to be sure to—" He stopped, his eyes widening.

"Yes?" Cecily prompted him.

Helm looked rueful. "I was to retrieve it from him before I left the house," he said. "But I forgot to do so."

"You were in a hurry," said Cecily.

"I was only concerned I would be late to supper. I have a tendency to become absorbed in my work."

"But you must have wanted to seek Sir Barnaby out before you left? To take your leave, at least?"

Helm avoided her eyes. "I did not wish to be of interruption," he murmured. He shifted and grimaced. "I must apologize to you, my lady. Your company, it has been of much cheer to me, but I find—I find I am compelled to lie down."

Helm looked pale, and Cecily could see his exhaustion was not feigned. The infusion was taking effect. His eyelids had begun to droop, and his jaw had slackened as the tension eased from it. Gently, Cecily took the empty cup from his hand and helped him into a reclining position. She asked if there was anything more she could do to make him comfortable.

Helm attempted a smile. "I am most eager for the continuing of my work, Lady Kay. If you could bring to me the specimen of the *cobra di capello*, which has the mark as of spectacles on its neck and is called also *le serpent a lunettes*. I must—I must make a count of its *scuta abdominalia* and *squamas caudales*. And—and if there are the recent editions of the *Philosophical Transactions*, I am wishing to read—Mr. Strachan's observations—serpent of Ceylon, green in color—and recent dissections of the *rattlesnake* performed by—by . . ." Helm trailed off. His eyes were closed and he had begun to slur his words.

Cecily spoke softly. "I am well acquainted with the comfort that can be found in work, Mr. Helm, especially when the subject is of great interest. But I am certain Inwood would insist that you rest a little longer before you resume your scale counting."

Helm's eyes fluttered open briefly. "Must inquire if you saw in your travels the serpent—common in Aleppo—mountains and rocks—color of sand with black spots—venomous and most intriguing—" His eyes closed again and he began to breathe deeply.

Cecily rose from the chair she had pulled up to the side of the bed. She surveyed in silence the space in which Walter Dinley had slept and worked. The curator must have dedicated most of his time and attention to his employment, for she could see almost nothing in the way of belongings. Only a small pile of books tucked halfway under the bed looked like they were there for his personal entertainment. Taking care not to disturb Helm, she picked them up and examined them. There were three: a history of China, a treatise on fruit trees, and an illustrated book of fossils. She was about to return them when she noticed the edge of a folded piece of paper tucked between the pages of the history. After glancing at Helm, whose eyes remained closed, she drew it out. She set the three books down quietly and left the room.

She waited until she was back in her chamber to unfold the sheet of paper. The shark jaw, familiar now, yawned over her shoulder from the wall. The document was a letter. *My dear sister*, it began. She skipped to the final page and looked at the signature scrawled with practiced confidence. *Anthony*

Holt. She stared at the name in puzzlement. What had Walter Dinley been doing in possession of a personal letter written by the celebrated traveler, recently deceased, to his sister? She turned to the first page.

> *I met a man in the market. How I wish you could have met*
> *him also, but perhaps one day you will, for he told me he wished*
> *to visit England to see the will-o'-the-wisps who lead travelers*
> *astray on the moors. He asked me to join him for tea, for which*
> *I was obliged to pay, and then did proceed to request from the*
> *shop their finest cakes and savory delicacies in portions that*
> *could have supplied a banquet. I would have felt taken advan-*
> *tage of, had he not gone on to entertain me with tales of such an*
> *absorbing nature, tales of peculiar events not unlike those fairy*
> *tales you so enjoy, that I happily sat with him until the sun set*
> *on the market and he walked away into the forest. That night*
> *at the inn, the villagers told me I had met a good friend of*
> *theirs. Not a man, they said, but a fox who comes from the*
> *forest once or twice a year and, pretending to be a man, tells*
> *them tales while they treat him to their finest teas and cakes.*
> *None of them wish to reveal that they see through his ruse, for*
> *they so enjoy his company that they do not mind the deceit. I*
> *would have thought they took me to be a credulous fool, except*
> *that I noticed the man's cap had sat oddly on his head as if it*
> *covered two triangle ears.*

The letter continued, each page spinning stories more exaggerated, more marvelous than those on the page before. Holt wrote of a pirate who once a month brought his ship to land and covered its whole hull in oil of cocoa nuts so that it slipped through the water faster than any other ship on the ocean. He wrote of double-headed snakes and conversations with anthropophagi. Invariably, he was the hero of every harrowing adventure. The letter concluded:

> *So you see you must not worry for me. I sail now for Chusan, where I am certain I will find much of interest to Sir Barnaby. A man with a deep purse and a voracious appetite for all I can think to send. Indeed he is the patron every traveler hopes to acquire. Be well dear one and wish hello to the elm tree and the old ghost in the attic.*

The words blurred before Cecily's eyes as she thought of their author arriving in Chusan, not knowing that it was the last land he would ever see. She blinked away her tears. The letter held tragedy, but it did not appear to hold answers. What she needed was to gain a better understanding of Sir Barnaby. She remembered Inwood's words to her in the study. *Sir Barnaby is here, now, still alive within these cabinets.* An idea occurred to her. Of course. She would go to the concentrated core of the collection. She would go to the registers in which Sir Barnaby had recorded those choices. It was the nearest she could come to speaking with a dead man.

CHAPTER 14

The house was being prepared for the following day, when Sir Barnaby's body would return to it. A subtle battle was in progress between Lady Mayne and Martha, with the widow issuing instructions from the confines of her shrouded room, and the housekeeper resisting almost all of them. Their most heated debate was over the appearance of the landings, through which the guests would have to pass to reach the master bedroom. Lady Mayne, citing the incompatibility of vulgar objects with pious reflection, wanted the objects on the landings moved into rooms where mourners would not see them. Martha argued that Sir Barnaby would never have condoned the rearrangement.

Lady Mayne, preoccupied with plans for the funeral to be held at the estate in a week's time, had yielded on the matter of the landings. The objects could remain where they were as long as they were covered in black silk. Martha had acquiesced to the compromise, but not before making dire predictions of boot heels and buckles catching on the black garlands, dragging them down, and pulling the contents off the shelves with them.

Martha had a point, thought Cecily, as she carefully avoided the heaps of cloth pooled treacherously in the dark recesses of the staircase. Many of the shelves were already partly covered. She passed the skeleton of a rat standing on its hind legs, its little bones wired together, its hollow cavity of a nose lifted to sniff the air. A corner of black silk was draped over it as if the skeletal creature had donned death's hooded cloak.

There was a table at the center of the library that had not been there before. Meacan was seated at it, her left elbow propped on its surface, her head resting heavily on her hand. Her other hand held a pencil poised over a page half-filled with writing. One of the blue-bound registers was open beside it. The rest of the registers were piled in crooked stacks on either side of her.

"The table is an improvement over the floor," said Cecily.

"It's one of the items John had to move from the carriage house," said Meacan.

"A more suitable surface for writing than the painted coffin would have been," said Cecily.

"The coffin is in the dining room," said Meacan. "And I will tell you, it is a strange thing to enjoy a mince pie in the company of a pharaoh."

Cecily crossed to the table. "How are you progressing?"

Meacan cast a critical look at the open register and fanned its pages. "I am empathizing with Athena when she was trapped inside Zeus's skull." With a sigh, she sat up straighter and stretched her arms. "And you? What brings you into the head of the late Sir Barnaby Mayne?"

"I thought I might assist you," said Cecily.

"By all means," said Meacan, gesturing to the chair opposite her. "Join me in the labyrinth. I assume, given your predilections, you'll want to begin with the items designated for the Plant Room. He used *HS* to indicate them in the registers."

"*Hortus siccus,*" murmured Cecily. "The dry garden."

Meacan nodded. She indicated a pile to her right. "The first volume should be there somewhere."

Cecily found it and sat down with it at the table. "I thought, instead of the plants, I would begin with the objects Sir Barnaby kept in his study."

Meacan's eyes narrowed. "Why the study?"

Cecily didn't answer. She had already opened the register. She slid her finger slowly down the column on the far right of the page, in which Sir Barnaby had recorded the location assigned to each object. She stopped when she came to a small astrological symbol. "This must be it," she said. "The sign for Leo, a pun on his name."

Meacan, who had been frowning at Cecily, now looked thoughtful. "Wait," she said. "Don't tell me. Leo. Mayne. The lion. Aha! The lion's *mane.* Leo. The den of *Mayne.* But you still haven't told me why you want to inventory the study."

Cecily took a sheet of paper and pencil from the stationery box. "Simple curiosity," she said. "His private study must have been where he kept the objects that were most precious to him."

Meacan absorbed the answer with a slight frown. Then she shrugged, took up her pencil, and returned her attention to the volume open before her.

Cecily's task was not a difficult one. Compared to the column containing a description of each object, which over the years had become dense with annotations and corrections, the column containing their locations was decisive and clear. She had no trouble identifying each appearance of the sign of Leo as she ran her finger down the page. Each time she saw the symbol, she copied the details of the acquisition onto her slowly lengthening list.

Sir Barnaby's study was smaller than the other rooms in the house, which meant that he had been obliged to consider carefully which objects deserved a place there. Cecily observed that often weeks or months passed before he added another article to its cabinets. She pictured him opening crates and sorting through bulk purchases, occasionally coming across an item that captured his imagination so thoroughly that he decided to keep it close: an opalized fossil of a nautilus shell, a skeleton of a bat, the hand of a mummy. As the years passed, more and more of these objects demonstrated his intensifying interest in occult studies. She began to see constellated rings, scrying glasses, beryl crystals, and grimoires.

Meacan's silence did not last long. As she came across names of collectors who were familiar to her, she would snort, and periodically offer a derisive anecdote. Cecily, only half listening, learned of Mr. Doddle, who was so remiss in returning borrowed books that the other collectors had made a collective decision to shun him, and of Mr. Wake, who was so offended by Mr. Atlee's criticism of his theories concerning the taming of beasts through music that he hired an arsonist to set fire to Atlee's collection. She learned also of Mr. Brome, who bragged of his drawers of carved Egyptian gemstones at every society meeting until the day it was discovered that a number of them were forgeries made of glass, and of the great feud between Plessey and Poff over the definition of a bezoar.

Eventually, Meacan's head began to nod, her chin slipping from her hand and startling her into wakefulness. After two hours, she declared she needed sustenance if she was to survive the tedium, and left in search of an unguarded pastry. Cecily, alone in the quiet with the great elephant skull, moved quickly through the registers.

She was nearing the end of a volume in which there had not been a single mark of Leo when suddenly she halted in surprise. Before her, the little symbol, written in Sir Barnaby's small, controlled hand, filled the column from top to bottom, accompanied each time by the letters EWC, which in other rooms stood for East Wall Cabinet. She turned to the next page, and the next.

The pattern continued on for twelve pages, and included more than three hundred objects. It was not only their location that they had in common. Each object had been added to the register on the same day, the first of September, 1699— almost four years ago—and each object was attributed to the same source, indicated by a single word: "Rose."

Cecily had encountered nothing similar in any of the registers. Where Sir Barnaby had acquired items in bulk, as he often did by purchasing or being given entire collections, he had separated them by subject into their appropriate rooms. Shells were kept with shells, books with books, serpents with serpents, and so on. That was not the case here. Every single object whose source was identified as Rose, be it shell, bone, stone, or coral, was kept in Sir Barnaby's study.

Overcome with curiosity, Cecily closed the register and left the library. She descended the dark, draped stairwell and entered the study. The open shelves seemed strangely familiar now that she had read descriptions of many of the objects on them. There was the bottle, its thick glass clouded and broken, the pink coral adhering to it in a tight embrace. There was the jasper cup, cool and translucent. There was the crystal ball, the silver talisman engraved with characters of Jupiter, and the mirror of black obsidian.

She crossed the room to the three closed cabinets set against the east wall. One by one, she gripped the handles, pulled, and experienced something she had not yet encountered anywhere in the house. These cabinets were locked.

CHAPTER 15

A stream of mourners ascended along the black-bound bannister to view the body of Barnaby Mayne and pay their
respects to his widow. It was not a smooth stream. Progress
was slowed by the many visitors who lingered at paintings
and partially covered shelves, craning their necks and straining their eyes to see all they could of the collection. Those
who tried to lift a corner of cloth in the hope of glimpsing a
rarity were firmly redirected by the servants and by Meacan,
who had been conscripted to help patrol the premises.

Over the course of the morning, Cecily discerned certain
words and phrases repeated like birdsongs within the general murmur of the crowd.

"Inwood, yes, yes, *all* of it."

"No trace of Dinley."

"Stabbed through the heart."

"Look here beneath the cloth—a skull, yes, but of what?"

"Isn't it wondrous?"

"Vulgar excess."

"Essential contribution to science."

"He looks almost alive."

The last impression was one Cecily shared. Sir Barnaby,
lying in his coffin, did look as if he might supply one of the

rare confirmations that a delayed burial could save the life of the seeming-dead. His presence still commanded. His expression remained authoritative. It was not impossible to imagine that only time was needed for that remaining spark of life, too small to be perceived, to catch fire again and re-kindle the blue eyes now hidden behind waxen lids.

Lady Mayne appeared more at ease now that black hangings covered every shelf in her room. A silver candlestick and the flame rising demurely from its candle provided the only gleam of light in the chamber. As she accepted Cecily's condolences for a second time, her eyes moved over Cecily's shoulder to take in with apparent gratification the long line of visitors still to come. Cecily didn't know whether the widow was more satisfied by the evidence of her husband's popularity or by the victory of social convention over the silent dominion of the shelves.

Cecily allowed the current of visitors to move her out of the room and back onto the stairs. When she reached the first-floor landing, she slipped into the library, where she found Giles Inwood standing alone at the table looking down at the open registers. He greeted her with a smile and an informal bow of his head, communicating friendship with the ease that appeared natural to him.

"Mr. Helm is much improved," he said. "Between John's infusions and the pleasure of your company, I anticipate a speedy recovery." His gaze shifted over Cecily's shoulder to the door. Cecily had pulled it closed, but the murmur and shuffling of mourners on the landing were still audible.

"There is a considerable crowd," said Cecily.

"I would not have expected anything different," said Inwood. "Sir Barnaby was one of the greatest among us. Of course, he would never have permitted so many in the house at once."

"Martha is doing everything in her power to protect the objects and preserve the order of the cabinets," said Cecily.

"I do not doubt it. She has been devoted to the collection since the beginning." Inwood looked thoughtful. "Perhaps she and her husband would consider an offer of employment in my own home. The transfer of the collection will be a mighty undertaking. Her assistance would be invaluable."

"I am not certain she understands that the collection is no longer Sir Barnaby's," said Cecily. "She speaks as if she is still receiving his commands."

Inwood's expression was serious. "But it *is* his, Lady Kay. It always will be." Dropping his eyes to the table, he touched a finger lightly to an open register. "Mrs. Barlow has devised a sound strategy for the inventory. Thorough, disciplined, and lacking unnecessary complexity."

Cecily concealed the pleasure the praise afforded her. "I will convey the compliment," she said. "I was surprised, though, when I heard that Lady Mayne had ordered an inventory. No matter the method, it will require significant time to complete, and I had the impression Lady Mayne was eager to relinquish responsibility as soon as possible."

Inwood's gaze remained lowered so that Cecily could not see his expression. "Some caprice is always to be expected from the bereaved," he said. "But tell me how your work is progressing. Have you located the books and specimens you require?"

His interest appeared so genuine that Cecily allowed herself an extended answer. Inwood was knowledgeable. They spoke for some time about the differences between the

Polium species of Smyrna and those of France, and about the uses of Origany of Crete by doctors on that island.

"I hope you know the Mayne plants, in addition to my own small collection, will be available whenever you have need of them," said Inwood. "Will you come to the tour of my collection next week?"

"I assumed you would be obliged to cancel it."

Inwood sighed. "Alas, I cannot. I have made commitments to my guests."

As Cecily promised she would attend if she could, she reminded herself that she had not sought him out merely to make conversation. She moved to the side of the table where she had been working. "With regard to the inventory," she said. "I wondered if you have a key to the cabinets that are locked."

Inwood raised a quizzical brow. "I haven't seen or heard mention of any keys to the cabinets. I never knew Sir Barnaby to lock any of them. He valued their accessibility, within the secure walls of the house, of course."

"Thus far I have found only three that I cannot open," said Cecily. "In the study. According to the registers, they are the cabinets containing objects Sir Barnaby acquired from someone called Rose."

"Ah, that must be *John* Rose," said Inwood, moving around the table to join Cecily at the register she had opened to the relevant pages.

"You know him?" asked Cecily.

"We all knew *of* him," said Inwood. "A traveler and a collector of some renown, especially in his youth. For a short time, I did know him better than most." There was a thoughtful pause before Inwood continued, speaking slowly as a person does who is describing one memory amid a crowd of others.

"I was traveling in the West Indies—four or five years ago—I was in Jamaica when I heard that John Rose was staying in a nearby town. I had always admired him, and enjoyed hearing of his adventures through Sir Barnaby, with whom he corresponded often over the years. I went to visit him. Sadly, I soon perceived that he was in no condition to receive me as a guest. Rather, he was in need of all the professional skill I could offer."

Inwood drew in a deep breath and let it out again slowly. Cecily imagined she saw in his eyes the wide blue sea, the crashing waves and haze of hovering insects, the suffering man. She remembered the date in the register, four years earlier. "There was no question of his ever returning home to England," said Inwood quietly.

Cecily allowed the moment of silence to rest between them before she spoke. "But his collection came here."

Inwood nodded. "In its entirety, I believe. I don't know when they agreed that Sir Barnaby would assume Rose's collection into his own in the event of Rose's death, but I believe the agreement was a long-standing one. Not unlike the one made between Sir Barnaby and myself." Inwood seemed to perceive Cecily's surprise, and smiled. "It is not such a coincidence, I assure you, Lady Kay. The self-importance of our little community has the effect of making it appear larger than it is. We collectors are all connected in one way or another. Each of us friends or enemies with the others. And we do what we can to preserve our efforts for posterity."

"Have you any idea why Sir Barnaby would have kept the cabinets locked?" asked Cecily. "When they were already secure in his private study?"

"I cannot think why," said Inwood.

There was a knock on the door and Meacan appeared.

"There you are," she said, seeing Cecily first. Her eye flickered to Inwood. "Ah," she said. "Mr. Inwood. May I beg your assistance? One of the drapes has fallen and movement up the stairs has come to a standstill around a small sculpture of a somewhat *priapic* nature."

Inwood, looking slightly bemused, followed Meacan out. Cecily was about to go after them when her eye caught movement outside in the garden. She moved closer to the window and peered through the thick glass and gathering mist. A man in a coat and wig was striding between the neat parterres toward the back wall. As she watched, he disappeared into the carriage house.

The resolution of his movement suggested that the man was not simply a stray mourner exploring the garden. He had gone to the carriage house with a purpose, and Cecily wanted to know what it was. To avoid the crowd, she went through the nearest connecting door to the adjacent house, which was supposed to be closed to visitors. Judging from the traces of mud on the stairs and floors, new since that morning, Martha's policy had not been entirely successful. Cecily wondered how many guests were now boasting to friends about the strange wonders they had seen during their illicit explorations.

By the time she stepped onto the veranda, the man was returning to the house. As he approached along the gravel path, she recognized the elegant tailoring and unremarkable features of Martin Carlyle. When he saw her he paused, then continued forward to join her. Tiny drops of mist silvered the edges of his gray wig and stood on the shoulders of his jacket.

"An oppressive atmosphere," he said, nodding at the

house. "I had to persuade that stern housekeeper to allow me out to take the air."

"I saw you from the window," said Cecily. "Going into the carriage house."

Carlyle shrugged. "I thought I heard a noise from inside."

"Was someone there?"

"Not that I saw, but I wasn't going to venture into the dark corners. Who knows where the mad curator may be hiding."

"Do you really believe he was mad?"

Carlyle did not look as if he cared one way or another. "Dinley? Could be. I don't know him."

"But you must have met him at least twice. Sir Barnaby mentioned you had visited the collection before."

A look of annoyance crossed Carlyle's face. "One does not become well acquainted with a man by listening to him lecture on proper labeling techniques and the surest methods to keep exotic fish from rotting."

Cecily hesitated. "I intend no offense, Mr. Carlyle, but for a man who makes a habit of visiting collections, you appear to find little within them that pleases you. I understand the collectors have many detractors who consider their efforts frivolous. Are you one of them?"

"I have no particular objection to the pursuit," said Carlyle. "But I cannot help but be dubious when I am expected to marvel at a piece of dirty muslin because its label says it is Pontius Pilate's wife's sister's chambermaid's hat. Or at the corpse of a mouse found starved in a wall. Or a common shell I might have picked up myself from any English shore."

Cecily remembered the last she had seen of Carlyle before the murder. "The antiquities, at least, appeared to be of some interest to you," she said.

"I admire beauty as much as any man." Carlyle's expression changed. He assessed her appreciatively. "And on the subject of beauty, I did not expect this morbid occasion to lead to a garden tryst with a married woman. Is your husband a jealous sort, Lady Kay?"

Carlyle's leer was familiar to Cecily. The last time she had seen it, he had been directing it elsewhere. "Have you seen Alice Fordyce among today's visitors?" she asked.

Carlyle smiled. "Ah yes," he said. "The Aphrodite who graced our group. Alas, I have not seen her again."

"Nor I. Do you know where she is staying?"

"Would that I did," said Carlyle. "What do you want with the maiden?"

"To call on her," said Cecily smoothly. "She will be shocked, I am sure, to learn that a violent crime occurred here so soon after her departure. Even I—" She affected a shudder. "We were all so near to it." She paused. "Did you see Sir Barnaby or Mr. Dinley after the tour was abandoned? Before the murder happened, of course."

"Not a glimpse," said Carlyle.

"I assume you spent the time perusing the rooms."

Carlyle regarded her for a moment in silence, then shrugged. "I had no intention of wasting the afternoon. I continued on the path the tour was to take. As you said, I'd visited before. I knew the way. My only real concern was to avoid that fool Warbulton. I did not intend to be trapped in *his* company until supper."

"And did you succeed?"

"I did. Fortunately for me, he had found a book in the library that commanded his whole attention."

"Had he?" Cecily recalled Warbulton's frenetic outbursts of interest. "I wonder what subject can have absorbed him."

Carlyle produced a short, derisive laugh. "No volume of science or philosophy, I assure you. It was Sir Barnaby's guest book. Warbulton is so desperate to establish himself in this circle that a list of names and personal details is to him what a new whale skull is to a real collector. I believe he was trying to copy every page. Otherwise he would have been bounding the rooms in search of company, I am sure."

"When I came downstairs, you were speaking to Giles Inwood in the dining room."

"And happy to be doing so," said Carlyle. "There is a man with whom it is easy to enjoy a conversation. Poor devil."

"Do you mean because he has lost his close friend?"

"That," said Carlyle, "and because he is now saddled with a burden the size of two houses."

Following his look, Cecily furrowed her brow. "You mean the collection? Mr. Carlyle, whatever your opinion, in inheriting the Mayne collection Mr. Inwood has received a great honor, in addition to a gift of immense value."

She was startled by Carlyle bursting into full-throated laughter. "A gift? What makes you think it is a gift?"

Cecily stared at him in confusion. "Lady Mayne told me that Inwood was to have the entire collection."

"Oh, he *is* to have it." Carlyle's laughter had subsided but he was still smiling. "But it isn't a gift. Inwood is to pay fifty thousand pounds to the widow for it."

"Fifty thousand?" Cecily heard herself gasp the number. It was an immense sum, a fortune, certainly an expenditure beyond the means of most gentlemen. "*That* was the arrangement between them?"

"Legally contracted, I understand," said Carlyle, nodding. "Inwood is to pay a king's ransom for these cabinets, added to which will be the expense of transporting it all and maintaining it, as he is contractually obligated to do."

"And that must mean," said Cecily, understanding coming to her, "that he cannot sell it."

"Not a single pickled fish of it," said Carlyle. "Oh, the collection may have some value. I do not deny it. But even if he did sell it, which would destroy his reputation among the others, he could never recoup fifty thousand. Not even the most passionate among them will pay for old bones what they would pay for items of actual, undisputed worth."

"I see," said Cecily quietly.

Carlyle looked up at the house again. "If you will excuse me, I must pay my respects and be off to my other engagements."

After he had gone, Cecily remained on the veranda, deep in thought. She reentered the house through the door that led into the hallway by the study. As she closed it behind her, a heavy form collided with her as it flung itself from the room.

"L-L-Lady—" Humphrey Warbulton abandoned his attempt at her name and stared at her uncomprehendingly. His face was still the same ghastly shade of gray white that it had been immediately after the discovery of the murder, and she felt for a moment that she had been thrown back two days and was about to be confronted with the same bloody scene again.

"Mr. Warbulton, had something happened? Are you unwell? Perhaps I could summon Mr. Inwood."

Sweat was standing on Warbulton's brow. "A—a—a cup of wine, perhaps."

Remembering a bottle of madeira in the dining room, Cecily led him there, selected a stone goblet from one of the shelves and, careful not to spill on the red label, filled it. She handed it to Warbulton, who took it with a shaking hand. "Th-thank you."

"What were you doing in Sir Barnaby's study?"

"His study? I—I—nothing. I was—I was lost. In my—my distress, perhaps."

"I am very sorry, Mr. Warbulton. I know you held Sir Barnaby in high esteem."

Warbulton appeared temporarily to have exhausted himself. He leaned against the table. Sweat stained the gray silk of his coat. His cuffs looked dirty. The scarf around his neck was carelessly arranged. He held out his empty cup.

Cecily refilled it. "Forgive me for prying, Mr. Warbulton, but this tragedy appears to have affected you very strongly. Were you perhaps well acquainted with Mr. Dinley?"

"Dinley," Warbulton echoed in a hollow voice. "No, no, I hardly knew the man."

"But you and Sir Barnaby enjoyed a close friendship."

Cecily had spoken sympathetically, but her words appeared to make Warbulton even more upset. He pushed himself away from the table, spattering wine on his coat and over the floor. "Not his friend," he said breathlessly. "No confidences at all. Hardly spoke to him. No close association." He looked fearfully around him and lowered his voice. "I shouldn't be in this house," he whispered. And with a final wide-eyed look at the walls, he fled the room.

By the time Cecily returned to the Plant Room an hour later, she was ready once more to close her mind against the puzzles and confusions of the human world. News of her presence and identity had spread through the house, and she had been cornered by several gentlemen who said they were eager to question her about her travels, but who in fact

wanted to tell her about theirs. She had caught no further
glimpses of Inwood, Carlyle, or Warbulton, nor had she recognized Alice Fordyce among the few female visitors. In the
mingling of black coats and cloaks and hats, with so little
light inside the house, she could not be sure of who was
there.

The Plant Room appeared as she had left it except for a
small piece of folded paper resting on top of the specimen
she had been prepared to identify next. Her name was written on it. She opened it, read its contents, and went to the
connecting door. Otto Helm was propped up in his bed, a
book open before him. He looked at her inquiringly.

"I'm sorry to bother you," said Cecily. "But have you seen
anyone come up here?"

"I did hear someone," he said. "A little while ago. I
thought it to be you. But when I called no one answered."

Cecily returned to the herbarium and read the note again.
*Lady Kay. You have questions to which I have answers. I know
the truth. To speak within the house is impossible. There is an old
elm in the field beyond the garden gate. Meet me there at the hour
of five. Trust no one. I will wait.*

CHAPTER 16

The house was beginning to empty, the mourners flowing like spilled ink out the front door. No one appeared to notice Cecily step quietly through the hall, past the study, and into the garden. Only the building itself seemed intent on her progress, its windows darkly gleaming, watching her as if she were an object that had escaped its shelves.

When she reached the sweetbay tree, she found it surrounded by a carpet of fallen petals, their white edges browning like burned paper. It was still spring, but the ground here had an autumnal look that conjured cold gusts and early nightfall. The sweetbay itself, despite its fading blossoms, maintained a posture of staunch confidence. It seemed in its solitude to declare itself the garden's protector, standing guard at the door to the outside world.

Cecily lingered, hesitant to leave the fragrant sanctuary. She drew the note from her pocket, not so much to read it as to study once more the curves and lines of ink, to search for a clue to the hand that had written them. A man? A woman? What purpose had guided it? What emotion had made it tremble?

She returned the note to her pocket and placed her hand behind the blossom closest to her on the tree, drawing it gently to her. She counted six petals, concave, not unlike those of a water lily. Numerous stamina embraced the conical pointal. It occurred to her then that she could remain where she was, and not take another step. She could limit her inquiries to the silent majesty of this flower, of the leaves near to it, of the branch supporting it and the roots sustaining it. Wasn't the puzzle of this tree, of its form and mechanisms and properties, enough to satisfy any inquiring mind? Shouldn't it satisfy hers?

Her attention shifted to the closed door embedded in the garden wall. From the house she heard, faintly, the chimes telling the hour before they were drowned out by the larger bells of churches. It was five o'clock. She stepped outside the protective circle of the tree and drew the bolt. The heavy iron was cold under her fingers. Remembering John's urgent call the last time she had stood here, she opened the door only just wide enough to slip outside, and closed it softly.

On either side of her, the rutted alley ran along the walls of other gardens. When the bells stopped tolling, she could hear cart wheels and voices, but she could neither see them nor determine their distance from her. The mist seemed thicker here, resting low and heavy on the field, as if there was not yet enough of it to spill over the walls into the gardens. It was darker than it should have been at that hour. Cecily wondered how soon it would be before the storm announced itself with thunder.

There was no one within sight. Though she was wary, she was not deterred by fear. It had never been in her character to seek out danger, but what she had witnessed of life had convinced her that death was as likely to be waiting in a nursery or in a castle fortified against attack as in any empty alley. Before her stretched the field. With a determined step, she started forward toward the elm.

The ground gave beneath her feet, the mud sucking greedily at her boots. What ruins rested beneath it, she wondered, what skulls and artifacts of ancient claims to that earth awaiting discovery and arrangement on a collector's shelf? She tried to keep to the firm tussocks of yellowed, sickly grass. The mist enclosed her so tightly she almost felt it squeeze her shoulders and curl snakelike around her throat. Other than her own body and the small patch of ground supporting her, she could identify nothing permanent in the shifting grayness except the elm.

It rose so high she could barely see the tops of its branches, but she could see that they grew densely, a sign of a distressed tree desperately seeking sustenance in the air that it could not find in the soil. The thin black lines were etched on the gray sky like scratched runes in a language she could not read. She was close to the tree now, close enough that she would have seen someone waiting for her beside it if anyone was there. There was nothing but insubstantial mist.

She thought of Alice Fordyce. It was no wonder the young woman's arrival at the back door had elicited shock from those who knew what lay beyond it. Cecily could not picture her clean, cream-colored cloak and translucent pink and white skin without thinking she must have been a ghost, an unhappy, lingering consequence of an unforgotten duel.

She had come to the base of the elm. Its bark was old and solemn as an aged face. Too late she realized that the great old trunk was wide enough to conceal the figure that had been waiting behind it. Too late to prepare for the hands that caught her arms and flung her down, down the short slope she hadn't seen, and down which she tumbled, her breath knocked from her chest.

As she rolled to a halt she tried to draw in air, only to retch at its fetid smell. She tried to rise, but her hands and knees sank into brackish water. She felt her legs grow heavier as the moisture soaked into her skirts. Beside her she heard the crack of a snapping branch. A human form loomed above her, but the sounds that came from it were guttural like that of a beast. She was on her hands and knees, trying to rise.

Then she felt the weight of a boot hard between her shoulder blades. She tried to brace her arms but her hands slipped and sank in the mire and her elbows buckled beneath her. The weight increased. She was able to claim a short breath before her face was submerged. Her nose filled with mud and water and she pushed herself up, half choking, only to be pushed down again and, this time, held. Light burst before her eyes, floating and spreading as pain flared in her lungs. Her body jolted helplessly against the implacable weight holding her down.

She heard a crack as if of lightning that seemed to come from inside and outside her head, and then the weight was gone. She heaved herself up, coughing and wiping the filth from her face as she drew in gasping, choking breaths. Too disoriented to stand, she began to crawl away from the water. She managed to get to her knees. Someone was striding toward her through the mist. She wiped enough of the mud from her eyes to make out the shape of a woman. She blinked and saw the brown-and-green-striped skirts, the raised arm, and the pistol clutched firmly in Meacan's hand.

Meacan's stride was not leading her to Cecily. Turning, Cecily saw someone else by the side of the pond, a man whose face she did not know. He was struggling to his feet. By the time he had stood, bending to clutch his thigh, Meacan had reloaded the pistol. His head swiveled to where Cecily kneeled.

"Not another step toward her," cried Meacan, raising the pistol with unwavering intent.

The man stumbled backward, regained his balance, and staggered away into the mists without looking back.

Meacan rushed to Cecily and helped her to her feet. Cecily was still out of breath, her vision still partially obscured by mud. "Close your eyes," Meacan ordered.

Cecily obeyed. She felt the gentle pressure of Meacan's fingers on her eyelids, followed by a firmer swipe across her cheeks and mouth as Meacan wiped the mud away. "Can you breathe?" asked Meacan. "How badly are you hurt? Did I arrive too late?"

"I'm not harmed," Cecily managed hoarsely. She started to step away, but her knees buckled and she stayed where she was, with Meacan supporting her.

"Not *harmed*?" Meacan exclaimed. "I should have killed him."

Cecily looked past Meacan's face, full of concern and flickering anger, to the space around them. There was no trace of the assailant. He had come from the heavy, swirling mist, and he had disappeared back into it.

Concern vied with triumph in Meacan's expression. "I was looking out the window and I saw you leave the garden. Whatever possessed you to come out to this place?"

With clumsy fingers, Cecily drew the paper from her pocket. It was sodden, but the words were just legible. Meacan read it in an instant, handed it back, and cast a watchful look around them. "I told you," she said, as she began to guide Cecily gently back toward the house. "I told you to stop asking questions."

CHAPTER 17

The household had gone to bed, but in the kitchen fireplace, a dancing flame crackled and hissed beneath a hanging cauldron. At the edge of the heavy table scarred by knives and branded with rings seared into it over the years was an assortment of vessels and plates. Cinnamon, mace, and nutmeg dusted a mortar and pestle. A pottle, empty but still coated on the inside with thick cream, rested adjacent to a pile of eggshells and a plate dusted with sugar.

Inside the cauldron a smooth brown potion simmered, its surface softly separating into milky islands. Meacan, who had been watching it closely from her position in front of the hearth, dipped a ladle into it and tasted. She cocked her head and smacked her lips quietly, assessing the flavor. She added a pinch of cinnamon and stirred.

Cecily was sitting in a chair that had been drawn from the table to be closer to the fire. She had washed and put on clean clothes earlier, but the curling mist of the dueler's field was only now beginning to release its grip. She was remembering being a girl of nine sitting in the kitchen in the gardener's cottage trying not to cry as she watched little beads of blood well on her skinned knee. Meacan's mother had cleaned and salved the scrape. Cecily recalled the yielding comfort of round arms, the neck warm with perspiration, the soft sway of skirts. The cottage had been a haven for any children who could find their way to it. Over the year it was occupied by Meacan's family, its windowsills had been filled with candied flowers, dried apricots, and preserved oranges and lemons as clear as glass.

Meacan dipped the ladle again, filled a cup, and handed it to Cecily. Only one sip was required to dissolve the final tendrils of mist that had seemed to remain twined around her spine. The warmth of the drink was not solely attributable to its temperature. "I don't remember your mother's posset containing *quite* so much sack," she gasped.

"She taught me to suit the recipe to the situation," said Meacan, filling her own cup and sinking into a chair opposite Cecily. "Don't you care for it?"

"Nothing has ever tasted better," said Cecily honestly.

Meacan took a sip herself, wriggled her shoulders, and settled back deeper into the chair with a smile. "Drink it down, then. It will counter the poison of that foul water he tried to drown you in."

Cecily obeyed. The rich, sweet drink spread warmth all the way to her toes. When Meacan reached for the jug of sack and added still more to the pot, Cecily raised her eyebrows but didn't object. Instead, she asked Meacan how she had come to possess a pistol.

"Ah," said Meacan, refilling her cup and stretching her feet out toward the fire. "*That* is a good story. It was six or seven years ago in the home of Lady Southeby, whose husband had recently passed from this world. The lady inherited his collection, but having inherited little else, her funds were sorely depleted. She needed an auction catalogue that would make all those dusty shells and pebbles look their best, and she had the good sense to hire me to illustrate it."

"I presume you leant the objects some additional allure," said Cecily.

"A touch of color here and there," Meacan acknowledged. "In any case, I found the pistol when I was in the library. It was hidden in an edition of *The Blazing World*—the pages were cut out in the center to make a box—and I was so taken with it that I bought the book from Lady Southeby myself. I saw no need to mention what was inside it, and she didn't ask. I learned to load and fire it and have kept it close ever since. Today isn't the first day it's been useful— Oh, don't look at me like that. I've never killed anyone."

"I'm relieved you weren't obliged to today."

Meacan shrugged. "Had he been the first, I wouldn't have devoted much time to regretting it."

Cecily didn't answer at once. In the wake of the attack, they had not had the opportunity to speak at any length. With their return to the house had come a flurry of social challenges that had required Cecily's complete concentration. First there had been the explanations. She had been walking in the garden and heard someone calling from the field. She had gone out—yes, she knew she had been foolish—and found no one. On her return to the house she had slipped and fallen.

Once her account was given and accepted, Cecily had addressed herself to the complicated business of a bath. A supper of excruciating duration had followed, eaten in the company of several lingerers-on from the viewing who were determined not to leave until they had accumulated suffi- cient knowledge of Sir Barnaby's death and of his collec- tion to impress their absent acquaintances. In the time since

John had sanctioned their use of the kitchen and shuffled off to bed, Meacan and Cecily had by tacit agreement limited their conversation mostly to quantities of spices and eggs.

Now, in the silence following the story of the pistol, Meacan leaned forward and gave the posset an unnecessary stir.

"Why were you watching me from the window?" Cecily asked.

Meacan set the ladle on its tray and sat back. "I wasn't watching you. I was merely appreciating the garden."

"But Martha had you monitoring the second-floor landing, and there is no window there."

"I required a moment's respite from the task."

Cecily paused. "That is understandable, but that it should be just when I left the house—" She sat back quickly as Meacan withdrew the ladle from the cauldron and gestured with it, dripping sticky posset onto the floor.

"Of all the obstinate, incautious, stubborn—" The words burst from Meacan as drops of posset flew into the hearth, sizzling as they struck hot stone. "Is it possible you have not appreciated the fact that you would never have been in danger today if you weren't so *set* on inquiring into what people *do not* wish to tell you? Can you not for a moment be content with what is known to you, and let be what is not?"

Cecily, who was beginning to relax into the warm embrace of the posset, surprised them both by giving a soft chuckle. "In truth, I am not certain I can," she said. "If I could, I wouldn't be here with you now."

"Of course you wouldn't," said Meacan. "None of this would have happened. That is exactly my—"

"I meant," Cecily interrupted, "that I'd still be in Smyrna."

Meacan's indignation vanished. "What? Why did you leave Smyrna?"

Cecily took a fortifying sip of posset. The fire was crackling eagerly, like a third person trying to be included in the conversation. "I didn't decide to leave," she said. "I was sent away."

"By whom?"

"By my husband, who didn't mind my questions as long as I directed them at plants. He *did* mind my inquiries into his mismanagement of company funds."

Meacan stared. Little creases appeared around her eyes before the smile appeared on her lips. "I should think he would," she said, dipping the ladle into the pot and refilling both their cups.

Cecily permitted herself to return to that day in her mind. She could almost smell the rain hitting the stone that had so recently been heated by the sun. She saw the ship and seahorse of the Levant Company arms carved above the library door. "I'd been obliged to put off an excursion to the valley of Nymphi," she said, watching the steam rise from her cup. "I'd read every book in the library, so I turned to Andrew's ledgers. I thought I might review his numbers, perhaps be of some assistance."

"And?"

"And my intention was to correct one or two miscalculations. Instead, I uncovered six years of fraudulent tariffs the port master and his corrupt accomplices had imposed upon the company during my husband's tenure, and of which my husband had remained entirely ignorant."

"Praise Hera for clever wives," said Meacan. "Your husband is a fortunate man."

Cecily didn't answer at once. She recalled Andrew's face quivering with defensive indignation as he declared her unfeminine, incapable of respecting authority and, by the end of his tirade, insane. Frowning at the memory, she picked up a poker and used it to shift a log that had burst into new flame away from the cauldron to keep the posset from being scorched.

"Ah," said Meacan, reading Cecily's expression. "He didn't like having his wife expose him as a fool."

"He sent me home on the next ship that sailed."

Meacan exhaled slowly. "I can see it," she said, her eyes on the sparks and caverns of fire in the earth, her imagination elsewhere. "You, pacing the length of the ship, lonely, humiliated and constrained to silence by your ignorant knave of a husband, staring out at the endless sea, with only those sad dried plants for company—"

"There is no need to insult the plants," said Cecily with asperity. "They—"

"Are fascinating, important, unique, yes." Meacan fluttered a hand impatiently. "My point is you arrived in England like a cat ready to pounce on the first string dangled before it. Your husband had refused your help, but there was no one here to stop you from seeking answers. That's why you bit down on the problem of Sir Barnaby's death and did not let go."

Cecily looked up sharply from the fire. Their eyes met, and Cecily recognized an openness in Meacan's expression that had not been there before. Wary of chasing it away, she lowered her voice almost to a whisper. "It wasn't Walter Dinley, was it?"

For a moment Meacan was still. Then she gave an infinitesimal shake of her head.

Cecily lowered her voice further. "How do you know?"

Meacan's expression became shuttered. "I can't tell you."

"Meacan, did *you* kill Barnaby Mayne?"

"No!" Once again the ladle flew upward, and once again posset sizzled in the fire.

"Then why?" Cecily demanded. "Why won't you tell me what you know?" When Meacan didn't answer, she continued. "You came to my rescue like a guardian knight. If you value our friendship enough to protect me, why not enough to trust me?"

Meacan opened her mouth to speak, then shut it. She turned her gaze down to her cup and stared into it for a long moment. "Because," she said at last, "if you cannot countenance an insect being drawn inaccurately or a crumpet being set on a book, you will not like, indeed will utterly condemn the reasons I have for knowing what I do."

"It wasn't that the bug was inaccurate," Cecily was compelled to point out. "It was that it was a *deliberate* obfuscation in order to—"

"And thus is my reasoning justified," said Meacan dryly.

Cecily was about to object, but changed her mind when she saw the twinkle in her old friend's eye. Meacan was going to talk, but she was going to make sure Cecily was as impatient as possible first. Cecily set her teeth and waited.

At last Meacan nodded. "Are you familiar," she asked, "with the name Covo?"

Cecily thought. She had not heard the name before, but she had seen it. "In the registers," she said, remembering. "He's someone from whom Sir Barnaby purchased objects for the collection."

"Sir Barnaby, yes, and many others," said Meacan. "Covo's coffeehouse is a favorite haunt of collectors. Not only does he procure and sell rarities, but he also provides services unique to the collecting community."

"What kind of services?"

"The collectors," Meacan replied, "have a tendency to be competitive, vengeful, petty, and prone to obsession. For a price, Covo assists them in winning their little battles with each other. Essential to his business are the agents he hires. Agents who can enter the houses of collectors with relative ease."

"Illustrators come to mind," said Cecily.

There was no trace of remorse in Meacan's smile. "Covo is a far more generous employer than the collectors."

"And what did he employ you to do in the home of Sir Barnaby Mayne?"

"Merely to gather some information. You need not look *so* critical."

Cecily raised an eyebrow. "How did you convince Sir Barnaby to hire you?"

Meacan was indignant. "I didn't have to convince him! I had already accepted Sir Barnaby's commission when Covo contacted me. I am not a *bad* illustrator, you know."

This was true. Cecily perceived that an apology was needed before Meacan would continue, and gave it.

Mollified, Meacan went on. "As I said, I was already working for Sir Barnaby, which is why Covo chose to contact me. That, and my untarnished history of success in our past collaborations. He wanted me to copy an auction catalogue, or rather to copy from an auction catalogue the objects on which Sir Barnaby intended to bid. He told me the catalogue was to be delivered to Sir Barnaby by a Swede, mostly likely on the day Sir Barnaby was to give his next scheduled tour of the collection."

"The Follywolle catalogue."

Meacan's brows lifted in surprise. "How did you know?"

"I saw it on Sir Barnaby's desk, and I've spoken to Helm—" Cecily paused.

Reading her thought, Meacan shook her head. "I had nothing to do with the attack on Helm. I had from Covo only the details necessary to achieve my object. I knew this Follywolle catalogue would arrive with Helm. I knew Sir Barnaby would mark the items he wanted. And I knew I was to make a list of those items before the catalogue left the house again with Mr. Helm at the end of the day."

"And did you make the list? What happened?"

Meacan, clearly enjoying Cecily's eagerness, took her time before continuing. "Once I had ascertained from Dinley that there *was* to be a Swede by the name of Helm on the tour, I did what I could to make a plan. My hope was to use the time when Sir Barnaby and his guests—of course I did not yet know you would be among them—the time when Sir Barnaby and his guests would be occupied with the tour to find the catalogue. Unfortunately, very little went as it was supposed to."

"Helm didn't accompany the tour," said Cecily. "Because he had to count his snake scales. And the tour ended early. And—"

"And Sir Barnaby died," said Meacan. "We have not come to that yet. It all *began* well. I was up early to keep watch near the front door, and was there when Helm arrived. I engaged him in conversation to make my presence appear natural. I saw Helm give the catalogue to Sir Barnaby, who said he would attend to it at once. I saw Dinley take Helm away to show him the collection and then ensconce him with the snakes. It was still very early in the day. It seemed likely that Sir Barnaby would finish with the catalogue and return it to

Helm before the tour began, which meant I would have the duration of the tour to find it and make my notes."

"But if you expected the catalogue to be back in Helm's possession, and you knew he intended to remain in the Serpent Room all day, presumably with his belongings, how did you mean to get access to it?"

"A small detail," said Meacan airily. "I knew I could find a way to distract him. I was more concerned with our interaction not being overheard by the household or the other guests. My secondary employment relies on my presence not being associated with these little—" She paused. "These little *incidents* between collectors. Out of caution, I decided that once the tour began, I would wait in my room until I heard footsteps on the ceiling above me. That would mean the tour had reached its farthest point from the study, and from Helm. I would go downstairs then."

Cecily pictured the location of Meacan's chamber. "The room above yours is the herbarium, if I am correct." Meacan nodded affirmation. "So if you heard footsteps," continued Cecily, "they were mine alone. The tour had already been disbanded."

"Yes," said Meacan. "But I was not aware of that. I heard the steps, and went down to the Serpent Room. To my delight, I found Helm's desk empty, his work abandoned, his bag unattended."

"Helm wasn't at his desk? What time was this?"

"It was about twenty minutes past five. I searched Helm's bag, but the catalogue wasn't there. I reasoned then that if Sir Barnaby had not yet returned it to him, it must still be in Sir Barnaby's study. I decided to look for it there."

"But it was his private study. Didn't you expect it to be locked?"

There was more than a hint of smugness in Meacan's smile. "I have learned," she said, "to circumvent such barriers. In this case, though, I didn't have to. To my surprise, the door was unlocked and swung open without a sound."

"But Sir Barnaby had already gone downstairs," said Cecily. "He must have been there when you entered."

"He *was* there," said Meacan. "He was lying dead on the floor just as he was when you found him nearly an hour later."

Cecily caught her breath. "He was dead already?"

"Unambiguously," said Meacan.

"And Dinley?"

Meacan shook her head. "Not a sign of him."

With a furrowed brow, Cecily raised her cup to her lips. She had been so intent on Meacan's words that her drink had grown cold. She replenished it from the cauldron. "But Dinley wouldn't have killed Sir Barnaby, left the room, and returned later to stand above the body as if the murder had just occurred."

"Of course he wouldn't have," said Meacan. "Not unless he really *is* mad. Which neither you nor I believe him to be."

"And there was nothing in the room to suggest who might have been there earlier?"

"Not that I could see, but then again I didn't stay long." Meacan hesitated. "All I noticed, other than Sir Barnaby of course, was a smell of vinegar."

Cecily thought this was odd. "I didn't perceive it," she said. "I thought the room smelled of camphor and roses. What did you do then?"

Now for the first time, a look of guilt crossed Meacan's face. "I left at once and returned directly to my room. I hadn't seen anyone on my way down, and I didn't see anyone on my way up. I could only hope no one had seen me. I thought of loading my pistol, but decided it would be better not to show I had one. So I took the axe and shield from above my dresser and waited to see what would happen."

Meacan was silent for a moment, her expression grave now, remembering. "I knew I would have to see it all again. I did what I could to prepare to feign surprise. But in the end I didn't have to pretend. I thought I'd lost *my own* mind when I was told you'd all but walked in on Dinley in the middle of committing murder." Meacan drew in a long breath and let it out in a rush. "I don't know what made the poor fool perform such a charade. But how could I say anything, given my reasons for being in the room earlier?"

"So you have known," said Cecily slowly, "or suspected, from the very beginning, that there was a murderer in the house that day whose identity was not revealed."

Meacan nodded. "I thought, and still think, that the answer must lie with Dinley. That is why I went out the next morning. I hoped to discover where he had gone. My first idea was to speak to Covo, but he was either out or not taking visitors. He cannot be relied upon, you know. So I visited every acquaintance Dinley and I had in common. That I knew of, at least, from my conversations with him last week."

Cecily, feeling the effects of the posset, gave Meacan a look of slightly exaggerated affront. "You mean you tried to discourage me from asking questions when you were doing the same thing?"

"I was doing it with finesse and experience," said Meacan. "*You* were all but asking each person who was in the house whether they'd killed Sir Barnaby, then striding away and presenting your back for a knife thrust."

"I wasn't so unsubtle as that," Cecily objected. "But did you learn anything about Dinley?"

"Nothing at all," said Meacan. "After that, I wasn't certain what I would do. I didn't think I'd be allowed to stay in the house, but I was worried if I left it, you would walk straight into danger. And I was proved right, wasn't I?"

"Then the inventory was your idea?"

Meacan shook her head. "No. I told you the truth about that. It *was* Lady Mayne who suggested it. I was happy when she did, though, and accepted at once. It was a way for me to continue, *tactfully*, to follow the course of events, and to keep an eye on you."

"It would have been easier," said Cecily, "if you'd confided in me instead of giving me oblique warnings."

Meacan sighed. "Not to trust too quickly is a lesson that has been impressed upon me a little deeper with each passing year. People do change, you know. I didn't know for certain who you'd become."

"No," said Cecily. "Nor I you."

"And so did not take me into your confidence either," said Meacan. She leaned forward. "But now that I have told you how *I* know Dinley didn't do it, tell me what made *you* start peppering us all with *where were yous* and *what did you sees* and *could it really have beens*. What made *you* suspect things weren't as they appeared?"

Cecily told her. As the fire dwindled and the level of the posset went down, she told Meacan about waking in the middle of the night and thinking of the bloody half handprint. She reported what Martha had told her about the missing Spanish pistol and how no one had actually seen Alice Fordyce leave the house. She told her about Anthony Holt's letter, the Rose collection, and the locked cabinets.

Meacan listened, nodding occasionally, a crease of concentration between her brows. "Any one of those three could have slipped that note among your plants," she said when Cecily had finished giving an account of her conversations with Inwood, Carlyle, and Warbulton. "And hired that man to kill you. He seemed to me the *hired* type. I would know. Covo employs them often enough."

Cecily was turning an idea over in her mind. "This Mr. Covo," she said. "I suppose he is very knowledgeable about the collecting community?"

"None more than he. And he likes to be called *Signore* Covo."

Cecily raised a brow at this. "I would appreciate an introduction. That is, unless you are going to renew your insistence that I stop prying into the matter. I know there is danger here, but I know also that at least some of the questions I have asked *must* have been the *right* questions. And I—"

"Stop?" Meacan's soft features all at once took on the solidity of a marble goddess. "Under other circumstances, I would be happy to let the titan collectors wage their wars over land and sea while we stayed clear of the crashing rocks and hurricanes. But someone tried to kill you today, and that cannot be allowed to pass. It's the two of us together, now. We're going to find the villain, and we're going to make it very clear that we are not such little creatures after all." This proclamation made, her face relaxed into a small smile of anticipation. "Tomorrow I'll take you to talk to Covo. I think he's going to like you."

CHAPTER 18

"Thomasin has left us," declared Lady Mayne when Cecily and Meacan entered her chamber on the following morning. Black silk still shrouded the cabinets, but had been removed temporarily from the windows. Light was required for the widow to review the proposed designs for funeral invitations, which were scattered on the table before her in a printed carnival of skeletons and winged hourglasses.

Lady Mayne continued in an aggrieved tone. "She has gone to find a new situation. It is a terrible inconvenience. Not only is there no hope of replacing her before today's mourners begin to arrive, but she was a *good* maid. Like my own Susanna, she had a neat appearance and a courteous matter, and she understood that cleaning floors and windows must in any *civilized* household take precedence over preening the feathers of dead birds. It is a trial, Lady Kay."

"You have my sympathy," said Cecily. "Did she give a reason for going so abruptly?"

"She did not need to give a reason," replied Lady Mayne with a sigh. "I cannot blame the girl for wanting to leave *this* house behind." The widow's gaze flickered resentfully over the covered shelves. "Would that I could do the same, but

I'll not shirk my responsibilities." She nodded toward the door of the master bedroom where Sir Barnaby's body lay. "He may have rejected the willingness of his wife to serve him in life, but he cannot deny me in death. No fault will be found in my loyalty." She turned to Meacan. "The inventory was very important to him, Mrs. Barlow. Essential, I understand, for the successful transfer of the collection. I hope it is nearing completion?"

Cecily observed with interest the demure professionalism that Meacan assumed in the presence of her employer. She wore a white cap pulled down tight to imprison her curls and discourage any association between herself and mischief, disorder, or irresponsibility. Her face was serenely immobile, but she maintained one deliberate crease across her forehead, a single line that communicated deference, honesty, and eagerness to please. "Oh, it's progressing very well, Lady Mayne. Lady Kay thinks I could have it finished in two months."

"Two months?" Lady Mayne gasped and began to shake her head. "I had no notion it would take so long. Can it not be hastened?"

"The estimate is short, given the size of the collection," said Cecily. "It will require two months at the very least."

Lady Mayne, frowning in displeasure, turned to Susanna, who was replacing the candle in the silver taper. "If Giles Inwood comes again today, tell him I wish to speak with him," she said.

Meacan glanced nudgingly at Cecily, who cleared her throat. "Lady Mayne, you have been so hospitable I hesitate to ask this favor, but if I might borrow Mrs. Barlow this afternoon to serve as my escort, I am expected to pay a call on my cousin and would prefer not to make the journey alone." She remembered Lady Mayne's initial expression of distaste for the city and added, "London is so dangerous."

"I suppose if you must," said Lady Mayne. "But before you go, and after you return, I expect Mrs. Barlow's complete dedication to her work here. Two months is too long. It is *too* long. I will ensure his contract is honored. I am pledged to do so. But he cannot have expected me to wait so long to be rid of it." Lady Mayne shuddered. "He *cannot*. Now please, leave me. The stationer requires a decision."

They accepted the dismissal and left the room. Once they were out of earshot, Meacan shook her head. "If she wanted the inventory completed in a week, she could have hired a flock of Warbultons eager to prove themselves in the collecting community. I am aware that I radiate efficiency and intelligence, but she knows I am only one person. I've never had a project commissioned by someone so ignorant of what it entails."

While Meacan went off to the library muttering, Cecily sought out John and Martha in the garden, where they were claiming the time they had before the arrival of the new day's mourners to attend to their own interests. John was weeding his plot of kitchen herbs, while Martha was taking advantage of a visible sun to clean an assortment of objects from the collection. As Cecily approached, she unrolled a red-and-gold-embroidered saddlecloth faintly speckled with mildew and set it out on the gravel to dry.

They were discussing Thomasin's departure. "It's hardly surprising," John was saying. "Of course she'd want to be off to more secure circumstances. She wouldn't want to stay in a house where there's been a murder."

Martha nodded an unsmiling greeting to Cecily as she picked up a large goblet set with colorful stones and began to polish it. "She didn't go because of what happened. She never liked it here. A wealthy household full of ladies needing their hair styled and their gloves perfumed. That's what she wanted. She would have left before any of it if she could have."

"What prevented her?" asked Cecily.

Martha turned the goblet over in her hands, scrutinizing the ornately worked silver for stubborn tarnish. She returned it to the cradle of her arm and continued polishing. "Her high opinion of herself. She didn't want to go unless she had the prospect of a good situation."

"And does she now?"

"Oh yes," said Martha. "Didn't you see her dress?"

Cecily shook her head. She had only seen the maid in the gray dress in which she'd first answered the door, and the black one she had worn since Sir Barnaby's death.

"Brightest blue silk I've ever seen," said John. "And colored ribbons. As if she was costuming herself as one of the master's butterflies."

Martha nodded. "She was always saying she'd leave as soon as she could buy herself a fine dress."

"*A fine dress secures a fine position*," said John. "She did like to say that. Must have been saving her earnings."

"Saved earnings or not," muttered Martha, "she shouldn't have been flittering off to the shops at Monmouth the day after the master was killed." Monmouth Street, Cecily knew, was a popular destination for purchasing secondhand clothing. Though scorned by the elite as a place for those who would rather have shabby finery than no finery at all, for a maid seeking a highly paid position, a gown purchased from its cluttered shops could open doors that would otherwise be closed.

"No," John agreed. "No, there's little respect for the deceased in that. And with that poor foreigner upstairs in need of care." He glanced up toward the garret room. "I sent her off on errands for the kitchen, and she came back with a gown." He stopped and let out a low cry. "My basil! And just after I'd moved them outside. Lucky I left some in safety." Muttering invectives against thieving starlings, he rose to his feet and went off to the greenhouse.

Martha watched her husband go, shaking her head. "A house of wonders, and he would spend all his time in the kitchen, the garden, and the greenhouse," she said. She set the goblet down and picked up another. It was made from what appeared to be an ostrich egg enclosed in silver. "I remember the day the master acquired this," she said. "It was a gift to him from *foreign royalty*." She turned the goblet over to show the red label pasted to its base.

Cecily leaned down and read it aloud. "'Presented to me by Peter the Great, Tsar of Russia, on the occasion of his visit, 14 October 1700'—the tsar of Russia came here?"

Martha nodded, her lip trembling. "On his tour of England. I saw him myself with my own eyes striding on these very paths." Angrily, she brushed away a tear. "Why that girl didn't think herself fortunate to be employed in this house I'll never understand."

Susanna's voice called then from the door. "Lady Mayne says the guests will arrive soon and you're to stop what you're doing and prepare for them."

CHAPTER 19

Signore Covo's Coffee and Collectibles, read the sign painted on a piece of driftwood artfully crusted with barnacles. The babble of emphatic voices inside the building was audible outside it, and a fragrance of coffee and tallow wafted from its seams. Through the thick windows glazed with rain, Cecily could see bewigged heads bobbing and nodding at one another like puppets.

Meacan led her past the sign and around to the back of the row of buildings. They approached the coffeehouse through the mews, and were admitted by a man with a dark beard parted by a ropey white scar. He grunted a greeting to Meacan, made a cursory assessment of Cecily, and nodded them through the door. "He is with a client," he said as they started up a narrow staircase. "You know where to wait."

The room to which Meacan guided them was a triumph of disorientation. It was lit by lanterns, its two windows covered by layers of silk and velvet embroidered with labyrinthine patterns. No portion of the walls or even the ceiling was visible. Objects, many of which offered no clue as to how they had been mounted, crusted every surface. No sooner had Cecily caught a shape she could discern—a sword, a shell, a skull—than her eye was carried to another place.

Even the door of the room swung strangely when Meacan closed it, as if it was straining its hinges, and Cecily saw that it was covered in colored tiles fitted together like scales of a thousand different fish.

Meacan surveyed the room impassively, her hands on her hips and her head tilted back. "It always feels to me as if I've crawled into a treasure chest and someone has shut the lid and locked me inside."

Cecily reached for an object near to her on the table, then paused. It was the kind of place that felt as if it had rules.

"Oh, pick up whatever you want to and put it back anywhere," said Meacan. "He doesn't keep any of it in order. I think he *likes* it when objects move about."

Cecily picked up the small sphere. It was a walnut shell turned into a box with a tiny golden clasp and tiny golden hinges. She opened it. Resting inside was a tiny pair of silk gloves.

"Ah, the walnut," said Meacan. "He told me once that the gloves were made to protect the paws of a hedgehog beloved by a Chinese princess. At another time it was the mouse of a Portuguese prince. If you ask him about it today, I expect he'll tell you something different."

They heard a door open and voices in the hall. "I do have your assurances, Covo? The sale is final? You will entertain no other offers?"

The reply to this question was delivered in an accent unlike any English accent Cecily had ever heard, or any Italian one. If the English familiar to her was a smooth pond, this voice was that pond with something glinting under its surface. "Be assured," it said. "And multiply the assurance a thousand times. The merman is yours. As soon as I receive the sum upon which we have agreed, I will wrap him in Paduan silk of deepest blue and deliver him to you myself."

Cecily and Meacan listened to steps pass by their room. Another door opened, briefly admitting the chatter of the coffeehouse below, and closed again. "Remember," whispered Meacan, "we trust him only enough to ask the questions to which we want answers."

The bearded man who had admitted them below reappeared and showed them to Covo's office. As Cecily's eyes moved over the chaotic clutter, she began to sense that it was not the result of an unintelligent or unfocused mind, but a deliberate attempt to confuse and overwhelm. For one, it was *too* chaotic, as if the patterns that formed naturally within disorder had been scrupulously disrupted. For another, it was clean. There was picturesque rust and tarnish, to be sure, but there was not a trace of cobweb or smudge of coal to be seen.

She looked at the man who had just finished writing an entry in a ledger. He was standing behind a desk, the quill still in his right hand. His left hand was extended, the long fingertips resting on the desk's surface. In the firelight the dark hair on his knuckles glowed copper. His jacket was of auburn brown silk subtly embroidered in red. He wore no wig and his dark hair, tied at the nape of his neck, had the look of a mane constrained.

His eyes went first to Meacan, then to Cecily, then back to Meacan with an inquiring lift of an eyebrow. They were intelligent eyes set in a face that balanced sharp-angled arrogance and easy humor. A face that said *you want me to like you*. Meacan crossed to the couch in front of the fireplace and sat. "Something to drink, Covo, and for my friend also."

The corners of Covo's mouth lifted in a smile. "Brandy or chocolate?"

Meacan considered. "Brandy, today."

Covo moved to a table covered in bottles of glass, wood, and stone. "How pleased I am you have come at last. I have waited in great anticipation and concern, and was most devastated to learn you came in search of me when I was occupied with other business." He poured three cups from a shimmering decanter. "A rare vintage," he said. "Seven bottles, found by the pirate Dampier in a cave on an uninhabited island. And the decanter—" he held the vessel up to the firelight to enhance the play of iridescent color over its faceted surface "—was made from the same sand that produced the chalice of Abadur."

"What is the chalice of Abadur?" asked Cecily.

Covo affected hurt. "I see I am not at my best today. Educated ladies and gentlemen never ask me to explain what something is when I pronounce its name that way."

"What way?"

"In a way that makes them worry they will appear foolish for not having known already. It is a trick of enunciation."

"You needn't try to use your glamor on her, Covo," said Meacan. "She is no fool."

"No friend of the divine *Meacanmara* would be."

Cecily glanced at Meacan. She hadn't heard her full name since they were girls. Meacanmara was the Irish word for the sea radish that grew on the windswept cliffs near the village where Meacan's mother had been born. It wasn't the root that inspired the name, Meacan's mother had explained, though a radish was a healthy, hardy vegetable not to be underestimated, but the flowers, clouds of golden yellow bright against the blue sea that danced when storms blew in.

"But please," said Covo, handing them each a glass of amber liquid, "introduce us."

"This," said Meacan, "is Lady Cecily Kay."

"Lady Kay, an honor," said Covo. "Of course. I understand you are recently arrived from Smyrna, breaking your journey in London to identify plants in the home of the late Sir Barnaby Mayne. You arrived on the *Unicorn*, if I am not wrong. Please sit down."

Cecily took a seat beside Meacan, appreciating the warmth of the fire. Pale curls of steam hovered around their skirts and the toes of their boots as the rainwater evaporated from them. "You are not wrong," she said warily. "But how do you know so much?"

Covo waved a hand modestly. "In this instance I cannot in good conscience boast of my aptitude for discovering what is hidden. Since yesterday morning, a significant number of the collecting community has passed through the Mayne residence. Of those who did, most have brought their ensuing conversations here to my little establishment. I need only open the hall door and listen. They find your and Mrs. Barlow's continued presence in the house intriguing."

"Cecily and I knew each other as children," said Meacan. "I've told her all about my business with you, so you can trust her as far as you trust me."

"With pleasure," said Covo.

Meacan pulled a piece of paper from her pocket and handed it to Covo. "As promised," she said. "Here are the items Sir Barnaby wished to acquire from the Follywolle auction." As Covo took the paper and moved with it from the mantelpiece to a brocaded chair across from them, Meacan's expression darkened. "But why you felt compelled to send your men to attack that poor Swede, I do not know.

Did you not trust me to accomplish the task? You see I've done a better job of it than you did. He didn't even *have* the catalogue with him. He'd forgotten it. When I saw him at the door, terrified, exhausted, covered in blood—and he'd done nothing, *nothing* to deserve such measures."

Cecily recalled Meacan's barely contained fury when Helm had appeared at the house. Now it made sense. She shifted her attention from Meacan to Covo, curious how he would react.

"Why," he asked mildly, "would I resort to crude violence when I have an agent of your subtlety in my employ?"

"Then you *weren't* responsible for the attack on Otto Helm." Cecily heard relief in Meacan's voice.

"I had no part in it, I assure you," said Covo. "And no story has reached my ears other than the one he himself told. A chance meeting with thieves in the night. It is not uncommon."

"Well then," said Meacan, accepting his answer. "I am inclined to ask you to add another coin to my payment. For unanticipated difficulties."

"And I would counter," said Covo, "that as my client hoped to use this list to frustrate Sir Barnaby's desires, desires that have now been, shall we say, *conclusively* frustrated by someone else, the list is useless and our contract is void."

"There is no need to make an argument of it," said Meacan. "Our original agreement will do."

"Good." Covo smiled at Meacan. His eyes glowed with amused respect, but there was more in his expression, an undefined hunger like that of a wolf drawn to a fire, uncertain whether what it feels is a yearning for the companionship of the people around it or a desire to consume them.

He unfolded the paper and scanned it. "Book, book, another book," he said. "Mummified hand, bezoar of a snake, the coral called *barba neptuni*, statue of Mars modeled in onyx, four eggs from the China pheasant, the robe of a—" Covo set the list on a table beside him. "Like reading the menu of his last meal. Poor Sir Barnaby."

Meacan looked skeptical. "You grieve his passing?"

"Of course I do." Covo settled his broad shoulders more deeply into the speckled black and gray pelt draped over the back of his chair. "Sir Barnaby was one of my most lucrative clients. Not only did he pay me to find and purchase a number of expensive items on his behalf, but he also brought me business entirely unbeknownst to himself. There have been times when I've owed a quarter of my income to him. I've been paid to secure the patronage of Barnaby Mayne, to arrange introductions to Barnaby Mayne, to settle feuds with Barnaby Mayne, to *prolong* feuds with Barnaby Mayne, to convince Barnaby Mayne to sell objects, and to convince Barnaby Mayne to buy them. To"—Covo glanced at the paper beside him—"To assist in petty revenges against him." He sighed. "Yes, I will miss the old obsessive. Let us hope this will be a lesson to collectors to treat their curators better."

"Do you know Mr. Dinley?" asked Cecily.

Covo nodded. "Oh yes, Lady Kay. I know them all."

Cecily tried to sound casual. "I had only known him a few hours, but he didn't seem—"

"—the type to murder anyone," Covo finished. "That is the general opinion."

"And you agree?" Cecily didn't turn, but as she spoke she felt Meacan shift on the couch. *Don't be overeager in your questions*, Meacan had told her. *If he becomes too interested, he will involve himself, and you don't want Covo involved if what you are after is truth and clear thinking.* Cecily reminded herself to be careful.

At the moment, Covo seemed simply to be enjoying the conversation. "Oh, certainly I agree," he said. "An earnest minnow of a man whose fiercest bite could do no worse than tickle the foot."

Meacan nodded in agreement. "My impression exactly. Gentle and quiet. Not one to get into a temper and kill his employer. But I suppose if he had some other reason, a hidden motive, you'd know about it?"

"You flatter me," said Covo. "But I know of no such secret. Strange as it may seem given Sir Barnaby's temperament, I believe Dinley *liked* the man, and was honored to be in his employ. Sons of parish clerks are not often welcomed into the anointed coterie of the gentlemen collectors. Whenever I happened to see the young man in my establishment, he was invariably engaged in some polite debate over the spelling of a plant name or the proper categorization of lapis lazuli. I hesitate to say it, for fear of tarnishing my reputation as a keen observer, but it seemed to me that Walter Dinley was *happy*." Covo turned thoughtful. "If he is caught, it will be edifying to learn what he says before he is taken to the noose."

As Covo spoke, Cecily had been perusing the walls in search of an object that would camouflage her next question. She found it in a cluster of concave disks, black and shining, reflecting the firelight like eyes. "Are those scrying glasses?" she asked.

Covo, following the direction of her look, nodded. "I would not have taken you for a credulous woman, Lady Kay. Do not tell me you accept the power of a charmed disk to show visions of the future?"

"I have never encountered any persuasive evidence that they can do so," said Cecily evenly. "But I did notice that Sir Barnaby purchased a number of them from you, indeed that you procured for him quite a few items pertaining to his studies of the occult."

Covo stood, removed a disk from the wall, and handed it to Cecily. "Whatever a collector wants can be procured."

Cecily took the disk. It was cool and heavy, its edges sharp enough to cut, its center a black well like a window into night. "I spoke with Mr. Inwood about Sir Barnaby's interest in the occult. He said Sir Barnaby collected these items to record man's gullibility, and to demonstrate the powerlessness of the objects."

"That is what Sir Barnaby said, yes," said Covo, watching her.

Cecily kept her eyes on the glass. "Was it true?"

"At present," said Covo, after a moment, "the study of the occult is merely out of fashion. But the line between harmless eccentricity and punishable blasphemy can shift under one's feet. A healer lauded for her novel approach one day can be burned as a witch on the next."

"You mean," said Cecily, "that if Sir Barnaby *did* take the subject more seriously than he admitted, he would have done his best to be circumspect about it."

"The meeting!" burst out Meacan.

Covo and Cecily both turned to look at her. "Apologies," said Covo. "Are you expected elsewhere?"

"No, no, no." Meacan spoke in a rush. "I was thinking of the meeting Sir Barnaby held in the dead of night. With the hats pulled low and the strange chanting."

Cecily turned to Meacan in surprise. "You never mentioned this meeting to me." She felt, in addition to her own curiosity, that if Meacan had wanted to avoid intriguing Covo, this was probably not the direction she should have taken.

Meacan seemed to have realized her error. She glanced at Covo, but his expression remained impassive. "The subject hadn't yet come up," she said. "It was on the second night I spent in the house. Sir Barnaby hosted a gathering. I'm sure I was meant to be asleep and not notice, for they arrived after dark and kept their voices to a murmur. They were in the Artifact Room, though, which is below mine, and I'm sure they were chanting."

Covo looked amused. "Allow me to enlighten you. Sir Barnaby belonged to many societies, of course, one for each of his interests. And yes, among these societies is one whose purpose is to study the occult with a little more *dedication* than its members are willing to admit in general company. I understand Sir Barnaby often hosted their gatherings."

Cecily looked down at the glass again, frowning. "Sir Barnaby was a man of science surrounded by men of science," she said. "Surely he cannot have been attempting to—to summon spirits with conjurations and magic circles?"

"I assure you, he was," said Covo mildly. "And is it so strange? Newton tells us that gravitation is an unseen force acting upon objects. Why then should there not be other unseen forces? Waiting to be discovered, perhaps, in knowledge that has been left behind in the mists of the past? Superstitions that have been too hastily overlooked?"

"You sound as if the idea appeals to you," said Meacan.

Covo shrugged. "I avoid having obsessions, myself. They make people easy to manipulate, a fact on which my business depends. But I cannot sell something if I cannot pretend to believe in it."

"And the occult was Sir Barnaby's obsession," said Cecily.

"Undoubtedly," said Covo. "Indeed, when I heard of his demise my first assumption was a botched blood rite or ill-conceived ritual potion."

"I assume," said Cecily, "that Inwood did not share his friend's interest. He seemed to know very little about it when I asked him. Or do you think he merely feigned ignorance?"

"Oh, Inwood's interests are of a very different nature," said Covo. He stood and went to one of the shelves embedded among the objects mounted directly to the wall. Cecily heard the clink of glass and metal as he sifted through items. "Ah," he said at last. "Here it is."

He returned to his chair and set on the table between them a wooden box with a tentacled sea creature carved into its lid. He opened it to reveal a broken glass vessel crusted in white coral, resting in a bed of tarnished silver coins. As he picked up the bottle, the coins fell away from it like scales. As they shifted, Cecily perceived sparkles of green and red and blue among them. "Tokens, merely," said Covo, "of the Spanish galleon that met its fate among the rocks that ring a distant isle. It waited there a century, its drowned crew and shattered hull a feast for shipworms until, seven years ago, an enterprising diver spotted a glitter of gold. They brought up pieces of eight by the thousands that day, and emeralds, sapphires, and rubies enough to armor Leviathan. The Duke of Albermarle, they say, had for his share sixty thousand pounds."

He handed Meacan the bottle. She turned it over in her hands. "It is a curious union of man's artifice and nature's art," she said. "I can see why it attracted you. I suppose you plan to label it *Poseidon's goblet?*"

Covo's eyes glittered. "I do now," he said. "And I am most

grateful to you for the suggestion." He scooped up a handful of coins and allowed them to fall one by one back into the box as he spoke. "There are certain gentlemen whose ears demonstrate a particular sensitivity to stories of sunken treasure, and a particular willingness to believe that devices will soon be built capable of lifting vast hoards from the watery depths. Giles Inwood is among them. It is this, not spells and spirits, that commands his attention."

Cecily nodded her understanding. She knew about the shipwreck speculators, and an idea was forming in her mind. "I know that not much escapes your attention," she said. "I wonder, is it possible that Giles Inwood has recently suffered a series of *failed* investments in these projects?"

A look of surprise crossed Covo's face. "Now how would you know that?"

Cecily kept her tone light. She saw that his attention was sharpening, and knew that each question she asked was another scrape of the blade against the whetstone. "I was just recalling Inwood's arrival at the Mayne house," she said. "When Mr. Carlyle asked him about the wreck of the *Nuestra Señora*, his reply was evasive."

Covo turned to Meacan, who gave a small shrug that said very clearly, *I told you she wasn't a fool.* "And what do you know of the *Nuestra Señora?*" he asked Cecily.

"On my journey back to England, I heard sailors speak of it. Two among our crew had recently returned from the expedition that was expected to raise that lost galleon. They were upset because they had been promised a share of the spoils, and despite the many promises made, no ship had been found."

Covo nodded. "Not a single doubloon."

"If Inwood was among the investors," said Cecily, "he could have lost a great deal."

Covo opened his hand in a gesture of beneficence, the auburn velvet of his cuff changing color as it moved through the firelight. "I would usually require payment in exchange for such information," he said. "But as you seem already to know the answer to your question, I will merely affirm it. Giles Inwood has had some acknowledged successes, but none of late. He is, as you say, in difficulties. To put it bluntly, Lady Kay, the man is ruined."

"Which means," said Cecily slowly, "that he will struggle to pay the fifty thousand he is obligated to pay Lady Mayne?"

Covo chuckled dryly. "Thus far, he has managed to conceal his circumstances from the collecting community, but I cannot imagine that will last much longer. He's calling in every favor owed him to raise the funds he needs. Reputation is of crucial importance, you see. He must protect the Mayne collection, as he promised to do. And he must pay the widow." Covo's expression turned speculative. "It is a shame for Inwood, a great shame, that Sir Barnaby died when he did. I am certain he wishes, for more reasons than simple affection, that his old friend had either released him from the contract, or stayed alive a little longer, until the next trove of Spanish gold revealed itself. But this has been a most unexpected and intriguing conversation. Tell me—"

Meacan stood up hastily. "We must be getting back, I'm afraid. Lady Mayne expects me to inventory the whole collection, you know."

After a moment, Covo stood also. "I do know," he said. "I trust you will inform me, should you find anything of particular interest."

"I will consider it," said Meacan.

As they left, they passed a rectangular box resting on a

pedestal by the desk. Inside was a twisted, dry creature no more than three feet long. Its shriveled head and torso appeared to be those of a man. The mummified tail to which they were attached was that of a fish. "The merman, I presume?" asked Meacan. She leaned closer. "It is better than your last one. I cannot see the stitching."

CHAPTER 20

The coffeehouse was located in Cornhill, one of the ancient hearts of London. Covo liked to say that the hill from which the ward took its name was molded and pushed into existence at the dawn of time by industrious moles of extraordinary size. Once blanketed in soft sedges and willows, the marshy soil now supported the stone and brick of one of the city's most enterprising neighborhoods. Cecily and Meacan waited to speak until they had climbed into the dark interior of a hired coach and begun their jolting journey back toward the relative tranquility of the West End's green squares and stately houses.

"I cannot help but feel slightly disappointed," said Meacan. "I thought that of any of them, Inwood was the most likely murderer."

Cecily tried not to bite her tongue as the coach wheels plunged from one depression to another. "I was less suspicious of him once I learned the sum he was to pay for the collection. That weakened his motive. And now that we know he is facing ruin and *cannot* pay, I do not see that he has any motive at all."

"At least not to our knowledge," said Meacan. "I'm

impressed, by the way, that you deduced all of that from the name of a ship."

"It wasn't only the *Nuestra Señora*," said Cecily. "It was also the inventory."

Meacan put out an arm to brace herself as the coach swung around a corner. "What does the inventory have to do with it?"

Cecily explained. "Lady Mayne has made it abundantly clear that she dislikes the collection, and wants to be rid of it as soon as possible. The first time I spoke with her, she told me she didn't anticipate it remaining in the house above a week. Why, then, would she commission you to complete an inventory? Even if she didn't expect it to take two months, she must have known it would take time."

Meacan considered the question. "She told me it's what her husband would have wanted."

"Yes, but I wonder if it was someone else who convinced her of that."

"*Inwood*," said Meacan. "Of course. He doesn't want to damage his reputation by admitting that he can't afford the contracted price, so he's trying to give himself time to raise the money."

"Precisely." The carriage turned onto a crowded market street and slowed almost to a crawl, making it easier for Cecily to speak. "My guess is that Inwood suggested the inventory and, to ensure that it would take as long as possible, recommended that Lady Mayne hire *you* to do it."

A laugh burst from Meacan. "Thank you very much for implying I owe my employment to an assumption of my incompetence."

"An erroneous assumption," Cecily assured her.

"As far as deductions go," Meacan went on, "I may not

have guessed the true inspiration for the inventory or recognized the name of a phantom shipwreck, but I *did* know
there was something wrong about Inwood. From the beginning, he has been too agreeable."

Cecily cocked her head. "I've never considered a person-
able demeanor to be an indication that something is wrong."

"Ah," said Meacan knowingly. "You spend too much time
with plants, and not enough with gamblers, many of whom
exist under a kind of curse. No matter how desperate their
circumstances, they cannot *help* but appear confident and
trustworthy. It's as if they are trapped behind a mask. And
the smiling, false face encourages those who have lent them
money to do so again and again, though it is to the detri-
ment of both parties. I've seen it before, and I've learned to
look for the hooks that fasten the mask to the face. I knew
I recognized something in Inwood's manner. I just didn't
know until now what it was."

The carriage had picked up its pace again. Cecily looked
out the window at the scrolling row of closed doors and
pedestrians glimpsed too quickly for memory to hold them.
"I suppose you are right," she said. Her mind was momen-
tarily claimed by a gentle sadness, as subtle as the brush of
a flower petal against her cheek.

Meacan read her expression and narrowed her eyes. "You
like him," she said. "We will have to be wary of your taste
in men."

Cecily raised her eyebrows. "And what of yours? I would
hardly call Signore Covo trustworthy."

"I can think of no one *less* trustworthy," agreed Meacan.
"But he's honorable in his own way." She grew serious. "I
do wish we'd learned more from him. Covo has a tendency
to *say* a great deal while offering very little direction. We

knew already that Sir Barnaby had a predilection for grimoires and pentacles. What we need is to speak to Dinley. The question is where he is hiding."

Cecily pictured the curator's anxious young face, and the humble accommodation he had built for himself out of books and blankets beneath the sloping ceiling of the Mayne house, in the company of silent antiquities. "I agree," she said, "that he is the person most likely to hold the answer to the whole problem, but if he is innocent, as we suspect him to be, then we must hope for his sake that he stays well hidden."

Her words drew a worried sigh from Meacan. "He's not so far in age from my own son. I thought of that when I spoke to young Hugh Ashton. There's another youth whose thirst for knowledge and adventure will get him into trouble one day if he doesn't temper it with wisdom. He is convinced of Dinley's innocence, you know. He told me so roundly, and looked sick with concern for his friend's fate."

"Hugh Ashton," said Cecily, trying to catch up to Meacan's thoughts. "He is the apothecary's son?"

"That's right," Meacan answered. "I've known the Ashtons for years, ever since they came to my husband to have their herbal printed. And it did very well, too. They ordered a second printing."

"They?"

"Peter Ashton and his wife wrote it together. You and Anne would get on well. You won't find a better authority on the medicinal plants that grow in this part of the country than she." Meacan recalled herself to the subject at hand. "Last week, Dinley happened to mention to me that he and Ashton were good friends. They would be. Two young men of similar temperaments and interests, though I'd say Hugh was the less responsible of the two."

"I see," said Cecily, understanding. "Hugh Ashton was one of the people you went to see the day after the murder."

"The first," Meacan affirmed. "Then I went to Lord Gitton. I'd drawn butterflies for him once, and Dinley had provided him some assistance when he moved his collection to a new house. Then I spoke to Dauncey at the Royal Society, who had arranged for Dinley to give several lectures there. And then Haydon, another mutual acquaintance. Dinley's family, by the way, is in Berkshire, and according to the constable, who sent a man there, they claim to know nothing of his whereabouts."

Cecily was still dwelling on the apothecary. "When you went to the younger Ashton, had he already heard about what had happened?"

"Of course," Meacan said quickly. "Everyone in the parish had by then."

"And you believe the friendship between him and Dinley was a close one?"

"That was my impression, yes. He did seem *very* upset about the murder."

"Do the Ashtons keep servants? Or an apprentice? Or did they leave their son alone with the shop?"

"He's alone." Meacan was looking hard at Cecily. "What is your idea?"

Cecily took a moment to compose her thoughts. "Do you remember," she said at last, "the way Thomasin looked when she went out to purchase the medicines Inwood required?"

Meacan considered the question, then shook her head.

"She appeared miserable," said Cecily.

"Well, we all must have," Meacan pointed out. "And she always looked that way. You must know she didn't like being employed at the Mayne house."

"I did notice, yes," said Cecily. "But there was a time when she presented a very different countenance. Upon her *return* from the apothecary, she looked almost cheerful. Consider, then, that the very next thing she did was to buy a dress and secure herself a new position."

"I saw the dress," said Meacan. "How she could have afforded a damask gown, and ribbons to embellish the petticoats, I cannot—" Meacan stopped. She clapped her hand to her head. "But what a fool I've been. To think that *you* thought of it and I did not, when I myself saw Hugh go pale as a sheet when I asked him where Dinley might have gone. Dinley was *there*. I didn't see him, but you think Thomasin did."

The idea took shape and color between them. "It would explain how she could suddenly afford a new gown," said Cecily.

"If we're right, the girl certainly has some presence of mind," said Meacan. "To blackmail them on the spot and know just what she wanted to do afterward. We must not forget her. She could be a rather useful person to befriend."

Cecily gave her friend a stern look. "*If* we're right," she said, "and Dinley is still there, they'll be doing a better job of keeping him hidden now that he's been caught once. Your friend isn't likely to give him up."

"Oh, young Ashton isn't my friend," said Meacan. "His *parents* are." She rolled her shoulders and inclined her chin into a posture of authority. "There's a difference, you know, and there's some power that comes with being the age we are. You leave it to me. I've dealt with unruly sons before. He has no hope of withstanding *Mrs.* Meacan Barlow."

★

Meacan was right. Hugh Ashton, a freckled youth in an ill-fitting wig whose expression seemed to fall naturally into that of someone in the middle of trying to remember what he was about to say, broke down almost at once. "Yes, Mrs. Barlow," he almost sobbed. "He was here. He isn't anymore. Please, *please* don't tell my parents."

The shop was dense with aromas of spices, herbs, and resins. Blue-and-white ceramic jars filled the shelves on the wall. Some labels were printed clearly on fresh slips of paper. Others were faded, blurred, and stained. They were arranged alphabetically, from aloes and ambergris and aniseed through senna and sulphur to wormwood. Drying herbs hung in bunches from the ceiling. In the center of the room was a long table scattered with leaves, flowers, powders, roots, bowls, baskets, and open books.

Meacan, her first object accomplished, altered her approach. Her expression softened as she relinquished the authority that came from being a friend of his parents, and replaced it with that of being a counselor and supplier of wisdom *other* than his parents. "You've gotten yourself into something of a scrape, haven't you, dear? Why don't we begin with you telling us where Walter Dinley is now."

"He—he's gone—" Ashton hesitated. He looked from Meacan to Cecily, came to a decision, and sighed. "He's gone to the docks," he said. "To try to board a ship to the Americas. But Mrs. Barlow, he *is* innocent."

Cecily spoke for the first time. "I think," she said, "that it would be best to start from the beginning."

The story unfolded in front of the hearth, where the three

of them sat, Meacan and Cecily attending to the various boiling infusions whenever Ashton became too caught up in his account. The more he confided, the more at ease he became. On the day of the murder, he had been mixing compounds, trying to keep up with the work of the shop while his parents were gone. They had even taken the apprentice with them, he explained, for training, so he had been left quite alone. He had been about to close the shop for the evening when Dinley burst into the room in a state of clear distress, and begged Ashton to conceal him.

Ashton, trusting without question, had done so. And just in time, for the constable and his men had come in minutes later asking if Ashton had seen Dinley. They told him that his friend had murdered Sir Barnaby. Ashton admitted to Cecily and Meacan that he had hesitated, in the moment, to impede the course of justice, but he had been and remained so convinced that Dinley could not have committed such a deed that he had lied and sent them away. As soon as they were gone, he had asked Dinley for an explanation.

"And?" Meacan burst in, unable to keep silent. "Did he tell you what made him confess?"

"He told me he didn't kill Sir Barnaby," said Ashton. "But I swear to you, Mrs. Barlow, he refused to tell me anything more."

"He told you *nothing*? But it's been three days."

"I did try," said Ashton. "The customers who came to the store were all discussing it. It was Mr. Cobb, here for a poultice for his wife's toothache, who told me Dinley had *confessed* to the murder. I was there at the table, the mortar full of sage and rue, and he told me all that he knew of the matter. When he left I demanded to know what had made Dinley own to the foul deed and what, if he was innocent, was preventing him from speaking—to *me,* his friend, at least."

"And?" asked Meacan.

Ashton took a pot from the flame, carried it across the room, and set it on a stand to cool. Meacan and Cecily followed him to the table. "And he still wouldn't speak," said Ashton. "It was clear in his voice he intended to take whatever secret he had to his grave."

Cecily looked at the open books on the table. One was certainly an herbal—the *Theatrum Botanicum,* she guessed, her eye moving admiringly over the thorough description of wolfsbane to which it was open. The other books, though, did not appear to be herbals, or at least not the standard ones. One, the pages of which were aged and stained, was open to a map held aloft by cherubs. "If Dinley wouldn't talk about the murder," she said, "tell me, of what *did* you speak?"

Ashton, following her look, turned the pages of the book to show its title, *China Illustrata.* "We spoke of what we always spoke of," he said quietly. "Of the distant places in the world, and of the plants that grow in them."

"China?" Meacan squinted down at the book, then shook her head. "Don't get him started on emperors and tea leaves," she said to Cecily. "He won't stop." She turned back to Ashton. "And you'd best get those ideas out of your head. For one, your father won't allow it. For another, everyone knows only the Jesuits are allowed into China."

"Yes," said Ashton meekly, his cheeks pinkening.

"You and Walter Dinley have been friends for some time," said Cecily. "What about *before* the murder? Did Dinley mention Sir Barnaby often? Did he speak of his employer's business?"

Ashton had moved away from the books and was pouring the still-hot liquid into a jar. Bay-scented steam rose in curls from it. "Yes," he said, spilling a little of the potion down the side. "Yes, he did speak of Sir Barnaby. Of his acquisitions, and the crates arriving, and the theories being published in the *Transactions*."

"Perhaps Dinley was concerned," prompted Cecily. "Perhaps Sir Barnaby had received some threat, or spoken of some enemy."

Ashton started to shake his head, then stopped. "There was nothing like that," he said. "But I suppose, that is, Dinley did—not complain precisely—but you mention concern."

"Yes?" Meacan prompted.

"He was concerned," said Ashton. "Dinley, that is, was concerned about the Rose collection."

The word struck Cecily's thoughts like a well-aimed stone. "Rose," she repeated. "You mean John Rose?"

Ashton nodded. "Sir Barnaby acquired his collection two or three years ago. And ever since he did, he's spent nearly all his time studying it. Dinley said he abandoned most of his other interests and insisted on staying in his study, alone, poring over the objects. Dinley didn't understand it at all. He asked Sir Barnaby on many occasions what it was that had such a hold on his attention, for Dinley perceived nothing of particular interest in the items, but Sir Barnaby offered no explanation."

"What about Sir Barnaby's interest in occult studies?" asked Cecily. "Did Dinley profess an opinion on that?"

Ashton's expression remained open. "Oh, he thought it a waste of time, though he would never have said as much to Sir Barnaby."

"And did Dinley speak of Giles Inwood? Or Humphrey Warbulton? Martin Carlyle? Otto Helm?"

Hugh considered the names. "Inwood, yes, of course. He came to visit not infrequently, and Dinley had a great respect for him. But Warbulton and Carlyle—no, I do not know those names. And Helm—I know he is the Swedish traveler who was attacked. Is he recovering? Do you require any more medicines?"

The question temporarily turned the tide of the conversation, and resulted in the quick preparation of a new salve. Ashton measured and combined ingredients. Meacan and Cecily helped, fetching jars from the shelves and returning them to their places.

Meacan opened a jar and sniffed. "Well, that's an agreeable perfume," she said. "You'll have to make more. The jar's almost empty."

Ashton turned to see what she was holding and blushed again. "That's—yes, it's very popular," he said. "It's for inspiring—that is—for bringing to mind thoughts of—that is—for—" Ashton's expression changed. "Now that you mention—"

"No need to explain," said Meacan, with a broad smile. "I believe I take your meaning. It *is* a pleasant fragrance."

"N-no," said Ashton. "That is, *yes*, but that isn't—I was thinking of something else. Dinley—I—I know it isn't important—but in case it—that is—Dinley was in love."

Meacan's eyebrows went up. "With whom?"

"I don't know who it was. He met her at one of the lectures of the Society. He mentioned on several occasions after that, though—" The furrow reappeared between Ashton's brows. "Though now that I think of it, he never once said her name over the past three days."

"What name?"

"I—I know he never told me her surname, only her given name. It's difficult to remember, that is, with all the names of plants and the customers, I— He said she was the most beautiful woman he had ever seen. Her name was—was—yes, I am sure of it. Her name was Alice."

CHAPTER 21

Despite Martha's best efforts, dust had begun to settle on the collection, dulling the polished cabinets and blurring the edges of objects. In the Bird Room, enterprising spiders, encouraged by the retreat of polishing cloths and brooms, had strung glinting strands of web between the birds hanging from the rafters. Pallid, insubstantial dust balls had formed in nests, tucked among unhatched eggs as if hidden there by spectral cuckoos. Meacan's inventory had progressed across half of one wall, and though she had replaced each object after examining its label, her minute adjustments to the display had given it a disturbed, uneven appearance, as if all the birds had just nervously ruffled their wings.

Meacan stood on tiptoe on a chair, holding the edge of a shelf for balance, squinting at the red label difficult to distinguish from the scarlet plumage of the bird before her. "*Cocco—*" she said. "*Coccothraustes Indica cristata*, or the Virginia nightingale."

Cecily, standing beside the chair, consulted the list that had become increasingly crowded with scribbled annotations. "Here," she said, as she made a neat mark beside the name. She tapped the pencil thoughtfully against the page. "If Alice met Dinley at a lecture in the autumn or winter, I expect she lives here in London, and is not only visiting for the season."

They had spent the last hour working together in the room, matching the items on Meacan's list to the corresponding objects on the shelves. At the same time, they had been discussing how to go about locating Alice Fordyce.

Meacan crawled her fingers along the shelf as she leaned to the side. "Not many women attend lectures at the Philosophical Society. We could make inquiries there. Someone must know something about her." She squinted at a label. "*Psittacus albus cristatus*, the—"

"—white crested parrot," Cecily finished, marking it on the list. She looked up at the bird, positioned on its stand with its black beak open as if it had been frozen in the middle of speech. The yellow feathers of its crest were still faintly lustrous. "We could also make a search of Sir Barnaby's correspondence," she said. "If Alice or her aunt wrote to Sir Barnaby to request an invitation to tour the collection, the letter might include an address, or the name of the aunt."

"If she even *has* an aunt," said Meacan as she stepped down from the chair. She was holding a solitary feather as long as her arm. "'A quill sent by Captain John Strong,'" she read from the label, "'who claimed to have met the bird on the coast of Chile, and was much amazed by the bigness of it.'" Meacan whistled under her breath. "He supposed it to be sixteen foot from wing to wing with a beak that could strip the hide from an ox."

While Cecily found the feather on the list and marked it, Meacan continued to run her finger thoughtfully along its edge. "When I first heard her voice calling so sweetly from the other side of the garden wall I thought she must be a wandering ghost. Opening the door and seeing her there in her white cloak with her great blue eyes did nothing to change my impression. Perhaps she *was* a spirit." Unexpectedly, Meacan chuckled.

"Something amusing?" asked Cecily.

"I was thinking of all of Sir Barnaby's books of spells. Maybe one of them was successful. Maybe she *was* an apparition, and he summoned her."

Cecily frowned. "I don't—"

Meacan, who had always struggled to see a joke through to its conclusion before starting to laugh, spoke through gasps of merriment. "After all," she said, "what ageing collector would *not* want to conjure a beautiful woman in the bloom of youth who yearns only to tour his collection and listen to him talk about it?"

Cecily's lips twitched. "And does your theory offer any insight into his demise?"

Meacan nodded eagerly. "Of course it does. Spirits are *always* turning on their summoners. He was remiss and left a word out of the binding spell. She slipped her mystical fetters and took her revenge."

Cecily met the unamused glare of an eagle and sighed. "It would make an entertaining story," she said, "but I don't think we will find our answers in it."

"Well, if we have come to the subject of stories," said Meacan, "one thing I do know about our mysterious Alice is that she has a gift for telling them. After I let her in, but before she went into the house, she regaled me with a fantastic yarn about the sweetbay tree."

Cecily raised her eyebrows in surprise and waited for Meacan to continue. Meacan's gaze became distant and she nodded to herself as the memory returned. "I'd set my drawing on the bench when I went to see who was at the door.

She noticed it, and naturally she complimented my work. Then she commented on the smell of lemons, and asked the name of the tree. When I told her it was the sweetbay, she lit up like a mirror when struck by sunshine. 'Oh,' she said. 'Oh, I know all about Sir Barnaby Mayne's sweetbay.'"

"There is nothing strange in that," said Cecily. "Sir Barnaby published a number of essays about it in the *Transactions*."

"Most girls of eighteen or nineteen do not read and memorize the *Transactions*," said Meacan. "*You*, no doubt, being an exception."

Cecily conceded the point. "How, then, had Alice heard of the tree?"

"I don't know," said Meacan, "What I *do* know is that her account bore no similarities to any I've ever heard. She told me Sir Barnaby's sweetbay came from a seed that was brought to England by a pirate, who found it on a deserted island."

"A pirate?" Cecily's brow furrowed. "I thought Sir Barnaby had it from a ship's surgeon who had traveled to the Carolinas."

Meacan nodded. "As I said, her story was not the usual one. But I always enjoy a good tale of piracy, so I asked her to continue. The pirate, she told me, had washed ashore after his ship was attacked and pulled to pieces by a monstrous squid, a creature with tentacles long enough to embrace it from deck to keel, and rows of round eyes like obsidian shields."

"And it was *she* who supplied these details?" asked Cecily, suddenly suspicious. The story thus far was not unlike those Meacan told when as children they escaped their lessons and deliberately lost their way in the garden maze. "They are not your own embellishments?"

"If anything," said Meacan, "I am leaving off some of the gilding. May I continue?"

It occurred to Cecily to protest that she didn't consider sailors' yarns to be a productive line of inquiry, but a glimmer of an idea, as yet indistinct, gave her pause. She gestured for Meacan to go on.

"The pirate," said Meacan, "searched every cove and cave and hill on the island, and soon understood himself to be entirely alone. Day after day he paced the beach, hoping for rescue, lamenting the loss of his companions and of the hard-won jewels that had gone to the bottom of the sea. One day, he saw something gleaming red on the ground. He picked it up, full of hope that one of his lost rubies had washed ashore, but when he saw the branches of a tree above him, he understood it was only a seed."

"If he thought it was a ruby," said Cecily, "he must have seen the aril *coating* the seed, and not the seed itself. It is only the aril that is red."

Meacan fluttered the feather impatiently. "This is a *tale*. Botanical anatomy has no place in it. As the months passed, the pirate grew fond of the tree, and of the lemon-sweet flowers that covered it in spring. He often spoke to it and told it stories of his home. He decided that if ever he should be rescued, he would reform, and be a pirate no longer. But no rescue came. Eventually, he resolved to escape the island using his own strength and craft. And when one day another storm lashed the waves into a frenzy and beat down upon the island with winds so great they uprooted the tree that had become a friend to him, he decided the time had come. He used the tree to make a boat, and set out again into the sea. And on that boat, with no compass to guide him or rudder to steer him, he was miraculously borne home. He came back to England, and out of gratitude to the tree, planted at the center of his garden the seed he had always kept in his pocket. And the tree that grew from that seed sired every sweetbay in London, including Sir Barnaby's."

Meacan set the feather down. "I didn't contradict the girl," she said. "It was a good tale, and well told. I did ask her whence she had it, but she gave no answer."

Cecily was deep in thought. The story itself was not familiar to her, but the manner in which it had been crafted, with such cheerful intention to fascinate, was. "It reminds me," she said, speaking half to herself and half to Meacan, "of a story about a fox."

"Oh?" Meacan looked intrigued.

"It was in a letter," said Cecily slowly. "Written by the traveler Anthony Holt to his sister."

Meacan smiled. "Sea monsters, pirates, deserted islands, jewels. Alice's account *does* have the ring of a tale an older brother would spin for his impressionable—" She stopped. Her eyes widened. "Do you think—"

The idea that had shimmered at a distance in Cecily's mind gained definition. "According to the captain who wrote to Sir Barnaby about Anthony Holt's death, Holt had been disowned by his father. But suppose Holt had a sister. A girl who loved her brother so much that she would defy her father?"

"Not Alice Fordyce," whispered Meacan. "But Alice *Holt*."

Cecily nodded. "If brother and sister wished to maintain a correspondence, might they not have done so through the man funding Holt's travels? Anthony could include letters to Alice in the crates he sent to Sir Barnaby, and she could send replies with Sir Barnaby's communications to Anthony."

Meacan leaned against the open cabinet behind her, careful to avoid the sharp beaks and talons extending over the edges of the shelves. "It doesn't seem in Sir Barnaby's character to facilitate so sentimental a correspondence."

"No, but it seems exactly in the character of a gentle curator in love with Alice."

"Dinley!" cried Meacan.

"I found the letter tucked in a book beside his bed," said Cecily. "He could have been keeping it to give to her."

"And she could have come to the house to receive it." Meacan's expression changed. "But do you think she knows that her brother—she *must* know by now—that her brother is lost?"

Cecily put her finger to her lips and looked meaningfully at the closed door. There were footsteps approaching. "We still have all the questions for her we had before," she said quietly. "What has changed is that we now have a good idea of where we must go to ask them."

There was a knock on the door. It opened, and John appeared. With him came a wafting fragrance of mint. In one hand he held a folded paper with a wax seal. "You two *are* returned," he said. "There's a letter for—" He held up the letter and squinted at it. "Ah, for you *both*," he said, and handed it to Cecily. Below the floury print of John's thumb was written in an elegant hand: *Mrs. Meacan Barlow and Lady Cecily Kay.*

John glanced around the room with only vague curiosity, scowled at a nearby starling, then shook his head and retreated to the door. "Supper's ready," he said. "I've had an idea for a salad of tansy, served hot, with spinach and green corn"—he left the room, still listing ingredients—"and primrose leaves. Violets, too."

When he had gone, Meacan's eyes dropped to the letter Cecily was holding. "That's Covo's seal," she said.

Cecily opened it and they read in silence together.

My esteemed friends. The games I enjoy in my little world of wonders can become tedious, the players and pieces uninspiring. Allow me to say that I found in your company this afternoon a renewal of interest and inspiration, dare I say creativity? I hope you will join me again. May I entice you? Tomorrow night there is to be a meeting of the society of which we made particular mention. The usual host being unavailable (ironic that he cannot be reached, given the subject in which they claim expertise), they have asked me to provide for them a space in which they can remain unobserved, and I have acquiesced. Perhaps you will also be my guests at that time, and we may continue our conversations.

Meacan gave a derisive snort. "They may *think* themselves unobserved," she said. "But there are no secret rooms in Covo's house into which *he* cannot see. A fact he knows I know." She sighed. "I suppose it's too good an opportunity to refuse. We may learn something of value."

"I am not certain I understand," said Cecily, frowning over the letter.

"It seems obvious enough to me," said Meacan. "Covo has invited us to join him for an evening of spying on occultists."

CHAPTER 22

Lady Mayne moved through the house so rarely that when Cecily heard footsteps and the crisp tap of cane on the landing the following morning, she didn't know who was approaching until she saw her through the doorway. The widow's pale gaze swept over the cabinets in Cecily's room with wilting disapproval. *Here, too,* the eyes seemed to say. *I should not have expected better.* Cecily supplied a polite greeting. Lady Mayne's mouth relaxed a little at the sight of her guest, neatly coiffed and attired in a tasteful gown of blue linen. "I hope I am not intruding, Lady Kay."

"On the contrary," Cecily assured her. "Your visit is most welcome."

This was not true. Cecily had been waiting, dressed and ready, for Meacan to join her. Finding the address of the Holt house had not been difficult. Meacan had ascertained it with a few strategic conversations with mourners on the previous afternoon. They had agreed to set out early before anyone could trouble them with questions.

"I am accustomed to exercise in the morning," Lady Mayne announced. "I prefer a garden, but as I cannot bear the city air, I must content myself with the indoors." With her free hand, she reached out and moved assessing fingers over the bed-curtains. Though they were worn and thread-bare, the blue velvet still shimmered like the surface of the ocean. "These should have been replaced years ago," she said, releasing them and shifting her attention down to the faded rug. "Five fewer stuffed crocodiles, and he would have had ample funds to furnish the guest rooms to a standard befitting the family."

Cecily was in the midst of assuring her hostess that she was very comfortable in the room when Meacan appeared at the door. "Ah, Mrs. Barlow," said Lady Mayne. "Good. I would speak to you both." She crossed the room and lowered herself to the window seat, where she sat with one arm outstretched, her palm resting on the carved handle of her cane. "On the matter of the inventory, I have decided that our current arrangement is no longer acceptable."

Cecily sensed Meacan freeze like a mouse that knows it must move quickly in a short amount of time, but is not yet sure which direction will be wisest. "I cannot imagine what change would be necessary," she said humbly. "I assure you the project is proceeding in an orderly—"

"I am not terminating your employment, Mrs. Barlow. I am simply making an adjustment in order to increase your pace."

Cecily and Meacan exchanged glances. If Inwood was indeed trying to delay the transfer of the collection, it seemed Lady Mayne meant to resist. Lady Mayne continued. "Of course I intend to do all that is required of me by God and by law to ensure the fulfillment of my husband's last wishes. I hope I have shown as much. I am sure I have." She directed a defensive look at the shelves as if she were responding to an accusation leveled at her by the silent bones.

"But I cannot think," she went on, "that he would have

wished to prolong my custodianship of his"—she paused and pursed her lips as if she had tasted something she did not like—"his *curiosities* over so many weeks. Therefore I took it upon myself to inquire among the visitors who have come to pay their respects whether any among them might be of assistance. I have since accepted the offer made by one Richard Thursby, Esquire, who not only impressed me with his gentility and decorum, but promised to commit not only himself, but his two secretaries to the endeavor. He believes that with the four of you working together, the inventory can be finished before the close of June."

"Ah yes, it would be Thursby," said Meacan with a knowing nod. "He does like to involve himself."

Cecily decided to risk voicing her guess in the hope that Lady Mayne would confirm the truth of it. "Have you mentioned this to Mr. Inwood? It was my understanding that he was the one who suggested an inventory be done."

"Yes, it was," said Lady Mayne irritably. "And yes, I have informed him of my agreement with Mr. Thursby. Mr. Inwood's only concern is that the inventory be thorough, and be accorded the full amount of time required for it to be so."

Meacan gave Cecily a knowing look that clearly communicated her thought. *Of course that would be his concern.*

"But as much as I appreciate Inwood's dedication to my husband's interests," Lady Mayne continued, "I see no reason why I should not take steps to hasten the project to its conclusion. I wish to make arrangements for the remainder of my own life, you understand. I wish to have this business concluded."

"Quite understandable," said Meacan. "When is Thursby to arrive?"

"He will be here at any moment. When he arrives, you

will acquaint him with your method, and the work you have done thus far. Then you may agree on how to proceed."

"Certainly." Meacan hesitated. "But I hope Mr. Thursby will be patient. I was to accompany Lady Kay on an errand this morning."

Lady Mayne shook her head. "Oh no, that cannot meet with my approval, Mrs. Barlow. Recall that you are in my employ. If you are to remain in this house, I must insist that there be no further delays. Am I understood?"

Outwardly, Meacan was all deference, but Cecily saw the mutiny in her eyes. "You are. My apologies, Lady Mayne."

Lady Mayne rose slowly to her feet. Her right hand gripped her cane. Her left went to the wall beside the window for support. "If you require an escort, Lady Kay, you may take Martha or John."

"Thank you," said Cecily. "But I will be quite—"

Cecily was cut off by a sudden cry from Lady Mayne, who had started for the door only to be jerked sharply backward. The veil attached to her tall widow's bonnet had caught on one of the sharp teeth of the shark's jaw mounted to the wall. Cecily and Meacan sprang forward to help as Lady Mayne fumbled in confusion with the snagged cloth.

The moment she was free, Lady Mayne confronted the shark with a look of furious hatred and embarrassment. "Vulgar perversion," she spat out. "The very walls of this house are malevolent." Refusing further offers of assistance, she righted her hat and smoothed the veil into place with shaking hands. "I will return to my room," she declared. "And I will not venture so far from it again. Not in this house."

When she had gone, Meacan touched a finger to the point of one of the shark's teeth and shook her head. "I told you," she said to Cecily. "The collection has a will of its own. That said, if Lady Mayne and this shark were to meet in open water, I am not certain the shark would emerge the victor. She looked capable of smashing the whole room to pieces."

Cecily was only half listening as she searched her trunk for a pair of gloves. "What do you know of the man who is coming with his secretaries?"

Meacan dropped her hand and heaved a sigh. "*Thursby*. One of the collectors, of course. As conceited and officious a pedant as you'll ever encounter. He will speak for two hours without cease on the subject of his *Plants of Cornwall* and the number of copies it has sold. When you meet him, you must ask him who provided the illustrations. You will have to ask him, you know, because you will not find my name printed anywhere in the—What are you doing?"

Cecily had found her gloves and was putting on her hat. "While I'm gone," she said, "you can observe the mourners. This is the last day they have to visit. Perhaps something of interest will occur."

Meacan frowned. "I am not certain I like the idea of you going to the Holt house alone."

"I will be careful," Cecily assured her.

"See that you are. Don't trust young Alice just because her face is fair. The knife that killed Sir Barnaby has a keen blade. Even her dainty hand could have driven it home."

*

William Holt, whose masonry contributed to London's weight upon the earth an impressive number of ornate fireplaces, lintels, and buttresses, owned a respectable house on Bread Street. From the portrait of him that hung in the entrance room, he appeared hewn from the same rock with which he made his living. He had the set, serious features of a man who applies himself to his work and who wishes it to be known, above all else, that he applies himself to his work.

After Sir Barnaby's crowded walls and Covo's deranged ones, Cecily found the inside of the Holt house almost disconcertingly spacious. Without the muffling abundance of material, sounds lasted longer, bouncing and echoing through the rooms. There seemed to be more air available for her to breathe. The house, she realized, was so normal, with its comfortable furnishings, tasteful artwork, and signs of family life—deeply etched scrapes on the floor where diners had pulled their chairs to and from the edge of the table, a blanket draped over the back of a settee by the fire, a basket overflowing with scraps of cloth and yarn—that she herself, her mind populated with skeletons and corals and mermen, felt like a curiosity that didn't belong.

The servant who answered the door apologized. The mason would be occupied at a building site for the rest of the day. When Cecily said she had come to pay a call on Alice, the servant responded that the youngest daughter of the house was not accepting visitors.

"Perhaps you might ask her if she would speak with me. Tell her it's Lady—" Cecily hesitated. Whatever Alice's condition, Cecily suspected she might need some further gesture of goodwill to gain admittance. "Lady Sweetbay," she said.

The servant complied, and upon returning pronounced that Alice would see her. He escorted Cecily up the stairs to a well-lit sitting room adjoining a bedchamber. Alice was in a chair by the window. The expression she turned to Cecily was glazed, the pink of her complexion replaced by blue shadows beneath swollen eyes. She rose slowly, dismissed the servant, and indicated a chair for Cecily.

"Lady Kay," she said, sinking back into her seat. Her voice was hoarse. "How did you discover who I am?"

Cecily sat down. "Mr. Dinley had in his keeping a letter written by your brother. I believe it was intended for you." She drew the letter from her pocket and held it out to Alice, who took it with a shaking hand. She unfolded it, glanced at the words without reading them, and folded it closed again as one might slam a door against the cold.

"I cannot," she whispered. But she set the letter in her lap and placed a hand over it protectively.

If there had been any doubt in Cecily's mind as to whether Alice knew her brother was dead, it was gone now. "I am very sorry," she said softly.

Alice did not answer. In the silence, Cecily took in the room around them. The tangle of ribbons that festooned the dressing table did nothing to brighten the grief that filled the space more convincingly than any black drapery in the Mayne house could. She turned back to Alice. "The house is not decorated for mourning," she said. "Do your parents know—"

Alice's mouth twisted. "Know what? That my brother is—" The sentence that had begun in anger ended in choked silence. Alice took a shuddering breath before she spoke again. "I have no mother. My father received word of it yesterday. I've known since the day of the tour, but I didn't tell him. I hoped when he did learn of it he would—we would grieve together. But he says Anthony's name is still forbidden in the house."

Cecily hesitated. "What was the cause of the estrangement between them?"

"Father didn't want Anthony to go to sea. He wanted him to stay here and become a mason." Alice turned her face to the window. "But Anthony had made up his mind the moment he learned there were shores beyond the horizon. When we were children, he would show me maps and journals full of wondrous accounts of adventures—" Alice's voice trembled and she cut herself off. When she spoke again, her tone was dull and constrained. "They quarreled every time they spoke. At first Father thought he could stop Anthony by refusing to give him money."

"But your brother found a patron in Sir Barnaby," said Cecily quietly.

Alice nodded. "Sir Barnaby said he would fund every journey on which Anthony embarked if, in return, Anthony sent him rare and curious objects. I have never seen Anthony so happy as he was the day Sir Barnaby made him that promise."

"And your father forbade Anthony from accepting Sir Barnaby's sponsorship."

"My father declared that if he didn't agree to stay at home and take up an apprenticeship, he could count himself a man free of his family name and inheritance." Alice paused. "Anthony left the next day. That was four years ago, and since then my other brother has been our father's only son. Now—now he truly is."

Cecily wished Meacan were with them. Meacan's expressive features would have moved at once in mirrored understanding of the young woman's feelings. Cecily's own face felt stiff and unnatural. She searched for words of condolence, rejecting the formal phrases that would chill the interaction and the informal ones that would presume an intimacy with the grieving girl that she could not claim.

Cecily was not aware that her eyes communicated intelligence, and a promise that she would attend to what she heard. Nor was she aware that the silver strands mingled with her dark hair and the fine paths traced around her eyes had the power to suggest to a despondent young woman that life could be endured. Evidently, Alice found in Cecily's quiet, composed presence an invitation to speak that none had yet offered her.

"I saw a painting of a shipwreck," she said. Her eyes were fixed on a distant horror. "I am told a Dutchman painted it. The sea was reaching up like a claw from below. The waves, like fingers, clutched the hull. Behind the pitching ship, clouds spread over the sky like angels of death. They permitted the passage of three yellow sunbeams from the heavens to the raging sea, as if to mock the fates of the crew. Around the ship were broken timbers and the rocks that were smashing it to pieces. And I—I think of him in that painting, Lady Kay. He must have been so frightened. And I was here"—she gestured bitterly at the hearth—"staying warm in the winter and daydreaming about pirates like a—like a spoiled—a spoiled, stupid child." She started to sob.

Cecily shook her head. "Your own safety is not something of which to be ashamed."

"I thought," said Alice brokenly as she gazed out the window, "that Walter would have come by now. I thought he would have been concerned. He—he has been my only confidant and friend and I—I expected . . ."

She doesn't know what has happened, thought Cecily. But why should she? How would the news have reached her, here on the other side of the city, alone in her room with her tears and her visions of shipwrecks? "Alice," she said. "Do you know that Sir Barnaby Mayne is dead?"

But Alice, lost in her own dark ocean of grief, looked un-comprehendingly at Cecily. "Sir Barnaby?" She spoke gasp-ingly, through tears. "No—no, it is *my brother* who is dead. Sir Barnaby is alive. Sir Barnaby invites no dangers to *his* door. He sends others out to meet them for him. To—to face the roaring seas while he waits with his cabinets like a—a *dragon* on his treasure, collecting and collecting and collect-ing." Alice was growing hysterical. "Anthony's life for—for *bones* and—and *trinkets*." She stopped suddenly. "Sir Barn-aby is dead?"

In clear, brisk sentences, neither dwelling on details nor omitting them, Cecily told Alice what had happened. She told her how, shortly after Alice's own departure, Sir Barn-aby had received a note from a courier that had made him cut short the tour. She explained how the guests had sep-arated. She described how she, Inwood, and Carlyle had come upon the body. Finally she told Alice of Walter Din-ley's confession and escape.

Alice listened calmly, almost gratefully, as if the account, however terrible, had ushered her back into a world away from the crashing waves on which she had tossed alone un-til Cecily's arrival. But at this last revelation, she drew in a sharp breath. "Walter? *He* killed— No." Alice's expression cleared. "No," she repeated. "He could not have committed such a deed. There has been a mistake. You say he *confessed?* But why would he—" Alice lifted her hand to her mouth. Her eyes widened. "He couldn't have thought—he couldn't have—that is I—I said— Oh, Lady Kay, I did *say*—"

Cecily saw that Alice was becoming increasingly agitated. "Why don't you tell me everything," she said. "Beginning with how you came to be at the Mayne house that day under an assumed name."

The calm authority in Cecily's voice appeared to soothe the young woman. She regarded Cecily through reddened eyes. "When my father said I could not write to Anthony, or receive letters from him, I was desperate," she began. "I seized every opportunity I could to hear news of his adventures. That is how I came across the notice of a presentation to be given at the Society. Someone was to read the most recent report sent by Anthony Holt to his patron, Sir Barnaby Mayne."

A note of pride entered Alice's voice. "I was determined to attend, and I did. My father never knew. I called myself Alice Fordyce and stayed very quiet near the back of the room. It was easy not to draw attention to myself. There was such a crowd there to listen. Everyone wanted to hear what Anthony had written, though the stories he gave to everyone else were not so wondrous as those he saved only for me."

Alice's voice shook. She steadied and continued. "I discovered that the man who read the report was Sir Barnaby's curator. That—that was how I met Walter—Mr. Dinley. I spoke to him after the presentation. He was kind, and he answered my questions so patiently. I decided to confide in him."

"You told him your real name."

Alice lifted her gaze, in which affection and grief mingled equally. "Not only did he promise to keep my secret, but he offered to be my servant. He told me that if I wished to write a letter to my brother, he would include it in Sir Barnaby's next missive to Anthony. And he promised that when Anthony's next box arrived, he would search it for a reply to my letter, and deliver that reply to me."

"And he was successful."

Alice nodded. "In the two years that followed, I have received three letters." Her gaze dropped to her lap. "Four, now," she whispered. She closed her eyes. When she opened them, Cecily saw that they burned with anger. "Every letter was precious to me," she said. "And yet I began to worry for him. Sir Barnaby was asking him to take bolder risks, to explore treacherous coasts and venture into inhospitable countries, only so Sir Barnaby could satisfy his appetite for rarities. As much as I loved to read of Anthony's voyages, I began to fear that he was exposing himself to danger only to please his patron." She paused, and in her fixed expression Cecily had a fleeting glimpse of her face as it would be when she was older.

Alice continued. "Three weeks ago, Sir Barnaby received a new box from Anthony. Walter, with whom I am now—" She hesitated.

"Friends," Cecily supplied.

"Friends," Alice repeated. "Walter proposed an idea. Sir Barnaby was soon to give a tour of the Mayne collection. I would attend the tour under the same assumed name I had used to attend the presentation at the Society. Thus, I could see for myself the objects that Anthony had wrapped and sent with his own hands, and if there was another letter for me, Walter could give it to me then. The plan was made, and I could hardly conceal my excitement as the day approached. I gave an excuse to my father. He even ordered a carriage for me. I stayed in it until it was almost at Bloomsbury Square. I walked the rest of the way so that the driver could not say where I had really gone."

"Which is how you came to lose your way and come to the garden door," said Cecily.

"Yes. In my excitement, I became disoriented. But Mrs. Barlow admitted me, and I thought all was well. I did notice that Walter was behaving strangely. He seemed several times to want to separate me from the group. But I was in such transports I paid him little attention."

"I expect he was desperate to get you away before the tour reached the second-floor landing," said Cecily. "He knew that when we came to the place where Sir Barnaby kept the crates sent by your brother, you would be subjected to the revelation there, in front of everyone."

Fresh pain misted Alice's eyes. "It would have been the same for me wherever I heard it. But you are right. When I fell and cut my hand, he insisted on taking me downstairs. I—I guessed something was wrong when he did not take me to the kitchen, as I assumed he would do, but led me instead to the garden—into a greenhouse. He tore a strip of cloth from his shirt and bandaged my hand with it—" Alice looked down at her palm. The wound had healed to a faint pink line. "And he—he told me. He hadn't learned of it himself until a few hours before. He said if he could have stopped me from coming, he would have. He blamed himself. He told me—" Alice's voice caught. "I—I cannot remember now. He was trying to be kind, but I heard nothing. I only remember saying, again and again, that I *hated* Sir Barnaby. That *he* should have been the one to die. He *made* Anthony sail too far. He forced him to do it so that he could fill his shelves. I told Walter that it should have been Sir Barnaby who died. I said if I had the strength I'd—" she lifted eyes full of guilt and confusion. "I said I'd—I'd kill him if I could." She looked up. "And now he is dead, and it is as if I *did* kill him."

"Unless you stabbed him through the heart," said Cecily, "I assure you, you did not."

Alice looked at her hand. "No," she said quietly. "No, I did not."

"When Dinley returned alone," said Cecily, "he told us he had put you in a carriage. That wasn't true, was it?"

"I was in no state to be put into a carriage," said Alice. "But he knew someone would come in search of us if we did not rejoin the group. He told me to wait there, in the greenhouse. He said he would return as soon as he could and take me home himself."

"And did he return?"

"I'm sure he must have, but I didn't wait." Alice shuddered at the memory. "As soon as he was gone I knew I could not stay there. It was like a prison. I wanted only to be home. So I left—I went out the same way I had come. I ran down the alleys and did not stop, even when I had no breath. I found my way home. Even now I am not certain how I did not come to harm. But I swear to you, that is how it happened. I didn't kill Sir Barnaby. I—I might have meant what I said when I said it, but I didn't kill him. And neither did Walter. But Lady Kay, I think Walter might have thought I—I think he might believe he is protecting me." A little color had returned to her cheeks and she uncurled herself slightly from the chair. "What should I do?"

"You should remain here, where you are safe. Do you have any idea where Dinley might have gone?"

"No, but if he comes to find me, I will not betray him to the authorities."

"We do not know the whole truth. He still *could* be dangerous."

Alice shook her head. "He is not. I know Walter."

Cecily saw the determined set to Alice's brow and knew she could not control the girl. "Mrs. Barlow and I are trying to find out who really killed Barnaby Mayne," she said. "And as far as I know, we are the only ones who are. If you hear from Dinley, telling us would be the best way to help him."

"Why?"

"Because while he may not know it himself, there is a good chance he possesses the information we need to identify the true murderer."

Alice considered this, then nodded. "I will tell you."

"Good. Now, did you notice anything that day that might assist us? Something you heard, perhaps, or something you saw that did not seem important at the time?"

Alice retreated into silent thought. Suddenly her eyes opened wide and she straightened in her chair. "There *was* something. Do you remember, right at the beginning of the tour, when Sir Barnaby showed us the emerald with the markings on its surface?"

Cecily pictured the wide, shallow drawers that comprised the lower half of the cabinets in the Stone Room. In preparation for the tour, several had been left open, jutting out like display tables, making progress through the room even more awkward. She remembered Sir Barnaby standing over one of them, pointing out his favorites among the rows of colorful stones. She recalled the dull gem that had glowed green when Sir Barnaby held it to the light. "I do," she said.

"Just as we were leaving," said Alice, "I happened to turn around. There was only one person still in the room. Everyone else was already in the hall. It was—I cannot recall his name—the man who looked as if everything bored him."

"Mr. Carlyle?"

"Yes, Carlyle. He had been bending over that drawer, and was just straightening up. When he saw me, he smiled and slipped his hand into his pocket. I wasn't sure of what I'd seen, and I haven't thought of it since. But now—" Alice paused. She concentrated for a moment on the memory, then nodded firmly. "Before he put his hand in his pocket, I saw a gleam of green between his fingers. I am certain it was the emerald."

*

The distance between Bread Street and Bloomsbury Square was a mere two miles. Cecily never liked to subject herself to a bruising ride in a coach unless it was necessary. Today, she found the idea of being enclosed in a dark box and relinquishing control over her own speed and direction particularly onerous. It was almost noon. The morning light had long since banished night's dangers, and there were many hours still before it would be time to prepare for their return. She decided to walk.

The sturdy Holt house doorstep abutted a busy thoroughfare like a stalwart boulder at the edge of a fast-flowing stream. Before abandoning it and stepping into the crowd, Cecily wanted to be sure she could picture the way back. As she traced her imagined path, her unfocused gaze took in a man standing in the shadowed entrance of an alley on the other side of the teeming street. Her attention slid over him, but his face remained in her mind. Among all the people her view from the doorstep encompassed, he was the only one who had been looking at her. She glanced back at the place where he had been standing. He was no longer there.

She told herself it was a small thing, easily dismissed, and started on her way. At first, simply traversing the street required her full attention. She kept to its edge, away from the thundering hooves and carriage wheels that churned dirt into ever-changing alchemies of offensive odor. Everyone else was doing the same. Her shoulders jostled against shoulders clad in silks, wools, cotton, rags, and leathers while her knees bumped against pigs and sheep being led to market. Overhead, carved and painted signs urged her to seek entertainment in *The Star, The Mermaid,* and *The Three Cups.* The sky was the same faded blue as the bed-curtains in the Mayne guest room.

Half her mind was dedicated to navigation, the other half to cabinets, emeralds, and occultists. As she walked, the latter subjects began to encroach upon the former. The more preoccupied she became with thoughts of murder, the more she allowed her preference for quiet over noise and for solitude over crowds to influence her movements. She continued northwest, but without noticing, she did so on smaller and smaller streets and alleys.

The first inkling of unease came when she stopped concentrating on Sir Barnaby's death long enough to notice that when her own thoughts quieted, the space around her did, too. Walls and corridors of stone now separated her from the thoroughfare, and she could hear it only distantly. Inadvertently, she had wandered into the dense network of shadowed alleys that filled the spaces between the city's palaces, boulevards, and squares. She chastised herself, and turned to retrace her steps.

Behind her, outside the open door of a tavern, a button peddler was urging his wares on a silent listener who was not looking at the wood and metal disks arranged like planets on black wool, but at Cecily. She froze. It was the same man who had been watching her when she left the Holt house. She was certain she recognized the sharp, protruding jaw and small eyes set beneath heavy brows. His features had the carved appearance of a seaman's, and he was dressed in the rough and shapeless clothes of a dockside laborer.

Their eyes met, and any thought Cecily had of coincidence vanished. He looked at her with recognition and, chillingly, with purpose. The alley seemed suddenly more enclosed than it had before. Cecily's eyes flitted over its other occupants. There was only the peddler, an old woman selling apples, and two inebriated gentlemen making their way to the tavern door with swaying steps. She could not depend on help.

She glanced quickly over her shoulder. The alley terminated in a closed iron gate. From where she stood, there was no way to tell if it was a dead end, or if a sharp turn to the left or right connected it to another alley. Even if there *was* a way forward, it would only lead her deeper into a maze she did not know. This struck her reasonable mind as the height of folly. She would have to go back the way she had come, which meant she would have to pass the stranger who had followed her. The peddler was still accosting him. It would be best to go at once, before he was left alone.

As she started toward them, the attack in the dueler's field crept into her memory and she felt again the choking mud and the pressure between her shoulder blades. Her breath shortened. The peddler began to shuffle away. The man remained where he was, standing beside the tavern door, his eyes on her. She drew closer, close enough to see that the whites of his eyes were bone yellow, and to smell his rank odor. She was almost level with him when, for the first time, he moved. She saw his hand slip beneath a ragged edge of his jacket. Dread filled her, slowing her steps as she watched the hand emerge holding a knife. He held it casually, as if in invitation.

Cecily had no choice but to walk almost directly toward the blade. Her heart pounded and her muscles tensed in readiness. Then, in one breathless moment, she was past him. Fear itched her spine as she hurried forward. Sculpted figures carved on church doorways followed her progress with frozen eyes. Perpetual gloom hung about her, as if she were in the place where night stayed hidden during the day, bitterly resenting its exile.

She almost fell into the bright bustle of Holborn. A small fruit market surrounded her with a mosaic of fresh and rotting colors. She looked over her shoulder. The man was not there. This time she did not hesitate to hail a coach, which she took to the door of the Mayne house.

As she knocked, another coach drew slowly past the house and stopped a little way beyond it. The horses stamped and shook their heads, but no one emerged from within. The door of the Mayne house opened and Cecily heard Martha's voice. She started to turn, then stopped. Something had moved among the trunks strapped to the top of the carriage. As she watched, a figure rose slowly from where it had been crouched between them, and descended easily to the ground. The carriage continued on. Martha was urging her to come in. Cecily stayed where she was, waiting. She knew that if it was the same man who had followed her, he would show his face. A moment later, he did. She thought, but could not be sure, that he gave her a small, malicious smile before he turned and walked away.

CHAPTER 23

The emerald had grown in a vein of quartz fed by the liquid heart of the earth. In the three thousand years between the day it was pried from its rocky setting and the day it became part of the Mayne collection, it had been given to kings and wrested from them. It had been embedded in one of the eye sockets of a sculpted god. It had glittered on the hilt of a sword wielded in sunlit battle. It had adorned the throat of a doomed bride. It had also acquired etchings: on one side the lion-headed Chnoubis, on the other a ring of Greek letters that spelled a long-forgotten name. The label written in Sir Barnaby's hand claimed that it had belonged for a time to the historian Tacitus, who had found it on the shores of the Baltic Sea.

Cecily stared down at the green stone in chagrin. She had remained in the Stone Room after Martha had admitted her to the house, and had gone directly to the drawer as soon as Martha had left the room. Instead of the empty space she had been expecting, she had found the emerald resting exactly where it had rested the first time she had seen it. To its right was a corroded gray nugget identified by its label as a curious piece of metal found in the ruins of Troy, to its left a few flakes of ash purportedly taken from Mount Vesuvius. It occurred to her that Alice could have been mistaken about *which* stone Carlyle had taken. She traced a finger along every row in the drawer, but nothing appeared to be missing.

As she slid the drawer closed, a carriage deposited a small group of mourners outside the front door. Visits to the house had become increasingly sporadic. Most mourners had elected to come on the first or second day, a choice due in part to excitement, and in part to the knowledge that despite the undertaker's considerable embalming skills, the experience lost charm with each passing hour. Martha returned to admit the newcomers, and Cecily went upstairs in search of Meacan.

She located her in the library, along with Mr. Thursby and his two secretaries. Thursby, a papery little man in spectacles, was already presiding over the inventory with an air of querulous self-importance. His secretaries, young and bewigged and difficult to distinguish from one another, were bent dutifully over their registers, their quills scratching across their separate lists almost in unison. Meacan, who had been attending to Thursby with a subtly mutinous expression, brightened when Cecily came in. After performing hasty introductions, she mumbled an indistinct excuse and pulled Cecily from the room.

In silent agreement, they descended to Sir Barnaby's study. Meacan closed the door behind them. She spoke before Cecily could. "The constable came here while you were gone. Walter Dinley has been captured."

The words tore through Cecily's carefully arranged thoughts. "Captured? How? Where is he?"

She had spoken too loudly. Meacan's eyes flew to the door, then back to her with a look of warning. She guided Cecily deeper into the room. "They found him at a wretched inn at the harbor," she said in a low voice. "Evidently the constable has had men asking questions there since the day of the murder. Dinley was waiting to board a ship to the Americas, just as Hugh said. They dragged him directly to a justice of the peace, and he's been committed to Newgate to await trial."

"Newgate." Cecily felt a sickening lurch in her stomach. The name of the prison evoked horrific tales of fever, torture, and corruption. She sank into the chair by the hearth.

Meacan picked up the stool from in front of the book wheel and positioned it so that when she sat the fabric of their skirts overlapped in a sea of blue and green linen. Their faces were almost touching. Meacan's expression reflected Cecily's feelings. "His chances of surviving until his trial are slim enough," she said. "There are three hundred prisoners trying to breathe inside walls built to hold half that number. He'll be starving and sick and surrounded by felons as likely to kill inside as they were outside. And some say the guards are worse." For the first time since their reacquaintance, Cecily saw tears well in crystal crescents along Meacan's lower lashes.

"As for his chances of surviving *after* the trial," Meacan continued, "they are slimmer still. And there is no hope at all if he pleads guilty."

"Can we speak to him?"

The question pulled Meacan somewhat out of her dejection, though her expression remained grave. "There's the official way—that's a permit from the Lord Mayor—but it would take time, probably more time than Dinley has."

"And the unofficial way?"

A small smile of approval ghosted across Meacan's lips. "A bribe at the gates. Of course we cannot count on being successful. It's no small thing to enter Newgate. But I thought we could make an attempt on the way to Covo's tonight."

Cecily nodded agreement. "And in the meantime, we will continue our efforts to discover the truth."

Meacan wiped her eyes and squared her shoulders. "That is just what I was about to say. So now you may tell me. Did you find the girl? Is she Alice Holt?"

"I did," said Cecily. "And she is. I believe we were right. Dinley lied to protect her. But I do not believe she killed Sir Barnaby." Cecily gave Meacan a full account of her conversation with Anthony Holt's grieving sister. She concluded it with the discovery that the emerald Alice claimed to have seen Carlyle take was not, in fact, missing.

"Carlyle a thief," said Meacan musingly. "I *can* see it. He seemed intelligent enough, and I did catch a glimmer in his eye that suggested a modest degree of artistry. But we can't accuse him of stealing an emerald that hasn't been stolen."

"No," Cecily agreed. "Nor can we save Dinley with Alice's testimony alone."

"Certainly not," said Meacan. "I expect the judge would say they conspired together and send them both to the scaffold."

"There is something else," said Cecily. "I was followed."

"Followed?" Meacan gasped. "Who followed you?"

"A stranger." Cecily told her what had happened.

"I don't like it," said Meacan darkly when Cecily had finished. "He sounds too similar to the villain I shot in the field."

"He didn't try to kill me."

"I don't find that sufficiently reassuring."

Cecily's eye was caught by movement over Meacan's shoulder. Someone was in the garden. She stood and went to the window. John was returning to the kitchen from the greenhouse, a bright posy of leaves and sprigs in one hand. The sound of the clock on the mantelpiece chiming four brought her attention back to the room. "Did you say it was about twenty past five when you found Sir Barnaby dead?"

Meacan had also risen to her feet. While Cecily was at the window, she had picked up a crystal ball from the mantelpiece and was now passing it back and forth between her hands. She made a humming sound and squinted one eye as she considered. "Twenty past or half past," she answered.

"That makes sense," said Cecily. "It was a few minutes to five when Sir Barnaby went downstairs. As far as we have been told, no one saw him alive after that, which means he must have been killed roughly between five and five thirty. It is a narrow window of time."

"But wide enough for a murderer to climb through," said Meacan sagely.

"Let us set aside the question of motive and speak only of opportunity," said Cecily. "Could *anyone* in the house have committed the murder?"

Meacan spoke slowly. "The servants say they were all together in the kitchen. Unless two are lying to protect the third, they have alibis. Otto Helm was not at his desk when I came in search of him, which means he *could* have been in the study stabbing Sir Barnaby. Alice told you she fled through the garden door, but no one saw her go. Dinley has given no account of himself, but we can assume, at least, that he was searching for Alice, having returned to the greenhouse to find it empty. Carlyle—" Meacan looked questioningly at Cecily.

"Claims to have been wandering the collection rooms alone," said Cecily. "According to him, Warbulton was absorbed by the guestbook in the library, but Carlyle only glimpsed him there. Warbulton could easily have slipped down to the study and returned without anyone noticing. Inwood says he was in the dining room reading, but we know he left it at least once, earlier, when he met Alice and Dinley coming downstairs."

"So we cannot eliminate any of them," said Meacan.

"No," said Cecily. "But to me, Helm's is the story that seems the most suspicious. He told me he was at his desk all afternoon, intent on his serpents, oblivious to everything around him. What was it that took him away? And why did he then depart the house with such haste?"

"I agree," said Meacan. "And being robbed doesn't excuse him from being questioned. He's alert, you know, and has been poring over books and specimens all day. What style of interrogation would be best? Should we challenge him, or put him at ease?"

"Neither. *I* will speak with him. *You* will resume your work with Thursby. Our task will become more difficult if Lady Mayne terminates your employment. How does it go with him?"

Meacan sighed. "It is not as terrible as I expected it to be. I have divined that Thursby simply wants an excuse not to work on his latest book, which he claims is going well but isn't. How could it? A compendium of all history, philosophy, and language—it is no wonder he's running from the project as if it has teeth."

While Meacan was speaking, Cecily's gaze had fallen on the smooth oaken sheen of the three closed cabinets. She waited until Meacan had finished, then nodded toward them. "I cannot help but think that the Rose cabinets are somehow connected to Sir Barnaby's death."

Meacan followed her look. "Rose. That's the traveler who left Sir Barnaby his collection."

"Yes, and remember that, according to Hugh Ashton, Dinley thought his employer was devoting an unwarranted amount of time to studying Rose's objects."

Meacan crossed the room and tugged the handles one by one. "Locked," she announced. "As you said."

Cecily joined her. "The objects are all listed in the register upstairs. They appear to be mostly shells, stones, bones, and birds. They come from distant places, but I saw nothing to indicate that they are of particularly high value."

"There must be keys somewhere," said Meacan. She surveyed the room, her face alight with new interest. She began to move along the shelves, shifting birds, peering into vessels, and turning over shells. Cecily did the same. Meacan let out a short exclamation when she reached into a porcelain vase glazed with blue dragons and pulled out a brittle brown object as large as her fist and pocked with holes. She sniffed it, grimaced, and handed it to Cecily, who examined it. "It's a sea sponge."

"I know," said Meacan. "But what is it doing in a vase?"

"And lacking a label," said Cecily, handing it back. "This is what I meant about carelessness even in the most orderly collections. It's the reason inventories are never as straightforward as you expect them to be."

Meacan dropped the sponge back in the vase. They searched for a few minutes longer, but without success. "It's like looking at a face and not being able to tell what it's thinking," said Meacan, staring at the closed cabinets. She tapped her knuckles softly against the oak. "Who is there?" she whispered. Her expression turned speculative and she touched a finger to the keyhole. "I *could* open it, you know. I have tools for just such occasions."

The sound of footsteps and voices reached them from the hall. Together, they stepped back from the cabinets. "Later," whispered Cecily. "You should get back to the inventory. I'll speak to Helm. As for John Rose, surely if anyone can tell us something more about him, it would be your Signore Covo."

Meacan brightened. "You're right," she said. "Covo will know. We'll ask him tonight."

★

Otto Helm was sitting up in the cot. He was surrounded by as many specimen jars as it had been possible to fit within his limited range of movement. They covered the floor, as well as a chair and a low table that had been drawn up close beside him. Inside the jars, coiled and still, snakes waited like supplicants at a lord's hall.

The bed was blanketed in books. Small stones and statuettes were being used as paperweights to hold them open. An army of illustrated serpents, patterned with diamonds and stripes and spots, seemed to slither over the pages. Some of the books were old. The illustrations were woodblock prints and the Latin texts told of oracular dragons and basilisks born of birds. Others were new, and boasted deft engravings and watercolor pigments that mimicked sun and shadow. The page nearest to Helm depicted a viper. The engraver and colorist had captured the sinuous heft of its form so realistically that its fangs appeared ready to sink into Helm's hand.

Helm's attention was on an open notebook, into which he was copying neat lines of text. When he heard Cecily on the stair he looked up, then back down. "A moment, Lady Kay, I must beseech of you," he said, continuing to write. He murmured under his breath. "Belly transversely . . . black and yellow . . . sides of neck alternately . . . head large—" Helm stopped and twisted to consult one of the books. The motion was too quick. With a gasp of pain he froze. His eyes squeezed shut.

Cecily hurried forward. "Mr. Helm? Are you alright?"

Helm opened his eyes and immediately set his pencil back to the page. "It is the *Vipera aquatica*," he said. "But this next, I cannot be certain." He tried to turn again, winced, and slumped back against the wall.

Concerned, Cecily removed two jars from the chair beside the bed and sat down. "You will aggravate your injuries if you do not rest, Mr. Helm."

With obvious reluctance, Helm placed the pencil in the crease of the notebook. "I wish to make use of time," he said. "And I am comforted when I am working."

Cecily understood the sentiment, and believed he meant it. She had seen that the instant he set his pencil down, the lines of suffering on his face deepened, as if work had been holding the pain at bay. "You are very thorough," she said, glancing at the notebook. It was a new one that had been purchased for him at the stationer's, and already it was almost half full. "I often think I will be able to remember more than I can," she went on. "I always regret my arrogance when I consult my notes later and find them lacking in detail. It must have been difficult for you, on the day of the tour, to maintain your concentration despite the many distractions."

Helm sucked in a short breath. Cecily could not tell whether he was reacting to a jolt of pain in his bruised ribs or to her words. "Always, there are distractions," he said after a moment. "It is necessary to learn discipline. To set the distractions aside."

"But you did at least find the time to leave your desk for a little while that day." Cecily perused one of the books as she spoke and did her best to keep her tone idle.

"To leave my desk?"

"When Mrs. Barlow went in search of you," said Cecily.

"Mrs. Barlow was in search of me?"

"To ask you a question about illustrating serpents," Cecily lied. "She said she was disappointed not to find you."

"But Mrs. Barlow has not come to ask—"

"Well, of course she did not want to bother you during your recovery. But I was surprised when she said she had failed to find you, as I'm certain I remember your mentioning you hadn't left the Serpent Room at all that day."

"I went to the library," said Helm. "I went to consult—" He cast his eyes over the books in front of him. "To consult the work of Mr. Gesner," he finished, pointing to one of the volumes.

Cecily set down the book she was holding and took up the one he had indicated. "*History of Four-Footed Beasts and Serpents*," she read. "*Describing at large their true and lively figures, their several names, conditions, and kinds*. Was there anyone in the library when you were there?"

"Hm?" Helm looked at her blankly.

"When you went to get this book from the library, did you see anyone?"

"Alas, Lady Kay, I am not remembering. My injuries, perhaps, are responsible. But allow me please to tell you the virtues of Mr. Gesner's book, which though it was published almost fifty years ago, is still of relevance. The anatomical drawings, you see, are most advanced. Still I would suggest if you wish to make a further study of serpents, that you allow me please to make other recommendations."

Cecily made several more attempts to ask Helm about the day of the murder, but he would not be diverted from the object of his fascination. At last, she brought the interaction to a polite conclusion and left him to his serpents. She carried from the room the feeling that, for a man dedicated to the advancement of knowledge, he had been singularly, one might almost think deliberately, unhelpful.

CHAPTER 24

Cecily and Meacan planned to stay the night at Covo's. Cecily, initially dubious, had allowed Meacan to convince her that navigating the city in the small hours of the morning after the lamps had burned out would expose them to far more peril than any they would face at the coffeehouse. Covo, Meacan explained, counted among the inconsistencies in his character an unbreakable regard for the rules of hospitality. No matter how many rainbow-painted butterflies, stitched chimeras, and sculpted fossils he sold to collectors eager for novelties, his views on the sacred trust between guest and host remained uncompromised. At least Meacan thought they did.

The excuse given to Lady Mayne was that they had been invited to join one of Cecily's cousins at the theater for a musical production of *Macbeth*. As it was an evening performance, and they had no wish to disturb the household with a late return, they had accepted the cousin's offer of accommodation. They would be back early in the morning so that Meacan could continue work on the inventory. Lady Mayne, busy with final arrangements for the funeral, made no protest other than to comment on the questionable morality of the stage.

It was true that *Macbeth* was showing that night, but as theatergoers shuffled down candlelit aisles in search of seats and singing witches practiced their infernal ditties, Cecily and Meacan were making their way by coach to Newgate Prison. They were as attentive to their surroundings as the fading light permitted. Several times, Cecily thought she glimpsed the man who had followed her, only to see the face change to one she did not recognize.

Night had fallen when they arrived. Clouds hurried across the sky as if they feared being caught on the points of the thin crescent moon. Light seeped from dirty lamps, pooling on mud and stone outside the prison walls. The grim structure seemed to Cecily to loom larger than it was, augmented by the shades of past walls that had been broken and burned over the terrible course of its existence. There were few who did not believe that ghosts wandered the shackle-lined halls, trapped in the dungeons from which not even death could liberate them.

Cecily's request that she and her friend be allowed to speak with a prisoner was met with disbelieving laughter from the guards at the gate. Meacan's offer of coins, though tactfully delivered, was also refused. She and Cecily continued to press their case until the amusement of the guards became tinged with suspicion. What were two ladies doing alone on a moonlit night trying to enter the gates of Hell?

Meacan signaled to Cecily that they would get no further, and requested that the guards agree at least to deliver a note to the prisoner. She offered to pay the same amount for this small service as she had been willing to pay to see him. This time, the bribe was accepted, and the small, neatly folded square of white paper was carried away like a beacon through the gate into the prison's black maw. Cecily and

Meacan had composed the message earlier in the evening. *The one you are protecting is innocent*, it said. *We suggest you begin admitting that you are, too. Maintain hope, and we will soon have you back among your books and your friends, this ordeal a fading memory.*

Around them, the figures passing the prison were indistinct, like shadows that had slid out from under its walls. It was time to continue to Covo's. They lingered only long enough to ascertain that the session at the Old Bailey was to commence on the following day. Meacan explained that this was good news. The schedule of trials would have been already set before Dinley's capture. "He won't be tried until the next session," she said as they searched for another coach. "I don't like to think of him languishing in there, but it gives us time."

A creaking coach stopped for them. Cecily's eyes lifted warily to its roof while Meacan peered into its dark interior. She nodded that it was safe. "I know a clerk," she said as they climbed in. "I'll send him a message and ask him to contact me at once if there is word on Dinley's case."

The coach shuddered into movement as if the horses were frightened. As it drew away, Cecily looked out the window. The implacable face of the prison, with its dim lantern eyes, looked back. Meacan's voice interrupted her thoughts.

"In a thousand years," said Meacan, in the tone she used for her dark musings, "when that monstrous dungeon has at last crumbled, I'll wager a collector will have a piece of rubble on a shelf with a label saying it came from the ruins of Newgate. And visitors will pick it up and wonder how many prisoners touched that very same stone with their emaciated hands before they met their cruel ends. I wonder if a stone remembers what it has seen." Meacan was silent for a moment. When she spoke again, her tone was at once lighter and more resolute. "A question," she said, "the answer to which awaits us at the bottom of a pot of strong posset after we've pulled Dinley from the jaws of that place and thrown the murderer into them."

*

That Covo had taken pains to ensure the comfort of his two visiting eavesdroppers was evident at once. The room to which he showed them was furnished with two comfortable couches made up as beds, each with a night table beside it supporting a candle and a neat pile of books. While the décor of the room was consistent with the rest of the establishment, two areas of one wall had been cleared of their ornaments. In front of each cleared section was a brocade chair.

Meacan gifted Covo with a chuckle of amused admiration as she set her eye to the peephole located at a convenient height above one of the chairs. "Remind me," she said, stepping away from the wall, "never to conduct private business in this house."

"Tonight's entertainment has not even begun," Covo replied, "and already you are drawing astute conclusions. On the subject of entertainment, I hope you will approve of the books with which I have populated your nests for the evening. A number of rare botanical tomes for Lady Kay, and a collection of stories for you. The tales are not to be published until next year, but I have persuaded their compiler, one Monsieur Galland, to provide me with an early manuscript. I hope they will serve, should you desire a reprieve from your spying."

Meacan recovered her cup of brandy from the mantelpiece. "I've never seen conjuration before. I assure you I have no intention of looking away if there's a chance they'll succeed in bringing a spirit into the room or opening a window to a fairy realm."

Covo's eyes glittered. His lips curved in a smile. "If the fairies decide to grace us with their presence tonight, I will not credit it to the pontifications of the occultists, but to the allure of the company now present in my humble home." He lifted his cup, a silver goblet with a jeweled stem, and bowed to them both before drinking from it. "Tell me," he said, straightening. "What news from the Mayne house?"

Meacan, who knew that the price of admittance to the secret chambers of Covo's coffeehouse was information, was ready for the question. Lit by firelight that enhanced her quick-changing expressions and lively gesticulations, she offered Covo one choice detail after another about the visitors who had flowed through the Mayne residence over the preceding days. Cecily was impressed by the number of them Meacan had recognized, and by the quantity of information she had overheard. Meacan reported on quarrels, alliances, acquisitions, dalliances, favors, assignations and, like sugar flowers artfully applied to an elegant confection, the occasional theoretical debate, including a simmering argument between a Mr. Gibbs and a Mr. Marten over whether Noah had kept a fishbowl on the ark.

Covo listened with the attention of a hawk scrutinizing a field, searching for the telltale twitch of a mouse's tail. His expression was guarded. Cecily could not identify which pieces of information interested him and which did not. When he did let slip a smile or a quirk of an eyebrow, it seemed that it was Meacan herself, and not the facts she was relating, that had inspired the change. Meacan concluded her recitation with the news of Walter Dinley's capture and imprisonment.

"Of that I am aware," said Covo. "Though I understand he has not yet stated his motive for killing his employer. If he takes it with him to the grave, we must hope an inspired storyteller will embellish the tale. At present it is rather—" Covo paused. "Rather *unsatisfying*."

"We believe it to be connected to the three locked cabinets in Sir Barnaby's study," said Cecily. Meacan and Covo both turned to her in faint surprise. Until then she had remained mostly silent, deferring to Meacan's better understanding of their sly host. But she sensed that Covo was toying with them, and felt compelled to resist the spell of distraction cast by the room.

"How intriguing," said Covo. "Have you unlocked them?"

"We cannot find the keys," said Meacan.

Covo raised an eyebrow. "I would not expect that to deter you."

Meacan, clearly taking this as a compliment, inclined her head in acknowledgment of it. Cecily spoke again. "According to the registers, the cabinets contain the collection of a man called John Rose. Have you heard of him?"

"Ah," said Covo. "John Rose."

Meacan turned to Cecily. "I told you he'd know."

Covo smiled. "You flatter me, dear Sea Radish."

They waited for him to continue. But he crossed his arms over his chest and gave a single shake of his head. "I am not a book to be opened and read," he said.

"Not a—" Meacan's expression turned stormy. "Do you *know* why Sir Barnaby kept those cabinets locked?"

The burgundy velvet of Covo's shoulders shimmered as he lifted both hands in mock helplessness. "I cannot say."

"We have been informed that Rose was a traveler," said Cecily. "And that he died in Jamaica. Can you not tell us more?"

Covo shifted from his position at the mantelpiece and moved to the door, his progress duplicated by candlelight shadows. "Allow me merely to suggest that Rose is a man, living *or* dead, whom I advise you to avoid. Now if you will pardon me, I believe the first members of the little gathering are arriving. They will require a welcome."

There were indeed sounds of footsteps on nearby stairs. Covo drew a mask from his pocket and fixed it over his face. "I do not know if they hide their faces," he said. "But I intend to do what I can to contribute to the atmosphere."

Meacan was frowning at Covo. It was obvious that she was simultaneously annoyed by his refusal to share his knowledge and intrigued by the way his mask complimented the angles of his cheeks and jaw.

They heard hushed masculine voices outside the room.

"The servant pointed this way."

"Are you sure? It's very dark."

"Something is moving at the end of the hall. Do you see it?"

"A mirror. Only a mirror."

Covo, with a smile, put his finger to his lips and left the room. "Good evening, gentlemen," they heard him say. "Please, a room is prepared for you. It is just here."

Meacan and Cecily sat down in the brocade chairs. Each set an eye to one of the openings. The room on the other side of the wall was lit by candles set in front of mirrors. Light caught on jewels set into the eyes of skulls arranged as decoration on a long table in the center of the room, alongside several mummified hands. The table was surrounded by chairs.

"Go in, go in," came Covo's voice as the door creaked open.

Three gentlemen, not in masks, entered the room and took seats at the table. One by one, more arrived. "*Non vi, sed mente,*" announced each new arrival with somber grandiosity, to the echoing reply of the others.

"That's Mr. Merden," whispered Meacan, as a tall man with hollowed cheeks and bushy white eyebrows entered the room and intoned the words in a rumbling baritone. "No surprise. I've always thought he had the look of a sorcerer."

Some drew out notebooks. Others set glinting objects on the table before them. These were difficult to see amid the shifting shoulders and voluminous wigs, but Cecily identified a box made of bones, a painted chalice, and an iron scepter. When they had all taken their seats, one was left unoccupied.

"Now that you are all assembled, I will leave you to your business," announced Covo. "Refreshments will be provided when you ask for them. Should you summon Mephistopheles, send word and I will have my servants prepare additional food." With these words, he left the room. He did not rejoin Cecily and Meacan. They heard him pass their door and continue down toward the chatter of the coffeehouse.

A man with round cheeks and several chins stood up and adjusted his spectacles. "It would be usual," he said, in a self-conscious voice, "for our leader to welcome us to this evening's meeting of the Philosophers of Night. But as he is no longer with us . . ."

A chair scraped across the floor as another man stood up, his prominent nose lifted as if to augment the effect of looking down it at his fellows. "I would put myself forward as temporary president of our group."

There followed a lengthy discussion of the formalities of nominations and elections, during which Cecily heard Meacan stifle more than one yawn. The men concluded at last that the one among them called Mercurius would be best suited to the position.

Mercurius, whom Meacan whispered was actually named Francis Bedgberry, suggested that it was time to call for refreshments. The next half hour was spent in the ordering and serving of wine, liquor, chocolate, and small dishes from Covo's kitchens. When at last this was complete, the new leader gestured with a hand holding a savory pastry to the empty chair. "I see we are missing young—what was his chosen name—"

"Angelicus," someone supplied.

"Ah, yes," said Bedgberry. "Angelicus."

"It's my opinion we'll do as well without him," said another. "Never quite *one of us.*"

"No, no," agreed Bedgberry. "And on the subject of those who are not with us, let us take a moment to acknowledge with due formality the recent grievous loss to our company."

The short silence that followed was broken by a man in a white wig that in the candlelight looked like a drift of snow lit by the lantern of a passing carriage. "Run through by his *curator*," he said.

"The loss to our group is serious indeed," said the man with the cherubic cheeks. "Only last month he loaned me a copy of the *Occultis Naturae*, which I considered very generous of him."

"There is no doubt," intoned the deep voice of Merden, "that his collection has served, and will continue to serve, as a precious vault of knowledge. But allow me to say without disrespect that I did think Sir Barn—"

"Ah—ah—ah—" interrupted Bedgberry. "His chosen name, please."

Merden looked annoyed. "The one we called *Leonatus* did bring to our group a degree of *engagement* with the subject of the occult that I—I will admit it now—I always found out of place, even *inappropriate* in our modern era."

The men around the table murmured agreement, their heads nodding and bobbing like starlings pecking for seeds.

"Always a source of discomfort, though I hesitated to mention it."

"There was a—a *credulity* to his approach."

"In truth I was embarrassed on his behalf."

A sense of shared relief emanated from the table. The men continued to eat and drink. "I don't suppose," said one, "that Inwood will agree to sell an item or two from the collection? I would be most gratified to add a *Consecrationum* to my own shelves, and I understand Sir Bar—Leonatus had a fine edition."

"I was hoping for a chance to acquire his beetles and butterflies," said another. "A box or two, at least."

Merden shook his head. "No chance of it," he said. "We all know Inwood. Man of his word. No, the Mayne collection will stay the Mayne collection even unto the end of time, and scholars not yet born will speak of him with admiration as the years roll on. Would that we all had such friends."

There was a collective sigh. Cecily felt an elbow prod her side. She sat back from the wall and turned to Meacan, who gestured her off her chair. "But they aren't *magicians* at all," whispered Meacan when they were away from the wall. "They're *collectors*. Nothing more. Here to discuss what they have and what they want. If they aren't chanting spells within the hour, I'm going to sleep."

Meacan was almost true to her word. An hour later she was in bed, but not asleep. Tucked beneath a luxurious silk blanket, her head on a brocade pillow, she held the book of tales Covo had left for her open to the candlelight and read with complete absorption until the light burned out.

Cecily remained at her post for the duration of the meeting. As Meacan had predicted, the occultists made no attempt to conjure spirits, raise the dead, summon familiars, or tell the future. They did pass various new acquisitions around the circle. Among the recent purchases were three silver rings engraved with the names of archangels, a number of jeweled sigils, and a round beryl crystal in a wooden stand. A new edition of *A True and Faithful Relation of What Passed for Many Years Between Dr. John Dee and Some Spirits* occupied them for some time. There was a brief argument over the relative power of hexagrams and pentagrams according to alchemists of the previous century. Bedgberry shared a circuitous anecdote of an argument he had witnessed between a farmer who claimed that his daughter had been cured of epilepsy by a magic ring and the local minister who insisted the ring was demonic and must be cast away. After three hours, the bottles and plates were empty and the group departed with pink cheeks and satisfied yawns.

The night passed quietly. In the morning, Meacan announced to Cecily that it had been the dullest meeting of warlocks she had ever seen. "Witches are vastly more entertaining," she said, as she splashed her face with water from a basin of translucent blue porcelain patterned with golden fish. "If I hadn't enjoyed Galland's tales so much, I would wish we had gone to see *Macbeth* instead." She patted her face dry and consulted a mirror framed by onyx dragons. "We learned nothing we didn't already know."

"But we did," Cecily replied.

Meacan swung around. "You think one of them had a connection to the crime?"

"Not someone who was there," said Cecily. "Someone who wasn't."

"Oh." Meacan frowned. "You mean the empty chair?"

Cecily nodded. "The phrase they used, *non vi, sed mente. Not by force—*"

"—*But by the mind,*" finished Meacan. "A fair motto for a society seeking to command without touch."

"On the day of the murder," said Cecily, "I heard the first part of the phrase spoken in greeting to Sir Barnaby."

"By whom?" Meacan demanded.

Cecily slipped the last pin into her hair. "If your Signore Covo can provide us with an address, I suggest we delay our return to the Mayne residence long enough to pay a call on Mr. Humphrey Warbulton."

CHAPTER 25

It was a chill morning. An unbroken gray cloud hung low and heavy over the city, its center dipped like the belly of a great whale swimming slowly overhead. Whitlowgrass and wall-pepper brightened walls with flecks of white and yellow that defied their drab surroundings.

The Warbulton house was so new that soot had not yet insinuated itself into its seams. The nests built by venturesome sparrows on the ledge of its uppermost story were the first ever to be constructed there. The front door, freshly painted and boasting a polished, ornate knocker, seemed to be calling out for attention, as if it could not wait to see a visitor's reaction to the grand staircase behind it. Purchased by the senior Mr. Warbulton, who had risen from an apprentice in a tailor's shop to a wealthy textile merchant, the house had become the London residence of his son, who had proven himself an astute businessman in his own right.

Humphrey Warbulton was not receiving visitors. This information came from a well-dressed servant whose meaningful glances and fidgeting fingers made it clear that he was bursting to say more, and was only barely restraining himself with the bindings of professional decorum.

"Tell Mr. Warbulton the matter is urgent," said Cecily. "Tell him Lady Kay and Mrs. Barlow must speak to him."

The servant hesitated. "But the master won't even—" He stopped, silently testing the various ways he could complete the sentence. Appearing to find none that constituted loyal behavior, he bowed and asked them to wait.

An odor of paint and polish lingered in the entrance hall. Unlike the Mayne residence, with its single, serviceable stairwell extending from kitchen to garret, the Warbulton house featured the new style of a grand staircase connecting the ground floor to the first in an elegant sweep of curving bannisters and airy space.

The entrance hall itself was more familiar. It was lined with shelves and cabinets of polished oak almost identical to the ones in the Mayne house, and the objects arranged on them were labeled with little red tags in clear imitation of the Mayne model. But where Sir Barnaby's shelves were full, Warbulton's were not. And where there was a confident, settled quality to Sir Barnaby's displays, which had enjoyed years of dedicated attention, the objects on these shelves were grouped awkwardly, like guests at a poorly planned party who cannot find a common topic of conversation. A marble bust looked uncomfortable next to a skull, which in turn seemed uneasy in the shadow of the towering porcelain vase beside it.

From upstairs, they could hear the voice of the servant. "A Mrs. Barlow, yes, *Barlow*, and a Lady *Kay*." Cecily thought she heard a reply, but it was muffled and unintelligible.

The servant returned. "My sincere apologies. He will not see you."

Meacan, who had been perusing the shelves, approached the servant and addressed him in a friendly voice, a conspiratorial tilt to her shoulders. "I've worked for collectors, too," she said. "I know all about their caprices. One obsession on Monday, another by Friday. Impossible to know what they'll want and when." She sighed. "Tell me, what is it that's preoccupying yours?"

The servant looked from one woman to the other. Neither of them had displayed the usual surprise expressed by visiting ladies when confronted with rows of stuffed birds and opalescent shells and sculpted deities. His eyes moved from Cecily, standing with squared shoulders and an air of authoritative intelligence, to Meacan, at once softer and sturdier than her companion, inviting confidences with the glint of humor and compassion in her autumn eyes.

Overcome by a desire to find out what they would do if they stayed, he lowered his voice to match Meacan's. "Mr. Warbulton has been closeted in his room for two days. We"— his eyes flickered downward and they understood him to mean a kitchen full of uncertain employees—"we've sent for his father to come for a visit. We couldn't think what else to do."

"Has he given an explanation?" asked Cecily.

The servant shook his head. "He only rails at anyone who comes near the door to leave him be. We've left trays of food, but he's eaten hardly any of it." The man lowered his voice further. "The chambermaid thinks he's afflicted with madness."

Meacan patted Cecily on the shoulder. "Lady Kay spoke to him, you know. Two days ago. Or tried to, but it was like trying to understand speech underwater, wasn't it?" She gave Cecily a look that impressed upon her the need to maintain solidarity with the servant, who was their only key to the upper floors.

"He did not seem mad at the time," Cecily murmured, half to herself as she remembered her interaction with the quaking Warbulton. "It seemed more that he was *frightened*."

Meacan addressed the servant again. "Let us speak to him through the door. Perhaps he will reveal something to us that he has not to you. And think, if he can be out of distress when his father arrives, thanks to your intervention, you may take credit for it."

The servant, persuaded, agreed to take them upstairs. They climbed the grand staircase to another, less ostentatious one, at the top of which he stopped at a closed door. A steady stream of words was audible from within.

"Is there someone in there with him?" asked Meacan.

The servant shook his head. "As far as we know, he's alone."

Meacan pressed her ear to the door. "It's *Latin*," she announced.

Cecily moved to join her. "Mr. Warbulton?"

The reply was instant. "Go away!" It was Warbulton's voice, but it was thinner now, like a stream choked by ice.

"We met at the home of Sir Barnaby Mayne," said Cecily. "Mrs. Barlow and I must speak with you. May we come in?"

"I will admit no one," came the reply. "I cannot be certain you are—" He paused. "*Yourselves*."

Cecily looked at the servant, who shook his head. "Said the same to me yesterday," he whispered.

"We are certainly ourselves," said Cecily. "If you are in distress, perhaps we may be of some help."

"No—no one can help."

Meacan and Cecily exchanged glances. Meacan mouthed two words to Cecily, who nodded and stepped aside so that Meacan could take her place at the door. "We have come," said Meacan, using the commanding affectation of royalty

Cecily remembered well from childhood games, "on behalf of the Philosophers of Night. In a token of our mutual
trust, I offer you these words." Meacan paused before she
announced with slow grandeur, "*Non vi—*"

There was silence. Meacan drew in a breath to speak
again. Then from within, high and nervous, came the reply.
"*S-s-sed m-mente.*"

"Good," said Meacan. "Now please open this door and
let us speak to you."

"Wait there," came Warbulton's voice. "Do not move."
They heard footsteps approach. The latch of the door rat-
tled. The steps retreated quickly. "C-come in."

The door swung smoothly open and Cecily found herself
facing a room that looked as if it had been the center of a
maelstrom. Books and papers covered the floor in complete
abandon. Clouded crystal balls were scattered over them like
beads from the broken necklace of a giant. Gleaming amulets were strewn about like autumn leaves. Cecily's breath
caught as her eye fell on a basin a quarter full of congealing
blood. The floor around it was littered with white feathers.
Drops of blood led from the basin to the window, through
which Cecily assumed the sacrifice had been tossed. A heavy
fragrance of smoldering bay hung in the air. The fireplace
was heaped with blackened branches twisted like charred
bones.

Warbulton was standing in the center of a chalk pentacle drawn on the floor. Around it were scrawled words and
symbols. His face was thin and pale. He wore a dressing
gown and a silk turban in place of a wig. As Meacan and Cecily approached, he shrank away. "If—if you are demons,"
he said. "I—I abjure you. You cannot cross this line." He
pointed a shaking finger at the chalk.

Meacan made a quick assessment. "He doesn't have a weapon," she said. Then she strode forward, touched her toe over the line, and stepped back. "You see?" she said. "Not a demon. Now—" She swept an arm to indicate the chaos around them. "*What* have you been doing?"

Warbulton remained where he was. "I—I— How did you know? About the Philosophers of Night?"

"That doesn't matter," said Meacan.

Cecily, hoping to ease the man into a more communicative state of mind, spoke gently. "You were missed at the meeting."

"Missed?" squeaked Warbulton. "Missed?" His face relaxed a fraction. "You—you mean they asked after me? Even Mr. Merden?"

Cecily nodded. "They wanted to know why *Angelicus* had not joined them."

Warbulton's eyes grew wide. "Did—did they say anything about—about the curse? About how it might be undone? Have they discovered a way?"

Before Meacan or Cecily could speak, they were interrupted by a yelp from the doorway. They turned to see the servant. His eyes bulged as he beheld the room. He shook his head in refusal. "Curses," he murmured, and took a step back into the shadow of the hall. "Curses and sacrificed geese. I'll not stay in a house to wait for Satan, not for all the comforts and fine clothing." With another shake of his head, he disappeared.

Concern vied with amusement on Meacan's face. She cleared her throat. "Your friends did not address with any, ah, specificity, the subject of a curse. Perhaps you would enlighten us as to what you mean?"

Warbulton looked aghast. "But—but how could they not speak of it?"

"I'm afraid we do not know to what curse you are refer-ring," said Cecily. "Has it to do with the death of Sir Barn-aby?"

"Of course it does!" cried Warbulton. "It has *everything* to do with it!" He looked at their faces. Seeing no understanding, he began to rub his arms as if he was cold. "You don't know," he whispered. "You don't know how to stop it. All rests with me. I must find—" He dropped to his knees and began to search through the papers scattered around him. "You have interrupted me. I must find the counter charm." He began to mutter feverishly as he turned over pages. "*Zorami, zai-tux, elastot* . . . figure of the talisman should be embroidered in silver upon poppy-red satin . . . steeped in blood of the mole . . . dipped in the juice of the pimpernel . . . when the moon is in her full light—"

"Mr. Warbulton," said Cecily firmly. "I understand an apology may usually be expected in advance of disillusion-ment, but in this instance I am convinced we are doing you a service. The Philosophers of Night are *not* magicians. They do not practice magic. They do not cast curses and, I am fairly certain, are in no danger of incurring them. They ac-quire talismans and grimoires because they have an interest in them, an *historical* and *theoretical* interest. If you believe Sir Barnaby's death was connected to a curse, you have been misled. It was a human hand that held the knife."

"The knife!" The word burst from Warbulton like a cry of pain that became a whimper. "If only—if only I'd never heard of that—that terrible blade."

Cecily made an effort to understand. "Are you speaking of the knife with which Sir Barnaby was killed?"

Warbulton wagged his head. "Yes—no."

"You are not making sense, Mr. Warbulton," said Meacan.

Warbulton's tongue flicked out to lick his dry lips. "It isn't the knife *with which* he was killed. It's the knife *that killed him*. Don't you understand? It was the knife *itself*."

A glimmer of light shone into Cecily's thoughts. She pictured the knife, the ancient appearance of it, the symbols engraved on its blade and the black gemstones embedded in its hilt. She spoke slowly. "Are you saying you believe the knife that killed Sir Barnaby carried a curse?"

"Yes." Warbulton sagged with the relief of having company in his realm of fear.

Slowly, with many stops and starts and digressions, his tale emerged. He had been overjoyed when, six months earlier, Sir Barnaby had invited him to join the Philosophers of Night. Warbulton had read every book Sir Barnaby recommended on the subject of the occult and, guided by Sir Barnaby, had become increasingly convinced that the power to summon spirits was within reach. The attitude of the other collectors had not dissuaded him. It was Sir Barnaby he wished to emulate, and Sir Barnaby *believed*.

"The meetings were always held at night," said Warbulton. "That—that is why I was so eager on the day of the tour. I'd never seen the Mayne house in daylight."

"I overheard one of these meetings," said Meacan. "The one that took place less than a week before Sir Barnaby died. Were you there?"

Warbulton, now sitting cross-legged in his pentacle, gave a tremulous nod. "I—I had no presentiment of danger. It was just like every other meeting. We each presented to the group the books and objects we had acquired on the subject of—of spells and spirits."

"Was that when you saw the knife?" asked Cecily.

"No. That is, yes. But only—only an illustration of it. Sir

Barnaby had made the purchase through an agent in Madrid, but the object had not yet been delivered. He had hoped it would arrive before that evening, but he had to content himself with—with giving us a description of it."

"And you are certain it was the same knife that was used to kill him?"

"An ancient blade," whispered Warbulton. "Perfected on the day of Venus, the moon being in the sign of Capricorn. A handle of white wood cut from a single stroke of a new sword. Engraved with glyphs of awful power. With it, a man can kill an enemy though they stand an ocean apart. The blade can cut the very fabric of the world and open doors to other realms. It might even unlock the gate to Hell."

Cecily glanced at Meacan. For all her previous amusement, Warbulton's words were having an effect. She looked chilled. Cecily felt it, too. The blood in the basin seemed redder than it had before. The papers rustled and whispered as if snakes nested beneath them.

Warbulton went on, lost now in his own horror and excitement. "When Sir Barnaby spoke of the knife, his eyes glowed in that peculiar way only his did. He was certain the knife would advance him in his studies, if only he could learn how to *use* it. But he knew it would be dangerous—" Warbulton swallowed. "According to the texts, the knife carried with it a dreadful curse, one that would smite any who came near to it and, knowing it for what it was, failed to become its master."

With an effort, Cecily shook the cobwebs of superstition from her thoughts and concentrated on what she wanted to know. "What happened on the day Sir Barnaby died?" she asked. "What did you see?"

The answer was disappointing. "I—I saw nothing," said Warbulton.

"Then you and Sir Barnaby didn't speak of the knife that day?"

"In truth, I had not thought of it since he'd described it at the meeting. I didn't know he had yet received it. It—it was not until Mr. Carlyle set it down so close to me and I *saw* it that I knew. I recognized it at once from the picture. I knew—I knew the curse had fallen upon Sir Barnaby."

"Why did you return?" asked Cecily. "On the first day the house opened to mourners, why did you come? And what were you doing in his study?"

Warbulton scrabbled through the papers. Seizing one, he slid it across the floor out of the pentacle toward them.

Cecily read the title aloud. "*A Spell to Lift Curses From Objects.*" She was silent for a moment. "You were trying to break the curse."

Warbulton nodded miserably. "I recited the spell, but I fear it has done no good. I did not know how to pronounce the words. And the components I have here—I am not certain they are correct. I was supposed to scratch into the circle here these words with the quill of a white male goose, but I am not sure the one I purchased *was* male. And I have not found a black cat. And I cannot help but think that if Sir Barnaby could not do it, he who knew so much, what hope have I of escape? And if Mr. Dinley was—was possessed by the curse, then my own death might come with a face I trust—a face I—" His eyes turned wary. "You—you must go now," he said.

"But Mr. Warbulton, you—"

"Go!" he shouted. "Be gone, demons!"

He was beginning to shake again and looked as if he might rush forward at them. Meacan took Cecily's arm and pulled her toward the door. "This is a trouble he'll have to solve himself," she whispered. "Come."

They reached the door. Just before they left, Cecily stopped. "Mr. Warbulton, were you in the library the entire afternoon? From the time Sir Barnaby left the tour until the time the murder was discovered?"

He looked slightly startled by the simple question. His face returned to a more normal set. "I—I was, yes."

"And during that time, did Otto Helm at any point come to the room?"

Cecily watched carefully. Whatever fears tormented him, they did not prevent him from answering her with calm certainty. "No," he said. "No, I am certain he did not."

CHAPTER 26

It was nearing eleven by the time they arrived back at the Mayne house. Meacan, who had expected a reprimand from Lady Mayne for her late return, was relieved to learn that the widow had ordered a carriage and gone out, taking Susanna with her. According to Martha, the unplanned errand was prompted by a letter that had been delivered shortly after Lady Mayne returned from church that morning. Of the contents of the letter and of Lady Mayne's intended destination, Martha was ignorant, but she said the widow had left in a state of considerable excitement.

Martha was cleaning the floor outside the study, which meant that further attempts to open the locked cabinets would have to wait. To Cecily's surprise, Otto Helm had made a painful journey down the staircase and ensconced himself in the Serpent Room. Thursby and his assistants had arrived earlier in the morning. As soon as he heard that Meacan had returned, he summoned her upstairs and set her to work in the library amid piles of lists and registers.

The appearance of the undertaker, come to bear the body away to await burial at the estate, incited a flurry of activity in the house that drove Cecily upstairs to the Plant Room. She needed a quiet place in which to think. Alone in the sanctuary of dry leaves, she worked patiently through the identification of another specimen. The pathways of her mind, warped by distractions and obfuscations, began to straighten.

An hour later, reoriented within her own thoughts, she was standing at the window where the light was best, studying a tiny cluster of petals, when she saw movement in the garden. Through the thick glass, she recognized the figures of John and Martha standing outside the open door of the greenhouse. It was clear from Martha's furious gesticulations and John's defensive ones that husband and wife were in the midst of a heated argument.

Cecily returned the specimen to its place and hurried downstairs. The quarrel had not abated when she stepped out onto the veranda, and it continued as she started down one of the gravel paths. John's eyes beneath their bushy brows flickered toward her as she approached the greenhouse. Martha, caught up in her tirade, didn't appear to notice her.

"Is this all?" Martha demanded. "Or have you more to confess? Perhaps you've used one of his fossils to replace the cracked brick in the fireplace? Or filled an ancient urn with your berry preserves? *Well*?"

John's hands, dusted with soil, extended in a placating gesture. "Now Martha, there's no reason to—"

"I'm the only one," snapped the housekeeper. "The only one in the house giving the collection the care the master would expect. The *only one*, now that he's gone."

"Please, Martha," said John. "You know that's not the way of it. See, here is Lady Kay. Let us put the issue before her. I'll wager she won't condemn me so harshly."

Martha swung around. Two spots of color burned on her

thin cheeks. "Yes? Is there something you require, Lady Kay?"

"Only a little air," said Cecily. "But I would be happy to contribute my judgment to whatever matter has led to such a difference of opinion."

Cecily's presence had altered the balance of the inter-action. Martha's anger, buoyed on the intimacy of endur-ing partnership, eased from her jaw. John, relieved that the storm had passed, wiped his hands on his jacket. "It is still my opinion that I didn't do any great wrong."

"How can you say so?" Martha pointed into the greenhouse. "Just look what my husband has had the effrontery to do."

Cecily moved to the open door. Inside the greenhouse, the ceiling of which was barely high enough to accommodate a standing adult, were a few raised beds and pots planted with herbs that filled the moist, heavy air with fragrance and added a green cast to the light. She guessed at once what it was Martha wanted her to see. Five bright baubles hung in front of one of the glass panes. There was a gold ring, three jewels that looked like drops of liquid color bisected by the thin twine looped around them, and a clear, faceted pendant that was casting a single, wan rainbow onto the basil leaves.

Cecily turned to John. "Are these from—"

"The cabinets!" cried Martha. "He's taken them and used them as ornaments! In the *greenhouse*."

Cecily turned to John. "*Did* you take these from the cab-inets?"

John shook his head adamantly. "I never did. I swear it."

Martha ducked into the greenhouse and pinched the twine of the jewel nearest to her, lifting it so that the stone became an accusing pendulum, twinkling as it swung. "Of course you did. Where else could you have come by them?"

John lifted his chin defiantly. "I do admit I found them among the master's things, but they'd been forgotten. There was no place for them. They didn't even have labels."

"What do you mean when you say they'd been forgotten?" asked Cecily.

John was eager to explain. "It was when Lady Mayne arrived. You remember there wasn't room for her carriage"—he nodded toward the carriage house—"and I had to shift that great painted coffin out of the way. Well, when I was doing so, I heard rattling inside. It gave me a turn. I assumed it must be old bones knocking about. I thought I'd look, though, just to see, as there was only a small latch holding the lid shut. So I opened it, and there were no bones inside at all, only these jewels. And I thought to myself, if I hadn't found them, they'd have stayed closed up in that dark place. And I thought, seeing as how I wasn't taking them from the property, what was the harm in putting them in the light when they shine so prettily?"

As he spoke, Cecily bent to look more closely at the objects. The ring was formed by two golden dolphins that held between them in their jaws a bezel containing a blue gem. Of the colored jewels, one was red, a garnet perhaps, cut roughly into the shape of a heart, through which light pulsed like living blood. The next was heather purple, and engraved with the proud figure of a man with the head of a jackal.

But it was the green jewel that arrested Cecily's gaze. It was as green as a translucent strand of seaweed soaked and glistening in the sun. On one side, surrounded in stars, was a creature with the body of a snake and the head of a lion, on the other a ring of Greek letters. She recognized the stone. It was the same one Alice Holt had seen Carlyle put in his pocket, the emerald that only yesterday had rested in its drawer in the Stone Room.

After a moment's deliberation, she turned to John and Martha. "I do think," she said crisply, but not unkindly, "that an effort should be made at least to *identify* the objects. A description of them should be added to the registers, if they are not listed there already."

"Good," said Martha, starting to untie the twine. "That is what the master would have wanted."

John shifted his weight from one foot to the other and looked embarrassed. "I had no ill intent," he murmured. "I only thought they would look well in the light."

"And so they do," said Cecily. "In my opinion, after Mrs. Barlow and I have given their identifications our full attention, I see no reason why they should not hang here until Inwood takes possession of the collection."

Martha's expression soured, but before she could object to the plan, Cecily had the gems in her hand and was promising to use every deductive faculty she possessed to do with them just what Sir Barnaby would have wanted done. She turned then and strode briskly back to the house.

There was no one in the Stone Room. Cecily crossed it as quickly as she could, winding between display tables covered in rocks shuffled from the shoulders of mountains, pebbles polished by the sea, and vials of sand taken from distant deserts. She knew the drawer she wanted. When she reached it, she pulled it open and stared down at the neat compartments filled with stones. None were empty. The emerald was still in its place. She compared it to the gem resting in her open palm. They were identical.

*

"Duplicates." Meacan sighed the word as she contemplated the ten jewels arranged on the table in Cecily's room. "False mermen I do not mind. But duplication—" She shuddered. "It makes me uneasy. A reflection shouldn't be able to leave its mirror. How did you find them?"

An hour had passed since Cecily had stood over the emerald in the Stone Room. In that time, she had located doubles of each of the items. Of each pair, only one was affixed with a red label. "They would have been more difficult to locate if they had been shells or skulls or plants," she said modestly. "But there are very few gemstones in the Mayne collection, and their color makes them easy to pick out from their more humble neighbors. The emerald, as you know, was in the Stone Room. The amethyst etched with the god Hermanubis was in the drawer below it. The pendant is a Roman Imperial gem. It was in the Antiquities Room, as was the golden ring. And this, the garnet heart, was in the Artifact Room. According to the label, it was found in a Germanic hoard."

Meacan touched one of the red tags. "The ones in the house were labeled."

Cecily nodded. "And the ones John found in the painted coffin were not."

Meacan's expression flickered between distrust and admiration as she picked up the two emeralds and held them to the light, one pinched between the thumb and forefinger of each hand. Cecily waited, wondering how long it would take Meacan to see what she had. Cecily had a keen eye for detail that she had honed over years of squinting at plants, performing such tasks as distinguishing sepals from petals, noting minute serrations, and spotting the telltale bracts that distinguish leaves from leaflets.

But she had underestimated Meacan, who had spent many more years than she learning how to spot deception. Meacan spoke almost at once, and with relief. "But they aren't identical at all," she said. "The color, for one, isn't quite the same. And the etchings aren't either."

"Try the rings," said Cecily.

Obediently, Meacan set the emeralds down and picked up the two golden rings. "This one is much lighter than the other," she remarked. "And the gold—" She scratched the tail of one golden dolphin with her nail. "It's only paint."

"The same is true of the other pairs," said Cecily. "In each set, one is a cheap trinket, and the other a genuine gemstone."

Meacan compared the rings again. "The one that has the label is the imitation," she said. "Which means that the one John strung up in the greenhouse was the true one." She clicked the rings together as she concentrated. "After Alice told you she saw Carlyle put the emerald in his pocket, we looked for the emerald, found it exactly where it was supposed to be, and so concluded that it had not been stolen. But if—" Meacan paused and closed her eyes.

Cecily, who wasn't going to begrudge her friend the moment of revelation, waited patiently.

Meacan's eyes opened, alight with triumph. "If Carlyle *did* put the real emerald in his pocket, surely *he* was the one who put the false stone in the drawer. I *told* you he seemed the type. He must have assumed that by the time the deception was noticed, it would not be possible to trace it back to his visit. After all"—Meacan looked at the emeralds again—"they are good copies. It isn't easy to tell the difference unless you can hold them beside each other." Her eyes lifted to Cecily's face and the triumph abated slightly. "You'd already come to the same conclusion," she said.

"I've had more hours to consider it," said Cecily. "And you did mention in the library the other day a collector recently embarrassed by the discovery that a number of jewels in his collection were forgeries."

"And I didn't think you were listening," said Meacan, looking gratified. The corners of her mouth tightened into a frown again as she resumed her thinking. "He would have needed to study the objects in advance in order to prepare the copies."

"I thought of that also," said Cecily. "He *had* visited the collection before. Sir Barnaby referred to it. I thought at the time that it was odd he would return to see the house again, given his apparent lack of interest in the cabinets. But Sir Barnaby also mentioned that on his first visit, he brought a sketchbook."

"That fits perfectly," said Meacan. "He must have made drawings of the objects he wanted to steal, and arranged to join another tour once he had the copies ready." She paused. "But how did the stones— the real ones—come to be in the coffin?"

"Carlyle put them there," said Cecily.

"How do you know?"

"Consider that afternoon. When Carlyle, Inwood, and I entered the study and found Dinley standing over Sir Barnaby's body, it was Carlyle who went in pursuit. I think he did so not out of determination to apprehend a murderer, but out of fear of being caught with a pocket full of stolen jewels. In that moment, all was confusion. He could not know whether a constable would arrive ready to make indiscriminate arrests. He realized that chasing after Dinley would give him an excuse to leave the room without inviting suspicion. When Dinley escaped through the garden door, it would have been the work of a moment for Carlyle to slip into the carriage house and drop the jewels into the coffin. And that would also explain why I saw him go into the carriage house on the first day of the wake."

"He was trying to retrieve the jewels," said Meacan.

Cecily nodded. "But by then, John had already moved the coffin and found them."

Meacan picked up the false heart-shaped garnet and turned it over in her fingers. "So it's to be a call on Carlyle, then?"

"I have another idea," said Cecily. "Tomorrow is the day Inwood is to give a tour of his collection. Carlyle said he means to attend. I suggest we do, also."

Meacan's eyes were suddenly catlike. "So we confront him there," she said. "We will have to come up with another excuse for me to leave the house, but that is easily done. The question is, do you think he's a murderer, or only a thief?"

Cecily tapped her fingers against the table as she pondered the question. "If Sir Barnaby had discovered Carlyle's scheme, it would give Carlyle a motive. But the timing does not make sense."

"How does it not?"

"Remember, Sir Barnaby had already been dead for some time when the murder was made known to the house. If Carlyle had killed him and wanted to be rid of the jewels, he would have had plenty of time to jettison them before the body was found. Why wait?"

Meacan set the rings down and leaned against the side of the bed, her arms crossed over her chest. "The lover, the gambler, the grieving sister, the madman, and now the thief. Each still as likely and as unlikely as they were before."

Outside, they heard the click of hooves and jingle of reins. Meacan looked out the window. "That's Lady Mayne returning," she said.

A few minutes later, Susanna came to the door. "You're to come to the dining room," she said. "Lady Mayne wishes to make an announcement."

CHAPTER 27

Lady Mayne sat at the head of the table, waiting in silence for the household to assemble. The ancient coffin loomed in the corner behind her, its smooth bulk making her look smaller than she was. Her shoulders, encased in black silk, appeared slight, the bones of her face pronounced and fragile. And yet, despite this seeming diminution, she held her position with the confidence of a raven on a promontory.

Cecily and Meacan took their seats in the places indicated by the widow's thin, commanding hand. Across from them, Thursby sat squinting through his glasses at the crowded walls, from which ballooned various musical instruments, their strings loose and untuned. His two assistants sat beside him in their identical wigs. Otto Helm, wan and bruised, occupied the more comfortable chair by the fireplace. John and Martha, the last to arrive, remained standing beside the door.

"Early this morning," Lady Mayne began, "I received news most unexpected and unsettling in its nature." Despite the gravity of the words, it seemed to Cecily that Lady Mayne was trying to keep the corners of her mouth from drifting up into a smile.

"I believe you are all acquainted with Giles Inwood," Lady

Mayne continued. "The man my late husband counted as his dearest friend, and to whom he entrusted his *great* legacy. Early this morning I received a letter, the accuracy of which I have since verified, informing me that Inwood has perpetrated a *gross* deception. Not only has he failed to uphold the terms of his promise to my husband, but he has taken advantage of my own unutterable grief to mislead and manipulate me."

"Inwood?" Thursby blinked through his glasses. "Giles Inwood? Surely you are mistaken. There's no better or more honorable man than Inwood among us."

"I, too, was taken in," said Lady Mayne. "He was ever gracious in his manner. He appeared most genuine. And yet it has been revealed to me that he succumbed long ago to sin. He is a *gambler*, Mr. Thursby."

Thursby gave a dry, affronted cough. "I've heard nothing of Inwood frequenting card tables or cockfights, my lady, and I would question the source—"

Lady Mayne cut him off. "It has been a trying day, one that has already required me to learn more than I ever wished to know about these vices. It is true that I am not personally acquainted with the author of the letter, but the courtesy with which Lord Wolfden expressed himself assures me he is a man of education and refinement. My husband's solicitor has since, after the most cursory inquiries, confirmed every detail."

"But *Inwood*," said Thursby, still dubious.

Lady Mayne sighed. "I assure you, I share your surprise. He seems far too rational a man to risk his fortunes and those of others on absurd speculation. For whom but the foolish would invest in rumors of sunken treasure?"

A spark of life revealed itself in one of Thursby's assistants. "Are you speaking of shipwrecks, Lady Mayne? I heard not a week ago of a Spanish galleon, lost these hundred years, found in shallow waters off the coast of Portugal. Full of doubloons, each and every one of its coffers!"

"No," said the other assistant. "No, I heard it, too, but then I heard they hadn't found it after all."

"And thus is Lady Mayne's observation upheld," said Meacan dryly.

Lady Mayne drew in a breath and delivered her next words with dramatic force. "I have it now on more than one authority. Giles Inwood is *ruined.* The sum—" She paused to allow the quiver of emotion in her voice time to make an impression on the room. "The sum my loving husband intended for the augmentation of my comfort in the twilight years of my life, the sum Inwood is *contractually obligated* to furnish, far exceeds his present means. What is worse, he has deliberately concealed his insolvency from me in order to protect his own reputation."

Meacan pressed a hand to her chest and shook her head in sympathy. "How upsetting this must be for you," she said. "And yet how fortunate that the veil of deceit has been lifted. I wonder, did the good Lord Wolfden explain what compelled him to write?"

"Merely his commitment to the truth," said Lady Mayne. "Dishonesty is abhorrent to him."

"I see," said Meacan.

"What do you plan to do?" asked Cecily.

Lady Mayne had her answer ready. "First, I will no longer lend my support to the extended charade that has been imposed upon me. The inventory was Inwood's idea from the beginning. I understand now that it never had anything to do with concern for my husband's legacy. It was only an attempt to prolong the time before Inwood had to make a payment. I will not be so used. Not for another moment."

Lady Mayne took a shuddering breath and drew her sharp shoulders back. She brought her cool gaze to rest on Thursby. "I am grateful for your assistance, but it is no longer needed."

"But—but Lady Mayne," sputtered Thursby. "Surely the inventory remains an essential step in the preservation of—"

"No. It does not." Lady Mayne's words sliced through Thursby's sentence. "No, now that I am freed of the influence of my husband's false friend, my mind is my own, as are all decisions connected to the objects in this house."

Martha stepped forward, pulling her hand from John's gently restraining grasp. "But what of the contract?" she demanded. "You aren't the one who controls the collection."

"If you wish to remain employed in *my* household," said Lady Mayne, speaking with the contented condescension of the victorious, "you will curb your tongue. My errand today was with not one, but two highly respected solicitors, both of whom assure me that, according to law, Giles Inwood has *broken* the terms of his contract with my husband. If he cannot pay for the collection, he cannot have it."

"Then the contract—" Thursby began.

"Is null and void," finished Lady Mayne. "And yet I believe, and the solicitors agree, that the way forward is clear. My husband intended for me to be the beneficiary of the sale of his collection. Therefore, the collection will have to be sold."

"But he wanted it to stay the way it is," said Martha. "The objects all together as he arranged them."

"It is a pity," said Lady Mayne, though it was clear she did not think it a pity at all. "I understand there is no person or institution willing to pay for such a responsibility. It simply will not be possible."

Martha, fists clenched as her sides, looked ready to throw herself across the table. Cecily spoke quickly. "If I might ask, Lady Mayne," she said, "what is it you intend?"

Lady Mayne's pale gray gaze flickered defiantly over the room. She seemed to address herself not to Cecily, but to the walls. "It has been made clear to me by those who graciously came to pay their respects that there are objects in this house of interest to the collectors of the city. What better course of action than to allow the collection to be divided between them?"

"But it will be broken all to pieces," said Martha.

"An inevitable consequence, I am afraid," said Lady Mayne. "To answer your question, Lady Kay, an auction is what I intend. I have already engaged a reputable firm to handle the business in its entirety and, as my presence will not be required, I have decided not to return to London after the funeral. In light of this, I'm afraid I cannot continue to provide you and Mrs. Barlow accommodation in this house after tomorrow. I'm sure you understand."

*

Evening crept silently over the city like a predator trying to catch it unawares before the lamps could be lit. Meacan sat on the window seat in Cecily's room. "For a woman with so little interest in collections," she said musingly, "she learned very quickly how best to dismantle one."

"Perhaps," said Cecily. "On the other hand, I suspect it is something she has been wishing she could do for a long time."

"A fair point," Meacan acknowledged. "And I understand

why Covo wrote to her. Auctions are good business for him. Collectors will pay to ensure they get what they want."

Cecily looked at her in surprise. "How do you know it was Covo who wrote?"

"The name," said Meacan. "Wolfden is one of his favorite pseudonyms."

The house was quiet. Thursby and his assistants had departed, though not before Thursby had, amid deferential coughs, asked if Lady Mayne would consider reserving on his behalf, when the time came, several small items of interest. A statuette of Hermes had caught his attention, and in addition a box of hummingbirds, and perhaps one or two peculiar fossils that he would consider a credit to his own shelves.

Cecily sat at the desk. She had restored the labels to the authentic gemstones, returned them to their places in the house, and rearranged the shells and urchins as they had been the day she arrived. "I cannot help but think," she said, "that the truth of Sir Barnaby's murder, and with it any hope of liberating Walter Dinley, will be irreparably fractured along with the collection."

Meacan's gaze shifted to the shark's jaw. "If only we could employ Sir Barnaby's spells and invocations to charm the skeletons into speaking. We could ask the shark what it has heard. And then ask what it was like to live beneath the sea, swimming through glittering silt and silver shoals."

Cecily regarded the silent, desiccated ring of teeth. The sound of rustling fabric made her turn. Meacan was pulling her hand out of her pocket. She held her fist out to Cecily and uncurled her fingers to reveal two slender pins lying crossed on her palm. "I believe it is time to see what is inside Sir Barnaby's locked cabinets," she said.

Cecily hesitated a moment. "We are still guests in this house. There are rules."

Meacan's brows shot up. "And you believe the rules forbid us from picking a lock? My dear old friend, I do not think you are quite aware of the game board we have chosen."

A memory presented itself to Cecily. She was standing on a pier, waiting alone to board a ship, enduring the silent shame of having been sent away by a husband who considered her a pest to be swept out with a broom. All because she had sought to expose a hidden truth. All because she had asked questions. What was this, here, in this moment, in the house of Sir Barnaby Mayne, but a chance to turn around and refuse to board the ship? Tomorrow, the house would close to her. Tonight, she could demand to know its secrets in the hope that it would save a man's life. She stood up. "I admit," she said. "I am rather looking forward to seeing how it is done."

"You'll have to watch closely or you'll miss it," said Meacan. "I've become quite adept at the art."

They met no resistance on their journey down to the study, though their progress was closely observed by the hollow sockets, painted orbs, and clouded spheres that made up the eyes of the collection. When they entered the room they could hear, faintly, sounds from the kitchen below. John and Martha were cleaning up from supper and preparing themselves for the following day, when they were to accompany Lady Mayne to the estate.

The room was lit with a purple glow as if the sun's final rays had been bruised. Meacan crossed quickly to the locked cabinets and, with a glance over her shoulder at the closed door, braced the sides of her hands against the polished wood and set her pins to the first lock. Her fingers trembled slightly. She rolled her shoulders and shook out her hands to relax them. "I feel as if I'm breaking into a beating heart," she muttered as she inserted the pins into the keyhole and began her deft manipulations.

The lock clicked open. Meacan, instead of looking triumphant, regarded the cabinet warily and did not open it at once. When she did, she stepped back as if she thought something might jump out. Nothing did. Together, they peered inside. Cecily felt a sudden sense of disappointment. She had expected the interior of the cabinet somehow to communicate the reason Sir Barnaby had kept it locked. What she had not expected was that it would look exactly as registers suggested it would.

Most of the shelves were fitted with lidless boxes that could be slid out like drawers or removed completely. Inside each box, specimens of the natural world were arranged with precision in compartments constructed to accommodate each object exactly. The lower shelves contained the larger items, which included specimen jars, skeletons, and birds. Each item was labeled not in red paper, but in white, and every label was written in a controlled, deliberate hand that was not Sir Barnaby's. It did not take Meacan long to pick the locks of the adjacent cabinets and expose the same structure in both of them. Once all three doors were open, Meacan began to lift objects out and examine them. While she struggled in the fading light to read the labels, Cecily set about lighting a candle.

"Stone carried by an eagle to its nest," said Meacan. She returned the spherical gray rock to its place and took up a stoppered vial. "Sand from the coast of Jamaica." She replaced the vial and continued her perusal. "Horns of an antelope of Barbary, shell of a checkered tortoise, head of a horned crow from the East Indies, tooth of a white shark, lignum aloe from Sumatra, gilt bronze brooch"—Meacan leaned in toward the small assembly of specimen jars— "prickled starfish from the Danish sea, and this one here is called the moon fish."

The candle flared to life, illuminating the silver disk of the moon fish in its jar. Cecily held the candle to the open cabinets, careful of its flame. "There *must* be a reason Sir Barnaby kept these cabinets locked."

Meacan had picked up a white shell to which was attached a long and detailed label. "The Venus shell," she read, "used by the French to adorn the bridles of their horses, by the Italians for the polishing of paper, and by the Egyptians to smooth their linen cloth—" Meacan stopped. "It is all very interesting, of course," she said. "But it's no different from— *Wait.*"

She had let the label dangle on its twine and was now holding the shell itself up to one eye. She squinted. "Bring the light here—look."

Cecily held the candle close to the smooth inside of the shell. "I don't—"

"If you tell me you can't see it I'll start to be frightened," said Meacan. "Look closer."

Cecily did. Etched into the shell so lightly it might have been only a trick of the eye was a symbol made up of crossed and branching lines, curves, and tiny circles. She stared. It had no meaning for her. "Do you recognize it?" she asked.

Meacan had already started to pick up other objects and examine them. "No," she said, "but there are others."

Together, they searched the objects for more symbols. Not every item was marked. Of those that were, some bore symbols similar but not identical to the one on the Venus shell. Some were etched with strings of numbers, some with dots that resembled constellations. Still others had words etched into them. "*Demaros*," murmured Meacan. "*Sameron, nerostiel, chrymos—*"

Cecily was frowning over a small skull identified by its label as that of a parrot. The symbol was etched onto the underside of its beak. "I *have* seen this before," she said, half to herself. But where? After a week in the Mayne collection, not to mention hours in Covo's crowded den, trying to place a single glimpsed image was like sifting through a dream. She had seen the skull. No, not the skull, a drawing of the skull. And of the symbol beside it. It had been in a book. She concentrated. Not a book. Not a *printed* book. Handwritten. A journal. A journal open to one page.

Cecily turned around. The book wheel loomed in the corner. She went to it, grasped the wooden frame, and turned. Its gears protested with a loud squeak. Meacan joined her and together, muffling the sound as best they could with their skirts, they turned the wheel so that the book that had been closest to the floor was visible before them. Cecily pulled it from the strap that had bound it in place. On the page to which it had been open was the drawing of the parrot skull and the symbol, framed in a dense network of notes.

"It's Sir Barnaby's writing," said Meacan.

"It's a journal," said Cecily, turning the pages. She recognized more items from the Rose collection, meticulously sketched beside the symbols and words associated with them. But it was the surrounding notes and figures added by Sir Barnaby himself that explained the importance the objects had for him.

"Spells," said Meacan. "This is the diary of a conjurer." She set her finger to a line of words wrapped around a pentacle.

"'Do thou force and compel the spirit into this circle, in a fair and comely shape, without injury to myself or any other creature, that I may accomplish my desired end, by the power of—'" Meacan stopped with a shudder. "Call me credulous if you like but I'm not so foolish as to complete *that* sentence."

It was Cecily who found the letter tucked into the back of the book. It had been read many times, its creases beginning to tear at either end from being folded and unfolded. Written in the same precise hand that had composed the white labels, the letter was addressed to Sir Barnaby.

> The years advance upon me and I find myself ever more distant from England. At the end of each day, as I watch the sun sink into the azure sea, and at night when the moon casts its path over the waves and the phosphorus dances like fire in the water, I express to the spirits of the air my gratitude that it is you, my dear friend, who will become caretaker of these small observations I have made of the world. I am told your cabinets grow in renown. What an honor it will be to occupy one humble corner of your collection, which will surely withstand time's hand, though you and I cannot.
>
> The moment has arrived when I must acquaint you with certain endeavors I have until now pursued in solitude. You wrote to me, long ago, of your conviction that the theories so popular among Society members—I refer to those rules that govern the movement of the heavens and of the earth—have been too quick to dismiss those ancient rituals and sacraments long-veiled in secrecy and persecution. I must apologize now for the response I gave you, offensive in its brevity, unworthy of a friend.
>
> Since that time I have traveled paths that led me at last to the wisdom you so generously offered, and I so ignorantly refused.

My friend, I have uncovered more than even you would believe possible. The powers of which you spoke exist. The tools with which to harness them are scattered through the world by a hand eager to bestow upon true followers the mastery of forces undreamt of by our predecessors.

The means cannot be given. They must be found. I fear I will not complete the quest before it is too late, and I have not breath left to speak the rituals. I must pass this burden to one worthy of taking it up. Upon my death, all that I possess will pass to you. I have left you all the signs I am permitted to communicate. It is you who must interpret them, and find the secrets within. Do so, and you will summon servants who will travel swift-footed and invisible through the air to do your bidding, who will build castles in the blink of an eye, who will defeat your every foe, including that greatest malefactor of all, that shadow Death himself.

The power is there to be claimed. Claim it, and when you do, perhaps you will remember your friend. Perhaps you will come in search of me. I will be waiting. I can say no more, only these names, with which to begin your journey. May Nizael, Estarnas, Tantarez, and Cassiel guide you.

Your faithful companion,
John Rose

CHAPTER 28

A sepulchral hush presided over the Plant Room the following morning as Cecily reassembled her bundles of specimens. Though strands of night still curled through the fog that pressed against the windows, the household was well on its way toward departure. Activity was concentrated in the lower floors. Lady Mayne's trunks had already been brought down, and Meacan had been conscripted to help pack kitchen utensils and food. Otto Helm had taken himself once again to the Serpent Room for a final session of observation and note-taking.

High above the bustle, Cecily pulled the straps tight around her presses and regarded the silent shelves. She could smell the paper and dried herbs. She could picture the flowers, leaves, roots, barks, and fruits sorted carefully within the piles, bindings, and drawers. How many answers waited here, ready for curious minds to come in search of them? She wondered with a pang how much of Sir Barnaby's painstaking curation would survive the auction, and how much would be lost.

She had slept poorly. The bad dreams Meacan had predicted on Cecily's first night in the house had arrived on her final one. She had seen a man she knew to be John Rose

standing alone on a desolate beach, his features shrouded in
sheets of rain, his arms raised as he shouted conjurations to a
stormy sea. With a twirl of a bony finger he made whirlpools.
With another he drew lightning in the shape of dead trees
across the clouds. From the roiling waters, skeleton sharks
breached, their white spines arching against the black sky.

Morning had restored clear thought, but it had not
brought new insights into Sir Barnaby's murder. The contents of Sir Barnaby's journal and of Rose's letter pointed
to occult magic, but Cecily, while acknowledging that the
world was full of mysteries beyond her understanding, could
not accept that a cursed knife was responsible for the death.

She picked up the first of her presses in one hand, gathered her cumbersome skirts with the other, and made her
way carefully downstairs. She was returning for the second
press when she heard the floor creak nearby. She followed
the sound to the Bird Room, where she found Martha. The
housekeeper's compact shoulders were outlined crisply
against the shelves. She was dusting and polishing, her
hands manipulating fragile objects with the deft familiarity
of routine. She looked over her shoulder, saw Cecily, and
turned back to her work. "I've cleaned the collection for
thirty years," she said. "I'll do it until the day every shelf in
this house is empty."

Cecily joined her at the shelves. "I understand you and
John are to accompany Lady Mayne to the estate."

"For the funeral," said Martha. "I'll see the master to his
final rest."

"And after?"

Martha wrapped her cloth tight around the tip of her index finger and gently stroked the dust from the long, smooth
beak of a toucan. "I'll come back."

"Will Lady Mayne permit it?"

Martha replaced the beak on the shelf and pulled open a shallow drawer. It was lined with the bodies of small birds, pressed together in an array of colors like the pieces of a puzzle, their eyes closed, their tiny beaks pointed like darts. Martha used her cloth to extract and crush a spider crawling among them. "Lady Mayne will not want me to remain at the estate, and she knows I won't want to be there. It's the collection I've served all these years, not the family. But if she has any softness in her she'll let me stay here until the end."

"And then you and John will seek a new situation."

Martha said nothing. She closed the drawer and opened the one below it, which was filled with delicate white bird skulls. Cecily thought of the parrot in Sir Barnaby's journal. "Did it trouble you that Sir Barnaby kept so many objects pertaining to the occult? Amulets, talismans, books of spells, items of that nature?"

Martha straightened and turned a clear gaze on Cecily. "You cannot make a record of the world without looking at the bad as well as the good. That is what the master said. There was dark and light in Eden."

"Did he ever speak to you of a man called John Rose?"

Recognition flickered in Martha's eyes. "We weren't so familiar that he discussed his friends with me."

"But you know the name."

Martha nodded. "Of course I know it. They had corresponded for many years. Sir Barnaby was always pleased when a letter came from Mr. Rose. And I remember as if it were yesterday when the Rose collection came from Jamaica. I saw it the day it arrived, so carefully packed, all those strange things from faraway places." Martha raised her eyes to the birds with outspread wings hanging from the ceiling.

"All these wonders. How could any housekeeper wish to spend her days beating carpets that look the same as every other carpet and polishing silver that looks like every other set of silver and cleaning stairs with only portraits for company?"

When Cecily left, Martha was cradling an ostrich egg in the crook of one arm, gently passing her cloth over the smooth surface like a midwife tending a babe. After Cecily had carried the other two presses downstairs, she went to the garden. John was pulling plants, shaking the dirt from them, and lowering them carefully into a sack. "The geraniums will be grateful for the healthy soil and sunshine in the country," he said when he saw her.

"Martha says she does not anticipate staying long at the estate."

John wiped a forearm over his perspiring brow. "Poor Martha," he said, glancing up at the house. "I hope you won't hold what she says against her. It was a terrible thing, the master dying so suddenly, and at Walter Dinley's hand, too. Now the collection is to be taken apart, and if you'll pardon my impertinence for saying so, for Martha it's as if the master is dying all over again."

"I understand," said Cecily.

John bent down to resume his work. "I'm sure it will be alright in the end. And I've had an idea for an infusion of chamomile and rose that should bring a bit of comfort to the house, if the cook at the estate will permit my interference."

Cecily thanked him for the nourishing meals, assured him that they had been greatly enjoyed, and went inside to find Meacan. She located her in the Serpent Room, where Otto Helm, a crutch leaning beside him, was once again at work.

"There you are," said Meacan. She fluttered a piece of paper in the air. "Here's a reply from the proprietor at the Dolphin. There is a room for us, and we can have it to ourselves. You'll like the Dolphin. The proprietor's wife makes the best scotch cakes you'll ever taste, unless they make them better in Scotland, and I cannot say whether they do or not." Her eyes dropped meaningfully to the hunched figure at the desk. "I was just asking Mr. Helm where *he* will be staying, should we wish to call on him."

Cecily approached Helm. He was bent over a book open to an illustration of a splayed and dissected lizard. "Will you be moving to an inn, Mr. Helm?" she asked him.

Helm spoke distractedly. "I am to be going home," he said. "As soon as may be possible."

"But surely you are not boarding a coach or a ship today," said Meacan. "You must be staying the night somewhere."

Helm looked up. "I am to be at the Elephant Weary," he said.

"*The Weary Elephant,*" said Meacan, with an approving nod. "No scotch cakes there, but the mince pies have few rivals in all of London. Well, then perhaps we will come to see you."

"I beg you do not trouble yourself. As I said, I am very soon to be going home."

Susanna appeared at the door. "The coach has come for Lady Kay and Mrs. Barlow," she said. She turned her small, stern face to Helm. "And Lady Mayne says to remind you that the house is to be closed by this afternoon. You must conclude your work."

Helm nodded over the open book. "But a few pages more," he said.

Since Meacan had already said good-bye to Lady Mayne,

she remained downstairs to instruct the coachman on what luggage was theirs while Cecily went up to bid farewell to their hostess. In the widow's room, the white cat was prowling along a high shelf, from which several objects had fallen to the floor.

"I am sorry you could not conclude your study," said Lady Mayne, after they had said what etiquette required. "But I am sure you are as pleased as I am to put this matter behind you. I have not yet thanked you for respecting my wishes regarding my husband's death. You see now that your interference would have been quite without purpose. The matter is all but concluded. The murderer is in prison."

"That is so," said Cecily. "But he may be found innocent."

Lady Mayne's white eyebrows lifted. "I think not," she said. "It is my opinion that Providence has seen justice done. I advise you not to let the sin of pride lead you to interfere in God's work, Lady Kay. And I do not speak only of justice. I speak also of nature. Your—you will pardon me—your *unfeminine* efforts to impose your order on His kingdom. My husband tried to keep the world on his shelves. Had he left to God what is God's, he might not have met the violent end he did."

Cecily met the other woman's eyes. "The hand that took your husband's life was human, not divine, Lady Mayne. And I assure you, Walter Dinley will not hang for a crime he did not commit if my *interference* can prevent it."

The sound of a small object shattering ended the conversation. The cat had swiped a shell from its place. It lay broken and scattered in sharp islands on the floor. "I believe your coach is waiting," said Lady Mayne.

As Cecily descended the stairs, she glimpsed once again the skeletal rat that had before been draped in black silk.

As she passed it, she thought she saw a smile on the tiny skull. She did not report this impression to Meacan as they climbed into the coach destined for the Dolphin. They had decided the previous evening to keep to their plan. They would attend Inwood's tour, which, if luck were with them, would lead to an edifying conversation with Martin Carlyle. Cecily looked out the window of the coach and watched as the house of Barnaby Mayne receded. From the outside, it looked just like every other house.

CHAPTER 29

It is often the case that the ruination of the rich is nearly imperceptible to the casual observer. This was true of Giles Inwood's manor house, which was situated on a salubrious stretch of riverbank beyond the reach of London's smoke and refuse. The rushing water glittered. Birdsong cut sweetly through the air. Insects flitted industriously from blossom to blossom. The trees that defined narrow walkways on either side of the house were haloed by spring's translucent green.

The carriage from which Cecily and Meacan alighted was not the only one on the wide gravel lane in front of the entrance. At the door, they were informed by the servant who admitted them that the tour had already begun. He led them over the black and white squares that patterned the floor of the entrance hall and up a grand staircase watched over by generations of painted patriarchs.

Once they were upstairs, the halls and rooms began to look more familiar. The shelves that lined the walls were not unlike Sir Barnaby's, though they were less crowded, and were arranged with more of an eye for aesthetic pleasure than scientific order. Bright-feathered birds were perched near windows where they looked more alive. Corals and shells were grouped by color. Compared with Sir Barnaby's collection, Inwood's featured a preponderance of art. Each chamber was furnished with couches and chairs thoughtfully positioned so that residents and guests could appreciate the displays in comfort.

They joined the group in a chamber dedicated to Greek sculpture. The tour was a large one consisting of twelve gentlemen of varying heights and volumes in wigs of varying heights and volumes. As the men swiveled to assess the new arrivals, Cecily recognized several faces that had been among the mourners who had come to view Sir Barnaby's body. She felt Meacan's elbow dig subtly into her side as Martin Carlyle smiled and bowed to them. He had a notebook tucked under one arm.

Inwood looked pale and thinner in the face than Cecily remembered, but when he saw her his eyes lit with friendship and he strode forward to greet them. "Lady Kay," he said. "And Mrs. Barlow." He addressed the group. "A moment, please, while I welcome these ladies."

While the gentlemen spread out across the room to examine the rounded marble bosoms and muscular male torsos of the pantheon, Inwood led them to an adjacent chamber. "It does me good to see you both," he said, speaking more to Cecily than to Meacan. "Have you come from the house? How fares Lady Mayne? I have no words to express my chagrin at being the cause of this further hardship to her."

He had left the door to the other room open. It was obvious that every ear was eagerly attentive beneath false gray curls. "Does everyone know?" whispered Cecily.

Inwood gave a rueful smile. "Oh, most certainly. The secret is out, and it will be a long while before I am extended credit from any quarter. But I expected much worse. I was sure no one would come today. Indeed, I would welcome a snub so richly deserved. But as you can see—"

"—Intrigue draws a crowd," murmured Meacan.

"I hardly think my rather common woes rise to the level of intrigue," said Inwood, a spark of self-deprecating humor in his weary eyes. "But tell me—is Lady Mayne well?"

Meacan's mouth quirked. "She's *more* than well. I've yet to see her in better spirits."

"She is to auction the collection," said Cecily.

"So I have been informed," said Inwood. "I do not blame her. Rather I blame myself entirely. Having failed to keep a sworn promise to my dearest friend, I must now watch as all that he entrusted to my care is broken to pieces."

Cecily thought back to the morning in the Plant Room. "Is there no chance someone else will purchase the collection in its entirety?" she asked.

Inwood shook his head. "It would be too unwieldy an acquisition for anyone of my acquaintance. But our thoughts run together, Lady Kay. Allow me to assure you that I am doing everything in my power to persuade those collectors I count as friends to encompass with their bids entire cabinets, even entire rooms. All that can be preserved of his order *will* be preserved." He paused. Grief rested heavily on his features. "It was foolish of me to try to keep my circumstances a secret. I deserve all the condemnation that can be heaped upon me. Sir Barnaby wished for his collection to be protected, preserved for the edification of scholars not yet born. It was his work, his legacy, and I, through my poor judgment, my pursuit of these wrecks that are but foolish dreams, have been its undoing."

"Do not trouble yourself overmuch," said Meacan with a touch of impatience. "In a world as cruel as this one, denying Sir Barnaby the satisfaction of having his shells forever called *the Mayne shells* is not so dire a crime."

"At least," said Inwood, "I have been given the opportunity to correct my behavior and, I hope, to restore my fortunes in a responsible manner."

"Mmm," said Meacan. "And if I were to tell you I'd heard of a lost Spanish galleon sunk off the coast of—"

Inwood cut her off by raising his hand in mock protest. The faint, self-deprecating smile returned. "I would tell you to leave it to the sea that claimed it," he said. "But I fear I am neglecting my other guests. Shall we join them?"

★

An opportunity to speak to Carlyle alone did not arrive until the tour moved to the gardens, two expansive green lawns that extended one behind the other away from the house and ended in a small wilderness. It was warm and still. The sun glared white through the clouds. Inwood ordered refreshments to be served outside and suggested his guests wander until the food was ready. As the group scattered over the lawns, Meacan and Cecily caught up to Carlyle and guided him subtly toward the trees.

Carlyle appeared in high spirits, aware that his clothes fit him well and that the other gentlemen were glancing enviously at the one among them framed by the billowing skirts of two women who appeared fascinated by his every word. He yawned when Cecily asked him his opinion on making botanical drawings from live plants as opposed to dried ones. He was much more eager to discuss Inwood's misfortune. "Inwood won't be paying off his debts any time soon," he said spitefully. "The amounts are monstrous. As for all this"—Carlyle gestured with poorly concealed envy at the grand house and gardens—"he is only barely maintaining appearances."

Meacan looked behind them at the stately edifice. "It seems to be holding on to its dignity as well as can be expected."

Carlyle shrugged. "The signs aren't obvious yet, but they will be soon. Didn't you see the floors in need of repair? The peeling paint? The broken latch on the back door? The servants are only day laborers from the village—he can't afford to keep his own. And if the lawn isn't trimmed this week it will begin to look decidedly unkempt."

Meacan glanced at Cecily with an expression that said her patience with their smug companion was at an end. They had passed through a wrought-iron gate into the leafy foliage of the wilderness. Cecily looked to be sure they were out of sight of the others, then nodded. At her signal, Meacan deftly snatched the notebook from under Carlyle's arm. With a cry of surprise he lunged after her, but she was too quick. She took two steps backward so that she was framed by the iron gate and clearly visible to everyone on the lawn. "You cannot attack me," she said, as pleasantly as if she had just remarked on the skill of the blacksmith who forged the iron trellis.

"That was not my intention," said Carlyle. He was trying to regain his composure but his self-assurance had deserted him. "Please return my book to me."

With Cecily beside her, Meacan opened the book and began to turn its pages. "Now, let us see what has caught your interest. Oh, yes, the amber amulet *was* very fine, as were the turquoise and the opal." She continued to leaf through the book. "Your tastes are certainly consistent. Jewels." She turned a page. "Jewels." She turned another. "Ah, here is a gold brooch. That's a change, but here—what a surprise. Jewels again."

"My interest is in objects whose values do not depend on a label," snapped Carlyle. "But that is none of your concern." He held out an elegantly cuffed hand for the book. "Please."

"This is a very fine likeness of Mr. Inwood's Egyptian emerald. You made this just now? I must say you draw much faster than I do. It is a good thing we have never competed for employment. As I was saying, the emerald. No doubt you've been looking for one ever since you were unable to retrieve the one you left in Sir Barnaby's carriage house. Tell me, do you keep your stolen jewels or sell them?"

Carlyle extended his arm toward the notebook again. "Give it back to me."

His tone was furious, but Cecily saw the fear in his eyes. Meacan saw it, too. "Tell us the truth," she said. "Or we'll cross the lawn right now and tell every collector gathered here who has allowed you to tour his collection to go home and give his drawers a *thorough* examination."

The change in Carlyle was remarkable. With the deflation of his confidence, his face seemed to rearrange itself. He looked all at once like a rodent. Cecily wondered whether his nose had always been so small. There was an oily sheen on his brow. "I don't know what you're saying," he managed.

"You were seen," said Cecily.

"Seen? Who saw me?"

"That doesn't matter," said Meacan. "We know about your duplicates."

Carlyle opened his mouth to speak, but he seemed incapable of collecting his thoughts and closed it again.

"I wondered," said Cecily, "what it could have been that

drew you to visit the collections when you appeared to have so little interest in them."

"You cannot accuse me," said Carlyle. "There isn't anything missing from the Mayne collection, or from this one."

"And what of Sir Barnaby's murder?"

Carlyle's eyes widened in horrified disbelief. "His murder? What about his murder? Dinley killed him. I had nothing to do with it."

Meacan closed the notebook. Instead of giving it back, she tapped the cover thoughtfully. "What if Dinley didn't do it? What if Sir Barnaby found out you were stealing his jewels? What if there was something in his study you wanted that you couldn't duplicate, so you went in and took it from him?"

"N-none of that is true."

"Then what *is* true?"

Carlyle swallowed, his throat working against his tight neckcloth.

"We *know*," said Meacan with a sigh. "There is no reason not to enjoy an opportunity to speak freely of your endeavors. You can even boast a little, if you like."

Carlyle daubed a cuff to his forehead. When he lowered his hand, he seemed to have regained some of his bravado. "I see no value in dry bones and stuffed birds. I see no worth in a pebble that a charlatan tells me is the very same stone that struck Goliath. Gold is worth what it is worth. An emerald is worth what it is worth. Yes, I took the jewels, but if you accuse me, I will deny—"

"But we have this," said Meacan. She waved the notebook. "So indulge my curiosity, please. How did you make the duplicates?"

Carlyle licked his lips and glanced across the lawn. "I— There is a lady who serves as housekeeper in the shop of a goldsmith," he said. "She has a talent for the craft."

"Well, you may tell her she has proved more deft with her handiwork than you were with yours. They are *very good* duplicates. Please pass along my compliments. And tell her should she need employment, I have a friend—"

Cecily broke in hastily. "What did you do after Sir Barnaby ended the tour?"

"I did precisely what I said I did. I continued through the rooms."

"And completed the remainder of your substitutions as you went."

Carlyle dropped his chin in a barely perceptible nod.

"You didn't come through the Plant Room because there was nothing in it of interest to you."

Again, Carlyle nodded.

"What do you know of John Rose?"

Carlyle looked genuinely bewildered. "John Rose? I've never heard the name before."

Movement caught Cecily's eye. The guests of Inwood's tour were reconvening at the back door of the house. She turned to Carlyle. "Did you see anything pertaining to the death of Sir Barnaby that you have not already disclosed?"

After a moment, Carlyle's eyes lit up. "Yes," he said quickly. "Yes, I did. If you want to know who has been keeping secrets about that day, I suggest you stop interrogating me and speak to the foreigner. Ask him what he was doing shoving a bloodstained letter behind a specimen jar."

"The foreigner? Do you mean Otto Helm?"

Carlyle nodded eagerly. "I saw him from the stairs. He was in the hall outside Sir Barnaby's study. He was reading a letter. It wasn't any concern of mine, but I know what I saw. There was blood on that piece of paper. And as I watched, he folded it and hid it up among the jars."

"Could you see whether the blood was in a particular shape?" asked Cecily. "The shape, perhaps, of a hand?"

Carlyle considered this. "Might have been. I only glimpsed it."

"And you said he put the letter up on the shelf?"

"He did. Stuffed it right there between the jars. Then he turned, and I think he saw that I was there, but he looked as if he was staring right through me."

"What happened then?"

Carlyle shrugged. "I went down to the Stone Room to see if there was anything more of interest there. I think I heard Helm go upstairs, but I cannot say for certain. As I said, it was none of my concern."

CHAPTER 30

The Dolphin was an old inn, the structure of which had survived the fire that had devoured so much of the city three decades before. Its worn beams and crooked windows made it a comfortably creaking establishment that regarded both guests and passersby with an expression of cheerful expectation. It looked as if it wanted to tell stories of what it had seen, and was waiting patiently for someone to realize it could talk. For Cecily and Meacan, it provided a temporary respite after the journey back into the reaching claws of city smoke.

Cecily was of the opinion that retrieving the bloodstained paper from the Mayne house should be their first priority, as knowing its contents would give them an advantage when they spoke to Helm. Meacan disagreed. She wanted to go directly to the Weary Elephant and confront him.

"He could depart the city at any moment," Meacan argued. "He's recovered enough to travel. The longer we give him, the more likely he is to slither off back to Sweden like one of those sinister snakes he so admires."

"I don't think you can hold his interest in serpents against him," said Cecily. She liked snakes. Every time she saw one curled on a sunny rock or stretched across a leafy lane she had to remind herself to keep a wary distance. She always wanted to look more closely at the diamonds and stripes and spots given definition by the mosaic armor of their scales, to observe the bunching and rippling of muscles, to see the forked tongues taste the air as if it held information for them that it did not for her. "I'm sure you'd agree," she said, "that you can no more hold all snakes culpable in the Fall than you can hold all women responsible for it."

"Oh, it's nothing to do with our departure from Eden," said Meacan. "*That* serpent *spoke*. If I encountered a *talking* snake I'd be much more at ease with it. It's the silent way they shift themselves that I find unnerving. If something with fangs is coming for me, I'd rather it announce itself first."

They were still debating what to do when there was a knock on the door. It was the innkeeper's wife, a capable proprietress armored in a dress of dark wool who gave the impression not only of being prepared for almost anything that could conceivably happen at an inn, but of having seen it happen before. "A note has come for Mrs. Barlow," she said.

Meacan took the proffered paper and opened it. Their new hostess, seeing her expression, tactfully retreated and closed the door behind her.

"It's from the clerk at the Old Bailey," said Meacan. "Walter Dinley has been tried."

Cecily thought she must have misheard. "But he can't have been. It's too soon. And what of witnesses? Wouldn't we have been called?"

"They made time for it because it was such a clear case," said Meacan grimly. "No witnesses were required after the constable gave evidence. It was over in six minutes."

It was clear from Meacan's face and tone what had happened. "Guilty," murmured Cecily. "And the sentence?"

"He's to be hanged at Tyburn."

"Has a date been set?"

Meacan began to pace the room. "Not yet. We still have time. There can be an appeal."

"We are close to the truth," said Cecily. "I know we are. I will go to the Mayne house and search for the paper. You make sure Helm stays where he is."

Meacan stopped and closed her eyes. "You are right," she announced as she opened them. "I don't like the idea of separating, but the two tasks are of equal importance. *I* should be the one to go to the house, though. If everyone has departed and it's locked, I'll be able to find a way in."

They agreed. Cecily would go the Weary Elephant, ascertain that Helm was indeed in residence, and take up a position in the tavern. Meacan would join her there after she had retrieved the paper from the Mayne house. Before they parted, Meacan subjected Cecily to an extensive and stern list of warnings.

"Keep to the crowded places," she said as she pulled on her gloves. "If you see the man who followed you, or another like him, point and shout *thief* and *constable* as loud as you can. When you arrive at the Weary Elephant, tell the proprietor you are friends with Mrs. Barlow and he'll make sure you aren't bothered. And tell him to save a mince pie for me. Be wary of the customers—it's a rougher establishment than this one." Meacan paused for breath, then concluded with a look that brooked no opposition. "And on *no account* are you to speak to Helm alone. He may be leaning on a crutch, but as he himself would be the first to tell you, the venom of an injured snake is no less deadly than that of a hale one."

★

It was nearing suppertime, and the Weary Elephant's famous mince pies had drawn a crowd eager to rest tired feet and wash away the day's doldrums with ale and company. The tavern was full, the noise cacophonous. Chair legs slid and tables rocked and it seemed to Cecily the only unmoving things in the room were the slumped candles that had not yet been lit. She didn't have to inquire whether Helm was there. She perceived him at once, sitting alone at a small table in the corner.

She corrected herself. He was the only person sitting, but he was not alone. Three hulking men surrounded him. The largest of them had his hands resting palms-down on the table. He was leaning forward so that his nose almost touched Helm's.

"He smells French," Cecily heard the man say as she approached. She glanced around the room in search of the proprietor, but she could not identify him amid the clamor and bustle.

Helm was shaking his head and trying to speak above the din, but the man confronting him slapped his hands on the table so hard it made Helm jump. "Why don't you tell him what we do with French invaders," he said to one of his companions.

The other man flicked the knot of the sling tied at Helm's shoulder to support his injured arm. "It looks like someone already started our work for us."

Cecily made the quick decision that her promise not to engage Helm before Meacan's arrival did not apply to the current situation. Allowing Helm to be reduced once again to bruises and broken bones by a trio of drunken bullies wasn't going to help anyone. She squared her shoulders and spoke with all the brusque authority she could summon. "There you are, Mr. Helm," she said. "The Duke apologizes for the delay."

Helm's eyes fixed on her in surprise. She saw his lips form her name. "The *Duke*," she said again, "asks you to meet him in your room. He had the proprietor take him upstairs so that you would be able to speak without interruption." She looked coldly at the leader of the men. His reddened eyes were now directed upward at the imagined nobleman pacing the floor of a room above them.

Helm rose to his feet. Cecily handed him his crutch. To-gether they made for the stairs. Cecily glanced once over her shoulder, and was relieved to see that the three would-be ag-gressors had taken the table and drawn out a deck of cards. Slowly, leaning heavily on the crutch, Helm led Cecily upstairs to a small chamber that smelled stale and musty. Its furniture was old and scratched, and by the number of trunks piled in the corners and clothes spread out to air, Cecily guessed it was a shared room. There was no one else in it now. She went in after Helm and shut the door behind them, abruptly muffling the noise from downstairs.

"I am most grateful for your assistance," said Helm as he lowered himself gingerly into a chair. He looked around the dingy room. There was a skittering sound from one corner, and they both saw a thin tail disappear into a hole in the wall. Helm winced. "I am sorry I cannot welcome you to a more comfortable place, Lady Kay. My funds provided only for modest travel, and since my misfortune, they are still more reduced."

Cecily remained near the door. "I promised I would not speak to you alone," she said. "But now that the opportunity presents itself, I cannot ignore it. I assure you, though, that if you make any sudden move toward me, I will open this door and call for help. I am certain those three men downstairs would not hesitate to come to my aid."

Helm shifted nervously in his chair. "I do not understand you, Lady Kay."

The room was silent except for the threatening hum of carousing from downstairs. "I know that when you left the Serpent Room on the day of the tour, you did not go to the library," said Cecily. "I also know that you took a piece of paper from Sir Barnaby's desk *after* he died, and hid it among the jars in the hall. Unless you can give me a satisfactory explanation to the contrary, I will be forced to conclude that you are the true murderer of Barnaby Mayne, and to summon a constable at once."

Beneath his unkempt wig, Helm's face contorted. "I beg of you not to do so," he cried. "I did not take any paper, and I did not kill him. I swear it to you."

"Will you tell me the truth?"

Helm's gaze dropped to the floor and he said nothing. Cecily opened the door just enough for the clatter and clamor of the tavern to swell into the room. Helm lifted his head. "Please do not call," he said quietly. "I will tell you everything."

Cecily shut the door and the room was quiet again. Helm took a deep, uneven breath. "I would have confessed it all to you before," he said, "if I believed it to be of importance to anyone but myself. I did not like to lie to you, for I have for you the highest respect."

Cecily maintained a flinty expression. "If what you are going to say relates to the murder of your host, I cannot imagine how you could have thought it was important only to you."

"But that is just it," said Helm. "What I have to say is in no way connected to the death of Sir Barnaby. On that matter, I know only what I have been told."

"If that is true, why did you lie?"

"Because I was ashamed of what I had done."

"And what exactly did you do?"

Helm did not answer at once. He picked at one of the frayed edges of his bandages. "You are a woman informed of the world," he said at last. "You are aware, then, of the great war being fought between my country and that of Russia?"

Cecily blinked as her mind tried to accommodate the unanticipated subject. In Smyrna, it had been the conflict between the Russians and the Ottomans that had dominated conversation, but she knew something of the war between Russia and Sweden that was slowly pulling one country after another into its orbit. "I do," she said slowly.

"But you question its relevance to the circumstances of the present," said Helm. "I will explain. Consider your own England's troubled history with France. As we saw in the threats of the men downstairs who mistook my accent for that of a Frenchman, it is a history that has kindled unquenchable hatred in English hearts. It is the same in my home, except that our history is with Russia, and is of late more troubled than it has ever been."

"I have heard," said Cecily, "that though your young king has shown himself to be a stalwart leader, the Russians have claimed a number of recent victories."

Emotion flared in Helm's eyes. "It is not only fortresses that have been lost, but towns, also, and small hamlets unprepared for war."

"I do sympathize with your distress, Mr. Helm. But what connection does this have to the day of the murder?"

Helm composed himself. "I came to the Mayne house with no expectation of any such connection. I was full only of anticipation, for I was happy to give to Sir Barnaby the catalogue he desired, happy to see an abundance of serpents very well preserved, and happy to accept the offer of Mr. Dinley to show me the rooms after I said I would not have time to join the tour."

"But something must have changed."

"Yes." Helm closed his eyes as if he was unwilling to return to the memory. With an obvious effort, he opened them and continued. "Mr. Dinley wished to be considerate of my feelings. He believed it his obligation to inform me that there was to be a man from Russia among the guests to attend the tour that day. He mentioned it to me because he did not know whether a cordial interaction between us would be possible."

"What did you say to him?"

"I thanked him for his solicitude, and I assured him there would be no unpleasant confrontation. I did not ask the name of this Russian, but I assumed him to be a fellow scholar. For the purpose of scientific collaboration, I believe the quarrels of countries may be set aside."

"But there was no Russian on the tour," said Cecily. As she spoke, she recalled Sir Barnaby's expectant looks out the window of the Stone Room while they waited for guests to arrive, and his words as the tour began. *Our company is not complete.*

"He did not arrive," said Helm. "I was relieved when the group came to the Serpent Room and I heard no Russian accent among the guests."

"But who was he? And what prevented him from attending?"

"I suspect it was merely the caprice of his nature that kept him away," said Helm. "And the effect of the strong spirits he drinks from morning until night." There was bitterness in his voice.

"You know this man," said Cecily.

"I did not then. I have since made his—" Helm hesitated. "His *acquaintance*." Helm touched one of the bruises on the side of his face.

"Your injuries," said Cecily. "Is *he* the one who attacked you?"

Helm grimaced and continued his account. "The day continued at first without trouble. Despite my fatigue from many weeks of travel, I worked with great attention and pleasure. Until I came to the snake that is called the Spotted Ribbon Snake."

"The Spotted Ribbon Snake," Cecily repeated. "I have not heard of it."

Despite the gravity of the situation, Helm's eyes brightened and he warmed to his subject. "There is little yet written of the species," he said. "In the books and letters I have read, it is reported that the Spotted Ribbon Snake is a species different from the Green Spotted Snake. But I suspect that, due to the variation in color depending on how recently a snake has shed—" Helm checked himself. "My apologies. The details are not of importance. What I wish to communicate is that I wanted to investigate the possibility that the two serpents were not two different species, but in fact *the same*. I had the Spotted Ribbon Snake before me, but there was no specimen of the Green Spotted Snake in

the room. It was then that I remembered the shelves in the
hall. That morning, after Mr. Dinley upset the jar, I had noticed that there were several serpents kept there among the
fish. I thought I might find a Green Spotted Snake among
them."

Cecily searched his face for duplicity, but saw none. "So
you went to the shelves to look for this snake."

Helm nodded. "I climbed onto the step stool and began
a search."

"At what time was this?"

Helm considered. "I am not certain. It was after five
o'clock. Perhaps a quarter of an hour past."

Cecily thought quickly. That would mean Helm was at
the specimen jars just after Sir Barnaby left the tour, but
before Meacan came downstairs and found him dead. "You
were outside the door of Sir Barnaby's study," she said. "Did
you hear any sound from within?"

"No," said Helm. "It was silent." He paused. "But just
before I went to the hall, I did hear footsteps and voices. I
heard a door close, and again footsteps."

"Did you recognize the voices?"

"No, Lady Kay. I was not attending to them."

"I see. Go on."

Helm did. "I was examining the labels of the jars when
I saw a folded paper that had been inserted between them.
I was curious, so I took it from its place. To my surprise, it
was a message that according to its date had been sent that
very day."

"And was it marked with a bloody handprint?"

"Yes. I did see the blood, but I assumed it to be connected
to the breaking of the jar that morning. I thought perhaps

Mr. Dinley had cut his hand on the glass. And then what I read in the letter drove the stain from my mind."

"What did it say?"

"It was very brief. The writer apologized for his failure to attend the tour. He was eager to reschedule his visit, but as he was soon to depart the city, he requested Sir Barnaby to reply at once to make arrangements. He supplied an address and—and a name. *Belyaninov.*" Helm's face twisted as he pronounced the word.

"Belyaninov." Cecily repeated the unfamiliar syllables. "I do not know who he is."

Helm cleared his throat. "General Kiril Belyaninov serves Tsar Peter of Russia. He is known to all in Sweden for his terrible efficacy on the field of battle. His name is only ever spoken in fear and in anger, for he has led every campaign most devastating to my county."

"And he is in London now?"

"On visit of diplomacy," said Helm in a choked voice. "When Mr. Dinley told me a man from Russia was to join the tour, I never guessed that it could be *that* man. When I saw his name, I was overcome. I consider myself a person of discipline, Lady Kay. Of patience. But in that moment, I was not myself. It came into my head very suddenly that I would kill Belyaninov. That I *must* kill him. But I had with me no weapon."

An idea struck Cecily. "The gun. It was *you* who took the gun from the Artifact Room."

Helm nodded miserably. "I had seen it earlier in the day. I went upstairs, and I stole it from its case. That is where I was when you say Mrs. Barlow went in search of me."

Cecily tried to steady the thoughts whirling through her head. "And that is the reason you departed the house before supper," she said. "You did not suddenly remember another engagement. You went to find Belyaninov."

"That is the truth, Lady Kay. Such was my emotion that it did not enter my mind to bid farewell to my host, or to retrieve from him the catalogue. So you see, as pertains to his death, what I previously have told you was true."

"What did you do after you left the house?"

"I inquired where to find the address given by Belyaninov in his message. I journeyed to that place on foot. I went to the door of his apartment and I—I challenged him." Helm lifted pained eyes and gestured ruefully at his bruised face. "I posed for him and his companions not even the smallest threat. They disarmed me with no effort. There was much laughter. I do not remember more, but when I came to my senses I was outside in the alley. I could not clear my thoughts. I wandered, and my path took me back to the Mayne house."

"As you told us," said Cecily.

"Yes," answered Helm. "I was most grateful to have my life, and since that time I have been determined to counter my wrongs by applying myself with renewed vigor to my work." He looked at Cecily sadly. "Now I have told you all. I must hope you forgive my foolish behavior."

"If what you have told me is true," said Cecily, "you have already been punished out of proportion with your crime. You may have believed your intention was to kill, but you were not the cause of harm to any person that day."

Helm attempted a smile. "You are kind, Lady Kay. But I do not understand why you have asked me these questions. Was not Walter Dinley the killer of Barnaby Mayne?"

"I believe Walter Dinley is innocent."

Helm appeared only slightly surprised by her words. After a moment, he nodded slowly. "I did not think him to be a man with violence in his heart," he said. "But I fear my story has been of no help to you."

"On the contrary," said Cecily. "You have drawn a clear path before me, and I have only one more request. Can you tell me where to find General Belyaninov?"

CHAPTER 31

General Kiril Belyaninov regarded Cecily through a haze of pipe smoke so dense that the contents of the room appeared stuck in it like insects in amber. That the general and his friends had not allowed the diplomatic purpose of their trip to curtail their enjoyment of it was evident in the tale of recreation written across the chamber. Playing cards peppered the floor. Toppled bottles and cups rose like ruined cities from tables. Paintings not only hung askew, but were pocked with puncture marks, an explanation for which was provided by the knife that had been left triumphantly embedded at the center of one bewigged brow. Discarded undergarments formed separate trails to every piece of furniture with a soft surface.

"But you are a *tall* woman with *dark* hair," said the general without rising from his chair. He was a man of advancing middle age, solidly built, with smooth, dark curls arranged loose almost to his shoulders. For all the limp dishevelment of his attire, his jaw was clean-shaven and firm.

Cecily remained on the threshold of the apartment with the door open, a precaution that had been suggested to her by the innkeeper's wife. The friendly-faced woman, raising beleaguered eyes heavenward, had declared she would have preferred to play housekeeper to a pack of wolves than to her current tenants.

The only action Belyaninov took upon comprehending that Cecily was not the hired company he had been expecting was to unsling one leg from over the arm of his chair and place both booted feet on the floor. "Kay," he said, pronouncing her name as if he were tasting it. "Kay. There is a Kay who is consul at Smyrna."

"That is my husband."

Belyaninov picked up a bottle from a table near him and shook it. He frowned, dropped it, and repeated the action with a second bottle and a third. He bellowed a name to a closed door behind him. It opened and a man entered dressed in trousers and an open jacket that exposed his furred, barrel chest from neck to navel. Belyaninov tossed the third empty bottle in his direction. It hit the floor and broke into pieces. The man grinned at Cecily. "Another bottle," said Belyaninov. "I'm to endure pleasantries with a friend of the conniving Turks."

The man's grin disappeared. He left the room and returned with a fresh bottle. As he set it on the table, he ground its base into the wood and fixed Cecily with a menacing stare. Belyaninov gave a bark of laughter and waved him away.

Cecily was reminded of days at sea when some quality of air and water imperceptible to her made the sailors stop their banter and apply their minds and bodies to their duties with grim purpose. There were set tasks for fine days and set tasks for stormy ones, she had been told, but when you didn't know what sort of weather was coming the best course was simply not to dawdle.

She spoke as if she did not expect to be questioned. "I

understand you were to attend a tour at the house of Sir Barnaby Mayne last week."

Belyaninov filled his cup. "Maaaayne." The word turned into a yawn that Cecily was grateful she was not near enough to smell. It seemed to make the air shudder. "Who is Mayne?"

"Sir Barnaby Mayne," Cecily repeated. "You were to visit his collection."

"Ah!" The exclamation burst from the general with sudden energy. "The collector. I had forgotten." He leaned forward in his chair. "Come into the light of the window."

"As I have no escort, I will remain where I am."

Belyaninov leaned back with a shrug. "Why does a lady I do not know come to speak to me of a man I do not know?"

"Then you were not acquainted with Sir Barnaby?"

Belyaninov picked up a second cup, filled it, and held it out to her. "Share a drink with me?"

Cecily shook her head. "Thank you, but no."

"A failure on all three counts," the Russian said with a sigh, and drained the cup himself. "The Tsar has a saying. Never trust a woman, a Turk, or a person who does not drink. I believe you are a woman, though you are tall and lack the shape of one. Through your husband you are affiliated with the Turks. And now—" He raised the empty cup. "You refuse the chance you had to rise in my estimation."

"We were speaking," said Cecily as if she had not heard him, "of the tour of Sir Barnaby's collection."

The general's expression turned bored. "I do not know this man Mayne. He wrote to me when I arrived in London. Three pages of obsequies. No less. The honor of the Tsar's visit to his house three years ago. The honor of discovering mutual interests. The honor of receiving a silver cup from the hand of the Tsar. The honor of beholding the Tsar's fine mustache."

Cecily nodded. "And?"

"And?" Belyaninov's mood swung again. Within the curls of smoke his eyes glittered with anger. "*And,* she asks me? *And*? As if she is General Commander. *And*?"

When Cecily maintained a steady silence, Belyaninov slumped back in his chair. "*And,*" he said mockingly, "*and come to my house.* That is what this Mayne wrote to me. Come and let me show you my turtle shells and my stuffed birds and my healing stones cut from the bellies of beasts. Come and let me give you a message for the Tsar."

A tingle of excitement moved up Cecily's spine. "A message? What message?"

"How can I know? It was not in the letter to me."

Cecily tried again. "You said Sir Barnaby and the Tsar had mutual interests. What did you mean?"

"I meant the cabinets, of course. Tsar Peter, like this Mayne, is a collector of curious items. Already his shelves contain greater wonders than any of your English ones. Soon they will be the greatest in the world."

"And does he have *particular* interests?" asked Cecily, thinking of the occult.

Belyaninov's lips extended into an unpleasant smile. "The Tsar's tastes run to the *anatomical,* my lady. Extracted teeth, double-headed beasts, unusual—"

Cecily cut him off. "And Sir Barnaby invited you to join his tour. The tour to be held on the twentieth of May?"

"*And* again," muttered the general. "Yes, yes, he asked me to come on the tour."

"Why didn't you attend?"

"But she speaks with such accusation!" exclaimed Belyaninov. He appeared to direct his comment at the destroyed portrait on the wall. The anonymous gentleman responded with a look of hauteur in his brown eyes, evidently unaware of the knife sticking out from between them. The odors and smoke filling the room were beginning to make Cecily feel slightly ill. To her relief, the general continued unprompted.

"I didn't attend," he said, "because the rogue canceled the event! A note from the man himself was delivered that very morning—and after I'd spent an hour tying a new neck scarf in the English fashion!"

Cecily's eyebrows drew together. "Do you have this note?"

Belyaninov snorted. "Why should I have it?"

"I only wish to understand," said Cecily. "You see, the tour was not canceled. I myself was there. It appeared to me very clear that Sir Barnaby was expecting you, and that he was surprised and disappointed when you did not arrive. Not only that, but I was told that Sir Barnaby received a message from *you* apologizing for not coming, and asking him to reply as soon as possible to reschedule your visit."

"I? I?" Belyaninov rose from his chair to a considerable height. His cry had brought the shirtless man back to the door. Another man in a similar state of dishabille stood behind him, fists clenched at his sides as if he carried his hands naturally as weapons. "I wrote no such message!" Belyaninov took a step toward Cecily. "Have I been the stooge in some mockery? Some prank?" Then, as abruptly as he had stood up, he sat down. He chuckled. "And I thought the English had no humor. Tell me. What trick have I abetted? A secret assignation of lovers? A cuckolding?"

"There has been a murder," said Cecily quietly.

Belyaninov seemed taken aback. "Whose murder?"

"Sir Barnaby's."

"The man is killed? Why did you not tell me so?" The Russian's astonishment appeared so genuine that Cecily felt a wave of disappointed frustration wash over her. She pressed him, but on the matter of Sir Barnaby's death, he had nothing to add. When she carefully broached the subject of the attack on Otto Helm, Belyaninov embraced the story with excitement. All accusations of womanhood and Turkish affiliation seemingly forgotten, he enlisted his two companions to help him relate to their new friend Lady Kay the story of the Swede holding out a gun he did not know how to use in challenge, and of the bloody ease with which they had dispatched him. Cecily's inquiry about a notebook filled with drawings of serpents was met with a torrent of inebriated laughter.

"If the Swede is alive," said Belyaninov, wiping tears of merriment from his eyes, "tell him his notebook pages were extremely useful in conducting business with our chamber pots. And thank him on our behalf. He provided some of the best entertainment we've had in London."

CHAPTER 32

Cecily reentered the tavern at the Weary Elephant to find it more crowded than when she had left it. Heat from the kitchen hearth rose up from the floor and combined with bodies and breath, turning the space into a stifling confusion of shifting shoulders, shuffling boots, and hands holding tankards aloft. Savory steam blurred the air over tables on which hot mince pies were being disassembled by butter-glossed fingertips.

Meacan wasn't there. Cecily circled the room twice, dodging elbows and casting covert glances at each table and shadowed corner. She noted the men who had threatened Helm hunkered over their cups. They seemed to have grown larger and louder, as if the approaching night was being pumped into their veins, bloating them with strength to stalk the city streets. She hoped Helm had the good sense to stay in his room. The proprietor, sweating and soot-smudged with a tray of pastries held before him, affirmed that he knew Mrs. Barlow, but hadn't seen her.

Cecily claimed a place with a view of the door and ordered a mince pie and a cup of ale. The warm food renewed her energy. It also increased her impatience. Half an hour passed. Outside she heard the parish bells chiming six o'clock, heralding the start of the day's protracted descent into night. It occurred to her that Meacan might have come in without the proprietor noticing, failed to find Cecily, and returned to the Dolphin. Resolved to look for her there, Cecily pushed her way through the heavy doors.

Outside, the air cooled her cheeks and she breathed more easily. The setting sun glared from a clear sky to the west at a storm gathering in the east. Wheeling gulls, illuminated from below by the sun's low rays, shone white against the looming slate-gray clouds. The yellow flowers of the stone-crop stood out brightly from cracks in brick walls.

It was only a short walk to the Dolphin. As she approached the inn, Cecily became more and more certain that Meacan would be there. But when she arrived, the innkeeper insisted he hadn't seen her. A cold sensation began to creep up Cecily's spine. She hurried upstairs. The room was as they had left it. The piece of cake Meacan had wrapped in a clean cloth and set on the mantelpiece that morning was still there, untouched. Cecily began to pace the creaking floors. Every time she heard a carriage she went to the window, but none stopped before the inn.

Time seemed to slow. Cecily had a remarkable capacity for patience and stillness when she had a plant before her, but it deserted her entirely when she was forced to wait with nothing to do. She had hated being closed in rooms from Venice to Istanbul to Aleppo to Smyrna while her husband and his colleagues made arrangements and agreements. She couldn't bear pacing from wall to wall, alone, suspended in useless ignorance.

The clocks had just struck seven when she climbed into a hackney and gave the driver the address of the Mayne house. The journey was slow. She braced herself as the carriage stopped and started and swerved through the crowded suppertime streets. At last the familiar terraced facades began to slip by the window. When the carriage stopped, she was out almost before the horses had halted.

The house looked abandoned. She perceived no ripple of movement behind the blank, expressionless windows. The cool curve of the door knocker at her fingertips brought her back to the day she had arrived, full of anticipation, readying her mind to accept new knowledge. She brought the metal ring down with a hard rap. No sound came from within. Of course, if Meacan was there, she had entered by stealthy means, and wouldn't respond to a knock at the front door.

A glance over her shoulder assured her that her presence on the threshold had drawn no attention from the street. She set her hand to the door and pushed. To her surprise, it opened. Her own momentum pulled her forward into the house. Quickly, she stepped fully inside and closed the door behind her.

Once again, her mind was pulled back, this time with dizzying force, to her very first moments in the Mayne house. She stared ahead of her in shock. The door into the hall was open as, she noted vaguely, was the door beyond it leading out into the garden. But between her and the exit was a glittering field of glass shards lit by a flare of sunset light. A faint smell of *spiritu vini* hovered in the air.

Cecily took a calming breath. The house remained silent and still. She advanced, stepping around pieces of glass. It seemed not one, but two jars had fallen or been knocked from their places. A long, pale serpent formed a curving path through the puddle.

She continued out through the open door onto the veranda. The marble Athena regarded her from its pedestal, cheeks streaked with soot as if from weeping. The gravel paths were disturbed, grooved and uneven as if something heavy had been dragged along them. Her eyes moved to the sweetbay tree and the circle of fallen petals around it. She squinted. There was an object among the petals, white like they were but larger.

By the time she reached the tree, her heart was pulsing in her throat. Lying crumpled amid the petals was a white cap. She picked it up, knowing already whose it was. She had seen Meacan pull it off her head and stuff it in her pocket several times a day, claiming she could not think with it on. Clutching the cap, Cecily ran to the door in the garden wall. It was closed but not bolted. She hauled it open.

The lane was empty except for wheel tracks and boot prints in the mud. Beyond it rose the elm tree, a forked, forbidding tower. Cecily shut the door and ran back to the house. She rushed from room to room calling Meacan's name. The white shrouds Martha had used to replace the black ones and protect the collection from dust billowed as Cecily opened and shut doors. As her fear increased she imagined birds rustling their feathers beneath the cloth and skeletons turning their skulls with little clicks. She moved from the garret rooms down past the sorrowful elephant skull and down to the kitchen. The hearth was swept and cold, the ceilings and walls denuded of John's bouquets of herbs.

Her search ended back at the shelves in the hall. She ran her hands along them, feeling for the paper Meacan had come to find. It was not there, but as she stepped down from the stool, Cecily's eye fell on a sodden strip of cloth emerging from under a display table. She crouched and pulled. The object that slid out was a sturdy cotton pocket designed to be tied around the waist and concealed beneath a skirt. It was heavy, and Cecily could already see the shape of what was inside it. Cautiously, she drew out the pistol. It was Meacan's. She reached again into the pocket and found the powder and bullets. Meacan had been prepared. She just hadn't anticipated the danger in time.

Cecily had already looked inside the study. Now she returned to it. The room had not been draped in white. It looked the same as it had since Sir Barnaby's death. The objects on the open shelves appeared to be in their proper places. And yet it seemed to Cecily something had changed. Her gaze fixed on the smooth surfaces of the closed cabinets. From the locks of three of them protruded three tiny keys. Cecily went to the leftmost one first. She did not need to turn the key. The door was unlocked. She opened it. Then she opened the two to its right. The shelves of all three cabinets were clean and empty. The collection of John Rose was gone.

CHAPTER 33

Fear and self-recrimination gripped Cecily's shoulders with sharp claws. Her thoughts staggered under their weight. How could she have failed to anticipate the threat? She had listened to Meacan tell her to be careful without giving a thought to the dangers Meacan might encounter. The Mayne collection was more than just the site of the crime. It was the *center* of it. Today, for the first time since Sir Barnaby's death, the house was abandoned. What better moment for the killer to return and conclude a plan of which the murder had been only one part?

Her gaze fell on the row of crystal balls arranged near her on the mantelpiece. Her own reflection, warped and distorted, stretched across the orbs. She thought of the countless hours John Rose and Barnaby Mayne must have spent staring into polished stones and black mirrors, convinced the correct words would summon spirits to grant their wishes. *Show me who has her*, she thought. *Show me where she is*. Nothing appeared within the clouded depths. From the emptied shelves that had held the Rose collection she could almost hear distant, mocking laughter. *You had the answer*, they seemed to say. *You did not see it, and now your friend is lost.*

She shut the cabinet doors. That was enough. What was

required now was clear thought and decisive action. She went to the window and looked out at the garden. The killer must have had a carriage waiting in the alley behind the house. Meacan may not have had time to use her pistol, electing instead to leave it as a message for Cecily, but the disturbed gravel and fallen cap suggested that Meacan had still been struggling when she had been taken away. She had been alive. If she still was—Cecily shoved aside the other possibility—she would be in grave danger.

The room was growing dark. Shadows crept toward Cecily from the corners as she rotated the book wheel, pulled Sir Barnaby's journal from its strap, and tucked it into the bag she carried. She left the house. Outside, the stone church towers were turning black against the pallid sky. The coachman she hailed looked at her dubiously when she told him where she wanted to go. A coffeehouse was no place for a lady, his expression said clearly as he nodded for her to climb up, and none less so than that of Signore Covo.

*

"You will have to wait." The servant with the scar through his beard blocked the entrance to the narrow staircase leading up to Covo's private rooms. His command of the position was evident from the patch of wall that had been left bare to fit a man of his exact height and girth. Leaning against it, he became part of the mad jumble. Amid the clutter that framed him, Cecily could make out an ivory skull, the hook of a bishop's crozier, a bird's nest, a paper scroll, and a fan of spun glass that reflected the crowded tables behind her.

Aware of the curious looks of the customers, Cecily lowered her voice to a fierce whisper. "I am not here to purchase Diana's crown or the stone that slew Goliath or the arrow with which Cupid struck Mark Antony or any of the other knickknacks your master sells to credulous customers. My business is urgent. If he does not see me at once, I will turn around and announce to the room that he is a fraud and a charlatan."

Frowning, the guardian of the stairs summoned a servant and sent him up into the darkness. "She's to come up," said the servant when he returned. The bearded man shrugged and waved Cecily past. She followed the servant upstairs. As they ascended, the conversations in the coffeehouse blended into a single murmuring stream punctuated by splashes of laughter. The servant brought her to the door of Covo's office and knocked.

"Come in, Lady Kay."

Cecily entered. The small fire and handful of candles did not quite account for the red and golden glow that filled the room. It was as if there were more flames illuminating it than she could see. Covo stood at his desk. In front of him rested an assortment of clocks, each set to a different time, and an hourglass in which the sand appeared to have been arrested in the middle of its fall.

"Chocolate or brandy?" asked Covo.

Cecily eyed him warily. In her experience, people with whom she was only slightly acquainted could not help but reveal a little more of themselves at the outset of every meeting. Encountered under new circumstances, they presented new details of their styles, moods, and manners. This was not the case for Covo, whose appearance and affect were identical to what they had been the first two times she had seen him. It was as if he existed changeless in this space where time did not pass.

"Let it be brandy, then," said Covo, and continued speaking as he poured two cups. "I have been called a fraud and a charlatan by those with significantly more influence over this city than you, Lady Kay, and it has done no harm to my business. My sensitivities are another matter. Your threat offends me, and I would not have you believe it was what earned you admittance to—"

Cecily interjected in a tone of quiet urgency. "Meacan is in danger."

The change in Covo's expression came and went as quickly as a flash of light on a facet of a spinning prism, but Cecily saw it before it was gone. He cared. She breathed a silent sigh of relief. "I understand there is no established trust between us," she said. "But I do not know where she is, and I need your help. When I asked you before whether you knew of the man called John Rose, you told me you did, but you refused to say more. I need you to do so now."

Covo studied her for a long moment. "Perhaps," he said at last. "But first I will require more information from you." He picked up the two cups and carried them to the table in front of the fireplace, moving with the controlled elegance of a predator who, with its prey in sight, tenses its muscles but does not leap. "Please sit."

Cecily shook her head. "There is no time—"

"Then you must speak quickly and not waste it," said Covo, with a sweeping gesture of invitation to a chair.

Recognizing that Covo did not intend to proceed in any way other than his own, Cecily composed herself and sat down opposite him at the table. "Meacan has been kidnapped," she announced. "By the murderer of Sir Barnaby Mayne."

A muscle in Covo's jaw tensed almost imperceptibly. "Most would say the murderer of Sir Barnaby Mayne is in prison. But I take it the person to whom you are referring is not young Mr. Dinley."

"No."

"I think, Lady Kay, that you should tell me all that you know."

Cecily was firm. "That will have to wait. There is too much to explain. What I *will* tell you is this. When Meacan was abducted tonight, the collection of John Rose was also taken. That is why you *must* tell me what you know about him."

A strange smile curved Covo's lips. The fire was reflected in his auburn eyes. "Very well, Lady Kay. But you will have to ask more specific questions, for what I know about John Rose would supply a bard with songs enough to entertain a thousand mead halls and a scribe with stories enough to fill a library. John Rose, you see, was my father."

The exclamation of surprise and disbelief about to burst from Cecily died in her throat as she realized that Covo was serious. She stared at him. "Why wasn't that your answer when we asked you before?"

Covo's gazed flickered over the encrusted walls and ceilings surrounding them. He smiled again, as if at a private joke. "My chosen profession benefits from a degree of ambiguity on the matter of provenance. There is power in a false name, just as there is in a false label." He picked up a small box and slid it open to reveal a tiny pair of scissors. Cecily read what was etched on a silver tag. *The scissors with which Delilah cut a lock of Samson's hair.*

Shaking herself from the strange spell of the revelation, Cecily pulled Sir Barnaby's journal from her bag and placed it on the table between them. "You asked me to be more specific. Sir Barnaby, like your father, was trying to master occult powers. What can you tell me about this?"

Covo made a quick examination of the book. His expression was faintly amused. "Do not tell me that you, a woman of scientific inclinations, have been persuaded to pursue witchcraft? Or rather, *do* tell me, for if so, I have a number of items for sale that may be of interest to you."

"Of course I haven't, but we are speaking of your father. He believed he had discovered a key to accessing the powers of the spirit realm." She leaned forward, flipped the pages of the journal, and slid the folded letter from its pocket.

Covo unfolded it. He touched a fingertip to the confident, curling letters. He read it quickly. Several times he chuckled softly. "Lady Kay," he said, looking up. "This letter *was* written by my father. I know his hand. But he was no occultist."

Cecily's brows drew together. "The meaning is clear."

"To me it is, yes."

Cecily tried to calm her rising frustration. "This is no time for your riddles and games. Meacan is alone. She may be hurt. We must—"

"On the contrary," Covo interjected. "This is precisely the time for riddles and games, though you err in thinking they are mine."

He continued. "My father was a singular man. One might say we had a certain affinity of personality. Much of what I know, I learned from him, though I saw him only rarely. His travels took him on one path. Mine, when I was grown, took me on another. Such was the nature of our separate venturing that each time we did meet, we accepted that it might be for the last time. That last time did come, nine years ago, when we traveled together to a library hidden deep within a desert that lies far to the east. We drank tea together while hawks the color of sunset wheeled above us, and we exchanged stories, some true, some not, of what we had seen in the intervening years. It was a pleasant time. I could not have chosen—" Covo paused, his gaze turned to the fire.

Cecily waited. After a moment, Covo went on. "Among the events in his life with which he acquainted me was his finalization of a contract between himself and an old friend to whom he had decided to leave his collection." Covo tapped the journal. "I refer, of course, to Barnaby Mayne."

"But why would it not go to you?"

The question made Covo smile again. "Because he knew I would not want it. My father and I shared some interests, but not all. I am not truly a collector. He was. And, like all collectors, he wanted his collection to be preserved. He selected Mayne because he knew Mayne had established himself as one of the most dedicated collectors in London. He trusted Mayne to care for his cabinets, and to assure them the prestige my father felt they deserved. My father had many admirable qualities, but humility was not one of them."

"I see," said Cecily slowly. "But what has any of this to do with the occult?"

"My father was not a credulous man, Lady Kay. He enjoyed a good tale, but gave no credence to amulets, talismans, and spells. He would have laughed at the fools who gathered here the other night to haggle over grimoires and debate the orientation of magic circles. Indeed, he laughed as he described to me what his correspondence with Mayne had revealed to him of Mayne's growing fascination with the subject."

"Then this letter—" Cecily's eyes dropped to the document.

"Is a lie," Covo finished. "He knew the strength of Mayne's desire to believe, and he used it."

"But why?" Cecily tried to understand. "Sir Barnaby had already agreed to take the collection, and as you just said, your father knew Sir Barnaby was a serious collector, the kind who would honor their agreement and protect the Rose collection."

Covo was thoughtful for a moment. "I would suggest to you, Lady Kay, that whatever else a collection may be, it is, inevitably, a record of a collector's existence. And, unlike those copies we make of ourselves in our children, a collection remains always within its collector's control, a faithful testament to what he has seen, and to his thoughts, his judgments, his choices, and his fascinations. The anticipation of its destruction can become, for the collector, another aspect of Death. The thought of its preservation, by extension, is a promise of immortality."

Understanding flared through Cecily's mind. She pictured Sir Barnaby's objects, each assigned so deliberately to a room, each so confidently affixed with a red label. "Your father wanted more than for his objects to be kept safe," she said slowly. "He didn't want his collection divided by another man's understanding of the world. He didn't want his labels replaced with new ones, or his birds moved to one room and his shells to another. He wanted them kept *together*, and he knew they would be so if their new owner believed they held a secret they would only yield if seen as an undisturbed whole."

"We all fear death, Lady Kay. Some of us merely choose more unique ways to dampen our fears than others." Covo looked down at the journal. "It must have amused him greatly to think of Sir Barnaby puzzling over his objects. He would have enjoyed this book."

The candle flames danced around them and the whole

room glittered like a dragon's cave. Cecily spoke softly. "Sir Barnaby spent his final years tormenting himself in search of a secret that wasn't there."

Covo's expression was unreadable. "As I told you, my father was not a humble man. Neither was he a kind one." Covo frowned. "I have told you what you wished to know, Lady Kay. I do not see how this will help us find Meacan, unless there is someone else who has been searching for occult secrets."

Covo's words hung in the silence that followed. Cecily closed her eyes. Her mind had begun to race. She opened them when she heard Covo's voice. "You are pale. Please drink."

She picked up the cup Covo slid toward her, but she hardly allowed it to touch her lips before she set it down. "I know where we must go," she said.

Covo's eyes narrowed. Cecily began to speak in crisp, clear sentences, in the same manner with which she might have justified the complex identification of a plant. As Covo listened, there appeared on his face an expression that was almost unknown to it.

"Lady Kay," he said, when she had finished. "You have done what few have ever been capable of doing. You have surprised me."

"Then you will help?"

"I am at your service."

"Good," said Cecily, standing up. "We will require a distraction."

CHAPTER 34

The hall was a deep pool of darkness broken by bands of moonlight. Bones, antlers, and crooked spires of coral reached for Cecily as she passed them. She had taken off her shoes and tucked them into the bag she carried so that her steps would be silent, but the floor was old and did not like intruders. Each time it creaked she froze, holding her breath as she listened for sounds of someone coming. Above her head, birds of prey with outstretched wings spun slowly on their strings.

She was on the second floor. Covo's voice still reached her faintly from below. "The greater the secret, the higher the price of keeping it," he was saying. "Just as a bright jewel is more difficult to conceal than a dull one, a valuable secret is more difficult to silence. You understand I am a business-man." He spoke in a voice Cecily had not heard him use before, a cold voice rimed with greed. She listened until she heard the reply. For now, the diversion was working.

The voices faded to silence as she continued her ascent through the house. Her destination was the single lit room she had seen from outside, its window glowing like an open eye in the night. She kept it firmly in mind as she made her way up narrow staircases and along hallways. The walls around her seemed to crawl with creatures animated by the pale moon. Lizards surrounded alligators like supplicants flanking their king. Horseshoe crabs and turtle shells studded the spaces between specimen jars, the floating occupants of which pressed their faces, claws, and paws to the glass as if trying to escape.

At last she reached the uppermost floor. There was a closed door at the end of the hall with a seam of golden light beneath it. She moved cautiously forward, tensing her body in her effort to be silent. Between her and the door, two marble statues stood facing each other. As she passed between them, she imagined she could feel their breath, cold on her cheeks like air hovering above a frozen pond.

There was silence from inside the lit room. Cecily turned the doorknob and pushed the door slowly open. She repressed a cry of relief as she rushed forward. Meacan's eyes, which had met hers with glittering fury when she first entered, widened in surprise. Through the cloth that gagged her mouth she made an incoherent sound of joy. In an instant Cecily had removed the gag.

Meacan's whispered words were harsh with her effort to restrain her excitement. "You *are* real."

Cecily assessed her anxiously. Meacan was seated in a chair with her arms behind her and her wrists bound. Her appearance was disheveled and there was a cut on her cheek surrounded by a swollen bruise. "Of course I'm real. Are you alright?"

"Not badly hurt," said Meacan. She squeezed an eye shut, testing the wounded side of her face, and winced. "And as to whether you're real, there's no *of course* about it. There has been far too much talk of spirits and demons for me to trust my eyes." She looked over Cecily's shoulder at the door. "Where is he?"

"Downstairs," whispered Cecily. "We must be quiet." She moved around to the back of the chair and began to work on the bindings. The rope was thin, the knots difficult to pick apart in the weak light.

"You know he killed Sir Barnaby," Meacan whispered.

"Yes."

Meacan twisted in the chair, pulling at the ropes. "Do you know why?"

"Yes. Stop moving."

Meacan stilled obediently. "All I know," she whispered, "is that he did it for *that*."

Cecily glanced up and saw that Meacan was looking at a group of boxes arranged neatly on the floor. She recognized the objects of the Rose collection at once. Nestled in the padded compartments designed to accommodate them, they appeared untroubled by their recent relocation. The room around them, she now realized, was lined with bookshelves and filled with maps and globes. In the moving light of candles, the duplicated surfaces of the world were spread in a bewildering display of wrinkled shorelines and painted oceans.

As Cecily returned her attention to the knot, wondering whether to search the room for a knife to cut it, Meacan continued to whisper. "He came for it when I was in the Mayne house. I think he would have killed me, but I was lucky. He asked me what I knew about the Rose collection. I told him that I knew *everything*, and that he'd be sorry if he silenced me. That's why he brought me here. I haven't said a word, though. It seemed wisest to pretend as long as possible to know more than I do."

Cecily had freed one knot only to find another. "We have to get out quickly. I don't know how long Covo will be able to keep his attention."

"*Covo* is here?"

"And he brought help. They're waiting outside. I didn't want to risk a confrontation before we found you."

"I hope he brought his strongest," said Meacan.

"Why?"

"You don't think I was overpowered by *one* person, do you? The villain has—"

The quiet was suddenly broken by distant shouts and crashes. Then Cecily heard a sound that made her breath catch. There were footsteps coming toward the room. "*Hurry*," whispered Meacan.

But it was too late. Cecily had time only to whisper a single sentence before two figures appeared at the door. The first was the man who had attacked Cecily in the field. As he entered the room, she noticed that he limped. When he recognized her his lips spread into a terrible smile, and his eyes glittered with promised violence. As he advanced toward her, a word from the door stopped him mid-stride. He retreated to a corner of the room, his gaze still fixed on the two women. The man behind him stepped into the light of the candles. With dread, but without surprise, Cecily beheld the face of Giles Inwood.

Even now, Inwood's face retained the expression of trustworthy charm that was natural to it. He spoke politely. "I must request that you cease your efforts to untie Mrs. Barlow. If you do not, I will be obliged to put an end to this more quickly than either of us would like."

Slowly, Cecily stood and came around from behind the chair. "Where is Covo?"

"Signore Covo is no longer of consequence to the evening," said Inwood. "Nor are his friends. I am curious how you—" He paused. A slightly rueful expression crossed his handsome features. "Ah yes, the broken door to the garden. I suppose I should be flattered that you were paying such close attention when you toured my collection."

Trying not to think about the possibility that Covo was dead, Cecily looked over Inwood's shoulder at the dark hall. "If you are thinking of attempting to overpower me," said Inwood, "I would advise against it. My associate has expressed his eagerness to address the very reasonable grievance he has against you and Mrs. Barlow. I have thus far dissuaded him, but I sympathize with the poor fellow. His leg pains him, you understand."

"It wouldn't if you hadn't sent him after Cecily," said Meacan.

Inwood was unruffled. "I had no *desire* to harm Lady Kay." He addressed Cecily. "Had you limited your inquisitiveness to the names of plants, I think we might have enjoyed many conversations in years to come. It disappoints me that we will not have the opportunity to do so."

He wanted to talk, Cecily realized. And he was confident. If she could keep him that way, her task would be easier. "I cannot think my company will be such a great loss," she said. "Now that you have what you wanted." Her eyes dropped to the boxes on the floor.

Inwood followed her look. "Attained at great cost and difficulty." He spoke wistfully, but the self-satisfaction in his eyes belied his tone. "I want you to know, Lady Kay, that I took no pleasure in what I did. Just as you forced my hand, so did he."

Cecily tried to look deferential. "I believe I understand,

but it would ease my mind to know whether my theory is correct. If this is to be our last conversation, may I request that it be an honest one?"

Interest flickered in Inwood's eyes. Cecily watched the battle between caution and arrogance play across his expression. Arrogance won. "Very well, Lady Kay. Tell me what it is you think you know."

For a moment Cecily hesitated. The truth was in her possession, but if they were to get out of the room alive, it had to be revealed in the proper order. Telling stories designed to fascinate was not her strength, and it occurred to her that their chance of survival might be higher if she and Meacan were in opposite places. She glanced at Meacan, and received in return a look of mystified encouragement that gave her strength.

She drew in a breath and met Inwood's eyes. "I believe that when you and Sir Barnaby had supper together on the night before the tour, he expressed his intention to end the contract between you. He no longer trusted you to protect his collection after his death, for the reason that he had learned your investments in the recovery of sunken ships had left you deeply in debt. Am I correct?"

Inwood's eyebrows lifted in surprise and appreciation. "I am inclined to blame your friend Signore Covo for spreading rumors about my private affairs. Indeed, I cannot bring myself to regret that his place in our community will soon be filled by another. Perhaps I may even exert some small influence over the choice, and ensure the installation of someone more sympathetic to my interests. But that will not concern you."

Cecily ignored the fear his insinuations inspired. She continued calmly. "Sir Barnaby was worried that you would not

be able to pay his widow, or to afford the expense of trans-
ferring and maintaining his objects. He could have altered
the contract, reduced the amount you were required to pay,
but I suspect his pride prevented him."

Inwood nodded. "He always had an inflated idea of the
worth of his cabinets. But I will give my old friend the credit
he is due. He had no sense that he was wronging me. In his
mind, he was doing me a kindness by relieving me of my
obligation. He expected me to be grateful. In the moment,
I was able to convince him that I was."

"But that was not what you felt."

"No, it was not." Inwood's gaze slid to the Rose collection
and he spoke with quiet fervor. "I had already waited longer
than should have been required of me. To lose it entirely—
that I could not accept."

Cecily willed his attention back to her. "You must have
been even more upset when he told you that he had already made other plans," she said. "Sir Barnaby was going
to propose a new contract, one by which the Mayne collection would be purchased, upon his death, by Tsar Peter of
Russia."

"Very astute," said Inwood. "How did you come by this
knowledge?"

"The possibility occurred to me when I learned that Sir
Barnaby had invited a diplomatic envoy from Russia named
General Belyaninov to join the tour. I knew from Martha
that the Tsar had admired the Mayne collection during his
time in London. He had expressed to Sir Barnaby his desire
to build his own cabinets, and to make them the most wondrous in the world. This year, the tide of the war between
Russia and Sweden has turned. The Tsar is now poised to
build a new capital, a city that will be the crown of his empire.

I suspect it occurred to Sir Barnaby that this was the perfect opportunity to offer the Tsar a jewel to set in that crown. What better way to ensure the preservation of the Mayne collection than to house it in the glittering walls of a royal palace? I believe Sir Barnaby meant to propose the idea to General Belyaninov, and ask him to convey it to Tsar Peter."

"It was an elegant notion," said Inwood. "But one I could not permit to succeed. Have you spoken to the general?"

"I have."

"You what?" the astonished question came from Meacan, whose attention had been flickering warily between Inwood and his grim accomplice. "I've been tied to a chair, and you've established diplomatic ties with a foreign nation?"

Inwood ignored Meacan. "That is unfortunate. I was hoping to keep him out of the matter entirely. But it is of no consequence. Whatever he thinks he was told by a—shall we say an *unconventional* woman—can be easily discredited. He and Sir Barnaby never spoke. That is the essential point."

"You knew," said Cecily, "that if Sir Barnaby presented the plan to Belyaninov, then even if it took months to formalize a contract, should Sir Barnaby die, your claim *could* be challenged. You had to prevent them from meeting."

Inwood nodded. "I would have preferred to take my time and accomplish the thing in a simpler way, but I had precious few hours."

"You sent Belyaninov a message purporting to be from Sir Barnaby telling him the tour was canceled," said Cecily. "But that only bought you time. You knew that Sir Barnaby would make another attempt to contact the general. You could not allow him to do so. He had to die."

Inwood looked grieved. "I did not want to do it," he said. "I had been so patient. The collection was coming to me. I was the younger man by twenty years. I was content to wait for my friend, for he *was* my friend, to go peacefully to his rest. I *wished* that for him. It was his own action that necessitated a different end."

Cecily tried to appear sympathetic. She needed to keep him at ease. "It must have been a challenge to plan it," she said. "With so little time, and in a house full of people."

Inwood's expression turned self-congratulatory. "Oh, it was indeed, Lady Kay."

"To accomplish it," Cecily continued, "you had to forge a *second* letter, one that would draw Sir Barnaby down to his study at a time you ordained."

"I wasn't certain it would succeed," said Inwood, with affected modesty.

"But it did," said Cecily. "He came downstairs as soon as he received your forged note. And you were waiting. As soon as you saw him go into his study alone, you went in after him."

"It was a terrible risk," said Inwood. "I knew I would have to endure the suspicion of those who knew the collection was to come to me."

"Yes," said Cecily, "but you trusted that suspicion would fade once word spread of the price you were required to pay for it."

"That is what I hoped, yes. Of course, we cannot fail to mention the remarkable turn of events that relieved a great deal of my fears."

Meacan spoke up. "You mean Walter Dinley's confession."

Inwood nodded. "I still don't know why the young fool did it."

"For love," said Meacan. "Something about which you know very little."

"Well, I am most grateful to him," said Inwood. "And if

there is any word I can put in to reduce the agony of his execution—a clean hanging, perhaps—I will of course do so."

"Dinley's confession was not your only piece of good fortune," said Cecily. "In the end, Lady Mayne's decision to auction the collection has relieved you of having to raise the money to pay her. Now you have in your possession the only part of the Mayne collection you ever really wanted. You have the cabinets of John Rose."

Inwood turned loving eyes to the boxes. "I could not risk them going to auction," he said. "What if Lady Mayne, bearing some animosity toward me, refused my bid? What if the boxes had been separated?" He closed his eyes as if the idea pained him. When he opened them, his expression was peaceful. "Perhaps you are right, Lady Kay. Perhaps it has all been for the best. Few threats remain, and they will soon be gone. Allow me to say once more that I regret it must be so."

He spoke with the polite contrition of a host obliged to bring an evening's light entertainment to an end. The illusion was broken by Meacan's exasperated voice. "But why? Why so much trouble and death for the cabinets of John Rose?"

Inwood looked slightly disappointed. "You do not know, Mrs. Barlow?"

Meacan's considered. "Well, we—"

"Rose told him," said Cecily, cutting her off. "Rose told him about the shipwrecks."

Inwood turned slowly back to Cecily. "Lady Kay, you do not cease to amaze. Yes, he told me."

"I imagine it was when you met him in the West Indies," said Cecily. "Shortly before his death."

Inwood bent down over the nearest box and plucked from a compartment the tiny, white skull of a bird. He turned it over gently in his hands. "I recall it as if it were yesterday. A storm had taken the island into a violent embrace. From his cottage we could hear the roar of the waves and the crack of breaking trees. The air was sharp with salt and sand. On that tormented isle, John Rose was the only creature who was at peace. The hour ordained by God for him to depart this world was approaching. I had no hand in his end, I assure you, Lady Kay. Nothing could be done. But thanks to the medicines I brought him, he felt no pain. If only you could have seen the gratitude that shone in his eyes as he lifted them to heaven, thanking God that in the very hour of his death, the Almighty had brought him a man worthy of the secret he had thought to carry to his grave."

Cecily concentrated her strength into her words. "John Rose had devoted his life to seeking out the remote paths of the earth. He had sailed into coves visible only from a single vantage point, and only when the sun and mist meet as lovers between spring storms. He had journeyed through deserts that had long ago been oceans, where the masts of ancient ships and hands of stone colossi reach up from beneath the sand. He had read every tale of an ill-fated voyage ever scrawled or printed, from accounts of treasures sent as gifts to win princesses that never arrived at their destination to diaries charting the courses of the ships that sailed victorious from Troy. He had listened to every rumor whispered by every sailor, captain, and pirate drunk and dreaming of unimaginable wealth."

Inwood listened, rapt. His eyes shone as if with fever, reflecting the glitter of a thousand jewels and the gleam of golden doubloons heaped high like hoarded suns. He spoke. "Rose never claimed the treasures he found, and he never spoke of them to anyone. Madness, perhaps, but what wondrous madness. Instead of taking them for himself, he hid everything that he found, every coordinate and distance and depth, here." Inwood touched a fingertip reverently to the markings etched on the beak of the skull.

"And he waited," said Cecily. "For someone he deemed worthy of the quest. As a younger man, he had promised his collection to his friend, Sir Barnaby Mayne, but Sir Barnaby had disappointed him. He was not deserving. So Rose told him nothing. But he told you. In time, the collection would be yours, and you alone would find what he had hidden there."

"You understand," said Inwood. "You understand I did what it was *necessary* to do. Rose chose me. He *meant* for me to have it. And now I *do* have it. I will find what he left for me. The lost wealth of ancient kingdoms will be mine." The mad glow did not fade from his eyes as he returned his attention to Cecily. "I wish you and I could journey together on this quest, Lady Kay. I regretted my first hasty decision to silence you. I was even pleased when he told me you'd survived." Inwood indicated his companion.

"And after that, you merely had me followed by another of your acquaintances," said Cecily. "But I doubt you would have hesitated to renew your efforts to remove me, had I threatened you."

Inwood looked at her sadly. "Unfortunately, you are correct, Lady Kay. And as I cannot trust you to cooperate—" He started to turn to his companion, then stopped. "No," he said quietly. "I believe I will do this myself."

Cecily stepped backward as Inwood advanced slowly toward her. She heard Meacan's sharp intake of breath. She met Inwood's eyes and held them. "You are mistaken."

Inwood continued his approach. "In what way, Lady Kay?"

"You will never find the treasure." Cecily took another step and felt the rustle of maps on the wall at her back.

Inwood smiled. "You doubt my intellect? I assure you, I am adept at solving puzzles."

"So am I."

For the first time, she saw Inwood's confidence waver. "What is your meaning?"

"There are no maps to hidden treasure in those boxes. There are no codes, and there are no clues. John Rose tricked you. The visions of shipwrecks he painted before your eyes were illusions."

Inwood's face changed. The charm drained from it like the color of sunset turning to cold twilight. "I am disappointed, Lady Kay. This attempt to confuse me in order to save your—"

Cecily cut him off. "It wasn't until *you* told *him* of your fascination with shipwrecks that he claimed to share your interest, was it?"

Inwood's voice was a snarl. "None of this is of any relevance."

Cecily's spoke softly, but her words struck Inwood like glass shards. "And it wasn't until *after* you had told him that you were to inherit the Mayne collection that he began to speak to you of hidden maps, was it?"

Inwood was silent. Cecily continued. "Did you know that Rose told Sir Barnaby a story as well? That his collection contained the secret to harnessing the power of the spirit realm?"

"You are lying."

"No, Mr. Inwood. I am telling you the truth. John Rose

wished to exist beyond the end of his life. It was *himself* he hid in these objects, not spells or maps to sunken treasure." She pointed to the boxes on the floor. "Sir Barnaby's obsession was with occult power, so Rose told him that he would find it here. Rose knew that as long as Sir Barnaby believed him, the objects would be preserved precisely as he arranged them. When he learned that you were to inherit the Mayne collection, he saw a chance to protect his cabinet beyond Sir Barnaby's death. Rose *was* grateful to you, but it was not only for the laudanum. It was for your gullibility. You presented him with another obsession he could use, and you gave him a final game to play."

Inwood stared at her. His face was waxy. "That cannot be."

Cecily drew from her pocket the letter that had been tucked into Sir Barnaby's journal. She held it out to Inwood, who took it and read it as if in a trance. The page fluttered in his trembling hand. "No," he whispered. "No, I have already begun to examine the objects. I have seen the symbols. The coordinates. The shapes of islands."

"Or are they shapes of occult sigils and talismans?" asked Cecily. "The obsessed see what they wish to see, especially when led by a guide who makes deliberate use of their fascinations."

Suddenly, Meacan laughed. Inwood swung to face her. "What amuses you?"

"You," she said. "You, who have speculated and stolen and murdered. And all for the sake of fairy fires kindled to keep you stumbling in the dark forever."

Inwood looked down at the tiny skull still in his hand. Cupping it as if it was a living baby bird, he stumbled backward until he hit the cluttered bookshelf behind him. He slid slowly to the floor. "No," he said. "No, it cannot be as you say."

The brute in the corner looked with some uncertainty at his cowed employer. Though he had little understanding of what had passed between the three, he had enough wisdom to suspect that the man who was going to pay him might not be intending to do so after all. His attention turned to Cecily, and she saw in his expression that he had decided to be his own master. His face hardened as he moved toward her. Inwood remained where he was, staring sightlessly before him.

"Stop." It was Meacan who broke the silence. She stood. The bindings that Cecily had succeeded in untying just before Inwood stepped into the room were on the floor. The gun that Cecily had slipped into her hands was leveled at the man. "I've shot you once, and it would be my pleasure to do so again. I will give you a moment to decide whether to lose your life, or to turn around, leave this house, and keep it."

The man made his choice quickly. As soon as she heard his footsteps descending the staircase, Meacan turned the gun to the unresponsive Inwood. "You were right to tell me to wait," she said to Cecily. "I didn't know how you were going to turn two threats into one, but I trusted you'd manage it."

Below their feet, the house suddenly shuddered with renewed activity. There were running footsteps on the stairs. Meacan and Cecily had barely exchanged looks before Covo appeared at the door, breathing heavily, a trace of blood on his sleeve.

"My apologies for leaving you alone so long," he said as he took in the scene before him. "I'm afraid his men had the upper hand for some time. I am most embarrassed. But the situation is righted now, and it seems you did not require my assistance." His eyes fell appreciatively on Meacan, who was still pointing the gun at Inwood, her expression only slightly softened by Covo's arrival.

Inwood was staring at the Rose boxes as a child might stare at a stage when the curtains open and the puppets that were there before have all inexplicably disappeared.

Covo addressed Cecily. "I take it you've acquainted him with all you told me?"

"He knows," said Cecily.

"Poor fool," said Covo. "What, then, shall we do with him? I thought we might leave the matter to the men he hired. They do not appear to be the type who take kindly to employers who don't pay."

The words seemed to penetrate Inwood's mind. His lifted wild eyes. "No, no, you don't understand. I will have the money. I will have it."

"That cannot be, Signore Covo," said Cecily.

Covo turned to her. "Are you sure? The justice of the courts is far less certain."

Meacan was glaring at Inwood. "As much as I am tempted," she said, "Cecily is right. We'll need him. It seems Walter Dinley is to live a happy life of sorting shelves after all."

CHAPTER 35

A sunny June day was a busy time in the physic garden of the Worshipful Society of Apothecaries of London. Gardeners tended the beds under the curious scrutiny of glossy starlings while robins wrestled worms from fresh-turned earth. Bright blossoms drooped with the weight of bees and sprang back up as the bees hummed away, pollen-powdered, to visit other blooms. Flitting butterflies filled the spaces between leaves, and squirrels spiraled up tree trunks in skittering flashes of auburn fur.

In the dappled shade of an elm, a group of apprentices formed a dense cluster around the Demonstrator of Plants, who was giving a stern lecture on the subtle differences between deadly hemlock and wild carrot. Most of the apothecaries-in-training had discarded their coats and left them flung over bushes or hooked on branches. Their sleeves were rolled up and their shirts had come untucked from their breeches after hours of leaning forward to examine the tops and bottoms of leaves and inhale deeply with eyes closed to test their memory of scents.

At the edge of a densely planted bed near the center of the garden, Walter Dinley balanced on his knees and one hand as he reached forward to cup a purple flower. His pallor had improved in the ten days since his harrowing incarceration had come to an end. At the recommendation of Peter and Anne Ashton, who had returned from their botanizing expedition to the tale of their son's brush with misadventure, Dinley had been offered accommodation at the garden while he rested and recovered. In exchange, he was happily contributing his skills to its somewhat disordered library.

Dinley sat back on his heels and turned to Cecily, who was crouched nearby, indifferent to the grass and dirt pressing patterns into the beige silk of her skirt. "The little flower you described," said Dinley. "Could it be *Thymbra spicata*? I recall the seed was sent from Crete, and I believe the empalements—" He paused and leaned forward once more into the dense foliage. "Yes, the empalements are five-pointed."

Cecily consulted her notebook. "And the tube of the petal is longer than the cup?" she asked.

Dinley's eager reply was muffled by greenery. "Yes, yes, without a doubt."

Cecily shifted until she was beside him, leaning into the purple blossoms. She reached out, pinched a leaf, and rubbed it between her fingers, gently bruising its silken surface. She raised her fingers to her nose. The scent of pepper and mint carried her as on wings to the parched ruins of a temple a day's journey from Smyrna. "This is the one," she said triumphantly. She wrote the name neatly in her book. "*Thymbra spicata*," she murmured, and tapped the page with her pencil. "And that's the last."

Dinley leaned back again. Smiling, he wiped the sweat from his brow with a sleeve. "John would suggest making a salad of it," he said.

They stood up together and dusted off their knees. Together they had identified from life the few remaining plants

she had been unable to name using dried specimens alone.
"I owe you a great deal of thanks," she said. "I would never
have arrived at *Helianthemum Ledi folio.*"

"I'm certain you would have in time," said Dinley. "And
you should not be thanking me, Lady Kay. Without you I
would be facing the gallows."

They started toward the boathouse that connected the
garden to the glitter and glint of the sunlit Thames. The
beds on either side of them were planted as neatly as possible under the circumstances. Many of the seeds had been
brought in crates by ships' doctors and travelers who had
given them to the garden with no sure knowledge of what
plants would grow from them. The gardeners and apothecaries had to wait and watch and wonder what would appear, and what properties it would have.

In the shade of the boathouse, Meacan and Alice sat
together on a stone bench watching the river slide past.
Though they had succeeded in communicating to Alice that
Dinley was safe and the true murderer found, this was the
first day she had managed to claim away from home. Days
of solitary grief had exhausted her, but with each answered
question and ray of summer sun she appeared to recover a
little more of herself.

As they drew nearer to the pair, Cecily reflected on the
preceding days. Upon his release from prison, Dinley had
received a warm welcome from the collecting community,
through which news of Inwood's guilt had spread quickly.
Dinley, despite the deprivations and fears that had left his
cheeks hollow and his eyes anxious, had dedicated himself
to guiding as much of the Mayne collection to safety as he
could. By now, though, what remained of it had begun to
drift apart like the cargo of a wrecked ship over the sea, likely

never to be joined again. Cecily had been gratified to learn that the contents of the Plant Room had been purchased in their entirety by an established giant of the collecting world renowned for his meticulous labels and catalogues. She herself had purchased a number of herbals and floras she did not have in her own library.

In addition, she had quietly and successfully bid on the golden ring, the pendant, and the three small gemstones that had so nearly become part of Martin Carlyle's private hoard. She had wrapped them carefully and sent them to Martha and John with a letter suggesting they use at least one of the small treasures to ornament a greenhouse. She had been inspired to add that, should they wish to reenter the collecting world, she would be happy to recommend Martha's skills to Humphrey Warbulton, whom she suspected had no notion of how to keep mildew off feathers or clean soot from coral, and would be deeply appreciative of Martha's expertise. Cecily and Meacan had paid a call on Warbulton not long after Dinley's release, and found him much improved. After learning the truth of Sir Barnaby's death, he had politely ended his association with the Philosophers of Night and declared an intention to concentrate his collecting efforts on safer subjects.

Alice was speaking slowly to Meacan, her forehead furrowed in concentration. "So the letter Giles Inwood used to lure Sir Barnaby downstairs was the one with the bloody handprint on it. But how did it come to be among the specimen jars?"

Meacan began to nod authoritatively before Alice had finished asking the question. "Inwood wanted to minimize the chances of the murder being connected to the Russian. That's why he took the message from Sir Barnaby's desk.

The trouble was that he had nowhere to put it. Do you remember he was wearing a pale gray suit? The letter was wet with blood, and he couldn't risk a visible stain. There was no fire lit to destroy it. He decided he should at least remove it from the room, so he took it out with him and hid it in the first place he saw—among the specimen jars in the hall. He came back for it later, but not before it had been seen by Otto Helm and Martin Carlyle."

"But it seems to me," said Alice, "that if he was so concerned about bloodstains, he would not have worn a pale suit when he knew he intended murder."

"Ah," said Meacan. "But he didn't expect there to be blood. The murder did not go as he intended."

Cecily made herself comfortable on a sunny boulder. Dinley remained standing. She watched his gentle eyes fix for a moment on Alice. Her blue ones looked to him just after he'd looked away. Cecily turned her attention to the row of turtles sunning themselves on a discarded beam from the boathouse.

"What did he intend?" asked Alice.

"It was the sponge that explained it," said Meacan. "And the odor. When I entered the room, I smelled vinegar. By the time Cecily came in, it had gone, but as she has such a sensitive nose, *she* smelled camphor and roses. Put them together and you have *Guy de Chauliac's soporific sponge.*" Meacan nodded toward Cecily. "She'd read about it, of course."

"The recipe is not used as often as it was in the past," Cecily explained. "But, as a physician, Inwood would have known it. A sponge soaked in a concentrated solution of poppy, henbane, mandrake, vinegar, rose water, and camphor. When applied to the lips and nostrils, it brings about drowsiness and numbs pain. Inwood had brought a sponge and a bottle of the solution to the house. His intention was to take Sir Barnaby by surprise, overpower him with the sponge, and complete the murder by suffocation. He hoped that this would make Sir Barnaby's death appear to have been a natural one."

Alice looked mystified. "Then why did he stab him instead?"

Meacan took up the story again. "Sir Barnaby showed more strength than Inwood anticipated, *and* he had a weapon available to him. As Warbulton told us, Sir Barnaby had recently acquired a knife that he believed to be of great significance to his personal interests. What would be more natural than to keep a new and intriguing acquisition, one so new it had yet to be labeled, on his desk?"

"Wrapped in a length of velvet," added Cecily.

"Inwood didn't expect it to be there," said Meacan. "But Sir Barnaby took it up and fought to keep his life. Inwood found himself in a struggle he never intended to have, and during the course of it, the knife slipped into Sir Barnaby's heart."

"The death could not have been made to appear natural after that," said Cecily.

"And Inwood would have found himself in a great deal more trouble," Meacan continued, "were it not for the confession of our gallant Mr. Dinley."

Both Alice and Dinley shifted uncomfortably, avoiding each other's eyes. "And all this because of John Rose," said Alice. "And what he told Sir Barnaby and Giles Inwood."

"Dangerous to play with the obsessions of others," said Meacan. "Rose's words were like weeds in receptive soil."

"I wonder," said Alice, "that Inwood did not begin to suspect the deception when he learned that Sir Barnaby kept the Rose cabinets locked. Wouldn't Sir Barnaby's evident fascination with the collection have made Inwood suspicious?"

"It seems you are more clever than Inwood was," said Meacan in an admiring tone. "Though it was not perhaps *quite* so obvious as you think. Dinley?"

Dinley nodded. "I was permitted in the study frequently enough to know that Sir Barnaby did not keep the Rose cabinets locked. I believe he thought it sufficient simply to keep the *room* locked whenever he was not there."

"It was Inwood who locked the cabinets," said Cecily. "He didn't want to risk their contents being inadvertently reorganized over the course of the inventory. He found the keys before we thought to look for them, locked the cabinets, and kept the keys himself."

"And was surely glad he did," said Meacan. "It must have been only hours later when the curious Lady Kay asked him where they were. I wouldn't be surprised if that's what made him decide to lure her to the dueler's field and eliminate the threat."

"Fortunately for me," said Cecily, "I was protected."

Alice looked out at the flowing river. "Anthony would have liked the story." Her voice trembled, but her eyes were bright and clear. She stood. Dinley scrambled to his feet and offered her his arm. They strolled together into the flowers.

"Do you think they'll marry?" asked Cecily, once they were out of hearing.

Meacan drew in a deep breath. "There's a good deal of grief between them," she said. "Could prove too heavy a weight on happiness. But who is to say when it comes to love? Often it's good that rots to bad, but sometimes the bad can blossom to good."

They were both silent, listening to the rushing water and the trills and twitters of birds. After a moment, Meacan spoke. "The auction ended today, you know." She had been following the sales with interest, delighting in news of new feuds, new favors, and new alliances, most of which were brokered by Covo. "The Rose collection has been purchased in full for an *extravagant* price, and you will never guess by whom."

Cecily raised her brows. "Someone I know?"

Meacan paused for dramatic effect. "Your *Russian*."

"General Belyaninov?"

Meacan nodded. "Apparently he's been frequenting all the Tower Hill pubs, and he's heard in bits and pieces the story of what happened. Everyone is talking, you know, about the hidden spells, and Inwood, and the shipwrecks. Who knows what he's gathered from the jumble, but it was enough to convince him that the cabinet of John Rose will be the perfect gift for the Tsar, who is very much taken with the macabre. A cabinet that has been the cause of obsession, betrayal, and madness? What could be more alluring? They are calling it *the murder cabinet.*" Meacan paused. "I wonder," she said.

"Yes?"

"I wonder if it isn't what Rose intended all along. Not *specifically* of course. But maybe, by telling Sir Barnaby that he had found the secret to occult power, and Inwood that he had found maps to lost treasure, maybe he hoped that eventually his collection would become so shrouded in mystery and fascination that it would turn his cabinet into a—well, I don't know quite how to put it. Into a—"

"An enigma that could never be solved?" suggested Cecily.

"*Yes.*" Meacan sighed. "In the end, I suppose he *was* a bit of a magician. Like a wizard who hides his soul in a needle in an egg in a rabbit in a bear, or however the story tells it."

They watched a painted pleasure barge glide by in a blur of gilding and fluttering velvet, its occupants oblivious of their regard. "I received two letters this morning," said Cecily. "It seems my husband is returning to England."

Meacan turned to her. "Is he?" she asked mildly. "Did one of his superiors discover that he cannot do sums or recognize swindlers?"

"He didn't give a reason, but he must have left soon after I did, for his message says he is already in Venice. He will spend the rest of the season there, but he gave instructions for having the house prepared for his arrival."

"Ah," said Meacan. "I suppose you'll be off to Lincolnshire, then."

"In good time," said Cecily. "The second letter I received came from the steward who has cared for my own family's estate for many years. He wrote to inform me that the current tenants have elected to quit the house, and to ask if I might come in person to hear their reason for going. He says it is of an unusual and puzzling nature. I wondered if you—"

"I accept your invitation," Meacan declared. "You *were* going to invite me?"

Cecily smiled. "The gardens will be happy to see you back," she said. "The trees have grown a great deal taller since we were little girls."

ACKNOWLEDGMENTS

The ideas that would become the foundation of this book were still in that chaotic, twisty-turny stage prior to being tamed by a plot when Doug Holland, the Library Director at the Missouri Botanical Garden, showed me the Garden's rare book room. As I marveled over the volumes, I felt for the first time that my as yet unnamed protagonist was sitting somewhere in time and imagination, concentrating on the details of a plant, ready to be pulled into an adventure. I am grateful to the Garden for that moment, and for the wealth of resources that were available to me later in the writing process, from biographies to herbals to herbarium specimens.

Established in 1673 by the Worshipful Society of Apothecaries, the Chelsea Physic Garden still sits at the edge of the River Thames in London, and still educates visitors on the uses of plants. The hours I spent wandering its paths making scribbled notes and sketches not only supplied essential historical details for writing *The Cabinets of Barnaby Mayne*, but inspired its final scene.

Publishing a novel is a group effort, and I am fortunate to have the guidance and support of a fabulous editor, Kelley Ragland, and agent, Stephanie Cabot. I'm also lucky to have a mother willing to turn her keen eye to tricky sentences, and a brother willing to share his insights into story structure. Finally, a way-too-big-for-a-sentence thank-you to my husband, Robbie, for talking through murder methods on weekend walks, for brewing experimental posset, and for reminding me always that words and imagination can transform one thing into another, no occult magic necessary.